MOLTEN MUD MURDER

MOLTEN MUD MURDER

AN
ALEXA GLOCK
MYSTERY

SARA E. JOHNSON

Published by Poisoned Pen Press, an imprint of Sourcebooks
P.O. Box 4410, Naperville, Illinois 60567-4410
(630) 961-3900
sourcebooks.com

Library of Congress Cataloging-in-Publication Data

Name: Johnson, Sara E., author.
Title: Molten Mud Murder / Sara E. Johnson.
Description: Naperville, IL : Poisoned Pen Press, 2019 | Series: An Alexa Glock Mystery
Identifiers: LCCN 2019020490 | (trade pbk. : alk. paper)
Subjects: | GSAFD: Mystery fiction.
Classification: LCC PS3610.O37637 M65 2019 | DDC 813/.6--dc23 LC record available at https://lccn.loc.gov/2019020490

Printed and bound in the United States of America.
SB 10 9 8 7 6 5 4 3 2 1

To Mom, with love and admiration

Chapter One

"Boiled? Boiled in mud?"

"No, ma'am. The chicken is sautéed, in chili-infused oil."

Alexa tore her eyes from the newspaper and stared blankly at the waiter of the Thai restaurant where she had stopped for lunch. She hadn't realized she had spoken aloud.

"More water?" the waiter added.

"Yes, please."

A *New Zealand Herald* had been left behind on the next table over, and she had grabbed it to keep herself company. Now it was all she could do to finish her curry. She was so absorbed by what she was reading that the wet wad of rice and lemongrass held midway from bowl to mouth slipped from her chopsticks and landed on her white T-shirt.

"Dammit."

She dabbed at her breast with a cloth napkin dipped in water and resumed reading. The front page was filled with grisly details of a murder in Rotorua, the very place she was headed for her friend Mary's memorial service. She had planned to call on Mary's family this afternoon after checking in to a cottage she had rented for two weeks while she figured out a way to prolong her stay in New Zealand.

A body had been found yesterday half-submerged in a Waiariki Thermal Land of Enchantment mud pool.

Boiled. Boiled in mud. The urge to finger her scar, to reassure herself, flashed like neon. She drank the water instead.

Rotorua, on the North Island of New Zealand, lay smack in the middle of intense thermal activity, like Yellowstone National Park in the States. Alexa read that the temperature of the mud pools reached two hundred degrees Celsius. *Hotter than water at the boiling point.* What would be left of the body? Teeth? She ran her tongue across her own and thought back to three years ago at the North Carolina State Bureau of Investigation when she had completed a second master's in odontology. Teeth were what had brought her to New Zealand.

Maybe teeth would be the reason she would stay.

An aerial view of the geothermal park took up half the page.

"Terrible, eh?" said a man leaning toward her from an adjacent table. He pointed to the paper while his companion, a woman roughly Alexa's age, late thirties, nodded.

"Gruesome way to die," Alexa agreed.

"Are you a Yank?" he asked, only it sounded like "yeenk."

"I'm from North Carolina."

The couple eyed her like she'd said "I'm from Mars." The woman was wearing conflicting colors, and the balding man had on a tank and shorts that showed too much hairy leg despite the sixty-degree breeze wafting through the open restaurant door.

"I've been working in Auckland for the past six months," Alexa added.

"We went to Las Vegas, yeah," the man said.

"Choice," the woman said. "But wouldn't want to live there. Crazy people."

Alexa, thinking not all the crazies were in the States, went back to her newspaper, but the man wasn't done.

"The dead guy must have royally pissed off a Maori," he said, stabbing her paper with his thick pointer finger.

"A Maori?" Alexa knew who the Maori were, but she was taken aback by this man's brashness.

"A native, eh. They used to boil the heads of their enemies."

Alexa shoveled down a last bite, gulped more water, and tucked the paper into her tote. She rearranged her afternoon schedule on the spot. Check in to her rental cottage. Stop by the police station to offer her services. *Then* call on Mary's family.

Maybe she had found her way.

—

Trout Cottage was tucked down a gravel drive on the outskirts of Rotorua. Alexa climbed out of the ten-year-old Toyota Vitz hatchback she had purchased when she arrived in New Zealand and leaned back to stretch. The scent of lavender spiced the air; she located their purple heads bobbing in the breeze to the left of the weathered, single-story cottage. The hum of the Kaituna River and the dancing lavender made her close her eyes and give thanks for the opportunity to be in this faraway land of abundant beauty. Eight thousand, five hundred miles was a long way from home.

The key was under the mat, just as the owner had promised. Alexa walked into a living area: wicker couch covered in wide black-and-white striped cushions, tan leather easy chair with ottoman next to a reading lamp, full bookcase, soft gray carpet, fresh white walls. She smiled, dropped her tote and computer bag, and checked out the bedroom.

A queen bed covered by a muted gray-and-yellow floral duvet was flanked by nightstands. Cracking the single window, she then probed under the bedding—yes, an electric mattress warmer. Spring nights could dip into the forties.

Spring in October. *Crazy.*

A small table and two chairs were all the furniture that fit into the kitchen. A vase of lavender sprigs brightened the windowsill. Alexa leaned over to inhale and then checked the cupboards where she discovered pots and pans, an electric kettle—she'd have to be careful, the water boiled almost instantly—plunger, salt and pepper, tea bags, and a canister of coffee that she opened, sniffed, and dumped. No smell, no buzz.

A trip to the grocery store had to be squeezed into the afternoon. She had started a mental list when her cell phone rang.

"Hello?"

"Terrance Horomia," a voice said. "I am Mary's brother. We heard you were in town for the funeral, and we'd like to invite you for tea. Five o'clock?"

She had called Mary's family yesterday and told them she'd be coming to Rotorua and would like to pay her respects. Mary had befriended her at Auckland University, or uni, as the locals said, and during her six-month visiting professorship, they had become close. Mary, who had worked as a biotechnician in an adjoining lab, was always eager to gab about biosecurity and conservation and New Zealand's wonders. She had enticed Alexa to stay longer, to travel as soon as her fellowship finished. "I'll take you round," Mary had promised. "We'll have adventures."

"That's kind, yes," Alexa said. "I look forward to meeting you all."

Terrance told her that Mary had mentioned her. "She said you were *whãnau*, like cousin, so come meet your family." He gave Alexa directions said *haere rã*, and the phone went silent. "*Whãnau*." Alexa said it out loud, tasting it, hearing it, seeing Mary's bright eyes.

A short two weeks ago, Mary had popped into her office and invited Alexa to drive from Auckland to the tip of the North Island. "Cape Reinga. Talk about tidal rips. At the lighthouse, you can watch the Tasman Sea meet the Pacific, man-sea meets woman-sea." Mary had laughed. "You know how that goes." But then she had turned serious. "It's the leaping point for spirits, the place the soul departs."

Alexa shuddered. What had Mary meant, leaping place for spirits? It must have been another Maori saying.

A single, never-married friend her age was rare. Often when people discovered Alexa had never been married or had children, their eyes scrutinized her like a magnifying glass, searching for hidden faults, cracks. The assumption that she grieved for the Prince Charming husband she'd never found or the baby she'd never cradled was below the surface, ready to pounce. It infuriated her.

Alexa should have dropped everything and said "yes!" to Mary's invite. But she prided herself in never shirking work responsibilities and had had final exams to give and the six- month fellowship to wrap up.

Days later, Mary was dead in a one-lane bridge collision. Dead.

I could be, too. Who would mourn?

Back home, she had blown it with her boyfriend, Jeb, when he mentioned marriage. "I like things the way they are," she'd answered.

Jeb had been incredulous. "We bought a couch together, and you won't commit? What's up with that?" He'd let it rip, and she knew she had hurt him. But Jeb hadn't been the right man. She doubted the right one existed, and when a colleague at the dental lab had posted the "Auckland University Seeking Odontologist Fellow" notice, she had thought "What the hell" and applied. Now she was here and determined to stay longer in New Zealand. Mary had had the right idea—explore. Why not? What else did she have back home? She'd never even been to Canada, and here she was in the Southern Hemisphere.

Alexa went back outside to unload the car, and after lugging in one large suitcase and one bulging backpack, she kicked off her Keds and sat on a porch chair in the sunshine to reread "Mud Pot Murder." According to the article, the body of a man, face and shoulders partially submerged in molten mud, was discovered by a busload of Chinese tourists at 8:50 Sunday morning. "We came from geyser and I was first here. I saw body sticking out but the head was in mud," one of the witnesses was quoted as saying.

Police were declaring the death suspicious and asking for information from the public. At press time, no missing person had been reported. "The victim's identifying features are indistinguishable," said district medical examiner, Dr. Rachel Hill. "All we know is that the victim is male, Caucasian, and forty to fifty years of age."

Couldn't a tourist have just gone rogue? Right before she had left the States she had read about a visitor in Yellowstone National Park who had ignored warning signs and wandered off the designated boardwalk, stumbling into a hot spring. All that was left of the guy was a Boston Red Sox cap. No remains had been recovered.

Her work visa was good for six more months, as long as she found another job. No office or classroom. No man to anchor her. A sudden breeze wrestled the paper out of her hands. She looked up, surprised, at the swaying, limbless trees topped by green pom-poms along the driveway. They were having a bad hair day. An urge to explore New Zealand's wildness—glaciers, the Great Walks, locations from *The Lord of the Rings* films, the bubbling mud pots right here in Rotorua—struck like a bolt. And Mary had said there was even a thermal waterfall near her hometown.

Alexa scooped up the newspaper and padded back into the cottage, found directions for connecting to the internet, and set up her laptop. A quick search revealed directions to Rotorua Central Police Station and the name of the inspector in charge of the investigation: Bruce Horne. Alexa clicked on the inspector's bio: born in Wellington, 1973, bachelor of science, Auckland University, special agent in charge of improving police efficiency, promoted to detective inspector in 2012, held in esteem by Maori community, outreach coordinator, married, two daughters, yadda yadda. A dark-haired man with intense blue eyes did not smile from a studio portrait.

—

The police station was new and modern. A band of red wood Maori carvings—faces with protruding tongues, fish, birds, and canoes—wrapped around the exterior. Inside, the welcome desk in the high-ceilinged lobby was vacant.

Where was everyone?

Alexa waited three minutes, staring up at a lightly balanced Calder-like mobile of six large birds—albatross? They had huge triple-jointed wings and cast undulating shadows.

"Be with you shortly," said a no-nonsense voice belonging to a severely bunned woman with cat's-eye glasses perched on a sharp nose. The restrained hair was an unnatural black. The woman busied herself arranging steaming tea in a Save the Penguins mug and then several files. Her "Kia Ora! My name is Sharon Welles" name tag straightened, she finally spoke.

"How can I help you?"

"I'd like to see Inspector Horne regarding the mud pot case."

Her eyes sharpened. "Is the *detective* inspector expecting you?"

"No, but I think I can be of assistance. Is he in?"

"He's on his way back to the station now. Have a seat," she answered, pointing to an empty bench along a wall of windows. "I'll phone to let him know you're here. Whom shall I say is waiting?"

"Alexa Glock. Forensic odontologist."

"Odontologist?"

"Teeth."

"You got here quickly."

Alexa smiled and took a seat. It was three o'clock. She let the floating birds capture her attention, pondered her personal albatross, and then let her thoughts migrate to her career. Seven years she had been with the North Carolina State Bureau of Investigation in Raleigh. She fished out her curriculum vitae: criminal psychology, crime-scene processing, trace evidence analysis, courtroom testimony. Three years ago, ready for a change, she'd left to earn a second master's in forensic odontology. "Comes in handy when face recognition is...not possible," she'd explain to friends. Pearly whites had shifted her career to teaching, first at the dental school in Chapel Hill and then—a convenient relationship escape hatch—to Auckland, New Zealand.

A voice jarred her back to the present.

"Detective Inspector Horne, remember I told you someone from forensics is waiting to see you." Alexa could hear the receptionist's voice, gone a bit syrupy, but not the reply. The clock on the wall read 3:22. After a few seconds of listening, the receptionist gave Alexa a puzzled look. Putting her hand over the voice piece she said, "Now just who are you?"

"Alexa Glock. I'm a forensics odontologist."

"Detective Inspector Horne says he is not expecting you."

"I'd like to offer my services. I can help him with the mud pot case." As the receptionist began to speak into the phone again, a tall, fit man with dark hair graying slightly at the temples appeared in front of Alexa. Shrewd blue eyes assessed her as his hand extended down.

"DI Bruce Horne. How can I help you?"

"I thought I might be able to help you," Alexa replied, rising. She took the man's offered hand in a firm shake. He had aged pleasingly since his bio portrait. "I'm Alexa Glock from North Carolina. I mean, I've just finished a job in Auckland, and I am looking for work." She took a breath and continued before the man could stop her. "I'm qualified in forensics, odontology, and crime-scene investigation. I read about the mud pot death in the paper. I'd like..."

"Hold on. You aren't from Auckland CSI?"

"No."

"You're from North Carolina? That's across the pond," he said, his forehead wrinkling. "What brings you to Rotorua?"

"A funeral. But I have a work visa and I'm highly qualified."

"A funeral?" The man's glacier-blue eyes stared at her until Alexa felt her face get hot. He was disconcertingly handsome.

She swatted that thought away like a pesky fly. "I'm expecting a forensics expert from Auckland in the morning. So I don't have any need of your services."

"In the morning? That's wasting time."

The detective inspector frowned as Alexa barreled on.

"I can ride out to the crime scene right now and do an initial analysis. I imagine safety is an issue." The number one rule in crime-scene investigation was to remove environmental hazards that could threaten investigators, but how could a bubbling mud pot be removed?

"As I said, we have someone coming. If you want a job, you need to apply online." He smiled briefly and started to turn.

"Here, take my résumé." She handed it to him but grabbed it back. "Oops. North Carolina number." Alexa dug for a pen and quickly drew a line through the number. "Just a sec. I can't remember what my new number is." She began to search her tote for the scrap of paper where she had written it, sure this would happen, removing sunscreen, an apple, and a scrunchie in the process. Horne stood patiently, watching her fumble around.

"Can I hold something?" he asked, one thick eyebrow rising in bemusement.

It was then she noted the curry stain front and center on her T-shirt. *Great.* "Yes, thanks." She handed him the apple. "Here it is." Number added, she traded her résumé for the apple and smiled into blue eyes. "I hope I hear from you."

Horne's left eyebrow flew up.

Chapter Two

Mary's childhood home was a modest brick ranch in a Rotorua suburb. Alexa parked on the street and, transfixed by the aroma of rosemary and garlic, walked down the driveway carrying a twelve-pack of beer and a bouquet of white roses.

A dark-haired man in khakis and a polo shirt was standing in the front garden at a barbecue. "Alexa Glock?"

She nodded. "Terrance Horomia?"

Terrance had Mary's eyes: topaz and voluminous. He pressed his nose and forehead against Alexa's in the traditional Maori greeting. "You had a safe journey from Auckland, I hope," he said. A tattoo of intricate spirals spilled from his short sleeves and ended at the wrist.

Alexa flushed, stepped back. "Yes, thank you. I am sorry for your loss. Mary was planning to bring me to Rotorua soon."

Terrance grunted. "She barely ever came back. Busy running from her roots."

Alexa didn't know what to say. "Where shall I put these?" She held up her offerings.

"Leave the brew here. I'll add it to the chiller. Go meet my wife and children. My mother and cousin are here too." He turned abruptly toward the rack of sizzling meat.

"Lamb?"

A nod as he brushed the crunchy skin with more oil and herbs.

The foyer opened to a den straight ahead, where she could hear TV garble and giggles, and a kitchen to the right. A plump, gray-haired woman was stirring a pot; a younger woman chopped mint.

"*Nau mai*, child," said the stirrer. "I'm Lorette Horomia, Mary's mother. It's good to meet her American friend." She let go of the wooden spoon and opened her arms, cloaking Alexa in an embrace.

"I am sorry for your loss," Alexa said into her soft shoulder and longed to sink deeper. Here this mother was, providing comfort when she should be receiving it. What would the loss of a child be like? Alexa couldn't fathom it, but she knew the loss of a mother.

Dressed in black leggings and a red-and-black swirly tunic, the other woman turned and offered her hand. "We will forge a new path. I am Mary's cousin, Jeannie."

No smile.

"What can I do to help? And where shall I put these flowers?"

A third woman, spilling out of a tight aqua sundress, walked in. "*Kia ora*." She introduced herself as Ellie, Terrance's wife. Her open smile revealed overlapping front teeth. "Come meet our children, Mary's niece and nephew."

Alexa returned the smile and followed her to the den.

Two dark heads turned from the flat screen when they walked in, Alexa still holding the roses. "This is Kala," said Ellie. "Our oldest."

"I'm almost nine," said Kala.

"I'm Kyle and I'm seven," her brother said.

"No, you're not!" said Kala. "You're six."

"Well, this is Alexa, Aunt Mary's friend from America," their mother explained.

The children eyed Alexa.

"I'm sorry about your aunt. There were pictures of you two on her desk." She hoped that was okay to say. Children were as unpredictable as dogs.

"I saw Auntie Mare dead in her coffin. She didn't open her eyes," Kyle said. "Are you someone's mum?"

"No. I..."

"Alexa is going to have tea with us," Ellie interrupted.

"Why do you have flowers?" Kala asked.

"They're for your family. Do you want to help me arrange them in a vase?"

"Okay," Kala said, jumping up. She skipped behind Alexa back to the kitchen.

The lamb was unveiled in the center of the crowded table. Dishes of roasted spring potatoes, mint sauce, steamed carrots, and green beans were passed around. Jeannie thawed a tad when Alexa complimented her on the mint sauce.

"Did my sister ever mention moving back here?" Terrance asked, setting down his fork.

"She talked about all of you. And about Rotorua. She had invited me for the holidays." A stab of panic. If she stayed in New Zealand, she'd be alone at Christmas.

"You can still come," said Kyle. "We'll have barbie and pavlova."

Barbie? Pavlova? Everyone laughed at Alexa's expression, and Ellie explained the Kiwi tradition of a Christmas day cookout and the whipped cream meringue dessert.

"Do you have snakes and lions and bears in 'Merica?" Kala asked.

"We have lots of snakes and a few bears, but luckily no lions," Alexa answered.

"You talk funny. We're having hokey pokey for dessert," Kyle said.

"Hocus-pocus? Is that a magic trick?"

"It's ice cream!" he screamed.

"Kyle, it's rude to say someone talks funny," his mom said. "You could say, 'Your accent is different.'"

"Your accent is different," Kyle said. Everyone laughed again.

Jeannie asked Alexa what brought her to New Zealand.

"I just finished a teaching fellowship in the forensics department at Auckland University. That's where I met Mary. Her lab was next door. I specialize in odontology. . .teeth."

Kyle stuck his tongue through the gap in his front teeth, and Alexa laughed. She didn't usually like children, but this one was growing on her. "I work with old teeth, not new ones like yours."

"Like Nana's?" Kyle asked.

Like dug-up skeletons and plane-crash victims. "Even older."

"Will you head back to the States now?" Jeannie asked.

"I might stay longer if I can find another job. My work visa can be extended indefinitely if I work in a high-needs field. I stopped by the Rotorua Police Department this afternoon. To see if they need help with the death at the mud pots."

"My class went to the Waiariki mud pots," piped Kala. "They're scary. The mud is alive. Jason said Maori used to cook people in them and eat them. And Samara saw bones poking out."

"Is that true, Mum?" Kyle asked in a worried tone.

A bang came from the end of the table. "That's enough, Kala." Terrance's voice drowned Ellie's response. "Do not desecrate your ancestors." Uncomfortable silence followed. Terrance, frowning, said no more, and his clan jumped up to clear the table.

Chapter Three

She lay in bed at 7:06 the next morning, cozy, only her nose cold, listening to the faint gurgle of the Kaituna through the cracked window and to a shrill *cheep cheep chirrup* followed by chattering. New Zealand, she had read in her guidebook, had been isolated from other lands and evolved into an avifauna full of wondrous birds. Many, like the kiwi and kakapo, were flightless because New Zealand had no indigenous land mammals as predators.

Alexa lay still, imagining an alien world with no mammals and trying to figure out why this was so. She concluded that the land was so isolated—twenty-five hundred miles from Australia, though people tended to lump the two countries together, and three thousand miles from Antarctica—that if you couldn't fly here (hence the birds) or swim (hence the seals, sea lions, and penguins), then it made sense that it would become an exclusive, birds-only party.

How utterly cool.

Alexa liked the guidebook story about Captain James Cook exploring the New Zealand coast in 1770. His ship was moored a quarter mile from shore. The dawn chorus of birdsong was so deafening that his crew begged him to anchor farther out.

But, she had read further, the bird party had come to a

disastrous clock striking midnight. The seafaring Polynesians who first inhabited New Zealand had killed off the moa and introduced rats, and the European settlers brought rabbits, possums, stoats, and cats. These party animals had blindsided the defenseless bird population, in many cases to extinction. No more laughing owl, huia, New Zealand quail, or bush wren. The past several decades saw the Kiwis (capital *K* for people, lowercase *k* for bird, Alexa had learned) working to eradicate the problem. Programs to erase invasive flora and fauna were underway. Mary had helped instigate biosecurity checks at airports.

Cheep cheep, chirrup.

Alexa closed her eyes for a few more minutes, happy for this bird's song, happy to be untethered, and then the urge for coffee made her hop up.

Mary's memorial service was to be at four p.m. at St. Faith's Anglican Church on the banks of Lake Rotorua. After breakfast, she would take a run along the river. And then maybe sniff around the mud pots.

She ate quickly and moved to the front porch despite the chill to sip fresh coffee and check her laptop for the latest mud pot news. The *Press*'s article "Group Tour Views Scene from Hell" included additional quotes from witnesses and a grisly photo of a body partially submerged in mud. "Only two feet were sticking out. I was sickened by the sight." The *New Zealand Herald* ran a similar front page article, "Tour Bus of Asians Discover Body," with another shocking photo. She didn't think a similar photo would be allowed in an American newspaper, well, maybe a tabloid. She also supposed the photos came from the Chinese tourists' iPhones and not from the authorities. The body was still unidentified.

Alexa rose, sipped the last of her thick, nutty coffee, and went to change. A run would warm her up and get her brain in gear. Then she'd head out to the scene of the crime: Waiariki Thermal Land of Enchantment.

After checking her phone to see if Detective Inspector Handsome of the Rotorua Police Department had called—he hadn't—Alexa discovered a path through Trout Cottage's side yard leading to the river. Dense spiky foliage and fern trees, cabbage, and silver crowded the path's edges and blocked the morning light. Between leafage, the Kaituna flashed green and roiling. A faint lemony scent wedded with river water perfumed the air. Taking deep breaths, Alexa stretched her hamstrings, first left, then the tighter right, and began to run the deserted path, slowly at first, her body acclimating after several non-running days. Then years of conditioning kicked in, and five minutes later, she was running strong and swift like the river. Many people who survive large burns end up with joint pain and difficulty walking or running, and Alexa was sure as hell not going to be one of them.

Running was thinking. She thought of Jeb—left to find someone else to share his life with. With a jolt, she realized she didn't care, felt lighter. Free. Was her heart frozen? Was something the matter with her that she couldn't form a lasting relationship with a man?

Rubbish.

Mary had always said "rubbish." Alexa thought of her instead of Jeb. Mary had befriended her week one in Auckland, popping her head in Alexa's office and saying, "I'm here to do the official welcome *haka*." She had made her eyes bulge and started stamping her feet when another colleague yelled at her to knock it off.

Now she's dead.

A lump lodged in Alexa's throat.

Think about today.

The mud pots. They were calling.

A reptilian shape across the path made her jump. Heart-poundingly high. Then she remembered: no snakes in New Zealand either. Another reason to stay.

After a bit more Alexa could hear the thunder of a waterfall and knew she was close to Okere Falls. There had been a page three article in the paper about a German whitewater-rafting tourist who had been helicoptered out from here the same day as the murder, injured while plunging over the seven-meter falls. The highest commercially rafted falls in the world, the article had claimed. Right here. Had the tourist survived?

When the roar became deafening, Alexa spotted a side path and veered. The path wound downward, narrowed, rock cliffs on either side obstructing light, the temperature cooler, dank, and ended above the falls. Three wooden steps led up to a viewing platform that jutted out above the river. Spray from the falls made her shiver as she climbed them and forced herself up to the edge, mindful of the slippery planks. She hated heights but pushed herself to conquer her fear.

Now or never, right?

She grabbed the flimsy safety rail, leaned over, and looked down. Her stomach flipped at the jumble of froth and force.

—

Showered and ready, Alexa found a brochure in the cottage describing Waiariki Thermal Land of Enchantment: an extraordinary landscape of hot spouting geysers, bubbling mud pools, and colorful sinter terraces. At $32.50 a pop, it was one of several geothermal parks in the area to visit, and the brochure made it sound like a theme park. She had never been to a geothermal area and was excited, as tourist and as scientist.

After twenty minutes of winding roads from the cottage, she found the entrance and drove up to the ticket booth. The only indication a crime had taken place was a handwritten sign taped to the booth: "Mud Pots Closed." Lowering the window, she handed over her American Forensics Association membership card, which had a decent photo of her in the corner, in hopes of avoiding the entry fee and asked the attendant for directions.

"Continue straight ahead, past the turnoff to Waiariki Geyser.

Then take the first right. Do you know when the mud pools will be opened?" the attendant asked. She looked Maori and had barely glanced at Alexa's card before handing it back. Security in New Zealand was a bit more relaxed than in the States.

"Perhaps soon, but there's no telling."

"The tourists want to go see where the body was found. Our numbers are up. Have they figured out who did it?"

"No comment. Thanks for the directions." Alexa pulled forward. Glancing in the rearview mirror, she noted more cars lined up.

Last night, after leaving Mary's family, Alexa had Googled Rotorua and found that it had a population of fifty-six thousand, and there had been two murders the previous year. Though rare, murder was not unheard of.

The turn, a narrow one-way blacktop, was blocked by orange cones. Alexa had to stop the car and move them out of the way, drive through, and then stop and replace them. Half a kilometer farther, a parking area appeared on the right. Two police cars and a white van were parked with no sign of people. Alexa parked next to the van and got out. Scrub and shrubs surrounded the lot; the land was low and eerie and reeked of rotting eggs. Yellow tape and a cordoned-off pathway pointed the way.

The noise. Alexa stopped abruptly after ten paces. She tensed, listening. *Sploosh. Plop. Gurgle. Splat.* Onomatopoeia come to life. She increased her pace, eager. Mud pots lay ahead, obstructed by ghostly clouds of vapor. When she reached a clear view, Alexa realized Kala had been right. The mud was alive, dancing, popping, sucking. Alexa moved forward up to a proper viewing area, separated from the living pond of mud by a hip-high fence and skull and crossbones warning sign.

She had never seen anything like it.

"You. This area is closed."

The voice came from behind. Alexa whirled around to find a female police officer. Her dark hair was mostly hidden by a uniform cap that shaded a broad, smooth Maori face and a blue lip-and-chin tattoo.

"Hello. I'm Alexa Glock, forensic odontologist. I'm here to take a look at the scene."

"Your badge. No one said you were coming." The stocky cop looked young, early twenties.

Alexa handed over the American Forensics Association card, hoping it would keep working. "Can you show me the scene?"

The cop scrutinized the card, comparing the photo on it with Alexa's face. She handed it back and said, "Follow me."

"What's your name?"

"Officer Cooper."

"Do you know who was the first officer on the scene?"

"I was."

Bingo. "Could I ask a few questions?" Alexa fought to keep her voice neutral.

"It's all in my report."

"I'm sure it is. How did you know to come here?"

"Dispatcher." The young cop looked at Alexa as if she were short a few. "Said there had been an accident. I was closest."

"Were you alone?"

Nod.

"What did you find when you arrived?"

"Chinese tour group. Twenty-eight people crowding and shouting on the platform up ahead."

The two women were walking uphill on a concrete path that led to another viewing area, this one above the molten pools. From here, tourists could look down into a bubbling Hades. Alongside the platform, a narrow gap led to a rocky hill. Alexa spotted another cop and two men in jumpsuits and booties standing below, within the largest of the taped areas, ten yards from the boiling muck. Yellow caution tape appeared in five different areas, which confused Alexa. A perimeter of a crime scene should be big. ("You can bring it in, but you can't pull it out," Dr. Winget always emphasized.) What was with these random areas taped off?

Clearly, she was needed.

Drifting steam clouds suddenly obscured the view. "Did anyone leave the platform and go down to the body?" Alexa hurried to ask more questions before they were spotted by the people below.

"No. I think some would have, but the tour director stopped them." The cop made for the gap leading to the rocky hill.

"Did the witnesses see anyone else in the vicinity?"

The officer stopped walking and turned to face Alexa. "Some did, some didn't." She shook her head. "We're still compiling the different statements."

"What happened next?" Alexa imagined a chaotic scene of foreigners trying to outdo one another with details.

"I removed them from the scene. Called for ambulance and backup." Officer Cooper folded her arms across her chest, the fabric of her short-sleeved blue uniform shirt stretched taut over thick arm muscles.

Alexa leaned toward her. "Did you go down to the body?"

"No. The ground around the pots is unstable. You can break through crust, fall into a new pot."

Why were people down there now? "So you left the scene unsecured?"

"Yes," Officer Cooper said, defiance in her voice.

Alexa didn't want to offend. "I'm sure you did the right thing."

"More people started arriving. I had to keep them from entering," the officer added.

"That's good. That way, the scene wasn't contaminated." It sounded as if the young cop had handled everything by the book.

"I got the tour group to wait in the bus until DI Horne arrived. Then I went to meet the ambulance. The EMTs had to lasso the victim to pull him out." Her face paled, making her blue lips brighter by contrast. Alexa had seen a sprinkling of Maori women in Auckland with similar tattoos. Mary's tattoo hadn't been on her chin but on her shoulder, a strange and beautiful image, part bird, part fish, and part woman.

"Did anyone take photos before they moved him?"

Officer Cooper nodded. "I did a livestream video. And we have many from the tour group." Her lips pressed together again, perhaps aware she had shared too much, and she started down the steep rocky hill leading to the people in protective jumpsuits. Alexa noticed one of the jumpsuits was Detective Inspector Bruce Horne.

Uh-oh.

A commotion above postponed their reunion. Two men, one clicking a Nikon with a gigantic telephoto lens and the other sweeping the scene with a TV 6 video camera, called out "G'day. Can we ask some questions?"

"Leave the area now," barked Horne. "Officer Cooper, why did you leave your post? Escort these men immediately."

"But," said the young cop, looking at Alexa, "she asked me to show her the scene."

Horne turned to Alexa, recognition dawning. "*She* is not authorized to be shown the scene. What were you thinking?"

"It's my fault," Alexa said. "I showed her my card."

"What card?" Horne's eyes burrowed into Alexa's, and once again, heat rose to the surface of her skin.

"My American Forensics Association card."

"Your what? Officer, show these men out and stay at your post."

The officer speared Alexa with her eyes and scurried up toward the media.

"Don't talk to them," Horne added. "There will be a press conference at five o'clock, and they can ask questions then."

"Yes, Senior."

"Thank you for perhaps compromising the scene," was Horne's greeting as he turned back to Alexa. His left cheek was smudged with mud, and so were his gloved hands. The tall police officer standing next to Horne scrutinized Alexa. The third man stood silent, watching. "You aren't suited up," Horne added. "What are you doing here?"

"I want to offer my expertise. Pro bono." Horne was right; she should be suited.

"Things are under control." The man's blue eyes flared. "We're about to attend the autopsy."

She decided to hold ground. Or mud. "Extra set of eyes and ears can't hurt."

"Is she qualified, sir?" This from the other suited-up man. "My wife..."

Horne ignored him and turned to the remaining officer. "Rangiora, go stand on the platform. Make sure no one else approaches."

"Right," the officer answered and cast a glare at her.

Alexa barreled on. "The heat of the mud accelerated rigor mortis, right?"

"We've determined that," the man next to Horne said. He was early thirties, marshmallowy in his white jumpsuit, and sweating. "We've just been given clearance. Geologists had to poke about, determine whether it was safe to be down here." An exploding missile of mud spattered his booties. He took a step away from the roiling pot. "They set up caution ribbon to mark where it's not safe."

Okay, Ms. Quick-to-Judge. That's why the caution tape is irregularly placed.

Alexa looked down to make sure she was on terra firma.

"Clever crime scene. Any evidence thrown into the pots has been eaten by acid," the unidentified man added. A new rivulet of sweat rolled down his forehead into his left eye. He pawed at it and appraised Alexa. "And you are?"

"Her name is Ms. Glock," Horne said. "She's a visiting dentist." Both men moved toward her.

She was impressed Horne had remembered her name. "I'm not a dentist. One of my degrees is in odontology. I've worked forensics for ten years. Most of them with the State Bureau of Investigation. In North Carolina."

"I'm Kit Byers, forensics investigator from Auckland," mystery man said. "Did you say Glock?"

"Yes." *Here it comes.*

"Like the gun?" asked Byers.

"Bull's-eye." The Glock 17 was the most widely used law enforcement pistol in the world. Alexa was used to the question, bored by it, really, and had a ready list of comebacks.

Horne's eyebrow shot up, and a smile appeared and disappeared lightning quick.

"What evidence have you gathered?" Alexa asked, hoping they'd keep talking. She nonchalantly pulled one Ked, formerly white, from mud she was slowing sinking in and stepped back. The heat and smell made her light-headed.

DI Horne's phone rang; he stepped away.

"A clean footprint cast. Soil samples," Byers said. "The victim's hands were duct-taped behind his back, so we have what's left of that. Duct tape was used around his mouth too, but that melted away. "

"I know duct tape." Alexa wondered if the murderer left prints on it. "Has anyone been reported missing?"

"No," Byers said, glancing toward Horne and then checking his phone.

"Were they able to fingerprint the body?" Alexa rushed to ask questions while Horne was occupied.

"The duct tape prevented the hands from clenching, so the fingertips are damaged," Byers answered, shuffling from one foot to the other and taking another look at his phone. "A few partials survived. Not enough to run."

Alexa thought about how burn victims were often recovered with clenched fists—pugilistic pose was the official term—which occasionally preserved fingertips. "Was he dragged down here or thrown from the platform?"

"Evidence supports he came down of his own volition."

"No signs of struggle?" Alexa looked around. Surely, the man didn't dive in voluntarily. Close to the pots, the ground was oozy, but farther away, the soil was dry, impressionable.

"Just there." Byers pointed a few yards from the mud pot. That area had caution tape too. "And further drag marks from the mud to where the emergency medics pulled him over here." Another taped area.

"How long was he in the mud?"

"Rigor mortis was maximal. Six to eight hours."

"Signs of putrefaction?" Alexa asked. Enzymatic decomposition was a secondary way to gauge time of death.

"Hard to tell," said Byers. "Place stinks even without a cooked body."

The DI rejoined the pair. "Hard to tell what?"

"She's asking about putrefaction."

Inspector Horne's eyebrows went up.

"I'd like to stand in during the autopsy. Help out." She looked from Byers to Horne. "The teeth will be key." She kept going. "Since the fingerprinting didn't yield results, dental configuration is the next quickest way to procure an ID. Was a stabilizer spray used before the body was moved?"

"A what?" Horne asked.

"I've heard of that, but we don't have it," Byers said. He turned to Horne. "It's a new product that forms a cast over a vic's jaw and prevents damage during transportation." His phone beeped, and before he answered, Byers took a breath and said, "If she's qualified, I need to head back to Auckland, Inspector. My wife is on bed rest and taking medication to stop premature labor." He checked his message. "But the labor isn't stopping."

Alexa couldn't believe her luck. She looked at Horne. Again that intense stare. Followed by a slow nod.

Yes.

—

Fifty minutes later, Alexa was suited up and standing at the foot of the naked mud pot man. Cloying formaldehyde and eau de cooked flesh overwhelmed her olfactories, whisking her back to her first autopsy.

Rex Hospital. Twenty-three years old and she had nose-dived. She understood the science behind a faint. Blood or drills or saws or bad news can slam the brakes on the pumping heart, reducing blood flow to the brain. Peripheral vision and hearing diminished. Sweatiness or clamminess. Room sway.

Crash.

Her boss at the lab had noticed her tendency to avoid autopsies and cornered Alexa until she had explained.

"Get over it. Fainting is empathy for the tenuous hold we have on life. The fainting self should be forgiven," the doctor had said.

Forgiveness.

As if it were easy. I haven't even forgiven my own mother for dying on me.

Alexa appreciated Dr. Winget's philosophy from way back when but now scanned the bleak room for a nearby bench in case she'd need to sit quickly. Burn cases like this were hardest. She involuntarily tensed, feeling the taut scar tissue from three reconstructive surgeries on her back protest. She'd been thirteen and even after twenty-four years, pain and despair flashed, forever close to the surface.

Detective Inspector Horne had introduced her to the pathologist, Dr. Rachel Hill, who had merely nodded at Alexa and continued readying her instruments.

Mud man, stretched out on stainless steel, was lobster red and swollen from the waist down: moderate belly fat, scar on right thigh, knobby-kneed, slack calves, long feet, ten toes.

The body had been washed; all traces of mud were gone.

Belly button on up, a farmer's tan gone awry, the skin tone segued from red to purple to fiery to blistered and peeling to denuded. What once was a face was a blackened skull with sunken sockets, missing nose, and a gaping hole with oddly protruding gray teeth.

Alexa kept her face expressionless. Horne was staring, gauging her reaction. She gave him a nod of assurance and went back to studying the cadaver.

Shoulder joints and humerus were blackened and exposed. Skin on the top sides of the forearms was hanging in strips. The hands, which had been bound by duct tape behind his body, seemed to have been somewhat protected from the thermal heat.

The tall, red-haired Dr. Hill put a Nikon away, pulled on gloves, goggles, and mask, and started talking into a tape recorder in a thick Scottish accent. "Badly burned body. Caucasian male." She abruptly turned off the tape recorder, pulled her mask down, and looked at Horne through her goggles. "I'm reminiscing," she said.

One of Horne's eyebrows rose.

"The eight-year-old lad who was rushed to the hospital from Kappi Thermal Park," the doctor explained.

"Two years ago, right? He died."

"After twenty-four excruciating hours. The boy climbed the barrier fence and jumped into a hot spring. Skin had peeled off his body before he even got to the hospital," she said, her voice softening. "There was nothing they could do to save him."

Jeez.

"Witnesses said he slipped, just playing around. It was Boxing Day," Horne said. "But this guy was dumped in."

Alexa, who had been holding her breath, let it go in a rush. Her scarred back muscles tightened, and she forced them to stretch by clasping her hands behind her back and straightening her arms as far as they would go. She hated boiling water.

The doctor eyed Alexa, readjusted her mask, and turned the tape recorder back on. "1.78 meters, 86 kilograms. Scar, 5 centimeters, above right knee. No visible tats. Approximately forty to fifty years old."

"How can you determine his age?" Horne asked, staring at the ravaged body.

The doctor gave Horne a patient smile. "I'll be able to tell with more accuracy when I examine the rib cage. The sternal end of the fourth rib will determine age. But for now, I'm going by pubic hair color, skin elasticity, and results from the X-rays we took prior to the autopsy. Slight arthritis in left knee is consistent with someone aged forty or older."

She began scraping each nail of the victim's right foot into evidence bags. Then the left foot starting with the big toe. "Fingernails are typically a better source of trace evidence, but look." She gently set the left foot down and moved to the victim's left hand. "The fingernails are deformed by the heat," she said. "Useless." She examined the wrist and then reached for tweezers. "I removed the duct tape binding the hands earlier. Looks like this was under the tape." She held the tweezers to the light and stared at a fragment. "Maybe glass?"

Horne appeared grateful when his cell phone buzzed. "Excuse me," he said, quickly leaving the room.

Next, the doctor plucked and bagged a few pubic hairs, murmuring into the tape recorder. She then stepped to the head and began probing. "No hair left on the skull," she said after a moment. "Melted away."

Her hands continued doing what looked like a scalp massage as Horne returned.

"Doc, I gotta go." He turned to Alexa. "If your credentials check out, you've wormed your way into a temporary contract."

"They will."

"Come to the station when you're done. There's a press conference at five."

The DI left, and the doctor gave Alexa a puzzled look. Her eyes were magnified by the goggles and looked like sky-blue discs. "There is significant cranial trauma. I feel a fracture." She manipulated the skull with both dexterity and gentleness. "X-rays will confirm it."

"You think he was dead before he was thrown into the mud?"

"It's possible, but I won't know until I check his lungs." Dr. Hill's gloves were covered in blackened ooze. She whipped them off and threw them toward a hazmat bin. "Who are you again?" She slipped on a pair of clean gloves.

"I'm Alexa Glock, forensics investigator."

"From Auckland?"

"Yes. Well, no. How long do you think he's been dead?" she asked, steering questions back to the victim.

"Tricky. The temperature of the mud accelerated rigor mortis. At the shoreline, it was ninety-seven degrees Celsius. Taking this into account, I'd estimate time-of-death window is between nine p.m. and midnight."

Why didn't America adopt the metric system? Alexa quickly calculated: ninety-seven degrees Celsius was two hundred four degrees Fahrenheit. Almost boiling. "Any idea what was used to fracture the skull?"

"I'll know more when I examine the X-rays. Let me get on with this."

"Did any of the duct tape around his mouth survive?" Alexa asked, ignoring the doctor's hint. Some tapes, especially those rated for attics and kitchens, could withstand heat to two hundred degrees Fahrenheit.

"It melted. What was left was damaged by acid."

"I'll need dental X-rays. Can we take those before you proceed?"

"Done," the doctor responded. "Pick them up on your way out."

Using a scalpel, Dr. Hill made a diagonal incision from each singed shoulder meeting in a V at the sternum and continuing down to the pelvic bone, explaining her movements into the recorder. She then ripped the blistered, blackened skin back on each side to expose the rib cage. Alexa's stomach churned up a bit of egg.

The autopsy took two more hours. The man's individual

organs were removed one at a time and weighed. "Interesting," Dr. Hill said. "The high temperature of the mud pit started to dry out the organs."

Congealed blood and tissue samples were taken from each and meticulously labeled for testing. When Dr. Hill finally got to the lungs, she looked at Alexa. "He was dead before he was thrown in. Look."

The lungs were clean—no muck—indicating the victim had not been breathing when he was thrown in.

"Let's see when and what this man ate," Dr. Hill said. The stomach and intestines were opened and explored. An escape of ghastly stink, like gangrene, assaulted Alexa's nostrils, and she flinched.

"Steak and chips for his last supper," Dr. Hill shared, bagging some and shaking her head. "Won't be able to use them to determine death like normal. They continued to cook postmortem."

For a change, Alexa wasn't hungry. "Last supper. Sad."

Dr. Hill left the victim's belly and moved on to his blackened head, first re-examining it externally and then making an incision at what was once the hairline, peeling what was left of the parboiled skin forward, exposing his skull, and finally, using a high-speed oscillating saw, revealing the brain. What would the inner workings of the mud pit man reveal? And why did someone kill him?

Alexa completed a postmortem dental chart on the victim as the doctor disappeared to check X-ray results. Of note was one gold alloy replacement, upper left molar, which survived the extreme heat of the pots, an untreated cavity in the lower left molar, and evidence of teeth grinding. A few minutes later, Dr. Hill raced back in, excited to have news that Alexa would have to keep to herself for a few hours.

She had a funeral to attend at St. Faith's Anglican Church.

Chapter Four

The Tudor-style church stood on the banks of Lake Rotorua. Alexa, who had raced to the cottage to shower and change into a silky gray shirt, black pants, and lavender sweater, arrived ten minutes early and walked in the open front doors. The interior, half full of whispering people, mixed Maori and traditional design. Ocher spirals were carved at the end of each wooden pew. Panels of geometric flax weaving adorned the stark white walls trimmed in bright red. A traditional stained glass image of Jesus in a forest of greens glistened from behind the pulpit.

Alexa slowly walked toward the colored light flooding through the glass, forming a beckoning path leading to a table of Mary memorabilia. There were her high school and college diplomas. A childhood photo of Mary and Terrance holding hands, a woven flax basket stuffed with envelopes and bills, and next to it, Tiki Man, the wooden statue Mary had had on her desk in Auckland.

Its iridescent eyes twinkled at Alexa.

Why did Mary die? She had made promises to Alexa. "We'll go bungee jumping and great white shark cage diving. And then we'll hike the Milford Track. People come from all over the world for Milford," Mary had said and made a reservation for them. "It's the world's most beautiful walk." Alexa resolved to complete these adventures in Mary's honor.

After she solved the mud pot case.

She was alone now in this foreign country. No friends. Tears bullied their way down her cheeks as she turned and found a seat, searching her tote for a tissue. The stab of abandonment made her think of her mother, who had died of brain cancer. Alexa had been six. Only vague memories remained. They had decayed a bit more each passing year until, at age thirty-seven, Alexa could only conjure a dark-haired shadow.

Deep yoga breaths.

"May I sit here?"

Alexa, swiping tears, smiled at a plain-faced middle-aged woman in a black pants suit and scooted over. "Hello. I'm Alexa Glock."

"I'm Sylvia Chapell."

"How did you know…?" the women said in unison and then laughed.

"I was her high school friend."

"I worked with her in Auckland."

"Mary always wanted to leave Rotorua for the big city," Sylvia said.

"But she talked about Rotorua all the time."

Sylvia shrugged and said, "She's home now. I can't believe she's gone."

The church was three-quarters full when a young priest, who introduced himself as Father McKinney, started the service with a prayer in English and then a prayer in Maori. He eulogized Mary Horomia as a seeker and learner. Mary's cousin Jeannie—the frosty one—joined him and sang the Lord's Prayer in English and then in Maori. Her voice was plaintive, clear.

Three men, including Terrance, dressed in white shirts and black coats, joined Jeannie on stage. The men began to dance a slow-motion *haka*, encircling Jeannie as she chanted in Maori.

Their eyes bulged and hands trembled. They stomped their feet and finally squatted, slapped their knees, and stuck their tongues out.

Mesmerized and confused, Alexa whispered to Sylvia, "Isn't that a war dance?"

"The *haka* is used in all kinds of ceremonies, even funerals," Sylvia whispered back. "It commemorates any significant event."

Father John said some parting words, and then the service was over. Alexa said goodbye to her pew companion, made a contribution to the basket, and found Jeannie.

"Your singing was beautiful," Alexa said.

Mary's cousin refused to meet her eyes or acknowledge the compliment.

What is up with this woman? Alexa surveyed the small groups of people talking, some laughing. Most were Maori like Mary, with dark wavy hair, bronze skin, topaz eyes.

Jeannie finally spoke. "Will you come back to the house for refreshments?"

"I can't." Jeannie's expression told Alexa she was waiting for an explanation. "I've offered my services to the Rotorua Police Department, and I need to attend a meeting in a few minutes."

"What services have you offered?"

"I'm helping with the mud pot case."

Jeannie frowned. "Why would you get involved with that?"

Alexa didn't answer. She found Mary's mother and Terrance, shaking hands or pressing forehead to forehead and nose to nose of departing guests, on the front steps. She joined them, giving a quick hug to each. She looked from Lorette's eyes to Terrance's and said, "Mary was so kind to me, and you both have been too." Terrance didn't answer and looked out at the lawn. Alexa followed his gaze. Kala and Kyle were running on the grass in the shadow of a huge angel statue.

"Will you come back to the house with us?" Lorette asked, her eyes heavy with grief.

"I'm sorry but I can't. I have a meeting at the police station. I've been offered temporary work on the mud pot murder."

Clouds drifted above, pushed by a stiffening lake breeze. Alexa pulled her sweater tighter. The angel statue had open wings and a beatific smile, but Terrance's face had gone stone-cold.

"Be watchful, Alexa from America," he said. "In Maori culture, boiling the head of an enemy is the ultimate revenge. It is the most potent curse one Maori can make to another, *Upoko kōhua*. People in the community think justice has been served and don't want *Pākehā* mucking about." Terrance stared into her eyes. "You should not interfere."

Mucking about. Mary's brother had a chip on his shoulder.

Circling the station lot twice, she squeezed the Toyota between a Channel Five van and an SUV, or ute, as the Kiwis called them. She grabbed her autopsy notes and hurried inside to where the press conference had been held. Reporters and news crews, talking among themselves and on cell phones, were filing out as Alexa snaked in, hating that she'd missed it. She was excited to share her news with DI Horne and found him at the front podium arguing with a man. A blond woman in a bright-blue suit stood next to him.

"You have no right to withhold the name of the deceased," the man with a Channel One cap said.

"As stated, we do not have a positive ID on the victim," Horne said and turned to the woman. "Your Worship the Mayor, thank you for coming. I'll be in touch."

"I expect to be kept up to date, Detective Inspector Horne," she answered, the vermilion border of her lips colored in by bright-red lipstick.

Horne spotted Alexa. "Ms. Glock. We meet again." His eyes lingered a second too long at Alexa's dressy outfit, and then he glanced at his watch. "Can you accompany me to my office?"

Not waiting for a reply, he turned and walked to the stairwell. "Hope you don't mind," he said, holding the door and following her in. "I always take the stairs."

"I do as well." Alexa took them two at a time, conscious she was being followed.

His office was on the second floor, in a corner, surrounded by glass. Horne motioned to a chair as he settled behind his desk after closing the door. There was a knock, and then the door popped back open. A uniformed cop said, "Senior, I have something."

"Can it wait, Officer Walker?"

The man stepped inside. "You probably won't want it to wait."

"Officer Walker, this is Ms. Glock. She'll be filling in for Byers."

"How's it going?" he said to Alexa and then turned back to Horne. "I heard Byers had to rush back to Auckland?" He patted at a wayward cowlick at the crown of his ginger-colored head.

Horne nodded but kept silent.

The young officer blushed. "We've a witness who said she saw a car leaving the mud pots early Sunday morning. On the phone now."

"Okay, good. Get her to the station."

The officer started to leave when Alexa said, "Wait a minute." She turned to Horne. "We need to get a search team back to the mud pots." She opened her pad and scanned it unnecessarily. "Dr. Hill determined that the victim was killed by blunt force trauma, most likely a rock, before being dumped into the mud pot. We need to search for the weapon."

"Sun's about to go down, Senior. Should we wait until morning?"

"No," blurted Alexa.

"No." Horne said, frowning at Alexa. "Might rain tomorrow. Take lights. Find that rock." The officer nodded and left.

"The perp probably threw it in the mud pots," Alexa said.

"Well...maybe he didn't. Other things on his mind. So you're telling me the victim walked down to the mud pots and *then* was killed? Why would he willingly do that?"

"Sounds as if he knew the murderer. But why were they there? At the mud pot? Late at night?"

They stared at each other, digesting, speculating.

Alexa broke the silence. "Do you mind telling me if I've been hired?"

"You got lucky. I called your past supervisor in Raleigh. Does Dr. Winget always get to work so early?"

Alexa shook her head to switch gears to the NC State Crime Lab. "She was always in when I arrived each morning."

"Didn't think she would be because of the time difference. What is it? Eighteen hours?"

"Something like that, depending on daylight saving time. We're living in the future here," Alexa said, her fingers playing with a pearl button on her blouse.

"What?"

"Nothing." Alexa dropped her hand to the folder on her lap. Something about this man made her say stupid things.

"She recommended you."

"I'm glad." Alexa thought of her former boss. A stickler but always fair. They had stayed in touch after Alexa left for the dental lab.

"Byers has to stay in Auckland. Our loss. I've worked with him before, and he's good. We can contract-hire you for the case if your license checks out. Our secretary, Ms. Welles, has paperwork for you."

"Do you have a lab and technicians?" She had once worked a case using a mobile crime van; it was better than working from the trunk of a patrol car but not much.

"Complete lab in the basement. One full-time technician, a newbie." He glanced at his watch again. "She's probably left for the day."

"Do we know who our victim is?"

"No missing people reports have been filed. I hope to God he wasn't a tourist. The mayor will have a fit."

"I've got dental X-rays since the fingerprints aren't viable. I'll start by contacting local dentists."

"What else?" Horne asked, his face darkened by stubble and worry.

"Our man had steak and *kūmara* the evening he was killed. But Dr. Hill doesn't want to use the contents in the stomach as time-of-death indicator because of the extreme heat of the mud. He had a gold crown, so I know dental records exist somewhere. But wait..." Alexa suddenly thought of the crime scene, of how blood is a fluid and responds to the laws of physics. "Sir, I should go back to the scene with your officers. Even if we don't find the murder weapon, any blood spatter will yield evidence. Perhaps handedness."

"Handedness?"

"Lefty or righty."

"All righty." Horne's left eyebrow twitched. "Post the dentals first. Call me if there's a match." He handed her a password for the lab computer.

"Camera, sir. I'll need a camera with lights and a crime kit."

"Go down to the equipment room for a camera. And then you can check out the lab, post the dentals, grab a kit. And I'll let Walker and crew know you'll be joining them."

"Thank you."

"My team calls me Senior."

—

Why were labs always in basements? Alexa was curious to see what kind of crime lab she had to work with. The one in Raleigh had been state of the art with new equipment and highly trained researchers, lots of them rookie eager beaver graduates of NC State's Forensic Sciences Institute, one of the best in the country.

Door was locked.

After running back upstairs to find someone with a key card,

Alexa impatiently gained access. The lab would do. A row of cabinets, work stations, two open cubicles, and multiple microscopes surrounded her. Two doors, one labeled Trace and the other Biological/Toxicology, were closed. A door to a large supply closet and another work station was open. Alexa felt like an intruder in someone's private space but brushed the feeling aside and sat down at one of the computers.

The central tenet of forensics odontology was that postmortem teeth can be identified by antemortem dental records. That was, if the person had records. Alexa had learned dental care was publicly funded for Kiwis until their eighteenth birthday. From the dental profile Alexa completed at the autopsy's end, she knew that this man's care had continued past then. The gold tooth was proof. But lately, he had slacked off. The cavity had probably been bothering him. And teeth grinding, or bruxism, often indicated anxiety. What was mystery man worried about? She spent thirty minutes sending a mass email with attached postmortem chart and X-rays to dentists registered in the greater Rotorua area. Maybe there would be a match in the morning. If not, she'd go countrywide. Then international.

She found a storage room in the lab, picked out the equipment she would need, and left.

In the Toyota, Alexa realized she was ravenous. It was six thirty p.m. and she had skipped lunch. She pulled out of the station lot, determined to find fast food. Mickey D's, she had noted in Auckland, had invaded Kiwi land like kudzu.

Ordering a Quarter Pounder, fries, and a drink at a McDonald's near the station, Alexa removed the pickles and decided to eat while driving. She turned the heat up in the car—springtime temperatures dropped quickly as the sun set—and navigated thirty minutes of wrong-side-of-the-road driving to the thermal park, allowing herself a victory smile for landing a job. Of course, it was at the expense of a murdered man.

My team calls me Senior. Alexa's smile widened.

—

In the mud pot parking lot, Alexa pulled a protective jumpsuit over her funeral clothes, glad for the extra layer. There was nothing she could do about her black pumps. She vowed then and there to store a spare pair of work shoes in the trunk. Boots for the boot. She gathered the equipment—camera bag, hand-held flash, tripod, and Maglite—and started down the path. Horne had assured her the team had the crime scene kit with them.

Darkness had descended; the path was barely discernible as it curved toward the boiling slurry. Alexa paused to let her eyes adjust and then proceeded slowly, the camera bag nudging her side. The whisper of plops and glops ahead and a scritch from behind spooked her.

Probably a possum.

Alexa stopped and looked over her shoulder. Nothing. Her heart was racing. Deep yoga breaths. She started again and in a few minutes made it to the second viewing area above the pots where she had stood just that morning.

Macbeth's witches worked below. Three ghostly figures, illuminated by spotlights, humongous shadows attached to each, shifted silently.

Get control of yourself.

"Hello," Alexa called. "Detective Inspector Horne sent me." She wondered if the police officers were trampling evidence. At least they were wearing suits. She brushed aside the fact that she herself might have contaminated the area that morning. "Could you come up this way?"

The three figures looked up and then conversed with each other. "We're working," one of them finally yelled.

"I need to speak with all of you. Up here," replied Alexa. She stooped to pull booties over her pumps and tried to banish thoughts that a search at this point, on ground already trampled by geologists, EMTs, and detectives and now a trio of

Rotorua's finest, was futile. Assume nothing, Dr. Winget had always reminded her staff.

"Shite," one of them said, stumbling. Alexa thought it might be the cop who had knocked on Horne's door.

The trio started climbing the bank. "Who does she think she is?" another voice, male, said. Reaching the platform, all three scowled at her. Alexa recognized Officer Cooper, the Maori cop. Next to her was the ginger-haired cop who had barged into Horne's office. The third guy, towering over his colleagues, was the one who had been with Byers and Horne this morning. She remembered his glare.

"I'm Alexa Glock, and I've been assigned to handle the forensics investigation. Which of you is in charge?"

"I remember you. You trespassed this morning," said tall guy.

"I asked who was in charge," Alexa repeated.

"I'm the senior officer."

"Your name?"

"Abel Rangiora. This is Officer Walker, and you already met Officer Cooper."

Alexa nodded.

"Everything is under control."

The senior officer had swirly dark hair, a wide nose, and a strong jaw. Hunky. Probably around thirty, Alexa guessed, Tongan, maybe, because of his size. But he could also be Maori. "How are you conducting the search?" Nighttime scenes, no matter how sufficient the lighting, were fraught with chances to err. Evidence seen in sunlight was easily missed and trampled on in the dark. Luckily, it wasn't raining.

"When we arrived, we set up the lights," Rangiora said. "We then divided the safe areas into sections. We're in section 2A."

"Find anything?"

"No weapon."

"I'm impressed with how you're conducting the search. But let me get down there and scout around for blood spatter."

"We've taken photos already. Obviously." Rangiora squared his formidable shoulders.

"I need to get to ground level and examine the soil for any darkening, which probably won't show up in your photos. There's BLUESTAR spray in the kit, right?" Alexa squared her own shoulders and jutted her chin.

"We've searched half the scene already," Rangiora countered.

"For the murder weapon, yes. I want to crawl around now, look for spatter."

"Yeah nah."

Alexa hated this odd Kiwi saying and fixed the senior officer with a stare. His arguing was fraying her nerves, but if she called him on it in front of Cooper and Walker, who silently watched, there would be hell to face.

"Walker, get back down there and man the lights," Rangiora finally said. Cooper mumbled something as Walker clambered down.

"Do you have something to add, Officer Cooper?" Alexa asked.

Blue lips pressed together.

"Go ahead and prepare the spray," she told the senior officer. BLUESTAR came in a tablet and needed to be dissolved in water. She loved the stuff that glowed in the dark when it came into contact with blood. "Do a double dose and then join me. Keep the lights on until we tell you to cut them," she called to Walker. Alexa climbed down just as a waft of sulfuric mist concealed the route. She slipped two feet, camera bag careening, but caught herself before landing on her butt. On level ground, she took a few moments to still her heart, busying herself with getting the equipment ready. She finally walked over to the corner of the squared-off area. More mist obscured the view. "You there?" she asked Walker.

"What, ma'am?"

"Never mind." Carefully, she lifted the ribbon, squatted, and started slowly sweeping the ground with her Maglite, which provided a brighter and more direct beam than the two portable lights. It was difficult discerning dark, muddy terrain from dark, bloody terrain. She got onto her gloved hands and knees and moved an inch at a time, the oozing mud pits sounding closer and louder. A rock jabbed her knee. "Dammit."

"You right?" came Rangiora's voice.

"Yes. Stay back there until I call you."

Meticulously, she swept the strong beam back and forth, crawling forward. Bloops and splats and gurgles became crazy background elevator Muzak. The breeze carried sulfur stink but then glided on, leaving the air dank and muddy again. Back and forth. Rangiora clearing his throat. Soft murmurs of the other two officers. A laugh. A plonk. A stink. The dark earth looked darker as she neared the center of square two. She shone her light back and forth to make sure.

"Officer Rangiora, follow the way I just came." Quickly, he was by her side, squatting.

"Spray here," Alexa instructed. She could hear Rangiora breathing steadily as he doused the area.

"Ready," he said.

"Lights off," Alexa called, tense and expectant.

An aurora borealis luminescence shone on the ground.

"Bull's-eye," Rangoria said. "Come here, Coop. Look at this."

Science—what was not to love? Alexa thought.

Officer Cooper had been standing beyond the caution ribbon. "Looks like glowworms," she said.

"Turn the lights back on, Walker. We need a negative control sample." Rangiora sprayed more BLUESTAR in the next grid, and he and Coop fist-bumped when nothing happened in the dark. Alexa set the camera on a tripod, readied the flash, and carefully pointed the shutter at an angle to avoid hot spots. Finished with the still photos, she switched to video and recorded the glowing area for ten seconds. The up and down was killing her knees, and the lights on and lights off gave her a headache. "Let's get this soil bagged now," she said to Cooper when she finished. "I'll run it in the morning."

She stayed and helped search the rest of the area, perhaps eking a crumb of respect from her new colleagues. The eerie explosions of plops and bloops faded into the new normal, barely discernible. An hour later, they had a single cigarette butt to add to the collection. No murder rock.

Chapter Five

She had timed it: it took twenty minutes to drive to the police station from the cottage, but Alexa had not factored in rain and rush hour traffic, naively certain that rush hour did not exist in Rotorua, New Zealand. She'd left at seven thirty, figuring that would leave her a few minutes to pop into the ladies', subdue her quarreling dark locks, and dab on lipstick.

But now it was 8:05.

Dashing into the station and ignoring the waving hands of Ms. Welles, Alexa took the stairs two by two. Out of breath, she knocked on DI Horne's office door.

No answer.

She heard voices coming from down the hall, licked naked lips, and entered a large meeting room. Detective Inspector Bruce Horne was standing at the front by a corkboard. Alexa quickly scanned the room and counted the three officers from last night plus two men in civvies.

All eyes turned to her.

"Ah, Ms. Glock," Horne said. "Let me introduce you to the team." She nodded as officers Rangiora, Cooper, and Walker were introduced.

"We've met, sir," Rangiora reminded Horne.

"And these two gentlemen are loaners from Auckland," Horne said. "Detective Trimble is undercover, and Detective McNamara is from homicide." Horne turned back to the team. "Ms. Glock will act as lead forensics examiner for the case. Any finds from last night's search?"

"What happened to Byers?" interrupted the homicide detective. His stringy ponytail, faded blue jeans, and loose beige fisherman's sweater contrasted sharply with the other detective, who was closely clipped and wearing a suit.

"Byers had a family emergency," Horne answered and turned back to Alexa.

"Possible blood and a cigarette butt, sir." The word "senior" flashed in her mind, but it was too unfamiliar for her to use. "No murder weapon."

"Good you got there last night before this rain washed trace away. Any word from the dental community?"

She had tried to check from home but hadn't been able to get a connection. "I'll check ASAP. Dental clinics are probably opening up around now."

Horne's eyebrows furrowed. "We still don't know who our victim is. Body was found three days ago. Why hasn't someone been reported missing?"

No answers.

"What did we find out from the person who spotted a car leaving the scene?"

"Dead end, Senior," said Walker. "She had her dates wrong."

"Figures. Are we done with crime scene witness statements?" Horne looked at Officer Rangiora.

"Bloody hell it's been," Rangiora answered. "Twenty of them didn't see anyone. Three claim a car was leaving as the bus pulled up, but they don't agree on the color or make. One insists she saw a bearded woman down by the mud pool. I think she has her gender pronouns backward. The rest don't speak English, so we're sending a Mandarin interpreter to meet up with them."

"One or two tossers have sold pictures to the newspapers," Walker added. "The photos have gone viral."

"Over a thousand hits," Rangiora said. "It's shambles. The tour group left the North Island this morning—we couldn't force them to stay any longer. They're on the ferry to the South Island. Impossible to do follow-up questions."

"The tour director was fuming that the group missed Tamaki Maori Village. They wanted their *hāngī* and *haka,* Coop, right? Doesn't your uncle run that place?" Walker asked.

What the heck is hāngī? Alexa wondered but kept her mouth shut.

Officer Cooper glared at Walker.

Horne began issuing directives when the detective with the ponytail interrupted again. "The bootprint found at the scene is the best evidence we got." He held up two clear bags. "This duct tape recovered from the body is too damaged to use."

Alexa was a duct tape geek. "Maybe not," she said. She knew tape was commonly used to bind victim's hands or mouths. It could be dusted for fingerprints, swabbed for DNA, or, if it looked like the criminal had ripped the tape with their teeth, used for dental comparisons. In a recent court case, she had superimposed the suspect's dental model with a duplicated model of the marks of recovered tape. Presto: busted.

When the meeting ended, she popped over to the loaner cops and started talking. "Mind if I see the tape?"

"The heat from the thermal mud destroyed any evidence," scowled Ponytail.

"The duct tape around his hands wasn't boiled. It might yield information," Alexa said, pulling out a chair and sitting.

"Where is it you're from?" asked Ponytail, scratching at some irregular beard growth.

"Auckland via Raleigh. In North Carolina, where I've worked in forensics for the past ten years." She remembered an exciting story. "Back home, we had one case where a body was discovered after being buried in a riverbank for a decade. The skull was wrapped in Scotch 110–3 Multi-Use like a mummy. That stuff is indestructible. I retrieved teeth-mark patterns, and they matched the husband's."

"And they lived happily ever after, eh?" asked Ponytail. His hair needed a shampoo.

"Lighten up," the other detective said. His wireless glasses had slipped down his nose as he scrutinized the tape.

"Mind if I look?" Alexa asked.

"Sure." Trimble pushed the two clear evidence bags over to Alexa. The tape in the first bag formed a wadded black blob. Dr. Hill had said it had mostly been eaten by acid. The tape in the second bag held more potential. She studied it. Flat, about seven inches long, one side covered in dried and flecked mud. The reverse side was slightly cleaner.

"Too bad it's not fabric. Prints adhere better," she said. Some steel gray peeped through dried mud. "Gray. Narrows it down to about one hundred brands. In the U.S., anyway. How about here?"

"Higgins carries six types of gray duct tape. We were about to head over there," Trimble said. He looked to be midthirties and had pale-green eyes and a bump at the end of his nose to catch his glasses.

"Looks heat-resistant. That will narrow it down," Alexa added. "I'll take it back to the lab. I can identify the brand, separate it, and check for bite marks. Lifting prints will be difficult. But not impossible."

"Waste of time," Ponytail mumbled, standing.

"Take it," Trimble offered, also standing. "We can use the photos. I'll head down with you. I want to check out the footprint cast."

Alexa, who was chomping to check email and test the blood spatter, followed Trimble down the hall, examining his neatly pressed suit. In her experience with the Raleigh Police department, homicide detectives wore suits and undercover agents were scruffy. This role reversal intrigued her.

"Why are crime labs always in basements?"

"Beats me, but I like it," the undercover cop replied. "Sunlight hurts my eyes."

Trimble opened the lab door and announced to a young woman standing at a microscope that Alexa was her boss for the mud pit case and asked for his boot cast.

The young Asian woman pointed to the cast and then turned her bright, eager eyes toward Alexa. "Hi. I'm Jenny Liang."

"I'm pleased to meet you," Alexa said. "What are you looking at?"

"I'm comparing several different soil samples collected from the scene. I hope that's okay. Evidence was piling up."

"Glad you took the initiative," Alexa replied.

Liang lowered her head and looked through the scope. "I'm seeing two unique patterns consistent with being from different locations."

"Excellent. Write that up. Let's meet in thirty minutes to go over what you have so far. Where can I test this tape?" The Raleigh computer system could access the FBI's National Forensic Tape File, which held samples of any type of duct tape known to man, woman, or hardware store. Would she be able to access it from a lab in Rotorua, New Zealand? And was the blood collected last night human blood? If so, whose? She rubbed her hands together and first logged into the lab computer to see if she had heard from local dentists. One reply only, and it was to solicit her business.

Alexa was soon using alcohol to clean a section of the tape and was happily immersed in the messy world of identifying the glue, fibers, and plastic backing of duct tape. She probably wouldn't need the FBI files anyway. And she couldn't wait to get to the samples collected from last night. A shoulder tap an hour later interrupted her happy flow.

"Here you are," Ms. Welles said sternly. "Didn't you see me waving at you earlier?"

"I apologize," Alexa said.

"Paperwork. You need to fill out paperwork if you want authorization to be using this equipment and have access to this lab. Come with me." Ms. Welles's forehead was bunched into two distinct knots.

Alexa mentally kicked herself. This was an opportunity she didn't want to jeopardize, so she obediently followed the straight-backed secretary.

The rest of the day passed in a blur. The bloodstained soil collected last night had occupied her for ninety minutes in the lab. Fundamentals of blood forensics: First, is it blood? The BLUESTAR indicated that it was. Alexa did a quick check to confirm the findings. Yes. Second, is it human blood? The quick serum protein check she ran indicated it was human blood. And finally, what blood type? The blood type test indicated type A, second most common blood type. Now she would send it off for DNA testing.

Assuming it was the murder victim's blood, Alexa hurried to upload the photos she had taken at the scene last night. The lighting was good. She studied the patterns of blue-green swirls on the computer screen. BLUESTAR evidence always told a story. Alexa puzzled over the plot. There were no drag smears, so she surmised the man expired on the spot. Had he been standing when he was killed? Or kneeling? An exclamation-shaped bluish blob indicated the man had been moving when he was hit, perhaps turning. The spatter measurements indicated he had been standing upright. Some of the story was unfolding.

This was way better than looking at dental bitewings.

Alexa readied a DNA sample and asked the lab assistant where to send it. Later, she and Jenny started working on separating the duct tape that Alexa had identified as Scotch general purpose duct tape in silver, made in the United States, "good quick stick to many surfaces, easy tear, used for splicing, waterproofing, bundling, tying, sealing, protecting," and, Alexa added to the advertising attributes, murder. It was unfortunately carried by almost every hardware store in the dual-island country.

"Because it's easy tear, we won't have teeth marks," Alexa said, more to herself than to Jenny.

Another disappointment had been that the prints on the slicker outer layer of the tape were too contaminated to be of use, just as Ponytail dude had predicted. Alexa was hopeful that the inner layers might yield prints. She had read about a case in the *Journal of Forensic Sciences* where tape was unwound using a tape-release agent and prints were viable from the inner layers. Jenny carefully dripped a two percent chloroform tape-release agent over the stuck-together area while Alexa painstakingly pulled the tape apart, bit by bit.

"I didn't learn about this at uni," Jenny said. "My boyfriend, Evan, is studying forensics at Auckland now, and I can't wait to tell him about this. He can impress his profs."

Jenny was a talker. Alexa learned that this was her first "real" job since earning a postgraduate diploma in forensic science from the University of Auckland and that she was sick of roommates and currently apartment-hunting. The nonstop chatter was pleasant, and Alexa found herself smiling and relaxed.

She showed Jenny how to lay the tape flat, sticky side up, to dry overnight. "We'll check it for prints first thing in the morning," she said when the lab door opened abruptly.

"Happy Smiles is trying to reach you," said Ms. Welles, her mouth doing Angry Frown.

Alexa stared blankly.

"I've transferred the call." Welles pointed to a wall phone and left.

Jenny shrugged, and Alexa, removing her gloves, picked up the phone. A man identified himself as Dr. Jason Paley of Happy Smiles Dental Clinic on Milton Road and excitedly launched into consent releases, proper warrant, a gold alloy replacement, and an amalgam restoration match. "I'll go ahead and tell you, his name is Paul Koppel. I'll release the records as soon as you fax the proper documents," Paley said.

"So he's local?" Alexa pressed.

"Yes."

"His address, please."

Though he shouldn't have, the dentist seemed thrilled to be involved and blurted the address. "Haven't seen him in a few, but his lads are regulars."

"Do you happen to know his blood type?" If Koppel had had any oral surgery, it would be in his chart.

"Type A."

Time to impress the boss.

Sprinting up two flights of stairs and down the hall, Alexa rapped loudly on Horne's door. He was in, wolfing a pastry at his desk. Her stomach rumbled at the sight.

"I've just received a call from a local dentist," Alexa said before he could swallow. "I know who our victim is."

"Right," Horne said. Crumbs littered his lips. "So do I."

Alexa's mouth dropped.

He wiped his lips, crumpled the napkin, aimed, and swished it into a trash can. He had missed a few bits. "A Mrs. Mindy Koppel called an hour ago to report a missing husband. When we asked if he had any identifying scars, she described the one on his right thigh." Horne paused and gulped, swallowing either pastry or the memory of mud pot man. "Officer Rangoria picked her up and went to the morgue. She recognized the scar. A fishing knife accident, apparently." He shook his head. "Family liaison took her home and called her parents and general physician. She's hysterical. There's two kids, boys. You can confirm with his dentals."

A flash of anger. "Why wasn't I informed?"

"I'm informing you now." His blue eyes challenged her.

This time, the heat flash wasn't anger but something else. Alexa flicked it away.

Horne continued. "Paul Koppel. Forty-two. Lives on Hanrahan Road. Real estate agent for Bowen Realty Group and a district councilor."

Alexa checked her scrap of paper. Yep. "Why did Koppel's wife take three days to report him missing?"

"She and the children just returned from their holiday cottage at Papamoa Beach. They hadn't spoken all weekend."

Alexa frowned. Domestic violence homicide was increasing back home. Was it here as well?

"Did Ms. Welles get you official?"

"Yes. I now have a temporary ID and a key card. But she doesn't like me."

"She doesn't like any woman other than herself. Haven't figured out why, but it's best to stay on her good side."

Alexa had already blown that with her early morning fly-by. "Roger." She grabbed an extra napkin on his desk and handed it to him, pointing at his mouth. It was hard to have a serious conversation with someone flaky. "Was it good?"

Now it was Horne's turn to be confused.

Alexa pointed to the wrapper. Georgie Pies, she had learned, were a Kiwi staple akin to chicken nuggets in America. Her stomach grumbled again.

Horne nodded.

"Wish I had some Bo."

"What the hell is that?" His eyebrows did a jig.

"Bojangles." Flirting was safe if a man was married. "Sweet iced tea. Biscuits. Fried chicken. Heaven. Where have you been?"

His smile made him appear younger.

"When do you think you can talk with Mrs. Koppel?" she asked.

"Doctor gave her something to calm her down and just gave his okay. It's paramount to get to her as soon as possible so her story is unrehearsed. I'm leaving"—he looked at his watch—"now."

"Why don't I go with you?"

Horne's left eyebrow went sky-high. "Don't you have lab work?"

"It's five o'clock. I've been working all day and have results I can share with you on the way."

"Let's go."

"Do you mind if we stop at a McDonald's for a take away?"

—

Between bites of her own Georgie Pie, Alexa, riding shotgun in the DI's unmarked cruiser, filled him in on what was happening in the lab. She explained the soil sample she'd taken the night before contained drops of human blood, type A, which matched Koppel's. He had probably been struck and killed in that spot before being dumped in the mud pot.

"You know we didn't find the murder weapon last night. Two soil specimens collected at the scene were inconsistent. The alien soil might indicate an area where Koppel or the murderer had been prior to the killing," Alexa said with relish. "The young woman in the lab, Jenny, she's good. She's contacting those geologists who checked the scene.

"Liang still needs guidance, but overall, she's been working out." Alexa mentioned the blood she sent for DNA testing along with the cigarette butt collected last night. "You have backlogs here like we do in Raleigh," she added. "Makes me feel at home."

"I'll give them a call to rush them," Horne interrupted. "This case takes priority."

Alexa added that she planned to run the duct tape for prints first thing in the morning and that Trimble had one usable bootprint cast that did not match the brogans Koppel had been wearing. "I agree with that Auckland detective with the ponytail. It's probably our best clue," Alexa said. "Size ten Lastrite workboot." She wiped her mouth and wished for water.

Her throat was dry.

Chapter Six

Paul and Mindy Koppel's house was a modest gray cottage partly obscured by boxwoods and blooming hydrangeas. A curved cement walkway littered with leaves and twigs led to a front porch large enough for a glider and two pots of parched petunias. A tall silver-haired man, shoulders squared, answered their knock.

"Hello. I'm Detective Inspector Bruce Horne of Rotorua Police Headquarters, and this is my colleague Alexa Glock." Horne showed his badge. "Mrs. Koppel is expecting us. I called ahead."

"I'm Jerry Russell, Mindy's father." He extended his hand to Horne and then Alexa. "Come in." He opened the door to a small foyer. "Mindy is in the den. I'd like to sit with her while you talk. Needless to say, we're all in shock."

"That's fine," Horne said.

A sudden shout came from a back hallway. "No! You aren't my mum. You can't make me." A carrot-headed boy shot into the entryway followed by a rail thin woman, her face strained.

"Pardon us," she said to Horne and Alexa.

"What's wrong, Ted?" Russell asked.

"Nana wants me to take a bath, and I won't. Only Mum gives me a bath. I want Mum."

"Of course you do. How dirty are you? Rugby or cricket?"

Caught off guard, the little boy looked down at his fairly clean T-shirt and shorts. "We played football."

"Football. No lad needs a bath after football unless he's goal-keeper. Did you tend goal?"

"No. Eddie did."

"See, Marge? He doesn't need a bath. Just a flannel behind his ears." Russell pinched Ted's ear and made him smile. "Then he'll be ready for tea. Off you go then." Before introductions were made, the boy and woman disappeared.

Paul Koppel's father-in-law smiled. "Management skills. That's all it takes. That was my wife, Marge. Ted's seven. We haven't let on yet about Paul, but he knows something is wrong. His brother, Casey, is five. Come into the sitting room."

Alexa wondered how Nana felt being undermined, but at least Russell had defused the situation. Who cares about clean toes when there's been a death? She walked with the men into a room of knotty pine paneling and stepped over a plush monkey with a missing eye. A worn beige sofa faced two floral armchairs. A woman wrapped in a crocheted afghan slumped in one.

"Princess, these are the police." Russell put a hand on his daughter's shoulder. "Please sit." He pointed to the couch.

Seated, a wilted pillow removed from behind his back and placed between them, Horne began. "Mrs. Koppel, we spoke earlier. I'm Detective Inspector Horne, and this is Ms. Glock from Crime Scene Investigation."

Mindy Koppel gazed hollow-eyed at Alexa and wiped her large nose with a tissue.

"I am sorry for your loss," Alexa said, wondering if Mrs. Koppel had ever considered rhinoplasty, and then chastised herself. Beauty was in the eye and all that.

"I understand this is a bad time, but we need to ask you some questions," the DI said. "First off, we need a recent photograph of the deceased."

Alexa realized with a start she had no idea what the victim

looked like. The man's blackened, denuded face flashed in her mind.

Russell strode to a bookcase and lifted a framed photo. He handed it to the DI and perched on the arm of Mindy's chair. "Taken at a real estate do, right, darling?"

Alexa leaned close to the DI, curious. Receding brown hair, glasses, forced smile, coat and tie. An average Joe.

"Who did this?" Mindy rasped. "Who hurt my husband?" She sat a little straighter, pushed lanky blond hair behind her ears, and sniffed.

"We don't know yet. We're doing everything we can to find out. Could you tell me about where you've been the last three days and how you discovered your husband was missing?"

"What do you mean?"

Horne spoke as if to a young child. "Start by stating your name and age, and then tell me where you've been since Saturday." He moved some magazines from the coffee table in front of them and placed a small recorder on it. Alexa pulled a pad of paper and pen from her tote.

"I'm Mindy Koppel. I'm forty—just turned forty." She stopped, fiddled with her hair again, and waited.

"Where have you been the last few days, Mrs. Koppel?" Horne prompted.

"We were at the bach."

Alexa reminded herself that "batch" was spelled "bach" and was Kiwi for holiday house. "The boys and I drove down Saturday." Pause. "Paul was supposed to come."

"Why didn't he?"

"Work. Some emergency meeting." Mindy blinked rapidly. "He's been working long hours."

"Was anyone else with you at the bach?"

Alexa admired the way he kept his voice even-tempered, mild. He had a face that most women would find attractive, and Alexa suddenly wondered about his wife, what she looked like, did she have a career, could she make her detective husband laugh?

"No. Just the three of us. And our dog, Abbie." Again she pushed hair away from her eyes. Alexa caught a glimpse of a collie dog in the garden through the open window.

"Do you usually go alone? To the bach?"

"Not often." She looked up at her father. "It's Mum and Dad's place. Most times, they come too. But Mum had a doctor's appointment."

"When did Paul find out about his meeting?"

"I don't know. Maybe Thursday. He told me Thursday night he couldn't come to Papamoa."

Surprise meetings and last-minute cancellations bugged Alexa. Mindy pressed her fingers to her lips.

"Were you upset?" Horne asked.

"What do you mean?" She straightened and looked him directly in the eyes. Her father put an arm around her.

"Were you upset that he couldn't join you for the weekend?"

"A bit." Pause. "Paul has been super busy. But that's good." She glanced at her father, who gave her a nod.

"What time did you arrive home today?"

"Around noon. We had to unpack and then go to the grocery. I called Paul to see what time he'd be home for tea. He didn't answer his mobile so I called the agency. Joan—that's the office secretary—said she hadn't seen him for a few days and didn't know about a meeting."

Alexa drew a star next to this in her notes.

Horne leaned forward. "What did you do then?"

"I popped next door to see if the Jacksons had seen Paul. They're both retired. They said they saw him pull out early Saturday but not since then. They thought he had gone to the bach with us. I got worried, so I called Dad, and he said I should call the police."

Alexa studied Mindy Koppel intently.

"So I did. I called the police."

Alexa had conducted a training for the Raleigh Police Force

on distinguishing between truth and lies, and she was good at it, or so she thought. Mindy Koppel could have killed her husband. Happened all the time, though most spousal homicide is committed by firearm, not boiling mud. Alexa mentally reviewed the classic signs of deception: holding eye contact, excessive blinking, not using "I" or "me" statements, giving brief explanations, vagueness, slow speech, grooming behaviors, and repeating questions before answering.

"When was the last time you spoke with your husband?" Horne asked.

"What?"

"When did you last have contact with Paul?"

"I texted to let him know when we arrived Saturday. He texted back, and I didn't talk to him since."

"Is that unusual?"

Pause. "Not really." More silence. "Neither one of us much likes yakking on the phone. Paul always says…" Once again, she stopped and thrust hair out of her eyes. Horne waited her out. Voices and the smell of sausage being fried drifted into the room; an unhappy wail made Mindy turn her head.

"When did you last speak to Paul?" her father asked.

"The last time we talked was Saturday morning while he was eating porridge and the boys and I left for the beach. He ran after us with Abbie's lead." Tears appeared, and underneath the afghan, she produced her phone, staring at it. "I keep calling, and he doesn't answer."

"We'll need to borrow that," Horne said, holding out his hand. Russell pried her fingers loose and handed the mobile to the DI, who slipped it into his pocket. "I also need your husband's mobile number."

Mindy looked panicked. "I…I don't know it. I have it on speed dial."

Digital amnesia, Alexa concluded. None of us memorize phone numbers anymore.

"That's fine. We'll retrieve it from your phone. Where is your husband's car?"

"I don't know. You've got to find it. Maybe..."

"We'll need the make and license."

Jerry Russell snorted. "I've told Paul he needed an upgrade. A ten-year-old Corolla isn't the right message to send clients."

"The car is fine," Mindy protested. Despite several checks made to her list, Alexa didn't think Mindy Koppel was faking shock and grief. But even murderers experienced these emotions.

"Did you and your husband argue before you left?" Horne said. "I imagine you were angry he couldn't come."

"No." Mindy Koppel's nostrils flared.

"Had your husband ever harmed you? Hit or slapped you?"

She glared. "No. Paul was a good husband. How dare you."

Her father hugged Mindy to him. "My daughter was never physically abused. She would have told me."

Alexa knew they would check out hospital records to confirm. She thought of the cigarette butt found at the crime scene. "Did your husband smoke, Mrs. Koppel?"

Mindy shook her head no.

The DI stood. "You've been helpful. I'll need you to stop in the station tomorrow morning to be fingerprinted."

"Why on earth...?" Russell spat.

"Procedure. For elimination. One more question."

Alexa knew what was coming even before Horne opened his mouth.

"Can you think of anyone who'd want to harm Paul?"

"No! Of course not. Everyone loves Paul." Tears streaked her pale face, and her nose began to run. She tugged the afghan tighter and shrugged her father away.

Not everyone, Alexa thought.

—

As soon as their belts were buckled, Alexa looked at Horne. "What do you think?"

"I'm withholding judgment until her alibi is verified." He started the engine, lowered the driver's window, and turned to look at her. "It concerns me that Mrs. Koppel went several days without speaking to her husband. That's unusual, don't you think? Wouldn't he call to ask after the boys?"

Having zero experience with the dynamic duo of marriage and children, Alexa rerouted. "She failed my lie detection checklist."

"Lie detection checklist?" His left eyebrow hit his hairline as he continued to study her.

She fought to hold his stare. "For three hundred bucks, I'll hold a seminar for your department. Most people lie three times within the first fifteen minutes of meeting someone new. Mindy Koppel blinked too much."

"What were yours?"

"What were my what?" Alexa asked.

"Your three lies. When we first met." His eyes deepened to a sapphire hue.

"You didn't give me my allotted fifteen minutes," she replied, her face heating up.

Stop flirting. I'm not interested in married men.

Horne broke the stare-fest. "Continue with your checklist."

"Mrs. Koppel repeated questions and kept touching her hair. Classic signs. My guess is she's holding something back but..."

"But what?" Horne had finally pulled away from the curb and glanced at her.

"I don't think she killed him."

"To rule her out, I'll make sure she was in Papamoa at the time of the murder. Check for witnesses. And I'll get Trimble to see if there's a life insurance policy. The Koppels have a modest lifestyle. Maybe Mrs. Koppel wanted more. Maybe she wasn't content with..."

Horne became silent, and Alexa wondered where his thoughts had traveled. To his own wife?

A toot from behind got him to pick up speed. "I have an APB on the missing car, and we'll talk with the Koppels' neighbors immediately. They may have seen something," Horne said. "I'm seeing Mark Haddonfield at nine o'clock tomorrow morning. He's deputy mayor of the district council and worked with Koppel, and I want to know what issues they've been involved with. Maybe something contentious."

"What kind of stuff is going on in Rotorua these days?" Alexa relished this exchange of information. It was all she could do to not rub her hands together.

"Big-time stuff. Should we raise the speed limit on Watawata Road? Should we grow more timber to sell to China? Add fluoridation to the water system? An art center just opened in the public garden. Maybe the groundskeeper is worried about his roses. I don't know. Trimble and McNamara are digging up everything they can find on Koppel. Bank records. Affairs. Real estate dealings. Parking tickets. Library card."

"Library card?"

"You never know what he'd checked out."

"People do their research on the internet now," Alexa said, thinking about how she had checked out the detective before they'd met.

"There's another press conference tomorrow afternoon, the mayor's coming, and I want something to report. People are afraid."

"My friend's brother..."

"Your friend?" They had pulled into the station parking lot.

"Mary." Saying the name was a stab of pain. "The one who died. Remember I came to Rotorua for a funeral? Her brother Terrance—that's his name; he's a Maori like Mary was—Terrance says this might be some kind of Maori hate crime or revenge."

Horne didn't laugh.

Alexa continued. "Terrance says that the phrase 'Go boil your head' is the most offensive curse a Maori can make toward another person." She gathered her courage to try the Maori phrase. "*Upoko kōhua.*"

They parted in the darkening parking lot.

Chapter Seven

Sprinting around a curve at six-thirty Thursday morning, Alexa knocked over a hooded youth holding—what were the odds?—a basket of eggs. The teenager sprawled to the ground, and eggs exploded like sunburst paint balls around him.

"My bad. I'm sorry," panted Alexa. She leaned over to help, and a spatter of her sweat dropped on his face.

"Bugger," he said, hopping up and shaking yolk off one of his Nikes, almost falling again. "Where did you come from?"

"Are you okay?" Alexa looked up at him. He was a six-foot beanpole. She dusted off the one unbroken egg and retrieved the basket. "I'm sorry. I was jogging and thought I had the path to myself. It's so early." She thrust the basket into his hand.

"Well, watch where you're going." He blushed scarlet in the budding light and brushed dirt off his knees.

"You're right. I will. I'll pay you for the eggs."

His giant brown eyes widened, parting his furry unibrow. How old was he? Fifteen? Sixteen? "No worries," he croaked. "I was taking them to some lady who's renting our cottage. She'll never know she didn't get them."

"Maybe she will. What cottage?"

"Trout."

"That's me," Alexa said. "I'm her."

"Her who?"

"The lady who's renting your cottage. I'm Alexa Glock." She offered her hand. The teen looked at it suspiciously, thought for a second, and then shook it.

"Here," he said, handing her back the lone egg and the basket. "Saved me a trip. Well, not really." They both laughed.

"What's your name?"

"Stevie. I mean Steve. Steve Ingall. My mum made me, I mean asked me, to deliver these...well...that." He pointed to the egg. "She's stopped by, but you weren't there."

"Tell her I love the cottage and everything's choice. Where do you live?"

"We're farther down Trout River Road about a kilometer, but you can cut through on the path just past Okere Falls. We've got a little farm, Mum and me and Sissie. Flying Fish Farm. Chooks and sheep."

"Tell your mum I'll drop by soon and return the basket. Her name's Sarah, right?" Alexa remembered this from the contract she signed for two weeks' rental. "I'm going to go back and cook this egg."

The morning light strengthened as Alexa jogged back to the cottage, careful not to jounce her breakfast.

—

Fortified by fresh fried egg and toast, Alexa left Trout Cottage early enough so that she arrived at the department at 7:50 sharp. She was excited about checking the duct tape used to bind the mud man's wrists. Fingers crossed, she strode through the main entrance and flew down the basement stairs. The hallway was dim. Alexa found the switch, flicked the lights up.

The lab door was unlocked, but when Alexa pushed it open, it was empty and dark. Jenny had said she'd arrive by seven thirty and set things up. Alexa grabbed gloves from the wall dispenser, pulled them on, and strode to the evidence shelf where she had stored the tape in a labeled plastic box.

No box. No tape. The bottle of developer lay on its side, a fallen soldier with nothing to guard.

What the hell?

The lab was silent except for the hum of a computer and overhead lights. Alexa scanned the room. The far end was dark except for a line of light seeping from the storage closet. Shouldn't it be locked?

"Good morning," she called. "Hello?" Silence.

Alexa scanned the lab again and came to a stop at Jenny's desk. A jacket and backpack were swung over the chair, and a takeout cup stood on the desk. She walked over and touched it, could smell tea. Barely warm.

"Jenny?" Alexa called out once more, her voice coming out raspy, low. "Jenny?"

This wasn't right. The light seeping from the storage room door beckoned.

She edged to the closet, the hair on her arms standing, the chemical reaction to fear pooling in her armpits. Taking a deep breath, she pushed open the door. One step in and she froze; Jenny's body, crumpled and slight, lay on the tile floor, and a trickle of darkening blood leaking from a tangle of long black hair pooled near her nose.

"Jenny." Alexa leaped, knelt, felt for a pulse on Jenny's neck and screamed, "Help! Help!" The pulse was faint. "Jenny, can you hear me?" She touched Jenny's cheek, pressed the clammy skin. No response.

Where the hell is a towel? A rag?

She jerked off her cardigan and pressed it to Jenny's head. Impossible to tell where the blood was leaking from. She had to leave her, get help. "I'll be right back."

Alexa sprinted through the lab into the hallway. Deserted.

"Hello? Help!" she screamed again. Where the hell was somebody? Down the hallway and through the exit door, she took the stairs two at a time and arrived breathless on the first floor lobby. Ms. Welles, taking paperwork from a nervous-looking woman with a tot clinging to her leg, turned toward her.

"Call 911!" Alexa yelled. "Jenny is hurt."

"What are you talking about?" Welles asked. The tot's eyes widened.

"Call 911. Call an ambulance. Call the police. Hurry." Welles frowned.

Alexa knew she wasn't making sense. She was *in* the police station, for God's sake. Place should be crawling with cops. And who knew what number to call in New Zealand to get an ambulance? *Not 911*. She slowed down. "The lab assistant has been attacked. In the lab, unconscious. And bleeding. Call an ambulance and DI Horne. Now."

Paling, Welles picked up the phone.

Finally.

Alexa dashed back to the lab.

—

"Tell me again what you saw when you arrived in the lab," Horne said thirty minutes later. Jenny had been rushed to Rotorua Hospital. The DI had ushered Alexa into his office and given her a bottle of water. She was seated while he, Jimmy Trimble, and Leo McNamara, the borrowed detectives from Auckland, paced like hungry vultures circling her chair. The office door was shut and the police station in lockdown. No one in. No one out. Ms. Welles was compiling a list of all people in the building at the estimated time of attack.

"I arrived at 7:50 and came down to the lab. The—" Her scar was itching.

"Did you head directly to the lab, right when you got here?" Horne interrupted.

"Yes. I headed right to the lab." The sudden thought that the attacker might have still been in the lab made Alexa's mouth go dry. She fumbled with the bottle's cap but couldn't twist it off.

"Go on." His face was expressionless, but the blue in his eyes had darkened to slate.

"The door was unlocked, but the lights were off. I thought that was strange." She wished the men would sit down or back up. Give her room to breathe. She struggled with the cap, finally got it to release its grip, and sucked down water as her eyes landed on a framed photo on Horne's desk. Two girls. Braces.

"Yet you still entered the lab," McNamara said. "Strange."

"Yes," Alexa replied. "I turned on the lights and went straight to the evidence shelf to get the…to get a sample we prepared yesterday. It was gone."

"What do you mean?" Horne asked.

"The sample wasn't where we left it yesterday. It was drying overnight." She stared at McNamara. "It was a portion of the duct tape we had separated yesterday. The box I had stored it in wasn't on the shelf. I looked around and noticed Jenny's jacket at her desk, so I figured she had to be here."

"Did anyone come in or out of the lab?" McNamara asked.

"Let her finish," Trimble said.

"No one was around," Alexa said to McNamara. "I called out Jenny's name and then noticed the door to the evidence closet was cracked and a light was on. I walked over and pushed it open." Alexa gulped more water, grateful for the hydrating coolness. "That's when I saw her. I checked her pulse and yelled for help, but no one could hear me. No one was in the hallway either, so I ran up to the lobby."

"Who was the first person you saw?" Horne asked, finally sitting behind his desk.

"Ms. Welles. She called for help, and I went back down to stay with Jenny."

"Why didn't you stay with Jenny and call for help with your

mobile?" McNamara asked. His face was hard, and his hands were clenched. "What if someone had come back and finished her off?"

"You're right. I should have."

"How many people knew about this tape you were testing?" the DI asked.

Alexa thought. She knew. Jenny knew. Who else? "I mentioned it to you on the way to interviewing Mindy Koppel yesterday. And Jenny recorded it in our preliminary report. I don't know if Jenny mentioned it to anyone." She had been excited to tell her boyfriend about the process, Alexa remembered.

"Someone knew about the tape," McNamara said. "And wanted it."

They all thought of the slight body being whisked away on a stretcher. Would Jenny Liang survive?

Horne sat quietly, lips pursed, and finally spoke. "We have to talk to everyone who was here at the station. See what they saw or heard. See what they were doing between seven a.m., when Jenny logged in, and eight. Find out who had access to the preliminary report. Check security cameras."

"I can help," Alexa blurted.

"Actually, no, you can't," Horne said. "Having found Jenny makes you a person of interest."

"A suspect," McNamara added.

"You're kidding, right?" Heat flooded her face. "Why would I attack Jenny?"

No one answered.

"The blood on the floor was congealing when I got there." She looked down and noted the tip of one running shoe splotched with egg. She hadn't wanted to wear running shoes to work, but her Keds and pumps were muddy.

The Egg Boy! Smacking into Stevie on the path this morning might clear her. "I can account for my whereabouts this morning to prove I wasn't at the station earlier."

Horne pushed a Post-it pad at her. "Name and number. And

then you can wait in the canteen. Have a cuppa." He spoke to Trimble and McNamara. "Let's get the interviews going."

The door swung open. "What the hell is going on here?" a man in a black silk suit demanded.

"District Commander Teal." Horne stood quickly. "I've been expecting you."

"I repeat." The two men faced each other, shoulders squared. The newcomer looked to be younger than the DI, his angular face unlined, but his hair a silken gray.

"Our lab technician, Jenny Liang, was attacked in the storage closet of the lab this morning," Horne said, his voice even and mild.

"Attacked in our own house? Is she dead? Who did it? Who are these people?" Teal looked at Alexa, Trimble, and McNamara.

"Liang was rushed to the hospital unconscious but breathing. I'll let my temporary staff introduce themselves."

Jimmy Trimble reached over to shake Teal's hand and introduce himself. "On loan from Auckland, sir." McNamara did the same.

Teal's quick once-over indicated he wasn't impressed with McNamara's ponytail and scruffy blue jeans. "How's Joe?" he asked, looking from Trimble to McNamara.

"Joe?" McNamara said. "Oh, Commander Inspector Nelson. Joe Nelson. He's holding down the fort back in Auckland. He's cleaning up the mess from one of our drug cops going bad. He's in court today."

"Heard about that. Bad PR. Who's to say we don't have a bad cop here too. And you are?" He turned to Alexa. A wave of aftershave, Hugo Boss maybe, made her lean back.

"Alexa Glock. I'm working forensics for the mud pot murder."

"Glock?"

"Yes, sir. Temporary hire."

"Like the gun?"

"Like the gun." *Pleeze.*

"Ms. Glock is the person who found the lab technician," Horne explained. "We were just interviewing her. We'll need to talk with you too. Perhaps Detectives Trimble and McNamara can take care of that now."

"Yes. Get on with it. We need this station opened. Come. Take a look." He waved them over to the large window in Horne's office overlooking the street below. A half dozen uniformed officers with five German shepherds and one chocolate Lab circled the parking lot like aquarium sharks at dinnertime. "The North Island police dog unit is scheduled to start training at nine o'clock. We've got to open. The press is going to go bonkers when word gets out."

McNamara, Trimble, and Teal left for Teal's office. Alexa was offended Horne considered her a suspect. As if reading her thoughts, he indicated the Post-it pad. "Give me some info so I can check you off the list."

Alexa fumbled for her phone, checked her contacts list for Sarah Ingall, and wrote her name and number. "I've never met this woman, but I bumped into her teenage son this morning as I was running. She owns the cottage I'm renting."

"Bumped into?"

"Literally. Knocked him down. I'm sure he hasn't forgotten me."

He held her gaze a moment too long. "You are hard to forget."

—

An hour later, Senior Officer Rangiora found Alexa in the canteen sipping bitter coffee with her right hand while her left contorted up and over her opposite shoulder blade like a double-jointed gymnast, mauling unsatisfactorily at her scar and pondering whether to leave. Mary's funeral was over. What was holding her in Rotorua? She didn't need the hassle. She quickly straightened, sloshing coffee on the table.

"Senior said your alibi checked out and the security camera confirms you entered the building after the attack occurred."

"No surprise," Alexa snapped.

"DI Horne said for you to go check on Jenny Liang. And then stop by the dental clinic for Koppel's records. Welles faxed them the forms. There is an all-hands meeting at one o'clock."

Who else had been caught on security camera? she wondered.

The tall officer escorted her to the door just as the station was opened and the posse of dogs and trainers entered the building. "Of all days to be overrun by dogs," Rangiora said. "We stationed a guard at Liang's door," he added.

The implications chilled Alexa and made her forget about abandoning the case. She had to help find Jenny's attacker.

In the parking lot, she found herself searching for the old blue Honda she'd left behind in Raleigh. It was nowhere. Her mind jumped from the horror of seeing Jenny crumpled on the floor to the horror of becoming a "person of interest" to the aggravation of having her car stolen. Finally, she recognized the silver Vitz hatchback and drove the three blocks to the hospital, replaying what Horne had said: *I'm hard to forget.*

She wasn't sure whether that was good or bad.

The three-story hospital was half the size of Rex Hospital in Raleigh, but the scent of iodoform disinfectant whisked Alexa straight back to childhood. She had spent three weeks in the burn unit, mostly flat on her stomach, and three months in physical therapy rehab. She'd been thirteen. "Activity and motion will reduce the pain," the physical therapist had insisted, while Alexa, enduring another round of physical "terrorphy," knew the opposite was true. A metallic taste had flooded her mouth.

She had bitten her tongue.

Alexa got directions from a stylish woman at reception. One floor up and past a nurses' station, a uniformed officer was sitting in a chair, toying with his iPhone. Alexa introduced herself. The officer slipped the phone in his pocket, stood, and asked for ID. He frowned as he scrutinized her temporary badge.

"There's no photo. I can't accept this, ma'am," he said. His badge identified him as Officer Scott Tulliver.

"Good for you. DI Horne won't mind a quick call to assure you I'm permitted." She looked through the crack in the door as Tulliver called the station. Liang's face, shoulders, and arms were exposed above a tight white sheet; her partially shaved head was ensconced in wires and electrodes.

"Yes, Senior. I know. Here she is." The officer handed his phone over.

"Glock—is that you?"

"Yes," Alexa said. She cleared her throat. "Officer Tulliver wants to verify that I can check on Jenny. I'd say he's doing a thorough job."

"Agreed. Put him back on."

"Yes, Senior?" Tulliver said back into his phone. He listened for a sec and then hung up. "You can go on in. He said it was okay."

"Thanks. Has her family been notified?"

"Her boyfriend is on his way from Auckland. Her parents are flying up from Christchurch."

"I'm glad. Thanks for being vigilant. Has anyone been by to check on her?"

"Just that Maori cop, the girl with the blue mustache and beard."

"I believe Officer Cooper has a *moko*, a form of tribal identity." Alexa scrutinized his face until he averted his eyes. Mary had explained the significance of Maori tattooing over beers one night when Alexa had asked about the blue lip-and-chin tattoo she had seen on a woman at the Four Square grocery store. Mary explained that all Maori women have a *moko* on the inside, close to the heart, and when they are ready, an artist simply carves it on the surface.

"What does your tattoo mean?" Alexa had asked, shocked by the word, *carved.*

Mary had glanced at her shoulder where her iridescent bird-fish-woman was hidden but hadn't answered.

Alexa pushed the door open. Why had Officer Cooper been by? Had she been at the station this morning? If not, how did she know Jenny was here?

Quiet hum of machine. Steady bleeps. Barely audible inhalation, pause, exhalation. Jenny looked twelve years old. Her blue-veined eyelids, void of makeup, flickered and then stilled. Alexa reached for her cool hand and squeezed gently. "Jenny. It's me, Alexa Glock. From the lab. I'm checking on you."

No response.

"Squeeze my hand if you can hear me."

No response.

"Your boyfriend is coming." What was his name? Eddie? Ethan? Evan. "Evan is on his way to be with you. Your parents too." She didn't know what else to say, hardly knew the girl, but stumbled on. "Be brave. I'll come back later. We'll find whoever did this."

No response.

If Alexa had arrived first at the lab, this would be her. An orderly bustled in, followed by a doctor who snapped, "She's not to receive visitors."

"I'm from the police department," Alexa countered, pulling out her ID. "Forensics. What can you tell me?"

The doc waved away her ID. "She was struck on the left temple by a blunt instrument. Brain is swelling. We're taking her for a CAT scan to see if we need to relieve the pressure. She's lucky she was only hit once. Otherwise…" He motioned to the orderly. "Get her going." He turned back to Alexa. "…she'd be dead."

"Can you tell what she was hit with?"

"Something flat, with a smooth edge."

—

Happy Smiles Dental Clinic on Milton Road, two roundabouts from the hospital, had sardine-packed parking around back.

The receptionist had received the proper warrants and had Paul Koppel's dental records and X-rays ready. A quick glance at the three-year old X-ray revealed one gold tooth, five fillings, and the merest white spot where a cavity was forming.

Only it didn't matter now.

Abracadabra Café was a block from Happy Smiles and had a parking space out front. No more McDonald's. Alexa wished she had her sweater—it was sullied by Jenny's blood and would have to be washed—and studied the patchwork of white and blue sky; the dark clouds she'd noticed on the drive to work had been blown like bubbles out to the sea that was never far away in this island country.

Inside the café, Alexa contemplated eating carrot cake for lunch, drooling over the glass case. The cake had thick cream cheese frosting embellished with sunflower seeds, coconut, grated carrots, and nuts. Alexa swallowed. No, but she could buy a piece for dessert tonight.

"Falafel salad and a flat white coffee, please," Alexa said to the woman behind the glass case. "And a takeaway carrot cake slice."

"Hotel California" was playing. (Was there no escaping the Eagles? Even in the Southern Hemisphere?) She wolfed her lunch. Her final check on the dental records would confirm the victim's identification but wouldn't explain why he'd been murdered.

What secrets did Paul Koppel harbor?

Chapter Eight

The case meeting was delayed. No DI Horne. District Commander Teal and the mud pot murder team paced about in the central meeting room, crunching water bottles, snapping gum, comparing notes. Tension was palpable. Alexa, after calling to find out the CAT scan results, counted heads. Senior Officer Abel Rangiora. Trimble and McNamara, the latter giving her the stink eye. Officer Cooper. Why had she gone to the hospital? The ginger-headed cop, Miles Walker, was shaking it back and forth. Alexa stepped closer to hear what he was saying to Rangiora.

"Bugger all. There goes my job."

"You'll be right," Rangiora said.

Walker shook his head. "I'm munted."

He looked like an overgrown Opie Taylor caught fibbing to Pa. Alexa wondered what he was worried about. Horne hurried into the room.

"Sorry to keep you waiting." The detective inspector looked harried and had files in his hands. "Just finished meeting with Mark Haddonfield, deputy mayor of the district council. He gave me a list of projects Koppel was working on. I'll get to them in a minute. Who has an update on Liang's attack?"

Rangiora spoke. "Twenty-seven people came in the station

between seven and eight a.m. Twenty-four have been interviewed or are one of us. We have three that we haven't identified."

The room went quiet; its occupants eyed one another.

"Find out who the unidentified are. Ms. Glock," Horne said, looking at her, "what's Liang's status?"

"She suffered a blunt force trauma. Her CAT scan showed ICP, so the doctor is performing a ventriculostomy."

"Speak English," McNamara barked.

"Her brain is swelling. The doctor is inserting a tube to drain it," Alexa said. "Her boyfriend and family are on their way. She didn't respond to my voice when I saw her earlier."

"What was she attacked with?" Horne asked.

"Something with a flat edge. I'll be able to tell more with photos of the wound and X-rays."

"Like a board?" Trimble asked.

Alexa shrugged.

"What else?" Horne scanned the team.

Rangiora and Cooper looked at Officer Walker, who stared at the floor.

"Get it over with, bro," Rangoria told him.

"Eh, bad news, Senior," Walker mumbled, shifting back and forth.

Horne lifted an eyebrow.

"The footprint cast taken at the mud pots was mine."

Alexa looked down at Walker's feet. *Yep*. Size ten Lastrite work boots. Most crime scene contamination came from the people who worked it.

"Blimin' idiot," McNamara yelled. "Are you bugger all kidding me? We've been going store to store."

"See me in my office later," Horne said and then turned to McNamara. "Have the tour bus statements all been verified?"

"Time of death of the victim was between nine and midnight the night before the body was discovered, so whether the three tourists saw a car leaving the mud pots the next morning is not worth pursuing."

"According to whom?" the DI asked.

McNamara shut up.

"Arsonists return all the time to the scene. Gives 'em a sexual jounce," Walker said.

"Jounce?" Alexa blurted.

Walker's cheeks colored.

"Some perps return to make sure it's a clean crime," Trimble added. "Could be someone who works at Waiariki Land."

"And sometimes—" Walker began.

"This is not Criminology 101," Horne interrupted. "Verify them."

"Probably back in frigging Chengchung by now," McNamara muttered.

"What did the deputy major say?" Rangiora asked before the DI lost his temper.

Horne started scrawling on the whiteboard—speed limit reduction , wastewater spraying—and stopped. "The local *iwi* say the spraying in Whakarewarewa Forest is contaminating the ground water and stunting the flax crop. Koppel is head of the committee to find an alternative location." He resumed—reconfiguring boundary lines, health and wellness conference. He underlined the last one twice. "The district council spent mega bucks sending Koppel to Morocco to attend an international conference on hot springs tourism. He was chosen to go because of his real estate background."

"Morocco? When?" Rangiora asked.

"The conference was..." Horne looked through his files. "Marrakesh. Three months ago. July fifth through tenth. Haddonfield mentioned the mayor and her husband also attended the conference." He hesitated. "The mayor is due here momentarily."

"Does Mayor Claiborne know the vic is Koppel?" Rangiora asked. From outside the room, a dog barked.

"Someone get those dogs the hell out of here," Horne said

and waited until Officer Cooper scurried away. "The mayor does not know. We plan to announce the victim's name at the press conference at two."

No one knew how to process this information. Was the mayor of Rotorua involved? What had happened in Morocco?

"One of us will need to speak to Mayor Claiborne about her whereabouts Saturday," he added.

"I'll do it," Trimble said.

"Catch her following the press conference." Horne checked his notes. He wrote *trespassing—Pirongia Island* on the board. "There's more. In August, Koppel and another person supposedly visited Pirongia Island and didn't get *iwi* permission."

"That's munted. Everyone knows *Pākehā* are forbidden on the island," Walker said, his coloring back to normal. "Boaties aren't even allowed close to shore."

"I'm a JAFA," Trimble said. "Why is this place forbidden?"

Alexa had learned JAFA stood for Just Another Fucking Aucklander, per their more rural countrymen. "They're jealous," Mary had explained. "People from the wop wops think Aucklanders are self-satisfied attention seekers ordering spicy soy lattes."

"It's an island a couple kilometers out into Lake Rotorua. It belongs to the Maori and is sacred. Some dude is buried in one of the caves," Walker said. "A bloke my brother knows…"

"Let's get back to my list here, Walker," interrupted Horne.

Walker colored again.

Alexa admired how Walker bounced back quickly. Like a whack-a-mole.

"Lee Ngawata has filed a complaint about the trespassing. He serves as our local Maori liaison officer." Horne checked his notes again. "Haddonfield said Ngawata believes the district council sent Koppel there to scope out development specs." He searched his notes for something else. "Age-old story of *Pākehā* cheating the Maori out of their land. But Haddonfield insists the district council had no knowledge or intention of developing the island." He shook his head. "Koppel might have gone rogue."

Alexa agreed.

"There was a dig there couple years ago. Someone vandalized the site, and the dig was canceled," Rangiora said.

"I remember that," Horne said. "It angered the Maori community."

"Do we have a date for Koppel's visit to the island?" Rangiora asked.

"Mid-August. After the wellness conference. Ngawata wasn't more specific than that." Horne drew a line connecting *health and wellness conference* and *trespassing—Pirongia Island*. "There might be a connection. Look into it. Finally, Koppel brassed off a couple fellow council members—a Glennis Kalman and Karen Fisk. About a report he lost or misfiled." Horne added *missing report* to the list.

The room was quiet; the list was heavy to digest. Wheels were turning. Theories tasted. Alexa immediately thought of what Terrance had said at Mary's funeral, that the boiling of a head was the greatest insult a Maori could make. The murder had to be symbolic. Alexa stole a look at Officer Wynne Cooper, who had slipped back into the room, standing alone. The only Maori present—unless Senior Officer Rangiora was; Alexa wasn't sure—*and* for some reason, she had shown up at Jenny's hospital room. Cooper was texting, her thumbs dancing. Had she tried to protect someone by stealing the duct tape? Alexa's speculations were interrupted by the mayor striding into the room.

"Welcome, Mayor Claiborne," Teal said, springing from the desk he had perched against.

"Gentlemen," the mayor said, scanning the room. "And ladies. I need an update. Why was the station on lockdown this morning?" She glanced at her watch. "In a quarter of an hour, we have a press conference."

"Unfortunately, we..." Horne started to say.

"We're on top..." said Teal at the same time.

"One at a time. Detective Inspector Horne?"

"To bring you up to date, we had an attack this morning in the lab that we believe is related to the mud pot murder."

Alexa liked the way Horne assumed control.

"In the lab? Here at the station?"

"Yes," Horne answered. "Our technician, Jenny Liang, was struck with a blunt instrument and is in serious condition at the hospital."

"Is she in danger of dying?" demanded Mayor Claiborne. Her turquoise suit reflected light like the pāua shells in Kiwi gift stores.

"It's uncertain at this time."

"Is this why there are dogs everywhere?" she asked. "I rode in the elevator..."

"No," Teal broke in. "The dogs are leaving. They were here for K-9 training."

"Why do you believe there is a connection with the murder?" The mayor directed her question to the DI.

"Ms. Liang and Ms. Glock—this is Ms. Glock, our forensics expert"—Horne nodded toward Alexa, and the mayor glanced at her—"were expecting to process results on evidence from the crime. The evidence is now missing," Horne said. "That's classified, ma'am."

"Is a police officer involved?" The mayor's darkly penciled brows bunched.

"We're looking into all possibilities," Horne answered. "An outsider could have entered the station. We're cross-checking security camera film as we speak."

"Anyone can walk into the station, right? I just did."

"Only at the main entrance, and we have security cameras there. All other access is locked and opened by scanning ID badges."

The mayor scanned the room. "Has the murder victim been identified?"

"Yes," Horne said. "The deceased is district councilor Paul Koppel, a local real estate agent."

The mayor went still. "Councilman Koppel?" Color drained from her cheeks.

"Yes. His wife identified him yesterday."

"I know him. I can't have my name associated with the murder victim. The opposition will capitalize on it."

"Opposition, ma'am?" Horne asked. No one in the room exhaled.

"Elections are coming up." Mayor Claiborne paused. "Mr. Koppel attended the Wellness Summit in Marrakesh that I attended. This past July." She shook her head. "The press will have a jolly go at this. Rip me apart."

"I'll let you decide what to tell the press, but my priority is solving Koppel's murder and an attack." Horne stood firm.

"This is appalling. You have got to find this murderer and find him quickly."

"Or her," Alexa said.

The press went rabid—pacing, pawing, panting—when they heard about Jenny Liang. To the mayor's advantage, their attention was focused on the attack in the station rather than the name of the murder victim.

"Who found her?" *The Press*.

"What's her condition?" TV 28.

"Did a cop do it?" *Rotorua Daily Post*.

"Was she intimate with the murder victim?" *The Aucklander*.

"Are citizens in danger?" TV 8.

Cameras rolled and lights flashed. DI Horne, sweating, looked pale but composed. Alexa, standing with the other team members behind him, battled against a sympathy surge and reminded herself that earlier, this man had considered her a suspect. The barrage of questions continued; Horne shielded himself and colleagues well, revealing little but bare necessities, speaking with dignity and, after eleven long minutes, answering a final question.

"No. No major suspects at this time. We'll keep you appraised. That's all. Mayor Claiborne, I'll turn it over to you."

"Thank you, Detective Inspector Horne." The mayor had regained her composure and nearly knocked Horne aside as she took the podium.

"Ladies and gentlemen of the press, I have complete faith in the esteemed Rotorua Police Department." Her Honor the mayor straightened her shoulders and spoke louder than necessary into the mike. "The inspector has assured me he will quickly arrest the person or persons responsible for these crimes."

No connection between the mayor and Paul Koppel emerged. The mayor spoke as if up for reelection.

"Crime in Rotorua is down for the third year in a row. Last year, there were only three murders in the area; two of them were solved within twenty-four hours. *Tatau, tatau*. 'We together' is our motto. We will keep you updated, but meanwhile, the citizens of Rotorua are safe at home and on the street. That's all. No questions." The mayor left the platform and snaked through the audience.

But were they safe? Alexa wondered, watching Trimble weave after the mayor.

DI Horne located Alexa in the stairwell. "Your landlady vouched for you."

She looked up at him, gauging his height at six feet two inches to her five feet seven. "She might evict me for being investigated by the police, and we haven't even met."

He laughed. "She said something about not putting all your eggs into one basket." Again, the laugh subtracted years from his face. "I'm short-staffed and need you to interview those two district councilwomen who were angry with Paul Koppel. They've agreed to meet you in a half hour."

It was rare that a forensics investigator specializing in odontology conducted interviews, but Alexa jumped at it, glad to be needed, glad to be working the field after three years dedicated to teeth.

Maybe she'd forgive the DI after all.

—

The drive to the district council offices was short, so Alexa barely had time to formulate questions. The two women were the fellow city council members holding a grudge against the murder victim for failing to produce a report. She'd start her questioning with the missing report.

Settled in a plain vanilla meeting room at council offices, Alexa killed ten minutes pushing the image of Horne's blue eyes from her mind and choosing a new ringtone (barking dogs because of the K-9 circus at the station) and wallpaper (waterfall) and checking messages (none) until Karen Fisk and Glennis Kalman entered in a blur of color.

"We drove over together, and traffic was chocablock. Hello, dear. I'm Glennis Kalman," the shorter and plumper of the two said, offering her hand. Large multicolored glasses dwarfed her round face, which was bordered by a brunette bob. She wore a Baltic-blue pants suit, military style, with big gold buttons.

Alexa wanted to salute.

"Gidday. I'm Karen," the other woman said, thrusting her hand forward. She was older, had short yellow hair fading to silver. Her bright-red coat and black-and-white striped blouse hurt Alexa's eyes. "What can we help you with? We know it's about our dear colleague Paul."

"'orrible. Just 'orrible. He's the first person I've ever known who was murdered," said Glennis. "By crikey. Boiled alive. The Maori call the mud pots 'brain pots,' you know. They used to cook the heads of their enemies." She sat down with a plunk across from Alexa.

"And leaving those wee boys. It breaks my heart," chimed

Karen, who sat next to Glennis. "Remember the little red-headed one at the council holiday party?"

"Yes. A dear poppet. And what about the dress Mindy was wearing?" Glennis said.

Alexa swooped in for redirect. "It's a terrible loss. What can you tell me about a missing report? Chairperson Haddonfield said you were both upset about a report Mr. Koppel couldn't produce." She opened up her notebook, pen poised.

The women clammed up.

Alexa leaned across the table. "You must tell me anything you know. It may help us figure out who murdered Mr. Koppel."

"That report can't have anything to do with the murder," said Karen.

"Oh no," chimed Glennis. "It was the spa report. Paul traveled to Morocco to represent Rotorua at the Global Spa and Wellness Summit this past winter. Early July it was. Here it is October and still no report. The council spent thousands sending him there."

"Yes, we are aware that Mr. Koppel went to Morocco in July."

"Marrakesh. Six days in Marrakesh," Glennis continued. "A global summit. Forty-five nations represented. Health and wellness tourism is a growing trend that we hope to capitalize on in Rotorua."

"People from all over the world were there. California, even," said Karen. "Mayor Claiborne and her husband went too."

"Were Mayor Claiborne and Paul Koppel acquaintances before the summit?" Alexa asked.

"They knew each other from town council meetings." Karen looked at Glennis for confirmation. Glennis nodded solemnly. "And he was supposed to compile a report and development plan to attract investors. He's a real estate agent, you know. I mean *was*. It's big bucks, the spa and wellness industry. I can find my notes and tell you exactly how much. But it's billions in tourist dollars, and since we're lucky enough to have hot springs in our area—"

"We're one of only four places in the entire world with such abundance of geothermal activity. Kamchatka, Iceland…"

"Don't interrupt, dear. You sound like a brochure," Glennis said to Karen. "The point is, we have the potential to grow Rotorua."

"GROW Rotorua is the name of our subcommittee," said Karen, ignoring Glennis. "There are people in the community who are against growth. The Maoris, for instance. A lot of Maoris live in Rotorua, you know, more than anywhere else in New Zealand, and they think we want to take their land. The report was supposed to include our survey results."

"We debated between a mail-in survey, which costs more, or electronic and decided mail-in would bring in more returns because, well, some people just aren't with the times, my own mother for one, and we included postage, so we got a seventy-two percent return."

Alexa had stopped taking notes.

"Well, like Glennis cut in, we went with the mail-in, and our results were to be included in Paul's report, and we worked hard to have our part ready first of September and gave them to Paul to include but he didn't," Karen said. "No report."

"It's not ethical to spring a report on people at the meeting. But Paul kept putting us off." Glennis's nose could not have been higher in the air.

"Wouldn't return our calls," Karen said.

"I'd like a copy of the survey results," Alexa said. "Do you think Mr. Koppel's report could be on his laptop?"

"Could be," Glennis said, "but I have the feeling he never took the time to write it. Once the excitement of the trip wore off, he didn't want to do the hard part. Either that or he was trying to get away with something."

"Any ideas about what he might be trying to get away with?"

The two women stared at each other again. This time, neither spoke. Dogs began to bark. Alexa jumped and then remembered her new ringtone. "Excuse me," she said to the women. "Glock here."

"Jimmy Trimble. Can you swing by the hospital? Liang is conscious. We need a statement."

"Yes. I'm finishing up this interview. " Alexa hung up and turned back to the women. "What might Koppel have wanted to hide?" They had had a few seconds to compose an answer.

"You just never know," Glennis said.

"What happens in Marrakesh stays in Marrakesh is what I think. Paul was up to something," Karen added.

Chapter Nine

The hospital door was ajar and no guard was outside. A young man was bending over Jenny.

Alexa rushed in.

The man stood quickly, startled. Jenny's eyes were opened, and she wore a weak smile. The left side of her head was covered in white gauze, and she was hooked to a monitor. She struggled to sit upright.

"Don't sit up," Alexa said. "I'm glad to see you've woken."

Jenny relaxed back into a pillow. "This is Evan."

"Who are *you*?" the young man asked. Tall and skinny, he had a head of wild brown curls.

"She's my boss at the lab," Jenny said. "Did you lift prints from the tape?" Her voice conveyed a strength that her body belied. Her pupils, Alexa noted, were dilated.

"How are you feeling?" Alexa replied, trying to calm her heart rate. "Why isn't anyone outside your door?"

Evan ignored her questions. "I can't believe what happened. Who hurt Jenny? Is she in danger?"

"Was there a police officer by the door when you got here?" Alexa asked, ignoring his questions in return.

"Yes. I don't know what happened to him."

"We were ready to check the tape for prints," Jenny broke in. "What did you find?"

"The tape has disappeared," Alexa explained.

"What? I was so stoked to get to work this morning."

"Why was Jenny attacked?" Evan repeated.

"First things first. Jenny, how are you feeling?"

"I have a headache that won't quit. The nurse is checking to see if I can have more meds. And I got eight stitches." She gingerly touched the bandage. "The doctor said swelling in my brain has been relieved. Maybe I can meet you in the lab tomorrow."

"Let's wait and see how you feel," Alexa said. "Evan, would you mind leaving while I ask Jenny some questions?"

His eyes searched Jenny's, and she nodded her okay.

"Tell me what happened," Alexa said as soon as they were alone. She pulled the lone chair in the room close to the bed and sat.

"I'm not sure. I got to the lab just past seven and put my things down. I went right over to where we stored the duct tape sample yesterday."

"Was it there?"

Jenny nodded and then winced. "I took it into the storage closet to ready the optical comparator."

"Who saw you heading to the lab?"

"I don't think anyone. I came in through the south entrance, swiped my card, walked straight downstairs. No one was around. I heard people in the canteen, but I had brought my own tea, so I didn't stop."

"And no one was in the lab?"

"Nope."

"Was the door locked?"

"Yes. I unlocked it and turned on the light. Then I found the tape and went to the storage closet. That's the last thing I remember. I must have heard footsteps behind me and started to turn. That's what the doctor says because of the location of the wound." Her hand reached up again. A monitor beeped. "It hurts." Her voice was weakening.

"Did you see who attacked you?"

"No. They snuck up behind me. Whoever it was wanted the tape, didn't they?"

"We believe so. Why do you say 'they'? Do you think it was more than one person?"

"Maybe." Her voice was fading, and her eyes looked feverish. "I don't know. Was it the mud pot murderer who attacked me?"

"Whoever it was took the tape, got what they wanted, so you're safe now. You need rest." Alexa stood. "One more question. Is Officer Cooper a friend of yours?"

"Who?"

"Officer Cooper. Young, Maori. She stopped by to check on you this morning."

"I've seen her around the station. She has the facial tats, right? But I don't really know her. I don't know many people at the station. I've only worked there for two months." Jenny closed her eyes. A single tear from the left one began to journey down her pale face. Then the eyes flew back open. "Do you think she attacked me?"

"Let's not jump to conclusions. You're safe now." Alexa looked around the room, wondering what had happened to the cop who was supposed to be guarding Jenny's door.

"Wait." Jenny raised her head. "We have more tape!"

"What? Where?"

"We were only separating a portion of the tape. There's more in storage. In a bin with the gravel samples and clothing."

"That's great."

Jenny looked ready to climb out of bed and rush to the station.

"I'll process it and let you know the results, okay? But remember—all this work on the duct tape might be for nothing."

Jenny's eyes closed again. Alexa waited a few moments and then quietly left the room, nodding to Evan, glad he could be

Jenny's guardian angel. She retrieved her phone and pushed redial.

"Trimble here," said a voice.

"Hi, Detective Trimble. This is Alexa Glock calling back. Can you find out where the cop is who is supposed to be watching Jenny's door?"

"He's not there?"

"That's correct."

"Let me look into it, and I'll call you back."

"Thanks."

Alexa found Jenny's nurse, who tracked down the X-ray technician. He willingly made copies for her to take back to the police station.

"What's your opinion about what might have been used as a weapon?" Alexa asked the bespectacled man. She figured asking was worth a try.

"Let me take a squizz."

Squizz?

He removed the original copy with a flourish and put it up to the light as if someone asking his opinion was what he lived for. "She has a slight skull fracture, see here?" The tech pointed to a faint white line. "Blunt force trauma. Ouch." He picked up a ruler and took measurements. "The weapon was flat and roughly five centimeters wide. A cricket bat or an oar. Those are my guesses." He whisked the X-ray away from the light and studied Alexa. "Don't quote me."

Her cell barked as she was exiting the hospital. Jimmy Trimble. "What did you find out?" she asked.

"Horne called the guard off. He decided since the attacker got what he was after that Jenny wasn't in danger."

"Tell him I don't agree," Alexa said, thinking of the hidden stash, thinking of the promise she had made Jenny. "Get a guard back here."

Chapter Ten

Oxymoronic when a police station feels hazardous. Alexa scurried through the lobby to the stairwell; she didn't want to announce her presence. No one knew about the extra duct tape but Jenny. Ms. Welles, who was talking to what looked like a reporter, didn't glance over.

Separating the duct tape single-handedly would be tricky.

The lab was dark and empty, giving Alexa déjà vu. She made sure the door was locked and then turned on a single overhead light. The evidence bin bulged with sealed and labeled plastic bags of various sizes. Soil samples, the single cigarette butt, rocks, stained clothing, hair, fibers, a sliver of glass, and finally, more muddy brown duct tape, sides stuck together. Alexa froze when she heard muffled footsteps from the hallway, but the lab door remained shut and the footsteps faded. She let go a stream of air, unaware she had been holding her breath.

The day was waning. Collecting the supplies she'd need to separate the tape, Alexa reflected on her duct tape knowledge. She had presented a "Fingerprints and Duct Tape" paper for a forensics seminar five years ago. One reason duct tape is a hotbed of fingerprints is that it is hard to manipulate while wearing disposable gloves. Criminals who wear gloves often whip them off when messing with duct tape. In one case, evidence that came into the lab included a latex glove stuck to tape. It had been easy to turn the glove inside out and get not only fingerprints but DNA. The accompanying photograph had made her audience laugh, but unfortunately, the fingerprints, when run through AFIS, had been unmatched, and the murder of an African American youth in a parking garage in Raleigh had not been solved.

Simple fact: sometimes murderers go free and walk among us. They're in the grocery store or picking up their children from school or sitting behind us at the movie theater. That man you smiled at on the treadmill next to yours? That fellow who works on your car? The guy at the other end of the bar?

Stop it, Alexa.

She walked over to the glove dispenser and slid a pair on. Carefully holding one corner of the soiled tape, mindful of her duct tape story, she removed it from the bag and placed it in a paper-covered specimen tray. Dried mud sprinkled the paper like allspice. Mud and any solution to wash it off would obscure the outer prints. That was why getting to the reverse side was important. Alexa propped the tape up, sprinkled droplets of chloroform tape-release agent into the crease, gently tugged it apart a centimeter at a time, and repeated the process.

"Damn," she said when the tape fell on its side.

The silence was creepy and the progress slow and clumsy; she missed Jenny's agile hands. Her ears were alert for more footsteps, and an involuntary shiver made droplets land on the outside of the tape, resulting in a tea-colored trail.

Deep yoga breath.

Pulling the two sides apart too quickly would tear the tape and damage any possible prints. A few more drops, a final tug.

There.

Now it would have to dry for twelve hours before she could administer the final steps and view the tape for prints. She was back where she had been twenty-four hours ago. Weird. Alexa surveyed the dim lab, considered taking the tape home with her, dismissed that idea, and found a cupboard. She hid the tray behind some bottles of epoxy, did a quick tidy up, and wondered if the DI was still at the station.

Upstairs, Alexa gave Ms. Welles a big wave and grin. "Is DI Horne still here, do you know?" It was five thirty.

Ms. Welles frowned. "I'm sure Detective Inspector Horne is very busy but I can call and see."

"Ta," Alexa said, adopting the local slang for the hell of it.

He was not in his office; Ms. Welles located him in the meeting room. He was conversing with Senior Officer Abel Rangiora, the hunk who had held the light for her at the mud pits. Alexa, approaching, could hear the topic, waste water treatment disposal, and remembered that issue listed on the whiteboard. She joined them.

"Officer Rangiora met with a local *iwi* rep about moving the wastewater out of Whakarewarewa Forest," Horne explained.

"*Whaka* what?" Alexa said.

The DI frowned. "Warren Womble, he's head of the Lakes Water Quality Association, said the city has five years to find an alternate location, so the fact that Koppel hadn't done so yet isn't negligent. And certainly not a reason to kill him. How's Liang? What did she see?"

"She's alert." Alexa recounted everything Jenny told her, except about the extra duct tape, and protested again about removing her guard.

"I put an officer back, but we're shorthanded. It's just for tonight," Horne said.

She decided to delay reporting on her conversation with Karen and Glennis. The missing Spa and Wellness report and the extra duct tape could wait until she could speak with him alone. Who was trustworthy?

Alexa was about to ask about Trimble's conversation with the mayor when Horne got a call. He looked at the screen. "Pardon me. I have to take this."

An uneasy feeling shadowed Alexa as she left the station.

Chapter Eleven

Groceries, her stomach insisted. Alexa made a unanimous decision that it was steak night. Followed by carrot cake. She'd run it off in the morning.

Grabbing a cart from the "trundler return" at the Countdown, glad to occupy herself with something other than duct tape and boiled heads, she began gliding down narrow aisles. First eggs. Located in the dog food aisle. It was a big shock when she first moved to Auckland to see unrefrigerated eggs; she imagined the salmonella tap dancing on the shells. But biotech Mary had explained that New Zealand farmers vaccinate laying hens to prevent the bacteria clustering on room temperature shells, so she relaxed. Next, steak hunting. One thick sirloin, free-range grass-fed when alive, aged when dead, expensive when in trundler. A kumara, or sweet potato as they called them back home, some spicy arugula, a pear, and a bottle of Australian Shiraz. Alexa's mouth was watering. She returned a loaf of sourdough to the shelf—a concession to the carrot cake slice in the car. Intent on yogurt and goat cheese, her cart smacked another.

"My bad," she said.

DI Horne, who had been zooming around the corner too fast, looked at her in amazement. Alexa realized, speed aside, she'd been driving on the wrong side of the aisle, USA style. "Don't give me a ticket."

"You're a dangerous person," he said, smiling that rare smile. Alexa surveyed his cart items: bread, canned beans, eggs, bacon, and an assortment of chips and cookies. Also a six-pack of Speight's, New Zealand's equivalent of Budweiser.

"Between you and me, we have the alcohol taken care of."

"Looks like you eat a little better with your drink," he replied, eyeing her items. "Most of this is for my daughters, who stay with me every other weekend. They come tomorrow."

"If you say so," she said, remembering the photos on his desk. *But wait. Every other weekend?* "They don't live with you all the time?"

"Their mother and I are divorced."

"But…" Alexa was about to advise him to update his police bio but stopped herself in time. "What are you fixing for dinner?"

"My specialty—eggs on toast."

A sudden thought.

No.

Oh hell—go for it.

"Why don't you add a steak to the pile and join me? We can talk about the case. I've got some information I wanted to share earlier."

He stood awkwardly for a moment, weighing his options. "I have to get back to the station after I drop these at home. Meeting with Teal. But I could stop by around eight, if that's not too late."

"It's fine. I live—"

"Trout Cottage. I know."

The ride to Trout Cottage was becoming familiar, a new kind of heading home, freeing Alexa's mind to ponder Horne. The *divorced* Horne. Now that she knew he was…well…single, the dinner invite took on more weight.

How did he know where she lived?

She concluded she wasn't ready to start a new relationship—her track record, her transience. Plus, a newly divorced man was surely gun-shy.

Glock shy.

Should be.

The spontaneous invitation was not a date. And besides, Detective Inspector Bruce Horne had daughters.

Her mind flickered to her stepmother. She had been a newly minted teen when her father had married Rita. After Mom had died, for the next six years, Alexa, Charlie, and Dad had been a team and then, just like that, the star player had been recruited by a rival. Team Rita. Alexa had been abandoned to the bench.

I hated her, and she knew it.

Alexa was glad, though, as she pulled up the long curving driveway that the days were growing longer instead of shorter like back home. Sunset would be around seven fifteen on this northern island in the Southern Hemisphere, giving her time to unpack groceries, take a run, and then shower.

—

DI Horne knocked at 8:05.

Alexa gave herself a last look in the bathroom mirror. She had carefully chosen an outfit to look nice but not a trying-too-hard nice: matching bra and panties, which of course would remain unappreciated, as would the scars marring her back (ha, always a jolt when a man first saw those beauties) the silky gray hip-length blouse she'd worn to Mary's memorial service over black jeans. Her thick, dark hair wasn't behaving—too freshly washed after her run, blown dry and ornery—so she thrust it behind her ears and quickly added large silver hoops as detractors.

Heart hammering, she scurried to the door as he knocked again.

"We located Koppel's car. Right in the Waiariki Thermal Land parking lot," Horne said. White stubble integrated with his five o'clock shadow. He was still dressed as he had been at the station: rumpled khakis, sky-blue button-down, tan jacket.

"Nice to see you too," Alexa responded.

"What? Ah, yes. Thanks for having me. Nice out here," Horne said, looking around. A Countdown grocery bag dangled from his hand.

She followed his eyes to the lawn, the lavender, and could hear the river humming. "I've been checking the yard for deer. I know there are no deer in New Zealand. We have so many at home, especially this time of evening, I can't help looking." Alexa was blathering. "Come on in."

Horne stood where he was. "We do have deer. Imported from the States. For hunting. For deer farming too. Mostly raised for export. The Europeans love their venison. There's a cave near here. Did you know that?"

"Near here?"

"Yes, Tutea's Cave. Just up the Kaituna."

Was it her imagination or was the river louder, more insistent?

"There's a side path as you approach the falls," he continued. "The entrance is barricaded because a tourist fell a year ago. It was wet and steep. She died. Maori women and children used to hide in the cave during tribal raids. They'd make their way down into the cave by flax rope." Now Horne was blathering.

"I'd like to see it."

"I'll show you sometime."

They stared at each other, suddenly silent and close, both aware spelunking wasn't normal procedure. He handed her the plastic bag with his steak and stepped backward. "I also brought dessert."

Alexa peeked in the bag at a box of Tim Tam cookies. "I've been wanting to try these. Thanks. Come in, sit down. Would you like a glass of wine or a beer?" She had added a six-pack to her cart, along with a second sweet potato. "Then you can tell me about the car. Strange it wasn't found sooner."

He followed her into the cottage, his scent filling the room: woodsy, musky, male. She could smell him all the way to her toes and didn't like it.

"Beer would be brilliant."

Alexa salted and peppered the second sirloin and slid it on the broiler pan next to her own and fetched two beers. *It's a work dinner*.

Horne sat on the couch, so she took the armchair. The frothy brew slid down easily; she was dehydrated and jazzed from her run. "Beer costs a fortune in your country."

The DI took a long sip and then sighed. "One of the disadvantages of being an island in the middle of nowhere. Most everything is imported." He considered the beer bottle label. "But Speight's is brewed here, and it's still dear. I gave Officer Walker a thrashing."

Alexa remembered about the bootprint at the crime scene. It had been Walker's. "Most contamination at crime sites comes from investigators."

"Been guilty myself. Lucky we caught it now and not later—or in court." The boot cast had been a hopeful bit of evidence, and they had to give it the boot.

Conversation started flowing like beer on tap. First, case-related: Koppel's car had been found in the overflow lot at the thermal park. The loaners had gone to the scene and checked it. "No obvious signs of violence. Trimble and McNamara are collecting samples and getting it towed to the station. We'll need you to analyze the trace first thing in the morning," he said. "If someone else left the car in the lot, there could be fingerprints."

"Any security cameras?"

"Unfortunately, no."

"How far is it from the parking lot to the mud pot?"

"About a kilometer. Hard to imagine he walked."

"What did Trimble find out about the mayor's whereabouts when Koppel was killed?"

"Sunday evening, she attended the Tulip Fest banquet at the

Energy Events Center. Said she was home shortly after nine p.m. Her husband can vouch."

"Yuck. Never trust a spousal alibi."

"There is CCTV at the EEC. We'll follow up tomorrow," Horne said. "She could have stopped by Koppel's between the event and arriving home. Needs follow-up, although I doubt the mayor of Rotorua is our murderer."

"You never know," Alexa said and then filled him in on her meeting with the two councilwomen. "What's the status on Koppel's laptop?" she asked. "Is the report on it?"

"Frankly, I don't know. Trimble is working it."

"One more thing. Jenny told me there was another sample of duct tape. I've prepared it so I can check first thing in the morning for prints."

He leaned toward her. "Who have you told?"

"No one. Until now."

"Keep it to yourself, and report the results directly to me. Don't even write it up."

He leaned back, and for a few minutes, the conversation drifted. Alexa waxed on about her job in Raleigh, and Horne perked up talking about his daughters.

"Denise is fifteen. She rock climbs, bouldering, really. It's a club sport. Samantha, my wife—I mean my ex-wife—and I call her Sammie. She's thirteen and playing netball for the second year, really keen. My daughter, not my ex." Horne's face had gone red. "Anyway, she's hard to live with these days."

The ex or daughter?

"Thirteen is rough, all those hormones," Alexa said. Horne's nervousness made her more relaxed. "That's how old I was when my father remarried."

"How did that go?"

"Disastrously." She had the scars to prove it.

"Sammie used to fish with me on the weekends, but she doesn't anymore."

"I think that's normal. The quest-for-independence kind of thing." She sipped her beer and thought of her father and the weekend hikes they'd taken in the years after Mom died: Eno River, Hanging Rock, Falls of the Neuse, her little brother, Charlie, bringing up the rear, complaining his feet hurt. She and Dad referred to Charlie as Tough Guy. Because he wasn't.

After Dad met Rita, there had been no more hikes.

"Do your father and stepmother live in Raleigh?" Horne asked, his left eyebrow rising.

"They moved to Florida five years ago." She should call Dad soon, update him. It was easier now that he had his own cell phone. He would be the one to answer. "My brother and his family—I have two little nephews—live on the other side of the state in the mountains. Asheville."

"I've heard of Asheville."

"Yep. Nice place. I'm starved," Alexa said, her beer drained, the conversation too intimate. "Let's get dinner."

Horne tended the steaks while Alexa took the kumara from the oven and tossed their salad with pear and goat cheese.

"A little butter, salt, and pepper is all these babies need," Horne said, sprinkling the steaks some more and looking around the counter. "And rosemary, if you have any."

She shook her head. "It's a rental place. How about lavender?"

Horne shook his head. "Where's a pan?"

"I was planning to broil them." The broiler was preheating, creating heat in the cozy space.

"Nah. Panfry. Eight minutes each side. And a glass of wine while they cook."

She never minded relinquishing control in a kitchen.

The Shiraz and heat loosened her tongue. She gabbed about Mary and their plan to hike the famous Milford Track, one of New Zealand's great walks, on the South Island in January. Mary had made reservations months ago.

"Nothing stopping you, is there?"

"I don't know about hiking alone." She was aware that she was enjoying herself.

"You won't be alone. The huts are full every night. People from all over the globe."

Horne's preferred method of panfrying the steaks had produced medium rare perfection, and they ate ravenously at the tiny table, knee to knee.

"This beats a Georgie Pie," he said. "Thank you."

Fork halfway between her mouth and plate, she stared at him until one of his eyebrows (they were ambidextrous) questioned her.

"Nothing." She half smiled. "Just thinking."

"Penny."

"Not worth it."

After they tidied the kitchen, she cut the carrot cake in half, and they carried the plates to the porch, sitting side by side in the plastic chairs, Alexa wrapped in her NC State sweatshirt, their talking spent. Darkness settled, and stars that refused to help Alexa gain her bearings filled the sky. She chewed slowly, savoring the cake, and then broke the silence. "I miss my familiar night sky. The Dippers, Orion. The North Star."

"No Dippers in the Southern Hemisphere. But look." Horne pointed. "There's Pegasus. See the wings?"

She tried but couldn't. A high-pitched screech made her drop her fork.

Horne laughed. "A ruru."

"A what what?" She groped for the fork, found it, wiped it on her pants.

"Our only surviving native owl," he said. "Also known as morepork. It's good to hear one. The Maori knew when they could hear a ruru that no enemy was approaching. The owl is watching over you."

River music burbled, and out of nowhere, Alexa teared up. Maybe it was the Shiraz. Maybe it was Mary's death. Maybe it was the tingling threat of a new relationship. Horne didn't notice and scraped his plate.

"Early day tomorrow." He stood, placed the plate on the railing, and thanked her again for dinner.

Alexa watched the car's taillights disappear in the darkness.

Chapter Twelve

Chirp-chirp-chirp. Cackle. Wheeze. Squawk.

What the hell? About to muffle the cacophony by burrowing under her pillow, the sounds repeated.

Chirp-chirp-chirp. Cackle. Wheeze. Squawk.

Alexa sat up and looked at the clock: 6:20. This was no sparrow. She threw off the duvet and padded to the window, searching the copse of trees to the right. A large, black-headed bird was perched on a branch. Its folded wings were iridescent blue, and a cotton ball was pasted to its neck like a bow tie. The bird began repeating itself: a Swiss cuckoo clock gone awry.

"Shoo!" she yelled through the crack, a smile on her face. Mary would know what kind...and then it hit her. No Mary. Her smile faded.

When she checked again, the bird was gone. In the kitchen, she fixed a cup of coffee and brought it back to bed. The first sip, nutty, strong, comforting, re-elevated her mood, last night's confusion thrown off like warm covers. She grabbed pen and notebook, pushed thoughts of Detective Inspector Blue Eyes out of her mind, and opened to a fresh page.

Time to make a list:

Why was Koppel killed?
Revenge? Passion? Greed?
Why throw his body in the mud pits?
Symbolic—makes a Maori look guilty.
Who attacked Jenny?
Someone within the police force?
What would the duct tape reveal?
Who wanted that duct tape enough to attack Jenny?
Was the mayor involved? Officer Cooper?
Mayor and Koppel attended same international conference.
Cooper visits Jenny in the hospital.

How many of the questions would be answered by day's end?

—

The conference room buzzed. By day five of a murder investigation—shock worn off—people were hungry to sink teeth into various hunches and hold on to something. Alexa scanned the room: no DI. Jimmy Trimble waved her over to a table where he, McNamara, and Officer Walker were standing around the bagged and spread contents of Koppel's glove compartment.

"Two unpaid parking tickets," McNamara said, jabbing a thick finger at one bag.

"District councilor, right on," responded Trimble. "Morning, Alexa."

"Good morning. What else did you find?"

"Owner's manual. Comb. Registration. Stash of serviettes. Stale biscuits. Rubbish. Condoms," Trimble recounted.

"Condoms? For a married man?" Alexa said.

Before anyone could respond, Horne walked in and scanned the room. "Who's missing?" he asked, looking at his watch.

"Rangiora got called away to an accident. Cooper is on her way. Teal said he would check in later." All this from Trimble.

"Someone else should handle the accident. We need all hands on deck." Horne, fists balled, strode to the front of the room. He turned to face the team and seemed to be avoiding Alexa's eye. "First an update on Liang. I spoke with her doctor ten minutes ago. She's going to be released from the hospital this afternoon but needs a couple days to recuperate, doc's orders. Glock interviewed her yesterday, and she could not identify her attacker. Who first?"

McNamara accounted for the finds in the car. "It was unlocked. The boot had a blanket, first aid kit, kid trainers, rope, and a few empty shopping bags. Found dirt and a stained towel, which are bagged and in the lab." He looked at Alexa. "We lifted prints from the steering wheel and boot latch, and they're also in the lab. There were rubbers in the glove compartment."

"Was Koppel fooling around?" Horne asked.

"We'll work on that today," McNamara answered. "We're trying to figure why the car went unnoticed. There's no attendant, just some bloke who rides around on a golf cart checking for parking passes. Said he didn't notice it until yesterday."

"Did Koppel own or have access to a boat? Get his wife in today. Does she know anything about that visit to the island? Why did he go, and who did he take with him? I want names, addresses. Was the visit connected to Morocco? Or his real estate doings? Interview his colleagues at Bowen Realty. We need a timeline of Koppel's last day. Who was the last person to see him alive? Have we figured that out yet?"

The DI's barrage was met with silence from the foxholes.

"What about his wallet and mobile?" Horne continued, his voice still steady but with a hint of anger. "Were they found in the car?"

"No, Senior," McNamara answered. "We suspect they were thrown in the mud pots. I'll work on his last day. We'll have his mobile records by noon. Maybe they'll provide some answers."

"Glock," Horne said, his eyes locking onto hers, "fill us in on your interview with the councilwomen."

Alexa recounted her interview as Officer Cooper arrived.

Everyone listened closely, and Horne began scrawling across the whiteboard again: *Morocco. Missing report.*

"Trimble, what have you found on Koppel's computer?" he asked. "Is this report on it?"

Trimble pulled out a list. "He's got 137 files…including his Morocco itinerary, sidewalk café regulations, kid's football schedule, cracked foundation report—his own house, by the way—property listings, mortgage figures…"

"Hell. A simple yes or no," said McNamara.

"Nothing is labeled Spa and Wellness report, but I'll keep looking."

"Get me that Morocco itinerary," said Horne. "I want to concentrate on that visit he supposedly took to Pirongia Island. Glock—when you finish in the lab this morning, follow up on this. Get on out to that island. Find proof of this visit."

"To the island?" Alexa's mouth dropped. "That forbidden island?"

"Scared?" asked McNamara.

Alexa didn't look his way, and no one laughed.

Walker shook his gingery head back and forth. "Bloody rash. It's Maori-owned, and *Pākehā* aren't allowed."

"This is a police investigation. Of a murder," Horne said. "The person murdered is suspected of visiting this island. There may be evidence to help us solve the case. Police have jurisdiction over Maori land."

Walker continued as if the DI hadn't spoken. "If you don't get permission, you'll be cursed. Or worse."

Horne paused as if doubting his ears, and Alexa wondered if he was finally going to lose his temper.

"Walker, enough. Shut it." His voice was firm and level. Then he spoke directly to Alexa. "Figure out what happened on the island. Search for evidence of the visit."

The supposed visit had been two months earlier. What evidence would be left?

"I'll set it up with Lee Ngawata, our Maori liaison, and get you a launch," he continued. "Officer Cooper, go with Glock. Use your ties. Next?"

Alexa stared at Cooper, who was staring at her boss, her face impassive. The Maori police officer refused to look her way. *Good.* It would give her a chance to ask Cooper why she visited Jenny in the hospital.

—

The lab was cold and empty. Alexa switched on all the lights and locked the door. There didn't seem to be anyone to fill in for Jenny, so now all the work was hers alone. She hurried to the cabinet where the tape was stashed and opened it.

Yes—still there—undisturbed.

She removed the tray but not before knocking over three epoxy bottles. *Calm down.* After righting them, Alexa gathered supplies and took the sample to the far side of the lab. The storage room would have worked, but it was still caution-taped due to Jenny's attack.

With great care, Alexa applied the adhesive-side developer to the separated tape. The few minutes it needed to soak in were eternities. Alexa practiced tree pose but couldn't keep her balance. She found a stable spot as focus point and tried again, holding the stretch, sucking in her stomach, thinking of the dark, starry sky last night and Bruce Horne sitting next to her. She lifted her leg higher and raised her arms.

I am not interested in a new relationship.

Her "branches" swayed. She gave up the yoga, rinsed the developer, and held the tape to the light, searching for prints.

There. A print.

But damn.

She'd have to breach the caution tape to retrieve the optical comparator from the storage room. Most labs had a single optical comparator given the seven- to eight-thousand-dollar price tag. Carefully, Alexa stooped under the ribbon and entered. She scanned the floor where Jenny had been, the rivulet and small pool of blood now an oily reddish-brown. Who would clean it? Alexa tiptoed past, hefted the comparator in both arms, and ducked out.

Placing the sample in tray one, Alexa plugged in and turned on the machine. In a few seconds, the image of a partial fingerprint was projected on the lighted screen. Manipulating the tape, she was able to locate a fuller print and centered it.

Classic spiral whorl.

Now for internet magic. Would the comparator make an identification from the National Fingerprint Database? The computer scanned her print and started humming. Alexa braced for disappointment.

The murderer, though making a statement by disposing of the body in a symbolic manner, did not come across as a serial criminal. Most likely there would be no fingerprint on file, unless he or she was a police officer, public employee, immigrant, or…

A red No Matches sign blinked. All that hard work and anticipation.

But "no matches" did clear her new colleagues. *That's good, right?* Nevertheless, Alexa decided the remaining duct tape would be safer at Trout Cottage—not in the lab—and dashed outside to the parking lot to put the evidence in the trunk of her car.

The next two hours were spent comparing soil samples, examining the stained towel from the boot, running the prints lifted from the car, which matched Koppel's, and cross-examining two hairs found on the body during autopsy that also matched Koppel's.

Upon request, the hospital had faxed colored photographs of Liang's head wound. Studying them made Alexa shiver. *This was Jenny's head. And she was attacked five yards from here.*

With blunt force trauma, the greater the surface area of the strike, the less the injury. Jenny's wound measured two and a half inches wide. Figuring out the type of instrument used would be critical to identifying the attacker. No abrasion patterns marred the wound, so the weapon was smooth. The X-ray technician had mentioned a cricket bat. Alexa wasn't sure what a cricket bat looked like, so she Googled it and studied images of flat-sided paddles made of cane and willow. Some were painted bright colors; the old-timey ones were brown and often had tape wrapped around the handle. Widths varied from seven to ten centimeters.

Too wide.

Wait. What about a police baton? In New Zealand, police officers didn't carry guns, but they did carry pepper spray and batons.

She Googled "police baton measurements," but the results were overwhelming and confusing: riot batons, polycarbonate batons, straight batons, night sticks, wooden sticks, Tasers, all with different measurements. She'd get quicker results the old-fashioned way.

Alexa scurried up two flights of stairs and entered a briefing room where two duty cops stood around a coffeepot.

"Hi," Alexa said to one of them. He was fully uniformed, dressed in a light-blue short-sleeved button-down. Layered over the shirt was a vest with pockets and badges. His pants were darker blue. Around the young man's compact waist was a black belt with pockets and clips and attachments. Hanging next to handcuffs was just what Alexa was looking for. "Can I borrow your baton, please?"

The cop put a hand over the weapon and looked confused.

"I work here. Down in the lab." Alexa explained who she was and what she wanted with the baton. "It's part of the investigation into yesterday's attack. Here's my ID."

After he studied her ID and looked to his colleague for reassurance, the young man detached his baton and handed it to Alexa. "Come down to the lab in half an hour, and I'll be done. Ta."

Alexa bounced back downstairs, playing ninja with the baton, almost bumping into Horne on the first floor stairwell.

"Coming through," she said, her cheeks reddening. Had he seen her jabbing the air?

"Speeding around corners again, are you? Where to?"

"Back to the lab. Doing a comparison." She pointed the baton at him.

He lifted his hands. "I surrender."

—

The baton did not match Jenny's wound. Something slightly wider was used. Alexa stepped back over to the storage closet and stood in the threshold, scanning the crowded shelves, file cabinets, mops, evidence-drying cabinet, and covered microscopes but discovered no weapon. Of course, the storage room had been searched. If the attack was premeditated, the perp would have brought the weapon with him. And not left it behind.

Overall, the morning's forensic results did not produce solutions. Much of forensics boiled down to elimination. Soil found on the dirty boot towel did not match soil from the crime scene. Fingerprints taken from car items and steering wheel matched Koppel's. DNA results were pending. Alexa wondered if Horne had remembered to call in a rush.

At half past twelve, Alexa finished comparing hair follicles under a microscope. Time to resurface and tackle lunch, Officer Cooper, and the forbidden island.

Over a flat white coffee and three-bean chili back at the Abracadabra Café, Alexa propped open her laptop and started researching Pirongia Island, careful not to drip the savory stew on the keyboard.

Horne had left her a voicemail that she and Officer Cooper had a two thirty meeting with Lee Ngawata on the beach of the sacred island, three kilometers from the Lake Rotorua docks. "He initially refused, but I told him it wasn't up for negotiation," the DI said in his message. She should meet Officer Cooper at the docks at two p.m., when a police launch was scheduled to take them to the island.

Through the windows of the café, she strained to glimpse the sky: nomadic gray clouds dragging strokes of blue. The weather refused to settle.

Lake Rotorua, she read, was formed by volcanic eruption twenty-five thousand years ago, resulting in a thirty-square-mile caldera now filled with fresh but often shallow water. In places, the water was heated by underground steam vents. Several islands dotted the lake, but only Pirongia, classified as a lava dome, had been used by Maori as a stronghold against warring tribes. A Chief Rangituata was supposedly entombed in a cave deep within the island; additional burial sites also reportedly contained human remains. There had been an archaeological dig there a few years earlier. Senior Officer Rangiora had mentioned it at one of the team meetings. Alexa clicked on the link and read the terse article dated September 2016:

> Important Archaeological Site Lures Hooligans. Pirongia Island, three kilometers from Rotorua docks, is the former stronghold of the northern island's most significant warring tribe and sacred burial spot of its leader Chief Rangituata. The island is off-limits to anyone but local *Ngāti* Hiko who were cooperating closely with a joint team of archaeologists from Otago University and Victoria University School of Maori Studies.
>
> "Evidence of human settlement is everywhere," anthropology professor Lis Jiles said. "Artifacts are oozing out of the ground. Shells, flax, bits of adze and moa bones. History abounds."
>
> Professor Jiles and her team had been working with local iwi and Rotorua Museum officials to better understand the Maori culture on the North Island, with emphasis on hunting

and warring practices when they discovered Saturday a sacred site had been disturbed and tonga missing.

The local iwi immediately closed the dig and have forbidden further research.

No wonder they don't want anyone coming to the island.

Alexa had an idea. Terrance, Mary's brother, would have the inside scoop on the island and maybe even knew Ngawata. She pulled out her cell and called him. He answered promptly.

"Horomia Plumbing."

"Terrance. It's Alexa Glock." She had never mastered small talk and got right to the matter. "Do you have time to answer a couple questions?"

"*Ae*. How can I help you?"

"It's about Pirongia Island. I'm heading there this afternoon." Alexa lowered her voice to make sure she wasn't broadcasting police plans to the two women chatting at the next table.

"Stay away from Pirongia. It belongs to the local *Ngāti Hiko* and is forbidden to *Pākehā*."

"What does that mean?"

"What does what mean?" His voice was flat.

"*Ngāti Hiko*?"

"*Ngāti* means descendant of and *Hiko* is the ancestor, the tribe of *Hiko*."

"Okay. So Pirongia is private land and closed…to the public. I understand. But as part of the mud pot investigation, I have an arranged meeting this afternoon there with Mr. Lee Ngawata, and I wondered what I might expect."

Silence.

"Terrance. Are you there?" Her voice had risen. One of the nearby women glanced her way.

"Meet with Ngawata in Rotorua," Terrance replied. "The island is *tapu* and does not belong in your investigation. Even Maori never go there unless they receive special prayers to do so."

"*Tapu*?"

"Sacred."

"Unfortunately, the island is part of the murder investigation." Alexa lowered her voice. "But I will be visiting with a Maori, Officer Wynne Cooper."

"I know her peoples. She is a descendant of Rangituata and named for Dame Whina Cooper, a respected *kuia*."

"*Kuia*?"

"Maori leader. Dame Cooper worked for the rights of her people, especially women. I hope her namesake is doing the same."

Alexa hoped so too. "Rangituata. He's the guy buried on the island, right?"

Silence.

"Terrance?" Alexa feared she had offended him.

"He is not some guy," Terrance said. "He was once the most influential chief of the North Island, wise and fair, highly intelligent, and with superior military skills. The island is his resting place, his jumping-off point, and must not be disturbed. There will be consequences if it is, like last time."

This time, Alexa was silent. Like last time? Had the so-called hooligans been found and punished? She'd need to do some more research or ask at the station.

"Another thing. There are many stories of how *Pākehā* have stolen onto the island and never returned."

Then the line went dead.

Chapter Thirteen

Whina Cooper's namesake perched like a wooden figurehead, stoic and silent, at the front of the skiff as they churned their way through Rotorua Harbor. Cooper had conveniently appeared, dressed in civilian clothes, just as the launch was ready to depart.

Had she been hiding and watching?

Lake chop was making Alexa anxious; she tightened her grip on the slippery console as she stood next to the captain, eyeing approaching whitecaps.

"This isn't a police launch, is it?"

"No. I do occasional search and rescue for the police, but I'm contract," the man replied. "Happened to be available this afternoon. Not many tourists yet." He was wearing a yellow slicker and matching rain pants and increased speed.

"Have you been to Pirongia before?" she yelled toward him. His eyes widened as he shook his head no. Another boat, scudding across their path, forced him to slow down and maneuver its rolling wake.

"First and last time, I hope. Getting paid extra for this jaunt." He pointed toward cliffs they were passing. Alexa followed his finger. A thirty-foot carved face of a warrior, fierce and Picasso-esque, returned her astonished gaze.

"That's Ngatoroirangi, a Maori navigator," the man yelled. "Tourists love it."

Alexa twisted her head, keeping the carving in view for as long as possible, not comfortable being watched from behind by the huge pupil-less eyes and two mouths full of teeth. When she turned back, they were in open water and humpback swells. White gulls followed the boat, screeching, circling. She pulled her jacket flaps closer together, thankful it wasn't raining, and fixed her eyes on a small green dot ahead, her apprehension growing at the same pace as the dot enlarged until it was impossible to fill her lungs, until the island loomed dead ahead.

She had a bad feeling in the pit of her stomach.

"Hold on," the driver said as he edged the skiff onto roiling pebbles. A wave lifted the boat up and propelled it farther onto a flotsam-strewn beach. "Right. Shake a leg. I'll be back in an hour."

"Aren't you going to wait?" Alexa yelled over the crash of breaking waves, trying to tamp the panic in her voice.

"Hell no." He could tell she was unnerved. "You'll be right."

Officer Cooper leaped onto the sand and trudged toward a break of trees above the beach, not looking back. A gray-green bird with orange feet and a mohawk squawked at her from a tree and dive-bombed, careening at the last second. Cooper didn't flinch. Alexa hopped into shallow water and sank. One of her freshly washed Keds got sucked off, and she just caught it before it drifted to freedom with a new wave. The tote she had flung over her shoulder dipped into the water, and she wondered if the plastic bags she had stowed the camera and tape recorder in would leak. The engine of the skiff roared in reverse, creating more foam and wake.

"Dammit," Alexa muttered. She step-hopped to shore and sat on the closest driftwood log. The beach was half a football field wide, banked by cliffs on one side and a jumble of fallen trees and boulders on the other. She poured water and gravel out of the Ked and slipped it back on, double knotting the bow. *Gross.*

Checking inside the tote, she was happy to see the camera and recorder dry in their plastic evidence bags. Her notepad and pen looked dry too.

Instead of hopping right up, Alexa took a minute to study her surroundings and calm her heart rate. Mr. Ngawata was supposed to meet them on the beach. Where was he? Was this the right beach? Where was Cooper? Closing her eyes, Alexa felt a need to calm herself. Deep inhalation. Hold. Exhalation. Hold. In. Hold. Out.

A shadow blocked the weak sun.

She blinked and rose simultaneously, losing her balance, stumbling backward over the log. Disoriented, she righted herself and stood, suddenly eye to eye with a man, midsixties, his facial *moko* faded to a dusky gray. The man wore a black jacket zipped to the neck, khaki pants, and sandals. His dark hair was slicked into a ponytail and gray at the temples. The furrow between his eyes deepened. Officer Cooper stood next to him.

"*Kia ora*," he finally said. His black eyes, like a snake's, did not blink.

"*Kia ora*," Alexa answered. "Are you Mr. Ngawata?"

The man nodded and spoke rapidly in Maori. All she could decipher was *tapu* and *Pākehā*.

"Thank you for allowing me and Officer Cooper to be here and ask you some questions," Alexa said when he ceased. She understood that Ngawata was a respected leader in the Maori community and served as their liaison with police. "He helps navigate cultural issues and works on improving police relationships with Maori," Horne had explained to her when she asked him yesterday.

Ngawata nodded his head and pointed toward an opening in the trees ten yards away. He began walking side by side with Cooper. Alexa followed. It was Ngawata who had made the complaint to the police department about Koppel and an unknown companion trespassing on the island. Such brazen disrespect, thought Alexa, squelching behind the two Maoris.

A cloak of silence descended as the trio entered thick woods. The birdsong and the sound of breaking waves clicked off. Velvety darkness and the scent of damp earth enveloped her. Stubbing her toe on a rock, Alexa paused to let her eyes adjust. Where were they headed? Were there buildings on the island? To her left, a fern tree towered, a giant emerald umbrella. Above it, another tree stretched to such height that Alexa wondered if it was related to a redwood. A sudden movement and harsh chatter made her whip around. Three birds burst from the fern tree and flew erratically back toward the opening as if making an escape. Alexa hustled to catch up with Cooper and Ngawata.

For a quarter hour, the three walked through earthy silence. Alexa could see no human trace, no sign of an archaeological dig. Pushing through two scratchy bushes, Alexa followed Cooper into a clearing, and light and sound suddenly switched back on. A steaming pool fed by a waterfall sliding down a cliff, as beautiful as a movie set, opened before her. Pulling her eyes away, she spotted two more men and tried not to act surprised: they were dressed as Maori warriors, bare-chested, holding spears, loincloths around their solid waists, a glimpse of tattooed buttock as one man turned profile. Their faces were covered in intricate spirals and symmetrical lines. The barefooted men padded to either side of Ngawata and stood staring straight ahead.

"*Ko wai koe*?" Ngawata asked her.

Alexa looked questioningly at Cooper.

"She does not understand Maori," Cooper said.

The elder threw both hands into the air, up above his head, and turned around slowly. As if he were a conductor for a symphony, birds began to sing, the waterfall increased in volume, and a wind blew steam from the hot pools toward them. "This is sacred land of our ancestors. *Pākehā* are not welcome," Ngawata said.

"I understand," replied Alexa. Her nostrils were assaulted by sulfur, her vision blurred. "I also understand that it was wrong that district councilor Koppel came to this place and brought a stranger. Can you tell me about that day? And would you mind if I recorded the conversation?" Alexa opened her tote.

"No photos. No recording." The man on Ngawata's right took a step toward her. He continued speaking, staring at her. "*Pokokōhua*! That *Pākehā* landed in a cove, and I caught him sneaking around."

"This is our island caretaker," Ngawata said. "He will describe the trespassing."

"How do you know it was Paul Koppel? Who was with him?" Alexa's questions tumbled out as she stared at the caretaker. He looked to be in his forties, and his *tā moko* had deeper hues than Ngawata's. Black ink lines were carved above each eyebrow in permanent malice.

"We have ways of knowing." He spat on the ground. "The councilman followed the other man through the island, and they rooted around the opening of *wāhi tapu* area. They dared to step into the cave, the sacred burial cave, disturbing the slumber of our mighty ancestor."

"Did they take anything from the cave?"

"They came out..." The caretaker held out a closed fist. Alexa held her breath as he turned it over, and stretched his fingers.

Empty.

"I followed them and watched them undress and sit in the golden waters." He pointed to the steaming pool and then spat on the ground again.

"Did you speak to them, ask them to leave?"

"I watched through trees. I did not speak." He turned and spewed a torrent of Maori at Ngawata.

"He has evidence the men came back again when he was not here to protect. Our ancestors have been once again desecrated," Ngawata said flatly. He turned to face Alexa, and his eyes contained all knowledge of wrongdoing, all trail of theft, rape, pillage linking white men and men of color. Alexa's shoulders drooped; she fought the urge to kneel, apologize, sacrifice.

Wait. The warring on this island—she had read at the coffee shop—had been mostly Maori against Maori.

Until recently anyway. She thought about the aborted dig and found her voice. "You understand what has happened to Mr. Koppel since that day, yes?"

"The spirits have acted."

"The spirits? You understand Mr. Koppel had a wife and two little boys?"

"The spirits have acted," Ngawata repeated. His stare was a cold blast, blank as that statue carved in stone.

"Mr. Ngawata." Alexa coughed. "Do you know who killed Paul Koppel?" Sulfur and steam were swallowing her.

What the hell was happening?

"You leave now, for your safety. The spirits are disturbed by your trespass."

"I will leave when you answer my questions." She glanced at the caretaker and the other man who stood silent. *Who was he?* She looked at Cooper, but the officer refused to meet her eyes or help out. "I need your names and for you to show me the cave the men entered. And if you have your ways—who was the other man?"

"Mā, mā." The caretaker pointed to his head. "White."

Another white man, she thought. That narrows it down. Then she noticed each of the warriors had clubs tucked into their waists. Green clubs, jade maybe, about two and a half inches wide. Her eyes widened.

Ngawata began talking in Maori to Cooper. They pressed their foreheads and noses together, and then Cooper spoke to Alexa. "We will walk out together, and I'll answer your questions. Mr. Ngawata will remain here." She strode toward the thicket and disappeared, her broad shoulders and straight back vanishing into the bushes.

Alexa, fighting an urge to run after Cooper, to run like a scared puppy, turned to look at each man directly, her heart pounding.

"I need to see the cave before I leave." Raindrops began pelting her skin with cold precision.

"For your safety, you must leave," Ngawata replied. The two men flanking him stepped toward Alexa, their eyes bulging and their chins thrust forward. She looked away, instinctively aware that meeting those eyes would provoke attack.

"I will make arrangements to speak with each of you again." Her voice shook. "On the mainland." Her parting words, directed to the ground, felt as feeble as her bravery.

Terrance had been right.

She shouldn't have come to the island, powerless against a force stronger than she.

She squeezed through the break in the bushes, wondering if she'd make it back to the beach, to the water taxi. Or would she vanish, another *Pākehā* never to return from the forbidden island?

But Cooper was waiting for her. Alexa followed silently. No boat was on the beach when they popped out of the forest nor on the horizon. The lake surf was louder, pounding fists upon the shore. Rain pelted. Cooper stood near the water, arms folded against her chest, her hair slicked to a black helmet against her skull. "Let's wait under the trees," Alexa shouted, turning from the bleak shoreline. The tote, heavy and useless, knocked against her as she trudged back toward the tree line. Cooper followed. "Okay. Time to talk," Alexa said. "I asked Mr. Ngawata if he knew who killed Koppel, and he started talking to you in Maori. What did he say?"

Officer Cooper turned her broad face and impassive eyes toward Alexa. Her blue lips parted. "He repeated that the spirits have acted. It is what he believes. He has no knowledge of who killed Koppel beyond that. Only that Koppel deserved it."

"What about the other man? Is he in danger from these 'spirits?'" Alexa made quote marks with her cold fingers.

"*Taonga* is missing. The spirits will act."

Alexa could not believe what she was hearing. All this crap about spirits.

"Who were the two men with Mr. Ngawata?"

"The one you spoke with is Ray Herera, the island keeper, and the other man is my uncle, Taylor Cooper."

"Your uncle? He didn't act like an uncle."

Cooper was silent.

"Officer Cooper. Talk to me. You're a cop. What do you think?"

"There's the launch." Her voice was urgent. "It is time to leave. Now."

The ride back was rough. Waves and rain assaulted the vessel and occupants; buffeting winds made the going stomach-clenchingly slow. There was no way to continue her conversation with Cooper, who sat on the bow again, holding tight to cleats, placing as much distance as possible between herself and Alexa, who had insisted on a life jacket. The extra layer added scant protection, and the captain remained silent, concentrating on maneuvering the small craft.

As the boat approached the dock, Alexa spotted a yellow-cloaked figure standing beside a piling.

It looked like Detective Inspector Horne.

Chapter Fourteen

Why is he here?

Before the boat bumped the dock, Cooper vaulted. Alexa waited until the captain cut the engine and started wrapping lines around the dock cleats. "Thank you," she said, handing him her dripping life jacket. He offered her a hand up, which in her shaky state she accepted but slipped on the wet wood anyway, landing on her ass.

"You right?" the captain asked.

"Yes, sure," she said, turning over and looking at him from all fours. She stood, heat flooding her face, and guardedly walked toward the DI.

"Has something happened?" she asked before he could comment on her grace.

His face was grave, but he shook his head no. They stood in the rain and watched Cooper disappear into the parking lot.

"I have more questions for her. But Officer Cooper's clammed up." Alexa's teeth chattered. Her saturated jacket was a pitiful reminder of how useless she'd been. Horne took off his poncho while scanning the dock area.

"I've put her in an awkward position," he said, turning back to her. "Family and work don't mix, but she was the only way

Ngawata would consent to you stepping foot on the island. She was your ticket and protector, you know." He handed her the poncho.

Instead of protesting, she struggled into it, disappearing and then reappearing, dropping her tote in the process. "I don't see how I needed protection. From what?"

DI Horne picked up her tote, slung it over his shoulder, and studied her, one eyebrow an inch higher than the other.

She knew he was right. The forbidden island and the three men holding court had been menacing. "We can talk in my car. Now you're getting wet, and I need to get the heater going. Or you can stop by Trout Cottage."

Alexa longed for a hot shower and dry clothes. It was five, and she couldn't face going back to headquarters. "Why are you here?"

"Go home. Get dry. I'll follow you in my car and explain." He handed over her tote.

Alexa drove fast through the rain. Even though her body was cold to the core, she was warming up to the man in the rearview mirror.

—

Turning on the electric kettle, she put Earl Grey bags in mugs and told him to fix the tea. "Back in a jiffy. I'll just take a quick shower." Her voice shook.

The hot water eased the shivers racking her body; the knowledge that Horne was in the next room prolonged them. She let go her restraint and imagined him showering with her, his nakedness pressed against hers, his mouth hot and hungry.

Cold water extinguished the vision.

Alexa toweled off vigorously, wiped a hole in the steamy mirror, and studied her hazel eyes. *Control. I do not want to get involved.* Her reflection was noncommittal, so she hurried to dress. Beige bra, granny panties. Last night's jeans, clean white T-shirt, and NC

State Wolfpack sweatshirt. Slipper socks. A quick comb through her combatant hair and she corralled it into a ponytail. A brush of lip gloss and she was armed.

"My cup of tea," she said, looking at the DI sitting on the couch and then at the steaming mug he'd set on the coffee table.

She popped into the little kitchen and arranged a couple of Tim Tams on a plate.

"I love these cookies, by the way." She set the plate down, picked up the mug, steadied herself, and perched on the edge of the recliner, hoping for the becalming effects of oil of bergamot. Why was her heart racing?

"Best biscuit there is." Horne stared at her, one eyebrow inching higher than the other. "You look ten years old." His large hands encircled his almost empty mug. "Do you drink tea in the States?"

"Hot in the winter, iced and sweet in the summer." *Was looking ten years old good or bad?*

He nodded. "What transpired on the island?"

"Why were you at the docks?"

He studied her, his blue eyes darkening. "You're a hard case." He swallowed the last of his tea. "I was at the docks because I had four phone complaints and two walk-ins about police trespassing on Pirongia Island. I was concerned you might have a greeting committee."

"You're kidding. Who are these people?" So he *had* been looking for someone at the docks.

"You know Rotorua has the largest indigenous population of anywhere in the country, right?"

"I think so." Mary had said there were a lot of Maoris in the area. The councilwomen had mentioned it as well.

"Over thirty-five percent of Rotoruans are Maori," Horne said. "Elsewhere in New Zealand, Maori makeup maybe ten or fifteen percent of the population."

"So people of Maori ethnicity complained?" Alexa thought of Terrance.

"Right. Let's just say my decision to get you on the island was shortsighted. I've disregarded the rules of *tapu*—the sacred Maori code. According to one elder who came in and complained, we have offended the gods."

"Me?"

"Not *just* you. The police department."

"But..."

"And the consequences are disaster, demonic possession, or death."

"Get real," Alexa snapped. "That crap doesn't belong in the twenty-first century. You don't believe that, do you?"

"It doesn't matter what I believe. What matters is that we have a segment of our population insulted and angry. I'm sorry to have put you—" Horne stopped.

"What?" Alexa knew what he was about to say. *In danger*.

"I'm sorry I wasn't more respectful of the Maori community. What happened on the island? Did you learn anything or find anything?"

Alexa recounted her trip, told him Paul Koppel and his buddy, another white guy, were suspected of making a second trip to the island and maybe stole treasures. She left out the strange transformation from silence to symphony with the raising of Ngawata's arms at the golden pools. She now doubted her memory—probably had imagined it—and described the Ngawata posse. "The two warrior men had green clubs. I wonder if a club was used to attack Jenny?"

"Clubs? You mean *patu*?"

"What?"

"*Patu*. Maori war clubs. Made of greenstone."

"Is greenstone the same as jade? They looked jade."

"That's greenstone. It comes from the South Island and is considered a treasure by the Maori. More valuable than gold."

"They looked like small paddles."

"*Patu* were used for hand-to-hand fighting. Most are made of whale bone or wood. Only royalty had clubs made of greenstone. They'd be worth a fortune. I wonder where they came from." He bit into a Tim Tam and chewed thoughtfully.

"Couldn't they have come from the caves where the chief was buried?"

"I wonder. Theft of artifacts. It happens. But I'm off track. Let's get one from the Rotorua Museum and see if it matches the weapon used in Jenny's attack."

"Good idea. First thing in the morning." Alexa then told him that the extra duct tape prints had yielded no match.

"That clears anyone from the department," Horne said. "We all have prints on file."

They talked about what would happen next, Alexa relishing the role of confidant. The DI had an interview scheduled with the mayor's husband. Full disclosure of Koppel's financial records had produced some unexpected deposits. Detective McNamara was meeting with the owner of Bowen Realty Group. And Koppel's phone records had been released.

Horne stood.

Alexa took the plunge. "Are you hungry?" She had an urge to rock this man's even keel.

"I have to go back to headquarters and then pick up my daughters." He checked his watch and then stared at her. "Rain check?"

—

The evening ahead stretched long and empty, and Alexa, restored by hot shower, hot tea, and hot thoughts, restlessly turned her attention to food. Rice and beans tonight. She would add garlic and onion and went into the wee kitchen to check if there might be cumin or red pepper hidden in the cabinets. Barking dogs made her jump. Her phone.

"Hello?"

"Alexa? It's Terrance."

"Hi."

"Are you okay?"

Alexa immediately remembered his concern from their lunchtime talk about the island. She should have called him. "I'm fine, Terrance. I was able to speak to Mr. Ngawata on the island, and Officer Cooper made a good guide." *Hardly*.

"I am relieved. But watch out for yourself. People are talking."

"What people? What are they saying?"

"My people. There is concern that a Maori may be unjustly blamed for this murder. Maori have been made scapegoats throughout history."

Like people of color in the States, she thought. "Please assure whoever you've been talking to that we are doing our best with the evidence we have. We aren't jumping to any conclusions or falsely accusing anyone. Trust me."

"I wish I could. But history is full of shattered trust."

"Evidence will guide us."

Silence.

"Terrance, did you call the police department about my trip to Pirongia?"

More silence. And then Alexa realized he had hung up. She stared at her phone for a few moments, shaken. *Watch out for myself?* Mary's brother meant well, but his call left her uneasy.

The little kitchen came with a rice cooker, which would free her up for a walk along the river to calm her nerves. The bergamot had failed. She measured rice and water, slowly and methodically, as the river beckoned.

The skies had cleared, as so often happens in the small island country; a "change," her colleagues in Auckland had called it. She grabbed the cottage umbrella, just in case, and headed for the door, checking her watch. Just past six—what time did it get dark? On impulse, she grabbed the little egg basket and decided to find Trout Cottage's owner and return it.

The scrambled egg incident seemed years ago, yet this was

only her fifth night at the cottage. What had Egg Boy said? A side trail either before or after the falls led to Flying Fish Farm. The air was fresh, clean, light, North Carolina's humidity a faded bad dream. Alexa inhaled deeply and hustled along the roiling emerald Kaituna, certain there could be no more pristine air anywhere.

I could live here forever.

She had switched to running shoes, the left one blotched with yolk, and dodged puddles.

When the sounds of the river intensified to standing ovation behind a curtain of vegetation, Alexa knew the falls were close. The cave Horne had told her about must be nearby, and she was tempted to search for it until she dropped the egg basket. Her thoughts jumped to the women and children who once hid from rival tribes, paralyzed. Imagine hiding in the dark, mothers clutching and hushing little ones.

Scooping up the basket, Alexa picked up her pace. A scrabble from behind made her turn. Another walker? Except for Egg Boy, she had not met a single person on the path. The thick, tall flax stalks quivered, opposite sides leaning toward each other in shadowy conspiracy.

But no one emerged.

Shortly after passing the falls, she came to the side path and veered onto it. In five minutes, she had climbed a small rise. Below, about fifty yards away, a clapboard gray house, weathered and homey, nestled near an outbuilding. Alexa started toward it when a commotion made her whip around. A flash of fur and teeth encircled her.

"Stop," she screamed. "No!"

A rumble of a fast-approaching four-wheel ATV drowned the barking. The Egg Boy was at the wheel.

"Back. Back down," Stevie commanded the dogs. "Sorry about that," he said, cutting the engine. "They won't hurt you."

Famous last words.

The two dogs jumped on the back of the four-wheeler and grinned at her, tongues lolling.

"We meet again," she said, her heart hammering. Even when dogs didn't ambush, she was nervous around them. "I want to meet your mother, thank her. I'm guessing the welcoming committee belongs to you?"

"Eh. They're friendly, I promise. This is Iris, with one blue eye." Stevie leaned back and patted her. The border collie returned the affection with a lick to Stevie's cheek, melting Alexa's heart a tad. "And this is Echo." Brown and scrawny, Echo barked.

"They look ready for action. How many animals do you have on your farm?" Alexa was thinking Flying Fish Farm might be larger than she thought.

"Six sheep. Three lambs. I was checking on them. And chooks. Look. There's my mum." He pointed toward a car pulling up the drive. "Wanna lift?"

"How could I resist?" The dogs hopped off as Alexa hopped on. "Sorry, guys," she laughed.

They took off with a jerk, the dogs barking and nipping the wheels. In a jiff, they were on the driveway next to a green compact car. A woman was emerging. Her sandy blond hair was swept into a topknot, adding inches to her frame, and her dangling greenstone whale-tail earrings caught the waning light and matched her eyes.

"Hello," she said, sending a questioning look at her son. "Who have you found?" A tween-aged girl got out of the passenger side and stared.

"Hi." Alexa waved. "I'm renting your cottage." She climbed off the ATV. "I wanted to introduce myself and return your basket. That was so kind of you to have Stevie deliver fresh eggs." Alexa wondered how much of the egg debacle Stevie had shared. "And I wanted to apologize for the phone call from the police yesterday. Just routine, I assure you."

"It's all good. Maybe you can fill me in sometime. I'm Sarah Ingall. This is my daughter, Lucy. Why don't you come in? I'll fix tea. Lucy—will you get the groceries into the house?"

Lucy glared.

"No thank you," Alexa said. "I have rice cooking and need to get back. But I'd love to come another time."

"Right-o. You're here for another week, eh? Maybe for a glass of wine instead of tea. Do you have everything you need at the cottage?"

"Yes. Yes to both. The fresh lavender in the vase is lovely."

"There's more growing alongside the cottage. If you have trouble sleeping, put some next to the bed."

"I will. Thank you again for the eggs." She handed Sarah the basket.

"You're welcome. You walked over?"

Alexa nodded and looked down at Iris, who had plopped on her sneakers.

"Why doesn't Stevie run you home? It's almost dark, and it would just take a second on the quad. You don't mind, do you, Son?"

Stevie revved the engine.

Chapter Fifteen

There was a dead bird in the cottage, right in the entry, its wings spread in a feathered fan behind its little body, arranged just so.

What the hell?

Alexa step-hopped to avoid squishing it. She had just waved Stevie off, the quad bike barely pausing, and walked into the unlocked cottage.

There had been no bird in the cottage before she left. How had it gotten here? How had it died? Flown in through the door and crashed into a wall? Alexa reached down and touched its brownish-red breast with her pointer finger.

Cold.

She pushed.

Stiff.

This bird—her mind fluttered to the three similar ones that had burst through the trees on Pirongia—had been dead more than a couple of hours. Rigor mortis was close to maximum. Someone had put it here, had come into the cottage while she was gone. Immediately, Alexa straightened and eyed the room.

Was that someone still here?

She backed toward the front door and pressed against it. Stood statue still and listened, her eyes scouring the living area and adjoining kitchen. Only the bathroom and bedroom were out of sight. Silence, except for the sound of her heartbeat, amplified against her eardrum.

"Hello," she shouted. "Come out."

Alexa counted to ten. Wished for a Glock. She crossed to the bedroom in four strides and threw open the door.

Empty.

Bed made, book on nightstand, wet Keds tossed in the corner. She peeked into the bathroom, still humid from her shower, soggy clothes piled on the washer, shower curtain closed. In a burst of courage, she whipped the curtain open.

Empty.

No psycho in the shower. No bird man. Heart jackhammering, she retrieved her phone from her pocket and tried to think of who to call. The police? Bruce Horne? Terrance? Jeb? She was a castaway on this remote island so far from home.

Home. *Right.* She didn't have a home.

What should I do?

She stepped into the bedroom and sank onto the bed, forcing herself to calm down, breathe. It was just a bird. She dialed Horne's number. "It's me, Alexa," she said when he answered. Shrill voices were in the background. Probably his girls.

"What's up?"

"After you left, I went for a walk, and when I got back, someone had entered the cottage and left a dead bird. In the entrance."

"Come again?"

"A bird. With its wings spread. It's been dead for hours, so I know either you or I would have noticed it earlier. Someone broke in." She could imagine one of his eyebrows rising.

"Okay—let me recount. After I left, you went out? How long were you gone?"

"Forty minutes."

"And when you returned, there was a dead bird on the porch?"

"No." Why wasn't Mr. Calm and Collected listening? "*In* the cottage. In the little entryway."

Pause.

"Bruce?"

"I'll send a patrol officer to check things out. Was the door locked?"

Relief. "No. My bad. New Zealand feels so safe, I didn't bother. Ironic, huh? Here I am working a murder case, Jenny is attacked in the police station, and I'm still under the illusion that Rotorua is safe." She forced herself to stop rambling. "I did a quick search, and no one is in the cottage, and it doesn't look as if anything has been disturbed."

"I'll see who is closest, and we'll get things checked out. You okay?"

"Yes." No. "Thanks. I'll see you in the morning."

After some deep breaths, Alexa felt fortified enough to check the rice. The cooker had kept it steamy and moist, the scent soothing. Chopping onions and garlic, glad for the knife in her hand, however dull, Alexa's mind jumped to the dead bird holding court in the little entryway. She wanted to scoop it up and throw it in the river but knew she needed to show whomever the DI lassoed into checking it out. "Whomever" would probably bag it.

Can you lift fingerprints from a dead bird?

Alexa put the knife down and went into the living area to take a couple of photos with her iPhone. For her own records. The wait for a police officer was interminable. Eggs could be laid and hatched while waiting for "Whomever." She locked the door (finally) and went back to fixing dinner, though her appetite was gone.

Rare, losing her appetite.

Garlic and onions sizzling, she wrestled open a can of black beans with a cheap opener and began rinsing them. Popping one in her mouth, she noted car lights in the driveway. When had it gotten dark? She dumped the beans in with the onions and garlic, gave a quick stir, turned the heat to low, and, avoiding the carcass, unlocked the door.

"We meet again." Senior Officer Rangiora, her cafeteria liberator, stood on the porch. "Detective Inspector Horne sent me to check out a possible intruder and, ah, a dead bird."

"Yes. I know." She stood back and gave him the lowdown as they stared down at the bird. She had forgotten how tall he was. Six three or four.

"A fantail. So you're certain it wasn't in the house before your walk?" Rangiora had on his uniform minus the hat.

"I'm positive." She didn't know whether to mention his senior had been there earlier. "I left the house around six to walk to the cottage owner's house. I returned at 6:45." A thought stabbed her. Someone had been watching the house. She wrapped her arms around her torso.

Officer Rangiora was thorough. After checking the cottage, he searched the property perimeter and rain-dampened driveway. His flashlight, which he held with his right hand, swayed back and forth near her car as she watched from the porch.

"Lucky for the rain. I can see tire treads," he called. "Looks like an ATV. Your own. Another set."

"Yes." Alexa went down to join him. "The ATV belongs to the cottage owner's son. He drove me home. The other set belongs to Bruce." *Jeez.* "I mean, Detective Inspector Horne. We had a meeting here this afternoon, to review my trip to the island."

And for me to imagine him in my shower.

Rangiora looked surprised. "DI Horne came here?"

"Yes. For a debriefing about Pirongia," Alexa said, her face flushing. "Do you see any other tire tracks?" It would be reassuring to know the intruder drove here and then drove away.

"No others that I can detect. Your bloke probably walked up the drive after parking on the road. I'll check for footprints on my way out." Rangiora surveyed the property. "No neighbors?"

"The cottage owner lives farther down Trout River Road, about a half mile. No one else lives between here and Highway 33."

"Isolated, eh?" He stared at her. "I'll stop by and see them. The owners. Maybe they noticed someone mucking about. Senior said to bag the bird and bring it in."

"I'll be glad to get rid of it."

They entered the small living area, now garlic and onion-scented, and looked down on the wee carcass. The protruding black eyes of the fantail beneath white eyebrows stared defiantly at them.

"*Pīwakawaka*," said Rangiora, slipping on a pair of gloves. He knelt and started to scoop the bird into a plastic evidence bag.

"No. Stop." Pīwakawaka, whatever that meant, had distracted her for only a millisecond. "It's biological. You need a paper evidence bag."

"I don't think it matters," Rangiora said.

"It does," Alexa insisted. Anyone with an iota of forensics training knew "wet" needed paper to maintain integrity. Plastic caused sweating.

Was Rangiora trying to contaminate the evidence?

The officer stood and left the cottage. In two minutes, he was back with a manila envelope. He knelt again. "Or *tīwaiwaka*," he continued as if he hadn't left. "Maori have lots of different names for fantail." He slipped the bird into the envelope, leaving a lone gray and white feather. He went silent but did not rise, the fabric of his uniform taut against his long thighs. The top of his head was a swirl of glossy black. "You know," he said, looking up at her, "in Maori culture, a fantail in a house is an omen of death."

Alexa's mouth dropped, but she quickly closed it.

"This might be the work of locals angry that you visited Pirongia. Word travels quickly. We'll have a patrol car drive by a few times tonight." He stood in a fluid motion and held the packaged bird out, looking at the envelope. "If someone had wanted to hurt you, they would have. This is a message."

The man sounded older than his years. Police work did that.

The evening stretched before her, long in tooth, full of Maori warriors and angry birds. She forced down a few bites of rice and beans, feeling uneasy sitting at the tiny kitchen table by herself. Solo dining was tricky after a few years of sitting across from Jeb. *And* when someone has left a dead bird in your living area.

The accompanying glass of leftover Shiraz went down easier than rice and beans and tamped her fear. After washing up, Alexa poured another half glass, moved to the living area, and stopped abruptly.

The duct tape.

Suddenly, she remembered the extra duct tape stashed in the trunk of the Vitz. Had the intruder known about it? Impossible. Only Horne and Jenny even knew it existed. And no one knew she had it in the car. She set the wine down and peered through the side panel windows flanking the door. Sliver of moon, scudding clouds, swaying trees. Unwilling to stand like a target, she grabbed keys and rushed into the yard. In under sixty seconds, she was back, heart thumping, with the duct tape evidence bag.

Get a grip.

She hid the bag in her mostly empty suitcase under the bed and returned to the living room, surveying it for home security. She pulled the curtains tight over the two side wall windows, but the door panels exposed her to anyone in the front yard or driveway. Should she cover them with towels? That seemed too much effort, so she double-checked the door was locked and sank onto the couch.

Alexa's wine-bleary frazzled thoughts turned to her mother, who surely had comforted her when she was little, held her tight and soothed away tears streaking her baby face. Only the vaguest of mommy memories remained: being on her lap, listening to *Curious George, The Very Busy Spider, The Pokey Little Puppy*. The tattered books had been lovingly stored in a closet in Raleigh. What would her mother think of her life? Would she be proud?

Or sad her daughter never married, had her own children? She wrapped up in the afghan, wondering how different her life would have been…

—

Blinding light jerked her awake.

Alexa sprang from the couch, tripping on the afghan, and searched for protection. The bright light dimmed, then only a single beacon shone, the table lamp a lonely lighthouse.

Gravel crunch of tires.

Alexa dashed to the door to see vanishing taillights. She turned the porch light on, angry that she hadn't done this earlier, and wanted to yell "Come back." Her watch showed two hours had passed. Neck pain from unplanned slumber made her wince, and the day's events flashed through her head: disappointing fingerprint results, Fantasy Island, Horne in the shower, the dead bird. Rangiora had kept his word, sending a cruiser to patrol the property. Checking a third time that the door was locked and turning off the lamp, she headed for the bathroom. Sleep would be elusive, but her teeth could be clean.

Chapter Sixteen

As soon as Alexa arrived at the station Saturday, DI Horne ushered her away. "Rawiri Wright is the curator of the Maori collection at the museum. He knows war clubs and their significance, and he's expecting you to arrive before the museum opens at nine." Pausing, he looked straight into her green-flecked eyes. "Anything else happen last night?"

"I finished our bottle of wine and..." Why had she said "our" bottle of wine?

"And what?" Eyebrow wag.

"Nothing. Never mind. Officer Rangiora thinks the bird is a warning from the locals."

"He could be right. Let's talk about it over lunch. Give me a buzz around noon. I'll treat you to a Georgie Pie."

She didn't know what Rotorua Museum would look like, maybe all glass and modern like the police station or a brick warehouse like many buildings on NC State's campus, but nothing prepared her for the timber-and-stucco mansion before her.

"Yowzah."

The flower-lined path leading to the entrance was wide. She had the forensics lab camera and was tempted to take touristy pictures. Post them on Facebook. Brag about spring in October to her twenty-seven "friends" from Raleigh.

She tore her eyes from the building to the surrounding green lawn and gardens: purple tulips, bluebells, and blooming rhododendron, a pond guarded by funky mop-top trees, gingerbread gazebos, quarreling ducks, and, as a reminder that molten lava lurked beneath the grassy surface, a venting fissure. Alexa vowed to come back as a tourist.

The main entrance was locked. A plaque next to the door explained that the Elizabethan building built in 1902 had originally served as a government bath house offering therapeutic treatment using thermal waters.

Alexa spotted an Employees Only door and found it unlocked. She ventured in—thinking once more how trusting New Zealanders were compared with Americans—and was not surprised to find a vacant lobby. She crossed a mosaic floor to a directory, mindful of the stillness, and found directions to Te Arawa Gallery. She glanced through a large picture window toward Lake Rotorua—gray and distant—and then climbed a curving staircase, formulating questions for Mr. Wright.

Te Arawa Gallery was also empty. At the threshold, she looked up to admire a carved wooden lintel. Three *tiki* figures with abalone eyes and protruding tongues were surrounded by complex spirals. Soft sidelights made the iridescent eyes sparkle knowingly.

"You like?" a quiet voice asked. Alexa turned to find a man, her height, sixty-ish, a ring of keys hanging from his belt loop. "Rawiri Wright. *Kia ora*." He leaned forward to press his nose and forehead against Alexa's. His kind eyes, behind wire rim glasses, searched hers. "We are part of the oneness of all that exists. I've been expecting you."

"Hello," Alexa said, confused by the intimate sharing of breath greeting. Terrance had greeted her the same way, but he was Mary's brother. "I'm Alexa Glock." She held up her new Rotorua Police Department ID badge with photo that Ms. Welles had handed her when she arrived at the station earlier. "I need to ask some questions that we hope will help us with our investigation."

Mr. Wright, ignoring her badge, turned his attention upward. His graying hair was combed straight back, exposing a broad expanse of forehead. "We are so fortunate to have this *taonga* back."

"What do you mean?" She could be patient.

"The lintel was a gift to Queen Victoria in 1886 and has lived in London in various museums until 2002 when, for reasons I can't fathom, it was sold to an antiques dealer. It could have been lost forever. Luckily, a private collector, a Kiwi, purchased it and returned it to Aotearoa last year."

"That is lucky." Alexa loved the Maori name for New Zealand: Aotearoa, meaning Land of the Long White Cloud. "Do you know who carved it?"

"Wero Taroi, a master carver, from the *Ngāti* Tarawhai tribe. He did most of his carving in the late 1800s. A piece like this belonged over the entrance to a meeting house. It is a spiritual guardian. Or, as *Pākehā* might say, a guardian angel. It wards off danger."

"I could use one at my cottage," Alexa blurted.

Mr. Wright studied her. "A lot of us need its protection."

"I know you're busy and the museum is opening soon. I have some questions about Maori war clubs."

Mr. Wright's eyes lit up like Christmas lights. "*Patu*! The thrusting weapon. Used to attack an enemy's neck, temple, or ribs. Executed correctly, a strike would crack a skull; a twist would disembowel a belly." He walked into the gallery.

Alexa imagined scrambled Jenny brain and paused under the lintel to allow good juju to penetrate before joining Mr. Wright, who had flipped on overhead lights and was standing between two glass cases full of such clubs.

"Perhaps this is the best collection of *mere* in the world." Mr. Wright beamed.

"*Mere*?" asked Alexa.

"Weaponry."

Teardrop-shaped paddles of various size and substance were displayed against cream velvet. Some were wooden, and others were made of bone or stone. Alexa's eyes stopped roving when she came to a club made of dark speckled greenstone.

"Can you tell me about this one?" Alexa asked, pointing. It looked to be about twelve to thirteen inches end to end and three inches wide. Grooves were carved into the handle, and the blade tapered to a sharp glistening edge.

"*Mere pounamu.* The most highly prized of all. Much harder than wood or bone, less likely to fracture on contact. Most greenstone *patu* belonged to chiefs. This one is very rare and has gained much *mana*."

"*Mana*?"

"Respect and power. From winning battles and executing enemies."

Executions? "Where is it from?"

"It is believed to be from Te Rauparaha, a celebrated South Island warrior chief. He was buried with it in a cave upon a bier made of sticks and rocks."

"What's a bier?" Alexa asked.

"A platform above ground. The defleshed body was laid upon the bier and covered with rocks, sticks, and mud in a pyramid shape. Two hundred years later when *Pākehā* disturbed the body and removed the club, it changed color before their eyes, darkened to the shade it is now."

"Really? It changed color?" She thought of the forest-green clubs hanging from the men's waists on the forbidden island. Had they been stolen from a burial place?

"Yes."

"Is it very valuable?" She spoke louder than necessary.

"Priceless."

"Well, yes, but what if someone had one on the market? What would it sell for?"

"An antiquity like this, from the nineteenth century?" Mr. Wright considered her question at length. "Twenty, thirty thousand dollars, maybe more."

"How did the museum acquire this piece?"

"Why is this particular club of interest to you?"

"Actually, it's not. Unless it went missing and then reappeared."

"It did not."

How much information to share? Mr. Wright had trusting eyes and had greeted her with warmth. "I met two men yesterday with greenstone clubs hanging from their waists." She wondered if Mr. Wright knew about her visit to Pirongia.

"Who were they?"

"I'm not at liberty to say. We also have a lab technician who was hit in the head with a club-like instrument at the police station."

"I heard about the attack. Are you saying she was attacked with a war club?"

"Please, this is confidential. The victim will recover. We aren't sure what she was attacked with, but I'd like to compare photos of her wound with this club."

"I could not let it leave the museum. And *patu* come in many sizes."

"I understand. But most of these in the case look roughly the same size. Could you remove it and let me photograph it?"

"Most *patu* are similar in size. Anywhere from ten to fifteen inches long. Thirteen inches is average. Any larger and they would have been unwieldy in combat. A larger one like this..." Mr. Wright walked over to the second case and pointed out a club twice as long. "A larger one would be used for show, perhaps in ceremonial dances. This is made of whale bone."

"How wide is the average club?"

"It varies." He stared at the whale bone one. "This one is five inches wide. Fighting clubs were two to four inches wide."

"I'd like to photograph this one," Alexa said, standing firm at the original case and pointing at the paddle that had supposedly changed color.

"As you wish. Mr. Horne is a respected officer of the law and fair to the Maori. Excuse me for a moment."

Alexa waited by the glass case and then wandered to a display titled *Ta Moko*: The Art of Tattoo. She read about the carving of skin with sharpened chisels. Both a straight-edged chisel and a smaller-toothed chisel made of bird bone were displayed alongside black-and-white photographs of men and women with facial *moko*. Alexa's face muscles twitched. She stepped back to the club case and stared hard at the greenstone *patu,* considering its size and weight.

Mr. Wright returned wearing cotton gloves. He unlocked the case and gently removed the club from its plush spot. "We'll take it to the back room. We have a stand where objects are photographed." He relocked the case, cradled the *patu,* and walked away. Alexa followed into a well-lit room where Mr. Wright placed the object on a small table covered with a tight blue cloth, encircled with lights.

"We have a saying," Mr. Wright said. "'*Ahakoa iti, he pounamu.*' Although it is small, it is of greenstone."

Alexa dug the digital camera out of her tote while deciphering the saying. Good things come in small packages? Mr. Wright handed her cotton gloves that she donned and began photographing the club, surprised at how tapered it was from side view, how blade-like. She borrowed a nearby ruler and photographed the club next to it from several angles.

Was the heat she felt each time she maneuvered the club imaginary? A feverish sensation penetrated the thin cotton gloves. She asked Mr. Wright to hold the *patu* against a light so she could capture it from beneath. The club became translucent; she saw black speckled tadpoles swimming in a deep green pond. "Gorgeous," she whispered, wishing the item was hers to keep, surmising that *patu* triggered greed. "Is it true that greenstone is found only on the South Island?"

"The Maori name of South Island is Te Wahi Pounamu. It translates 'place of *pounamu*.' All *pounamu* comes from the South Island along the west coast or in rivers, Arahura River especially. *Pounamu* came to the North Island as barter or war bounty. The Europeans had their gold, we had *pounamu*."

She was reluctant to part with this club of mystique. She ran her gloved finger along the surface one last time.

"*Mere* were designed to kill, you know," Mr. Wright said softly, reclaiming the club.

—

Back at the lab, Alexa's fantail was waiting for her on the specimen table, tagged with date and location. A wave of anger coursed through her body. Who dared enter her home? Her sanctuary? She opened the cooler locker and placed the bird in, knowing she would have to decide quickly what to do with it before it decomposed, and then worked comparing the photos of Jenny's wounds, to the uploaded museum photos. The dimensions of the club were similar to the dimensions of Jenny's wounds and the surface of the paddle matched the abrasion-less wound. There was a strong possibility a Maori war club made of greenstone had been used to attack Jenny. She'd make a 3-D image to confirm. Anxious to tell the DI, Alexa also wanted time to figure out what it meant. Follow up with more research. But clues pointed to an obvious assumption: a Maori killed Koppel. There was the mud pot itself and the symbolic way Koppel had been "boiled." Terrance had said that the gravest insult a Maori could inflict is "boil your head." There was the sacred Maori island that Koppel trespassed.

But wasn't all the Maori-ness just a bit transparent? Was a *Pākehā*, or white person, trying to make a Maori look guilty?

Alexa decided to recommend Horne get the three men from the island into the station as soon as possible. She called him but got his voicemail. Whoever they were dealing with was brazen and willing to take risks. *Brazen enough to leave a dead bird in my house.* What if Horne got fingerprints from the men and they matched fingerprints on her bird? Could you lift fingerprints from a bird?

A quick Google search revealed the recent article "Scientists Discover How to Recover Fingerprints from Bird Feathers." Alexa eagerly read. The forensics scientist from Abertay University in Scotland said the findings would help catch people guilty of wildlife crimes.

Maybe murderers too.

She loved this job and its endless surprises. Now she was eager to fetch her fantail. The article was general, written for a newspaper. Later, Alexa would savor the research paper it came from in the journal of *Science & Justice*. But the article revealed what fingerprint powders worked best on feathers without damaging the evidence: red and green magnetic fluorescent. The scientist had dusted six different birds of prey, but Alexa wagered it would work on insectivores as well.

She went in search, fingers crossed, to the supply cabinet. Black powder was the most commonly used dusting powder, and every lab had a bucketful, but other colors worked better on certain surfaces. White, for example, worked best on glass. Alexa could see a jar of white, a jar of aluminum, and one of bichromatic. She had used bichromatic, a mixture of black and white, on a multicolored phone protector in Raleigh with clear results. There were even some spray powders. But no fluorescent. She'd need a UV lamp too, or a blue light and goggles. She already had the camera.

Her bird wasn't repulsive anymore. Alexa called Ms. Welles from her cell.

"*Kia ora*. Rotorua Police Department."

"Hello, Ms. Welles. It's Alexa Glock from the lab."

"Yes?"

"There are some important materials I need to aid in the investigation. How can I get them?"

"We have a well-stocked lab."

"I agree." Welles's was touchy. "But I need a certain type of fingerprint powder that is not stocked. And a UV lamp."

"I'll have to run this by District Commander Teal. He's just left for the day. It's the weekend, you know."

"I need these supplies today. For the *murder* investigation." By Monday, her bird would stink. "Do you want me to ask Bruce?" *Damn—a mistake.*

"Bruce?" Ms. Welles' voice went cold. "Are you referring to Detective Inspector Horne?"

"Yes. I know he'd want me to finish my testing as soon as possible."

"I'll speak to Detective Inspector Horne and let you know. Bring me a list. It will be difficult to get supplies delivered on a weekend."

"Thank you so much," Alexa said all sugary. Welles was speaking the truth. She thought of the Auckland forensics lab just three hours away. It was sure to have what she needed. Her mind was already zooming in a car up to Auckland, dead bird riding shotgun. But first, she had a lunch date.

Chapter Seventeen

Alexa was loathe to ask Ms. Welles for the DI's whereabouts and decided to find him on her own. She almost didn't recognize District Commander Teal on the stairwell. He was dressed in jeans and polo and looked ten years younger than his Monday through Friday suit-self. Perhaps he was hiding from Ms. Welles. "Ms. Glock. How are you?" he asked, stopping midstep. His premature white hair had to be professionally styled.

"Fine. Just finishing up some lab work."

"What's this I hear about a threat?

"Threat?"

"I heard there was a break-in at your residence and a threat conveyed."

How did Teal know? "Someone did enter my cottage and left the carcass of a bird. I'm not sure what to make of it. I guess it could be teenagers."

"Yes. That's true. But make sure you lock up and add more lights to the property. Have you thought of getting a dog?"

Lock up and lights on, yes, but she wasn't planning to traipse to Sarah's house to demand floodlights and borrow Iris. "Thanks for the tips."

Past noon, her stomach insisted. She found Horne and the

loaners in the conference room. Alexa joined to hear McNamara recount his interview with the owner of Bowen Realty. "Guy Bowen is the owner, took over for his father last year. He's trying to revamp the agency—make it bigger and better. Has new ideas like virtual tours and online bidding. What a-hole would buy a crib online? But sales have flat-lined. Trimble has the money report."

"Koppel earned forty-one thou last year. That's down from his two previous years," Trimble said. "He also earns three thousand a year for being on city council. The Koppels have a joint account. All the money that goes in flows right back out again."

"Living paycheck to paycheck," McNamara said.

"Does his wife work outside the home?" Alexa asked, thinking of the wilted widow in the floral armchair.

"No." Trimble's glasses caught the light and glinted. "But in August, Koppel opened a new account at a different bank. One of those on-call accounts. Two deposits of one thousand dollars each and a five-hundred-dollar withdrawal money order made out to"—he checked his stack of papers—"to Wei Zhong."

"Who the hell is that?" McNamara said.

"Mrs. Koppel is coming in at one thirty," Horne said. "She may be able to shed some light."

"The deposits were made at around the time he supposedly trespassed on Pirongia," Alexa pointed out. "Were they cash deposits?"

"Yes, cash deposits, so no trail," Trimble said. "Paul Koppel did have a small life insurance policy but hardly enough for the wife to off him." He looked at Alexa. "What's up about a break-in at your house? Is it related to the case?"

Bird news was fast-flying. "I don't know. When I was out, someone entered my house and left the body of a bird."

"Probably flew in when you opened the door," said McNamara, stuffing a banana wrapped in bread into his mouth.

"I don't think so." Alexa could smell peanut butter and stepped back. She had vowed not to engage with Ponytail man.

"What's up in the lab?" the DI asked.

All three looked at her expectantly. "Nothing fishy from the contents of Koppel's car. But the dimensions of Liang's wound are compatible with a Maori war club."

"Liang was attacked with a war club?" asked Trimble.

"Possibly. The dimensions of the wound approximately match the size and weight of the greenstone club I photographed at the museum this morning. No pattern transferred to Liang's skin, so the weapon was smooth." She looked directly at Trimble. "Are you familiar with CAD?"

"Sure, yeah. Computer-aided drafting. It renders crime scene drawings. Looks professional in court. Jurors love it."

"It can render a possible weapon, too, given wound dimensions. It created an object similar to a Maori war club. So characteristics of a club match Liang's wound."

"I used CAD last year to reconstruct a bullet path," McNamara interrupted.

"But unless we locate the actual object, we can't be a hundred percent sure. According to Mr. Wright at the museum, none has gone missing from the collection, but greenstone clubs are worth a lot of money. Did you get my message about getting Ngawata and his posse from the island to come in to the station?" she asked Horne.

"Posse?" He actually smiled. "We're working on it. They're hard to locate."

"One of them is Officer Cooper's uncle, Taylor Cooper. She can probably help you find him. We'll need their fingerprints."

"Fat chance," Ponytail said, smacking his lips, his breath now reeking of Jif.

"Never hurts to ask," Horne answered. "Law says they'd have to volunteer unless they're in custody. If one of these blokes attacked Jenny or killed Koppel, then he won't be willing. I'll watch their reactions. Could be revealing. Let's break for lunch. Trimble—get up with Officer Cooper about her uncle. Meet back at two."

As the Auckland loaners filed out, he turned to Alexa and said, "How about that lunch date?"

McDonald's was two blocks from the station, and they opted to walk. The air was scented with lake breeze, and the sidewalk was bustling with Saturday shoppers like a yesteryear village. In the States, all these people would be driving to Costco or shopping online. Alexa wanted to discuss Officer Cooper but decided to wait until they were eating. She window-shopped instead, searching for boots and thinking how Bruce—when had she started thinking of him by his first name?—how *Horne* used the word "date" and how uncomfortable that made her feel. Hot cold. On off. But it was only McDonald's. No one went to a McDonald's for a date.

They both eyed the movie playing at Regale Screens: another superhero remake.

"Took Sammie," he said, catching her eye. "*She* liked it."

The McDonald's near the station could have been a Mickey D's from home except for the group of loud girls squished into a booth, all wearing navy and maroon Rotorua Girls High School sport uniforms. The menu was different too; it included Georgie Pies.

"They aren't on the menu in the States."

"I wonder what a McDonald's in Paris sells," Horne said. "Baguettes and Brie?"

"With supersized wine." They both laughed and ordered.

She let the DI pay.

"What was that thing McNamara was eating?" Alexa asked when they sat across from each other in a booth.

"Monkey roll," Horne said. "My daughters love them."

"Gross." Two bites in, Alexa decided this Georgie Pie would be her last. Chicken 'N Vegetable pie was gross too.

"Not hungry?" he asked between bites of his own pie.

"I'm always hungry," she said, sipping her almost ice-less Coke. She pointed to it. "What? Is there a shortage of ice in a country only a six-hour plane ride from Antarctica?"

"Typical Yank, complaining. And loudly. What lab results do you have?"

"I'm still waiting for DNA results from the trace evidence we collected from the body. Did you put a rush on it?"

"No." His first pie, a steak and cheese, had vanished. "I'll do it when we get back. What did you do with your bird?"

"It's in the cooler. I discovered prints can be lifted from bird feathers. It would be worthwhile, but we don't have the right powders in the lab."

"Let's get what you need. Sharon Welles can put in an order."

"Welles said it would take a while, this being the weekend. I called the Auckland Forensics Lab, and they have what I need." She paused and crumpled up her pie in its wrapper. "I might drive up this afternoon. Take my birdie with me."

"I was hoping you'd sit in on the Mindy Koppel interview. Helps to have a female present, I've found. And she's already met you." He eyed the crumpled pie with sorrow and started in on his second.

"No problem. I'll sit in and then head to Auckland. Spend the night and dust the bird first thing in the morning." Alexa was curious to see Paul Koppel's wife again. What did she know about that investor and her husband's new bank account?

"Auckland's a long drive."

"Three hours. I'm throwing this away and getting a Quarter Pounder." So much for embracing Kiwi cuisine.

Four minutes later, she was back in the booth, removing pickles and chowing down. After a few bites, she put the burger down. The DI was eyeing her discarded pickles. She pushed them over. "I've been meaning to bring up Officer Cooper."

"What about Officer Cooper?" His eyebrows rose, and defense colored his voice.

"First of all," Alexa said, pausing to wipe her mouth. "First of all, where was she when Jenny was attacked? Her uncle has a greenstone club."

"Wait a sec. We don't know definitively that a club was used."

"Secondly, she was the first officer on the murder scene, right? She could have chucked any evidence into the pots. And she totally clammed up on the island. Barely spoke—it was like prying words from a statue."

"I put her—"

"And finally," Alexa interrupted, "Cooper visited Jenny in the hospital, and Jenny, who was unconscious at the time, doesn't even know her. Why would Cooper visit her?" Alexa couldn't make herself say what she was thinking: to finish what she had started in the lab closet. By suffocation instead of blunt force trauma. The officer stationed outside Jenny's hospital room might have saved her life.

"Wait a minute," Horne snapped. "I've know Wynne Cooper for seven years. I sponsored her when she was an angry high school kid, headed for trouble. We have a program that connects at-risk teens with career opportunities. Shadow a teacher. Shadow a plumber. Shadow a cop. She shadowed me. Didn't say much, but she came alive, had a spark, a goal. You could see it in her demeanor."

"That's a worthy program. But—"

"I helped her qualify for *Taumata Raukura*—a police training program." They were taking turns interrupting each other.

This is not looking good.

"Cooper is the first one in her family who's ever been to uni, and she's been with us as a full-fledged officer for eighteen months now. Why would she risk all her hard work?"

"Sometimes family trumps career." Never had for her. "All your effort into her aside, look at my points. Where was she when Jenny was attacked?"

"She was not logged in at the station and was not caught on security camera."

"Okay. But that doesn't mean she wasn't there. She could have wedged a door open or ducked the cameras."

"Are you going to argue with our security? Hang Cooper on conjecture? Or worse, because she's Maori?" Eyebrows flatlining, pickles untouched.

"It's easier for a cop to get in the building unseen than Joe Blow off the street. It's no conjecture that Jenny was attacked, right? And what about Cooper happening to be the first person on the scene at the mud pots?"

"She handled it well for a rookie."

"Except when she let me enter the scene, remember? Is that handling things well? Maybe she was hoping I'd contaminate evidence."

"Again—conjecture. Someone had to be the first on the scene. It was coincidence."

"I don't believe in coincidence." She was surprised they were having this heated conversation and took a deep breath. "Yesterday on the island, Cooper chose to ignore me rather than work as a team with a fellow officer."

"You're not a fellow officer."

Touché.

"I put her in an awkward position. I used her family ties to get permission for you to visit the island," he added.

"Cooper doesn't get to pick who she works with. That's dangerous. And explain why she went to see Jenny."

"Maybe to support a fellow officer. I don't know."

"She doesn't strike me as the warm-fuzzy-here's-a-box-of-candy type. You need to talk with her."

DI Horne had to face facts. The next bite of burger tasted like mud, and Alexa wrapped it up to toss. So much for the pleasant lunch "date," the lunch she had skipped leftover rice and beans for.

The walk back to the station was silent.

—

Mindy Koppel and her father were waiting in reception. Ms. Welles pried her eyes away from father and daughter at the sight of Alexa and DI Horne entering the station together. Disapproval made her nose rise up like a marionette string was pulling on it. "They've been waiting for ten minutes, Detective Inspector Horne."

"Thank you, Sharon." The DI turned to Mindy and her father. "I'm sorry we've kept you waiting."

Mindy Koppel looked worse than when Alexa had last seen her sunk in an armchair. Her shoulders were hunched, her lifeless hair hung in oily clumps, and her nose was bulgy red. She looked every bit the grieving widow down to an oversized sweater, probably smelling of her husband, dwarfing her frame.

"We need to speak with your daughter alone this time. We'll just be down that hall," Horne said to Jerry Russell. "Unless you want a solicitor with her?"

"Why would she need a solicitor?"

"I am not saying she needs one, but one would be allowed to sit in as we ask questions."

"I don't like your implications," Russell replied. "My daughter is the victim here."

Paul Koppel might not agree with that, Alexa thought.

"And you're the ones who need an attorney," Russell continued. "We plan to sue over those newspaper photographs. You had no right…"

"We apologize the newspapers ran photos of the crime scene. They did not come from the department," Horne said.

Alexa remembered the *National Enquirer*-like photos of the murder scene. She didn't blame Russell for being angry. "Mrs. Koppel, why don't you come with me so that your father and Detective Inspector Horne can talk?" she intervened.

Mindy rose obediently as a child and followed Alexa to the interview room down the hall.

"Sit here, Mrs. Koppel."

"Thank you." The room had a long table and four chairs.

Alexa held one out for Mindy. "Would you like something to drink? Tea or water?"

"Water. Ta."

DI Horne joined them as Alexa was returning with a cup of water and box of tissues. He swung his leg over a chair across from Mindy, turned on a recorder, and started. "Thank you for coming in, Mrs. Koppel. We'll be taping this interview. Do you remember Ms. Glock from Crime Scene Investigation?"

Mindy gave Alexa, who sat next to the DI, a nod. "Have you found out who killed my husband?" She put her blue suede tote on the table, gripping it with white-knuckled fingers. Her diamond engagement ring lay sideways, too defeated to stand upright.

"Not yet. That's why I need to ask you more questions. I appreciate you coming in today. How are the boys holding up?"

DI Horne looked genuinely concerned, and Alexa remembered the carrot-top fellow refusing to be bathed by anyone other than his mum.

"Dad has explained to them about Paul, but they don't believe it. Casey thinks it's a game where someone falls dead but then gets up." Her eyes welled.

Alexa pushed the box of tissues toward her.

"Ta," she said, crumpling one to her face.

"I am again sorry for your loss," Horne said. "We have people here who can help you talk with the boys. I'll give you a number to call."

Mindy blew her nose and looked at him, her eyes red-rimmed, puffy.

"You've had some time since we talked to you last. Can you now think of anyone who might have wanted to harm Paul?"

"No."

"We have located your husband's car. At the Waiariki Thermal Land of Enchantment parking lot. Why would he have driven there?"

"I don't know. We've never been there, never taken the boys."

"Had there been any angry phone calls or emails Paul mentioned?"

Mindy thought a moment. "He was being harassed by two

women on the town council. He said they kept calling him and badgering him about some report." A little color appeared in her cheeks, and she sat straighter.

"The Spa and Wellness Summit report. I know the women you're referring to," Alexa said. "They were upset that Paul had not submitted his report about the Wellness Summit he attended on behalf of the Rotorua City Council in Morocco."

"If Paul had a report to do, I'm sure he did it."

"Apparently, he did not submit it, and the councilwomen felt it was overdue," Alexa said.

"I don't know anything about that. He was busy. A new listing came up while he was away, and then he had those meetings with the investor he met. That's a lot to ask for someone who volunteered his time and efforts." She pushed hair out of her face.

"He received a stipend to serve as town councilman and did enjoy a free trip to Morocco, yeah?" Horne said.

"It was a work trip. Not a *vacation*."

"What do you know about the investor he met in Morocco?" Horne asked with the slightest of zeal.

"They met on the flight coming home, not in Morocco. Paul met with him several times. Council business."

"Was the investor a Kiwi?" the DI prodded.

"No, I don't think so."

"Tell us everything you know about him. It's important."

"Paul was excited to show him about. They went out to dinner, looked at land, and had meetings. That's all I know." She gulped water from the paper cup.

"Did you meet this person?" Horne asked.

"No."

"Do you know his name?"

Mindy shook her head. Dark circles pooled beneath her eyes.

"Can you provide the dates Paul met with this person?" His voice now had a hard edge.

Mindy's forehead wrinkled. "Early August, I think. A weekend. Deputy Mayor Haddenfield would know, wouldn't he?"

"Did you know Paul went to Pirongia Island in August?"

"What are you talking about?" Mindy stared at the DI. "That's rubbish."

"So do you know anything about him visiting the island?"

"No. He wouldn't. That's a private island." No pausing or blinking or tics. The sound of laughter came from the hallway, and she flinched.

"Did Paul have a boat?" Horne asked.

"No."

"Did he have access to a boat?"

Mindy hesitated. "My father has a boat." She finished the water and squeezed the cup to a misshapen hunk of wax.

"Where does he keep it?"

"Rotorua docks. Sometimes we tow it to the bach."

Alexa knew they'd be searching the boat. But would it yield evidence two months later?

"We'll need access to the boat," Horne said. "I'll explain that to your father. Mrs. Koppel, were you aware that your husband had opened a new account at Kiwibank in August?"

Mindy looked surprised. "Why are you looking into our bank account? Shouldn't you be looking for who killed Paul?"

"There's always a chance there is a link between money and murder. Do you know anything about this account?" The DI handed her a bank statement with highlighted items. Mindy studied the statement, her brow furrowing.

"I don't know why Paul opened this account. Maybe something to do with work." Her cheeks had faded back to pale.

"Who is Wei Zhong?" Horne pointed to a money order receipt. "Is it the investor he met?"

"I don't know who that is. What will happen to that money?" Mindy looked desperate.

"All accounts are frozen until the investigation is complete. Were you and your husband experiencing financial hardships?"

Mindy flared. "Guy Bowen hired two new agents last year, and there weren't even enough listings for Paul, I mean, for the rest of the agents."

"So money was tight?"

"Paul feels that I, well, *felt* that I always compared him to Jason, my brother, and to my father, you know, with the bach and boat. They take expensive holidays." She blew her nose. "We were, and the house needs…, well, the market has been horrible. I…"

The DI waited patiently, but Mindy had run out of steam.

"This is difficult to ask, but are you on birth control of any sort, Mrs. Koppel?" The DI actually squirmed in his seat.

Alexa knew he was thinking of the condoms in the glove box.

Mindy was stunned. "What business is my personal health to you?"

"Nothing is personal in murder, I'm afraid. Were you and your husband planning on having more children?" Horne pushed.

"I do not understand what this has to do with Paul's murder." Mindy pulled the baggy sweater tighter with one hand and grabbed her purse with the other. "I'd like to go now."

"Is it possible that your husband was seeing someone?"

"No." Mindy's chin jutted. "Paul was a good man. He loved us."

"Had you and your husband had an argument before you took the boys to the bach, Mrs. Koppel?"

"How…no. When will I get my phone back? I need it."

"We can pick it up on your way out. We're done with it. Thank you for your time. And let me get that phone number of our social worker for you."

Alexa sat still, thinking, in the silence of the room. DI Horne handled the interview well. The questioning had made Mindy Koppel defensive and indignant but reaped juicy information: The Koppels struggled financially. Paul met someone on the plane, maybe a foreigner. And Paul had a boat at his disposal.

Horne popped back in after five minutes and leaned against the open doorway. "That was hard," he said. "Her phone records didn't amount to anything suspicious. They confirm she texted Koppel last Friday afternoon and made no communication after that until Monday."

"But she could always have used a different phone if she had anything to hide."

"Are you considering her a suspect?"

"No, except statistically." Alexa didn't believe Mindy killed her husband, but she could have discovered he was fooling around. "Did anyone see her at whatever beach she went to? What was it called?"

"Papamoa Beach. Trimble is on it."

"Did you ask Mindy's father about the boat?"

"Yes. He told us where it's located. I'm sending someone to the marina right away."

"That's good, although evidence will probably have eroded."

"I plan to talk to Mr. Russell alone. I want his impressions of his son-in-law. And I plan to get a warrant for that flight manifest. Who did Koppel meet on the plane? But it will take forty-eight hours."

Alexa stood. "I'm going to leave for Auckland now."

DI Horne looked as if he wanted to say more but just studied her, their luncheon argument a Berlin Wall.

Chapter Eighteen

In the lab, Alexa set the featherlight bird bag in a box, gathered the camera bag, and hurriedly left for home. She did a quick scan at the entrance to the cottage. No bird. Everything normal, and as she picked up the afghan still on the floor and folded it neatly, she realized getting out of town was a good idea.

The dead bird had sullied her nest.

Alexa forced herself to open her laptop and make a hotel reservation. For a millisecond, she had thought about surprising Mary, just showing up at her apartment. *Mary is dead, stupid.* Who would empty her apartment? Her office? She wondered if she should offer to help as she placed a call to the Auckland Forensics Department to make sure someone would be there in the morning. *Nah. Stay out of it.* Finally, with overnight necessities, she flew the coop.

The calming voice of an Aussie GPS app helped Alexa navigate out of town. The Thermal Explorer Highway skirted Lake Rotorua and headed northwest to Matamata, home to the renowned *Lord of the Rings* Shire. In the States, when she'd mention her New Zealand fellowship, people had asked: "Are you a Tolkien fan?" "Will you go to the Shire?"

Pay good money to see creepy elves and bearded gnomes?

No way.

With a pang, she remembered Mary had been an anti-fan of the *Rings* hoopla. "Rotorua used to be the number one tourist attraction on the North Island. Now people go to the Shire instead. It's hurt my cousin's business."

"What's his business?"

"Tamaki Maori Village. You know—song, *haka, hāngī* feast."

"Feast?"

"Lamb, kumara, pumpkin, cabbage. The food is covered with flax and leaves and then steamed over hot stones."

"So you'll take me there?" Alexa had asked, her mouth watering.

"Well, maybe. It's embarrassing to see my *whānau* with painted faces and no shirts sticking their tongues out at tourists. But the food's good."

Out of Rotorua's stinky clutches, the state highway became an undulating ribbon pulled through quaint villages, pastures of sheep and lambs, one-lane bridges, and hills. Alexa's peripheral vision caught a blur of earthy browns, emeralds, spring greens splattered with pink and purple. Eye candy.

The narrow highway had scarce traffic. Maybe she'd do the Village thingy on her own after the case was solved. And the Shire, why not? Today, she'd drive by. In three hours, she'd be back in the City of Sails.

—

Alexa pulled up to the SKYCITY Hotel in the central business district at six thirty p.m. The rate for her room was decent, but she hadn't factored in the cost of city parking—another twenty dollars for one night in a low-ceilinged garage beneath the hotel. She considered what to do with the bird she had christened Fanny: hotel room or trunk? She pressed her nose to the box and decided to leave it in the dark, cool trunk; the spring night would not hasten decomposition. Plus—it would be hard to sleep with this particular roomie.

Her room was eleven stories above the city, with seductive views of the boat-speckled harbor, the arched bridge, and the slowly revolving Sky Tower. She squinted at the tower, amazed to watch a form jump from the top, plunge straight down, and then jerk halfway back up. The bungee-jumping idiot made her stomach flip-flop, so she erased the view with a swish of drape and flopped on the huge bed. Tension dissipated as she fluffed a second pillow, shoved it under her neck, and promptly fell asleep. Dreamland was not her intent. She'd passed some enticing restaurants on Queen Street—Bistro Enchant, Zomato, Lord of the Fries—and had been excited about a hearty meal and popping into shops if they stayed open late on a Saturday night.

It was nine p.m. when she awoke, groggy and disoriented. *Where am I?* She wobbled to the bathroom and splashed water on her face and then called the front desk, hoping for room service.

"We have a snack case in the lobby."

Alexa stayed up another hour, munching a Moro bar and a pack of Krispies and watched two *Parks & Rec* reruns while taking stock of her six days in Rotorua and the unexpected roller coaster ride it had become.

Chapter Nineteen

The Auckland Department of Forensics was a standalone building adjacent to the Auckland Central Police Station on Cook Street. The main entrance was locked, though Alexa could see people entering the police department next door. She rang the after-hours buzzer and studied the concrete building with interest. Even though she had taught two courses to budding odontologists—Introduction to Forensics Odontology and Forensics Odontology: Research Methods—she had never been here; the lab at the dental school had been adequate.

No two forensics departments were ever the same. Alexa was excited about seeing New Zealand's premier lab. A bespectacled man peered through the glass and spoke through an intercom.

"Ms. Glock from Rotorua?"

"Yes."

The door clicked open. "Dan Goddard, chief forensics examiner," he said, holding out his hand. Alexa shifted the bird box to her left hand and shook and then handed him her ID. He gave it a casual glance and handed it back. "I was expecting you. How can I help? Something about a bird?" He was boyish, wearing jeans, an untucked navy polo, and red tennis shoes.

"I hope you didn't come in on a Sunday morning just for me," Alexa said. "I need access to your prints equipment."

"No, no, I'm on call, getting caught up on paperwork. Nice when the lab is quiet. Come on—I'll show you around and let you get started. Are you American?" His oversized round glasses slightly magnified his bright eyes.

"Yes." Alexa followed Goddard down a corridor that opened into a two-story atrium.

The lab spread in an arc. From the open area they were standing in, Alexa could see office cubicles and signs for various departments: firearms, biological, trace, prints, toxicology, even a vehicle examination bay.

Goddard smiled. "It has an open design, as you can see. Enhances safety, according to the design committee, if you can see what your fellow workers are doing."

"Looks brand new." Alexa noted the TV monitors, security call-assistance buttons and, when she walked past an emergency eyewash station and the lights came on, motion detectors. A call-assistance button would have helped her in the Rotorua lab, that was for sure.

"Ten years old. Hard to believe."

A muffled bang made Alexa almost drop Fanny.

"That's Jack, our ballistics expert. He's in the firing range." Goddard pointed toward the firearms section. A closed door had a homemade sign on it: *Loose Cannon—Do Not Enter*. "I'm not sure he's working on a case. I think he just likes to shoot." Another faint blast.

"Why do you need ballistics experts in New Zealand?" Alexa asked, thinking of all the gun violence back home.

"Yeah nah. Mostly, we don't. Less than two percent of violent crime involves firearms, but we've had an increase in hunting accidents."

"How many people work here?"

"Including myself, eight full-time." Goddard had bright brown eyes and contagious energy.

"I met Kit Byers when he was sent to Rotorua to help with the mud pot murder."

"Good man, Kit. He's on paternity leave. His son was born prematurely."

"I hope the baby will be all right," Alexa said and wondered if there might be a job opening here in Auckland. She'd like to stay in New Zealand longer. "What are you working on?"

"Our big case—you probably read about it—is the discovery of two bodies, a woman and girl. In a tidal basin. Buried in salt and mud."

Alexa thought of their teeth. "Have you been able to identify them?"

"DNA is pending, but they match the description of a pair who went missing ten years ago."

"Were they murdered?"

"No. They got lost while hiking. Washed off a trail in a storm."

"Must have been some storm."

"A real southerly. But today, I'm compiling a paint analysis. What can I say?" His smile revealed a slight overbite. "It's not all glam, is it? What have you got?"

"A bird. I want to take prints from a bird carcass, and we don't have the fluorescent powders and UV lamps."

"I didn't know you could lift prints off a bird."

"Me either." Alexa excitedly shared the results of the Scottish report.

Goddard's eyes gleamed. "Call me in when you get it set up. This I have to see! I'll be in my office." He pointed to one of the cubicles.

Goddard took her to the latent prints department. "The storage closet is here," he said, unlocking it. "Keep a record of what you use on one of these forms." He handed her the paper. "I hope you find what you need."

He left her admiring the space. She set the box and her camera bag on a fifteen-foot workbench and surveyed her surroundings: a refrigerator, sink, secured evidence locker, and shelves full of reference material and manuals. The storage closet was like a candy store and had its own smaller workbench. Alexa drooled over the array of rainbow print powders and chose green fluorescent, which would fluoresce a neon Granny Smith color under UV light. She would dust Fanny right in the storage room, because total darkness would allow her to best see the results, just as BLUESTAR had detected the blood at the mud pots.

Supplies rounded up: camera and tripod, fluorescent powder, portable UV lamp, feather duster, lifting tape, black backing card, magnifying glass, specimen tray. Alexa set the camera on a flexible tripod with a shutter release cord and slipped on gloves. It was fantail time. She opened the box, removed the bird from the evidence bag, and slipped it onto the sterile specimen tray. She carefully dipped a feather duster into the talcum-ish powder, just the smallest dip—too much powder would fill in ridges—and then gently twirled it onto the bird's small breast, resulting in a mildewy blotch, a blight marring Fanny's down. Turning off the lights, reminding herself to breathe, Alexa turned on the UV lamp.

It was an amazing sight.

Under the magnifying glass, she could see a luminous topographical map and, off to the side, in ridged detail, a partial fingerprint.

She debated whether to turn the lights back on to add more powder in hopes of enlarging the print but decided not to tempt fate. Another swirl could wipe it out. Alexa fumbled the camera on, adjusted the angle, and released the shutter. Zooming in and out, she took a series of photos. They looked clear and brilliant through the lens, and she would enlarge them back in Rotorua. Before she would try lifting the print, which wasn't recommended with fluorescent powder, she had to show Goddard. Turning the lights on and camera off, she bounded off.

"Wicked," Goddard said. "Send me a copy of the photos. I'll share it with our wildlife specialist. We've experienced kiwi poaching. One dude put a live chick in a suitcase."

Alexa shook her head and asked, "Can you tell if my fantail is a male or female?"

"No idea. Male and female fantails look alike. You realize it's only a partial, right? It won't hold up in court," Goddard said.

"True." Only ten percent of crime scene fingerprints were usable in court. "But a partial can still further the case." *Especially if it matches the duct tape print.*

"I'm surprised you don't have fluorescent powders in Rotorua," Goddard said. "We've been using Lumicyano for a year now."

They spent ten minutes discussing advancements in fingerprinting. Dan Goddard was a kindred spirit.

"I'm just working on contract for the mud pot case."

"It's all over the news. The bird figures in?"

She nodded. "Anyway—my contract is for this one case. Are there any openings here in Auckland?"

"Do you have a work permit?"

"Yes. It's good for another six months and then could be renewed."

"If you don't mind travel, I could use you. Byers doesn't want to rove the countryside, now that he has a wee sprog."

Wee sprog?

Goddard continued. "Most towns are too small to have a forensics lab. There are only five in the whole country—Auckland, Wellington, and Rotorua here on the North Island. Christchurch and Dunedin on the South Island. If you're interested, send me your résumé."

Alexa left the lab neat and tidy and lingered in the atrium, thinking she'd feel right at home here.

Excited to get back to Rotorua to do a print comparison, Alexa was also reluctant to leave the country's largest city so quickly. She had slowly been learning her way around its busy streets when her fellowship ended and now decided to spare an hour for shopping. Everyone promised summer was coming—but for six-plus months, it had been one sixty-degree day after another, so she wasn't sold, but she did need boots and a yoga mat. Central Mall was on the city outskirts, and she hoped its shops would be open Sunday morning.

They were bustling.

Alexa parked and located her need-to-buy list: yoga mat, boots, raincoat. She added sandals and short-sleeved tees.

The yoga mat was most pressing. Practicing yoga was a way to keep limber and reduce skin tightening that plagued her burn scars. In Auckland, she had joined a yoga studio, but if she was going to be traveling, she'd have to use a yoga app on her phone.

Her first yoga therapy class had been in eighth grade, thanks to Ms. Turner, a kindly school counselor who knew about the accident and noticed her hunched-over walk, not a great look for making friends or attracting boys, but it had relieved pain from scar tissue busily creeping like ivy to every crevice and ridge not covered in skin grafts. The memory of that first class, lying on her mat, hating her grotesque adolescent body, fighting tears and rage, flashed across her mind.

Don't go there.

There was a purple mat at Farmer's, a target-twin without red dots, anchoring the mall at one end, but Farmer's shoes and raincoats were thumbs-down. Alexa then detoured to lingerie and tried on a midnight-blue bra and pantie set that lifted and padded perfectly, the bra anyway. She thought of Mr. Blue Eyes as she assessed her image in the dressing room mirror and sucked in her stomach.

Not. Bad.

Stop it.

The man is close-minded and stubborn. And you'll be leaving soon.

A few minutes later, the pricey set was wrapped in tissue and tucked in her tote. Hutchins Hardware had a display of different-colored gum boots lining the front window. They weren't the black leather boots, she envisioned but gum boots ("We don't call them Wellies," Mary had scolded) were more practical. Plus, they were very Kiwi; every other person in New Zealand was wearing a pair. Alexa settled for Red Brand at eighty-five dollars and left the mall pleased with herself.

The future was looking up.

—

At half past three, she parked at the Rotorua station, grabbed Fanny and camera bag, and walked through the front entrance. Sharon Welles wasn't working. A uniformed police officer was sitting at her desk, messing with his phone. He waved her over and studied her badge without speaking.

"I'll be in the lab." She suddenly wanted to let someone know where she was. "I'll check by on my way out."

The lab through the small door window was dark and empty. Alexa unlocked it, turned on the lights, and made herself check the storage closet. The caution tape was gone, and the blood had been cleaned. Lemon disinfectant lingered in the air.

Alexa slipped Fanny, who now wore a hint of Eau De Rot, from her box into a plastic storage bag. Opening the evidence freezer, she rested Fanny within and shut the door.

Bye bye birdie.

Time to upload the photos. They were better than she imagined and revealed at least thirteen minutiae.

With a full print, twenty-five or more minutiae points like ridges, islands, spurs, and cores were used to verify a match. The computer would reject a print if it contained fewer than thirteen minutiae. Totally absorbed, Alexa ran the partial through the data bank and held her breath, hoping against hope they might match the duct tape prints or someone on the police department payroll. Cooper? Rangiora?

But seconds later, a No Match notification deflated her hopes. Whoever left the bird in her house had no fingerprints on file and was not the same person who bound Koppel's face with duct tape. Another clue flies the coop. Dead as the moa.

She emailed the print to Goddard and thanked him for his lab hospitality, attached her résumé, and added a note that she was interested in working with him.

Done.

Alexa considered checking to see if DI Horne—Bruce—was in his office but decided against it. Her trip to Auckland had been for naught, and she wanted to use her new yoga mat, stretch her taut muscles. She locked up, climbed the stairs to the lobby, and waved a goodbye to the officer on duty.

—

Trout Cottage looked forlorn, as if Alexa had been away two weeks instead of twenty-four hours. A fierce wind buffeted the lavender stalks as she dropped her new boots and yoga mat on the front porch and fumbled for keys.

A fluttering note was taped to the front door.

Her heart skipped a beat. A threat? Alexa unfolded it and read:

Sunday—Pop over for a glass of wine. Five-ish. Sarah.

Relief. An invite from the cottage owner. Egg Boy's mother. It was ten to five. The yoga mat would have to wait. In her haste to visit her landlord, she lost any apprehension about entering the cottage.

Everything was fine.

Alexa decided to spruce up. She changed from baggy jeans to tight black ones, pulled on a rose silk turtleneck, and wrapped a wispy Monet's water lily scarf around her neck. The natural waves in her sable hair looked tame for the moment, and, pleased, she locked the house at 5:05, scanned the property, and hopped into the car. No trail along the river this time.

Sarah opened the door before Alexa knocked. "No one could ever sneak up on us," she said and scolded the barking duo at her feet. "Echo and Iris, hush! Lovely to see you again. I'm glad you spotted my note. Come in. I can't tell if we're soon to have more rain or if this wind is chasing it away."

Alexa stepped into the small foyer and offered her hand for the dogs to smell. Iris licked and Echo pranced. Something savory was simmering. Soup? Stew? Alexa's stomach rumbled.

"Lucy and Stevie won't be home until six, so we have the place to ourselves. Let me put these guys out, and then you can fill me in on why a jiggy police officer stopped by after tea the other night. We're in a spin, not used to heaps of excitement. Go sit down." Sarah pointed and disappeared.

The den had the same coziness as Trout Cottage plus the rubble of children: unzipped backpacks, dirty trainers, a stack of Wii games. Alexa walked over to the bookcase and started reading titles.

"Are you a reader?" Sarah asked. She returned bearing a tray of crackers and cheese. Her fair hair was exploding in a topknot again, adding inches to her height, and the dangling earrings were copper today.

"Yes. But not so much lately."

"I could talk heaps about books, but sit down and tell me what happened that night. Officer Tall, Dark, and Handsome came an hour or so after you returned the basket and asked us questions. I almost did a poppie afterward, but I thought a knock at the door late at night would push you over. Do you always create such a twiddle? But wait—let me get wine first." She disappeared and whirled back bearing a Marlborough Savvy and two glasses. "Cheers," Sarah said after pouring each of them a glass.

"Cheers," Alexa replied, toasting her neighbor, not sure how to start, and then set the wineglass down and smeared a cracker with cheese. She chewed and swallowed. "This is delicious."

"Cambozola. Blue mixed with Brie." Sarah watched impatiently while Alexa smeared and ate a second cracker. "I'm waiting," she said. "Why a call from the coppers one day and a visit the next? Should I be worried?"

Alexa didn't blame Sarah for being curious and launched into the attack at the station, the bird carcass in Trout Cottage, and her involvement in the mud pot murder. "I'm afraid there's a connection and the bird was a warning to back off."

Sarah stared for a moment and then said, "That's an obscure warning, yeah. Like fishing for symbolism in *The Garden Party*."

"The Garden Party?"

"Short story by Katherine Mansfield. She's a Kiwi. The hat Laura wears supposedly symbolizes class consciousness. But maybe Mansfield just wanted Laura to wear a lovely hat."

What the heck? Alexa preferred biographies and the occasional romance. "The case is intertwined with Maori culture. The cop that you met told me fantails are a Maori omen. Did Steve see anyone after he dropped me off?"

"No. The officer asked him, and he said he didn't. It's a lonely road. No traffic to speak of, and if anyone does drive down—usually it's a fisherman looking for a spot on the river—the dogs let us know."

Alexa, weary of speculation and symbolism, changed the subject. "Tell me about yourself. What do you do besides manage property and two teenagers?"

"I teach art at Rotorua Lakes High School. I make jewelry too. Glass and metals." She shook her head to make her earrings dance back and forth.

"Those are fun." Alexa admired the copper slivers, comparing them to the simple silver hoops she wore daily to avoid morning jewelry dilemmas.

"Trout. Tourists go mad."

"I liked the ones you had on when I first met you. Were they greenstone?"

Sarah nodded.

"How do you get the greenstone?" Alexa sipped her wine and thought of the magical paddle at the museum, the way it glinted in the light as if alive from within.

"I used to buy raw greenstone from a supplier in Christchurch, but it's gotten too dear. I've switched to Canadian jade. It's cheaper even with shipping."

"How come?"

"Five years ago, the government returned the greenstone mining rights to the Ngāi Tahu *iwi* on the South Island. Since then, there's been no mining. That's jacked up the price of greenstone already on the market. Supply and demand."

Rawiri Wright had not mentioned the soaring price.

Sarah was a talker. Alexa relaxed into a plush recliner, picked a dog hair off her thigh, and listened. "My husband died four years ago. Cancer. He was a farmer and a pharmacist. We've sold off most of the stock, and Stevie takes care of what's left. It's teaching him way more about responsibility than any lecture from me. Lucy, on the other hand, lives to get out of any work at all. Her job is to help me clean Trout Cottage between renters. Ha." As if on cue, Alexa's cell phone barked at the same time as Iris and Echo started a frenzy of their own. It was a confusing moment.

"My phone," Alexa explained.

"My children," Sarah explained. "I'll go greet them."

"Hello?" Alexa said.

"This is Horne," came the reply. "Have you returned from Auckland?"

"Yes."

"I need you at Ponga Point on the lake. We have a drowning."

"A drowning? Where's Ponga Point? Will my GPS find it?"

"I don't know." Alexa could hear a voice in the background.

"Hang on, Sammie. I'm on the phone," Horne said. "Sorry. My daughter is upset that she has to return to her mum's house.

Come to my place, and we'll drive to Ponga Point together. I'll radio for a forensics kit."

"Who drowned?"

"Male adult is all I know." He gave Alexa his address and hung up.

She stuffed another cheese cracker in her mouth, thinking this would probably be dinner, and was chewing as Sarah returned.

"Thank you for having me. That was work so I need to be off."

Sarah searched Alexa's face. "More mud pot?"

"A drowning. It's not related." Alexa met Lucy, who was yammering about play practice, on her way out.

"Be careful," Sarah called.

A common refrain, Alexa thought. Stevie waved as he was walking toward the barn and she toward her car.

A lonely mist descended as she drove the deserted road. Sarah's home, warm and bright, full of "What's for tea?" and "Have you fed the dogs?" tugged at a raw spot. What price had she paid to be here and now? To make the decisions she had along the way?

Chapter Twenty

The GPS voice—Sheila, Alexa had christened her—calmly directed her through Rotorua traffic lights, roundabouts, side streets, and finally "You have reached your destination." Six two-story attached town houses stood beyond the parking area, each with a patch of grassy front garden and a second-floor balcony. Maybe there was a lake view.

Alexa parked and was opening the car door when she heard Horne's voice.

"Good timing," he said. "Sharla just picked up my daughters. Not a happy scene."

Sheila, her GPS woman, driving Horne's daughters away? "What?"

"Sharla is my ex. Why don't you ride with me? It'll be easier, and we can talk."

"Sure," Alexa said, surprised by his friendliness. Had he forgotten their spat? She followed him to a battered Ford Ranger truck and couldn't help noticing he looked attractive in jeans. They buckled silently.

The DI looked her way as he pulled out of the drive. "Mindy Koppel's alibi pans out. Two people saw her and the lads at Papamoa Beach—a neighbor and a store clerk."

"I'm glad." She hadn't wanted the boys to suffer the loss of both parents.

"There's no hospital or medical records of spousal abuse," he added.

"Have you located Officer Cooper's uncle and the island caretaker?"

"Yes and no." He paused. "Cooper contacted her uncle. Taylor Cooper is coming to the station in the morning. Lee Ngawata is joining him. But no one has been able to locate the caretaker. He lives on the island and has no mobile. We're hoping the cooperating gentlemen can communicate our message to him."

"Smoke signals?"

"Beats me." He smiled as he drove down Littleton Street.

"He actually lives on Pirongia? Is there a cabin?"

"I don't know. I was going to ask you." The lake was ahead, and he turned left.

"The parts I saw were completely wild. But I didn't see all of the island. Can I sit in on the interview?"

"Nine o'clock sharp. What happened in Auckland?"

Alexa brightened thinking about the glowing green print extracted from Fanny's breast but recalled the No Matches result. "Dead end," she said. "But it's a modern lab, and Dan Goddard—he's the director—was interested in the technique. Were you able to talk with Paul Koppel's father-in-law?"

"I stopped by unannounced. Posh place. Russell didn't think highly of Koppel, didn't think he was good enough for his daughter. Called him dull and unmotivated. A poor provider for his darling daughter."

"That's harsh."

"Russell is outspoken, used to controlling his family, I'd say. Mindy married Paul against his wishes. He thought she could do better."

"You don't think…"

"I asked where they were when Koppel was killed, and he and

his wife, Marge, alibied each other. The wife defended Koppel, said Paul was a loyal husband and father, and it wasn't his fault the housing market tanked."

Silence followed, broken by Horne's cell. He fished it out of his pocket without taking his eyes off the twisting lakeside road. "I'm on my way. Maybe fifteen minutes," he barked. "Any ID yet?" He listened and then tossed the cell in a cup holder. "The drowning victim is Maori. No ID on the body. Probably a fisherman. A wife or friend will report him missing soon." He glanced at her. "Drowning stats are down for New Zealand as a whole but up for Maori. They live in an island country and believe the sea and lakes and rivers are *taonga* left by their ancestors. I respect that. So why don't they learn to swim? Teach their kids? What's so hard about putting on a life jacket? It's frustrating."

Alexa listened to him explaining a program the police and Parks and Recreation departments co-sponsored to teach Maori kids swimming and water safety and thought of North Carolina drowning stats: most victims were male, African American or Hispanic. She hoped a similar program was available back home. But then she became distracted by the nearness of the DI's thigh and turned to study the lake, close and restless.

The wind had abated; the waters of Ponga Point were rock-skipping calm and pink from the dipping sun. She unbuckled and shook off an urge to walk into the water and lie back, float on the pillow-top reflection of sunset.

Life is not a sunset, Glock.

Her head back in forensic mode, Alexa surveyed the scene: empty dog park, an arm-in-arm couple walking up from a lake-side trail, a playground in which two small children and a man stood like statues, the arms of all three akimbo, studying the commotion on the shore.

She followed the DI from the parking area to the fleet of one ambulance, a fire truck, and two patrol cars, all flashing lights, which formed a semicircle around a ribboned-off beach area.

Portable lights were set up and turned on in preparation for soon-to-be darkness. Voices drifted from the fleet, but the emergency personnel stood back. There was no one to save.

The body, faceup, was clad in pants only and slightly bloated. Waves lapped a meter from bare feet. A police officer stood above it. Why hadn't the body been covered? As she and the DI approached, a voice from behind said, "Bruce Horne. What can you tell me?"

Alexa turned around and recognized Dr. Redhead, the mud pit pathologist. What was her name?

"Just arrived myself, Dr. Hill. Rachel. How are you?"

"Busy, Bruce. You heard about the fatal wreck on Highway 33? Two teenagers, one inebriated. So frickin' sad." Dr. Hill spotted Alexa. "Ms. Glock. We meet again."

"Good to see you, Dr. Hill." She didn't like the familiar way Dr. Hill said "Bruce."

The doctor caught up as they reached the body and asked the officer, who turned out to be Senior Officer Rangiora, if the body had been moved. No drag marks led from the water.

"No. I only turned him over to check for a pulse. I wore gloves. We'll need to move him quickly if the wind starts up again."

"Who found the body?" The doctor's Scottish brogue was annoyingly delightful.

"A lad walking his dog. He's over there." Rangiora pointed toward a bathhouse where a young man, seated at a picnic table, was speaking with another officer. A cocker spaniel was tangled in a leash held by the man.

"How did the body get beyond the water level?" Dr. Hill asked.

"The wind was kicking until half past five. Southerly blowing through. They've calmed. See that log?" Rangiora pointed up shore. Dr. Hill and DI Horne followed his finger and both nodded. "Same thing happened to it. Left behind when the wind calmed and water receded."

While this weather report was going on, Alexa studied the

drowning victim's face, half obscured by sand, tats showing through the bare areas. She walked closer.

"Ms. Glock. Please stand back," Dr. Hill said.

Alexa couldn't believe it. She ignored Dr. Hill and leaned in. "Detective Inspector Horne, I recognize this man."

Chapter Twenty-One

The body smelled of algae, amniotic fluid, fish. Alexa thought of water's dual nature: power and calm, life and death, womb and birth. Water cleanses a body at birth, and water cleanses a body at burial. The new. The old. The yin, the yang. The man before her had fake brows chiseled in ink above the natural, slightly thinning brows. Even if this man had smiled, his expression would convey eternal anger. Alexa remembered those menacing black arches from the island. She had spoken to this man two days ago about Koppel and his guest. Alexa caught her breath and looked up at Horne. "It's the caretaker."

Horne's eyebrows hit the sky. She could imagine the conversation in his mind. The very same guy we wanted to talk with in headquarters but couldn't reach. Dead on a beach. No way it's a coincidence.

"You know this man?" Dr. Hill frowned at Alexa.

"I met him two days ago, on Pirongia Island. Officer Cooper said his name is Ray Herera."

"Pirongia?" Dr. Hill glanced toward the open water and snapped on gloves. She squatted next to Alexa, who stood and backed up. "You saw him alive forty-eight hours ago?"

Alexa nodded. Questions pop-rocked her brain, but she remained tight-lipped, not wanting to influence the doctor.

"That's significant. Generally, a body will reach the lake bottom slowly as the organs and lungs become saturated. Deeper water compresses the organs, forcing out air, speeding up the sinking. Unless something gets in the way, the body reaches the lake bed." The doc was tugging at the victim's eyelids. "Bruce, how deep is Lake Rotorua?"

Where was she going with this?

"Not deep in most places," he said. "Ten meters average."

"What's the water temp?"

"Sixty degrees—give or take—somewhat warm for New Zealand lakes because of underwater geysers."

"It's strange he washed up so quickly. He shouldn't have popped up this soon. Like I said, it takes a while to sink. Then gases have to form to make a body buoyant again. If he's been dead less than forty-eight hours, he should be a log on the bottom of the lake. With other causes of death, say a heart attack or drug overdose, the lungs won't fill with water and the body will stay afloat, wash up quicker. I'll check his lungs. This may not be a drowning."

Alexa and DI Horne regarded each other. Was this another murder? The scene changed quickly, like New Zealand weather. The DI called in reinforcements. This family beach would now have to be processed in a different way, but it was unlikely to be the scene of the maybe murder.

The expanse of water was closer, louder, more menacing than minutes before. Alexa watched a gull calling ha-ha-ha-ha in alarm as it skimmed the now gunmetal-gray surface. She thought of what she knew about water deaths. Submersion in water could mask the cause of death. Water washes away fingerprints and DNA. Why didn't more murderers use the cloak of water? Somewhere out there was the scene of the crime. Had it been on the forbidden island? Whoever killed Herera, if he had been killed, probably thought the body would not be discovered so quickly. Or ever. Gears were cling-clanging in Alexa's mind as she listened to Horne issue orders.

"I want him fingerprinted right away," he was saying. "Where's the forensics kit I ordered?"

"Here, Senior," Rangiora answered, nudging it with his foot.

"Glock, get to work and then go to the lab with the prints, see if we can make a positive ID." Horne turned back to Rangiora. "When she's ready, drive her to her car so that she can get to the station. It's at my place."

"Yes, Senior," Rangiora answered, his eyes ping-ponging between his boss and Alexa.

"If the press talks to either of you, we are considering the drowning an accident."

—

At half past eight, the lobby area was deserted, the floating albatross white silhouettes against a starless ceiling, the front desk unoccupied. Alexa debated whether to find someone, let someone know she was here. Then thoughts of Jenny's attack crowded in. Maybe it was safer to come and go quietly.

Only the echo of her footsteps sounded in the stairwell to the basement floor, thin and empty.

She looked both ways down the basement hallway, annoyed the fluorescent light nearest the lab was blinking on and off, and unlocked the door with her key card. Horne had said that Jenny would be back in the morning. Good. There was plenty of work. She switched on the lights and locked the door from the inside. Alexa toyed with the idea of turning on the radio but decided she'd rather keep her ears alert. Paranoia clung to her as she pulled gloves out of the dispenser. She readied the comparator, carefully extracted the lift card with Herera's prints, and laid it on the viewing platform. It had been easy taking prints from the lifeless hand, and Alexa let auto focus do its work. The middle tip of the right hand was optimal, although the prints were slightly enlarged from swelling. Turning on the scanner, Alexa waited, reminding herself to breathe, and in sixty-six whirring seconds of internal compares and contrasts of over a million prints gathered from criminals, suspects, government employees, school teachers, immigrants, and police officers, she was rewarded with a green light.

Bingo.

A noise aborted her victory dance. Footsteps in the strobing hallway. A shadow. Movement at the opaque door window. A slow turn of the door handle. A jiggle. A push.

Alexa bit the inside of her cheek.

The lock strained. Held.

Jenny's attacker? Alexa tasted blood, reached into her pocket to retrieve her phone.

Empty. Pocket empty.

Where the hell was her cell? A frantic search of the other three pockets. Empty empty empty. The shadow leaned toward the window, enlarged. Alexa ducked below the counter as a face pressed against the pane, features distorted, grotesque, alien.

In her tote.

Her cell phone was in her tote. By the glove dispenser. Out. Of. Reach.

The lab phone was even further away. Another turn of the handle. A rattle. Footsteps. Footsteps fading. Silence. Whoever it was did not have a key card to unlock the door. Breath expelled from Alexa's lungs like a storm surge; she remained crouched, spent.

Okay, okay. It could have been anyone, right? Night watchman. Did police stations in New Zealand have night watchmen? Did police stations anywhere have night watchmen? Alexa stayed on the floor three interminable minutes and then stood, stiff and cautious, her back scars screaming. Why didn't this lab have emergency buttons like the one in Auckland? Sprinting over to her tote, she fished out her blasted cell and punched redial.

"Horne here."

"It's Alexa."

"What?"

His abrupt tone stunned her to silence. "Are you there?" he demanded.

"Yes." She gulped and then plunged. "I have results from the prints, but I'm not safe down here in the lab. Someone just tried the door."

"What are you talking about?" His voice softened. "Are you hurt?"

"No. I'm alone in the lab." She heard heavy breathing. And then realized it was her own. "The station was deserted. I locked myself in the lab, and someone just tried the door. Tried and then left." She didn't add that he or she could be waiting in the hallway or stairwell.

"I'll get an officer down there immediately. Don't unlock until you hear three knocks."

"Thank you." A flood of relief. "And, um, Bruce? We have a match. The prints match the ones found on Fanny."

"Who the hell…?"

"I mean on my bird. The fantail left in my cottage." She hadn't registered the implication until now. The drowned man, Ray Herera, had left the bird in her cottage.

And now he was dead.

Chapter Twenty-Two

An eternity passed before someone pounded three times on the door and she heard a muffled "Ms. Glock. It's Officer Rangiora."

"You again," Alexa mumbled, opening up. Panic bloomed in her chest. Had Rangiora tried to get into the lab? He knew she was here, maybe even followed her after dropping her off at DI Horne's with that snide comment about "another private meeting, eh."

Officer Rangiora kept popping up. Her cottage. The beach. The mud pots. Here.

"I've been upstairs since I dropped you off at your car," he said, breathing hard. "Detective Inspector Horne said someone tried to enter the lab, yeah?"

"Yes. I locked myself in. Someone tried the door a couple times, pushed their face against the glass, and then left."

"Could you see who it was?" Dark shadows ringed Rangiora's eyes.

"No." Alexa left out that the face had looked extraterrestrial.

"I didn't pass anyone as I came down, but I'll take another look. In the morning, we can check security cameras."

Alexa followed him.

"Need to get this light fixed," Rangiora said as they walked from one end of the basement hallway to the other, opening each door. Past the lab were two rooms: a storage room jammed with boxes and a unisex bathroom. Opposite the lab, there was a room of similar size housing a maze of silver heating and cooling systems. All were unlocked and provided places to hide. Alexa followed Rangiora like a puppy as he scouted, using his flashlight, even getting on his hands and knees to look under an HVAC unit.

"Nothing," he said. "No one here."

At the end of the hallway, the emergency evacuation door was ajar.

"What the...?" Rangiora said, rushing at it and pushing it wide. Cool night air tumbled into the hallway. The stairwell was dark and led one level up to the parking lot. Rangiora stared at Alexa. "This is a bloody 'mare," he said. "Any frickin' person could walk in."

"Or did walk in," Alexa reminded him. He started to pull the door shut.

"Don't!" *Was he trying to sabotage evidence? Again?* "I'll check it for prints, see if they match the ones left on the lab door handle."

Having a plan calmed Alexa down.

"My prints will be both places," Rangiora said, looking at his hands.

"I know. Do you think you can get someone down here to stand by while I work? Then you can search the rest of the building."

"Detective Inspector Horne told me to call him back," Rangiora said. "Then I'll find someone to stand guard."

Every kid who dreams of becoming a detective dreams of dusting for fingerprints, but this round was overdose. The door handle and exit door bar were slick surfaces, so Alexa used a magnetic brush. Brush wasn't the right word—no bristles were involved. The device gently blew a coating of powder over print deposits, snapping them into view and yielding clearer results than traditional dusting.

Alexa would photograph the results and then lift the prints with sticky tape, readying them for the comparator. There would be a traffic jam of prints to cross-check and eliminate. She wasn't even certain the mystery visitor at the lab door entered from the outside anyway. And perhaps he was wearing gloves.

She started at the evacuation door, standing in the night air, using light from the hallway to work, happy the young officer whose baton she had borrowed stood at the other end of the hall, flickering weirdly in the fluorescent strobing. She waved and then worked.

An hour later, she had lifted thirteen full and partial prints. Brain-dead and aware of probable futility, she decided to wait until morning to run them. The baton officer walked her to her car.

The drive to Trout Cottage was dark and desolate.

Chapter Twenty-Three

Alexa entered a buzzing conference room at 7:55 the next morning and, sighting Jenny Liang in the back of the room, went to her. "Welcome back. How are you feeling?"

"I'm okay. If I get a headache, I need to go home." Her wound was hidden by a knit beanie, and her face was pale. "Have you found out who attacked me?"

"We're working on it. I'll fill you in later."

Alexa clutched an envelope to her chest and studied the people in the room. The entire team was present, everyone standing except Ponytail, who was straddling a chair and talking into his phone. A photograph of the dead Pirongia Island caretaker, a head shot, was thumbtacked next to the photo of Paul Koppel on the corkboard at the front of the room.

DI Horne, freshly shaved and smart in a gray suit, strode in. "Good morning," he said, his eyes making rounds. "Everyone is aware we have a second body connected to the case. We will obtain permission from our Maori liaison to return to Pirongia."

"We don't need permission," McNamara said. "It's a crime scene, and New Zealand law has jurisdiction on Maori land. Unlike in the States with Indian reservations." McNamara threw a scowl at Alexa.

"Thank you, Detective, for that legal review, but we have no idea if Pirongia is a crime scene, and as per the Historic Places Act 1993, it behooves us to get permission first." Horne wasn't backing down.

"The delay..." McNamara said.

"There won't be a delay. Ngawata is voluntarily coming to the station in half an hour." The DI looked at his watch and then at his team, his eyes pausing at Alexa's and then moving on. "Okay, everyone. First—welcome back Ms. Liang."

The team clapped, and Jenny cringed. "Ta," she said.

"Rangiora—where are we on Liang's attack?"

"We're down to one unidentified person on the security cameras, and we've also found a security breach that we're factoring in."

"So basically nowhere," Horne summed up and walked over to the corkboard, pointing to the photo of dead man number two. "The body is Ray Herera, resident caretaker of Pirongia Island. He washed up on Ponga Point and was found at precisely 5:28 yesterday evening. I'm treating it as a suspicious death rather than an accidental drowning, but we are keeping this information from the press."

"Why?" asked Trimble. He was holding a cup of coffee that Alexa eyed jealously. She had slept until seven and had to rush.

"The killer wanted it to look like an accidental drowning. Let's play along."

"How did we identify the victim?" McNamara asked.

"He was identified by Ms. Glock, whom I'd called to the scene. Cooper and Glock met him on Pirongia."

"He claimed to have witnessed Koppel's trespassing," Alexa said.

"His body will undergo an autopsy ASAP to identify time and cause of death," Horne continued. "We searched the beach for evidence last night, and I have two officers repeating the process this morning."

"What do we know about him?" Trimble asked.

"Not much. No arrest record." Horne looked toward Cooper and paused, giving her a chance to share any information. Her blue lips stayed firmly pressed together.

"Ms. Glock has information that indicates a connection between Herera and the break-in at her house. Ms. Glock?"

"Yes. Good morning." Alexa paused as she removed photocopied prints from the envelope and went to the corkboard to hang them. "The prints of the man whose body washed ashore last evening match prints on the bird left in my house."

"Wait. Can you lift prints from a bird?" Trimble asked.

"With the right supplies, yes," Alexa said. "There was no database match for those taken from the bird until I entered Herera's last night."

"So the drowned guy left a bird in your house," Trimble said. "A dead bird."

"That sums it up," said Horne. "Anything else, Ms. Glock?"

Alexa decided not to broadcast the face in the lab door. "No."

"This is how I want to play it. Ms. Glock, as soon as I get permission from Ngawata, go back out to the island with Senior Officer Rangiora and Officers Cooper and Walker."

"I'm carked," Walker said.

"Take crime scene kits. Search hard and find where Herera lived, how he lived, if there are indications of a struggle. I'll arrange a police launch."

"Might as well report me missing ahead of time," Walker added.

No one laughed.

"Not to worry," Rangiora said. "Coop and Glock made it back."

"Pushing luck," Walker said.

"That's enough, Officer Walker," Horne said. "Unless you'd rather be on traffic detail?"

"No, Senior."

"I'll be interviewing Ngawata and Taylor Cooper shortly.

They were both with Herera three afternoons ago and hopefully can shed some light on the latest victim. I'm now considering them suspects."

Cooper's face remained impassive. Had the DI talked with her privately?

"Detective Trimble, stand in at the autopsy." Horne looked at his watch. "It's about to begin. Get over there and call as soon as cause of death is determined. Detective McNamara will attend the interview with me."

The DI left the room before Alexa could get his attention. She turned to Jenny. "Let's head to the lab. I'll fill you in on the case and what needs to be done before I head to Pirongia."

The lab had been transformed into a chamber Alexa dreaded; Jenny probably felt likewise. But this morning, after turning on the lights and radio, Jenny eager to resume work, the lab felt safe again.

Alexa left Jenny tapping away at her computer and went to collect the prints from last night. She'd have Jenny run the results and do the cross-checking.

"I'll need a list of whose prints they are and which, if any, match prints taken from the exit door. When Trimble gets back from the autopsy, you'll have plenty of work. Start with fingernail scrapings if there are any. I don't know when I'll be back." She then updated Jenny on her theory of the attack weapon.

"A Maori war club? I was hit with a war club?" Jenny's eyes widened. "Why hasn't anyone told me this?"

"We don't know for certain, but the computer-generated comparisons match," said Alexa. "Is there anything else you remember? Now that a couple days have passed?"

"I do remember hearing footsteps behind me. That's why I turned."

"I'm going to ask that a police officer be stationed down here today. Call me if you find out anything you think is need-to-know."

Alexa left the lab determined to find the DI. Looking down at her outfit—the same black jeans she'd worn when he came for dinner and a cotton button-down—she'd also need to find waterproofing. Why hadn't she bought a raincoat in Auckland? Why did she forget to put her new gum boots in the car? She stared down at her freshly washed Keds and then looked up. Rangiora was in the hallway. "Officer Rangiora?"

He stopped and turned. "Ms. Glock. I was heading to check the security cameras. See who was here when you had your face-in-the-window last night."

"I'll join you. Have you found out when we need to be on the docks?"

"Detective Inspector Horne said he'd text me when he set it up. Figured this would be a way to kill time while we waited. Did you get prints from the door handles?"

"Yes. I haven't run them yet."

The officer scrutinized her face for a second and then resumed walking. They entered a room with a Communications Office sign on the door. It was high tech with switchboards, TV monitors, and a row of computers. A non-uniformed Maori woman was stationed at the switchboard, talking into a headset, something about the ambulance arriving in a few minutes, stay on the line. Alexa realized this was the 911, or rather the 111 emergency line. She had made a point to find out.

"Why is there just one person here?" she whispered to Rangiora.

"I don't know. Usually there are two."

"What if there's more than one emergency?"

"The calls get rerouted to one of three central communications centers. Closest one to here is Auckland."

"Are there surveillance cameras in the hallways?"

"No. The CCTV monitors are just at the entryways."

"That's right," the woman who had been talking on the phone chimed in. She had hung up and swiveled around in a wheelchair. "Howzit." She offered her hand. "I'm Aria Thompson."

"Hi," Alexa said, shaking her hand. "I'm working contract forensics. Alexa Glock."

Aria continued. "The station has CCTV cameras at three locations only: main entrance, west side employee entrance, and the exit at the rear of the main floor."

"Are they monitored?" Alexa was scanning them as she spoke. A middle-aged couple entered the main entrance.

"We watch them as much as possible, depending on how busy we are," Aria said.

"There's no camera at the basement emergency exit?"

"No, just the three I mentioned."

"We need to look at last night. Eight until ten," Alexa said.

Aria wheeled over to the TV monitors and pressed a few buttons on a central control panel. "Warp speed or regular?"

"Warp. We don't have a lot of time," Rangiora answered.

"This is becoming a regular activity," Aria said. "I was called in overtime to examine tape the other morning too. When the lab girl was attacked."

Aria worked the controls, and for the next twenty minutes, the three watched a fast-forwarded black-and-white parade of comings and goings from the three different security cameras. Rangiora IDed people whom he recognized, including himself, and Alexa, who perched on the edge of a chair, wrote down names and times. Aria was able to ID one. "That's Shirley Weeks. She works in here. Must have been heading home to her kiddies." That left one unidentified man along with Alexa, Rangiora, Jimmy Trimble and Leo McNamara, Wynne Cooper, and a rookie cop named Cyrus Shelley.

"Can you zoom in on the person we can't identify?" Alexa asked. He was the only one who used the main entrance. He was wearing a hoodie, and his head was down.

"Sure. Give me a few minutes. I can print out stills too."

Rangiora moved closer to the picture. "Hold it. Looks like the same unidentified POI we have for Liang's attack."

Before Alexa responded, she glanced up at the main entrance camera. Ngawata was entering. A chill ran down her back. No sign of Officer Cooper's uncle. Alexa had been shelving the leaden lump of apprehension she'd felt ever since Horne announced her return to the island. She thought back to the two men on either side of Ngawata, Cooper's uncle and Ray Herera, their bulging eyes and threatening stance.

And now one of them was dead.

She continued watching the camera. Ngawata was ushered away by Sharon Welles. Alexa turned to Aria, who was fiddling with controls. "One more thing. There's an emergency exit door in the basement that Officer Rangiora and I discovered had been propped open last night. Who is in charge of security for the station?"

"Security? In a police station?" Aria's earnest face was void of *moko,* and her finely tweezed eyebrows rose in unison.

"Who checks to see if doors are locked up? Things like that?"

"The janitorial staff. We use Castle-Corp. They come in daily, handle trash pickup, cleaning, and general building maintenance."

"Who was on duty last night?"

"I can find out."

"I need to speak with whomever it was," Alexa said.

"I'll get you the number."

"Here's another question," Alexa added. "I need some waterproof clothing. Where should I go look?"

"Equipment check-out desk would be my guess. Where are you headed?"

"Pirongia," Alexa said.

"Classified information," Rangiora said simultaneously.

Aria's eyes widened as Officer Rangiora's cell pinged. He checked it and then looked at Alexa and nodded. "Got a boat lined up. Time to go," he said. "We'll stop at my locker. I've got an extra slicker."

"Was that Detective Inspector Horne?" Alexa asked, standing.

"Yes."

"Would you call him and get a guard sent down to the lab?"

"There's no need for that," Rangiora said.

"I think there is. I'll call him if you…"

Aria's eyes widened again at this early morning drama.

"Okay," Rangiora snapped and started punching his phone.

"Aria?" Alexa turned back to the woman. "Would you make that phone call for me? Find out who was on duty last night and when the basement door was checked last."

"Will do."

"Here's my number. Text or call when you find out. I appreciate it." She wrote her name and now memorized number on a Post-it and stuck it on Aria's desk. "I'll stop back by for the monitor printouts this afternoon." She turned and followed Rangiora.

Reluctantly.

Chapter Twenty-Four

Those limestone eyes again. Alexa balanced like an old pro as the police skiff skimmed past the towering Maori face carved in the cliffs.

Pupil-less. Haunting. Watching.

A tour boat close to the carving looked like a bathtub toy. An even smaller boat, a kayak, was right next to the cliff. Alexa watched in horror as a swell smashed it into the rock wall, flipping it. She was about to shout to Officer Rangiora, who was skippering, when the kayaker popped up and righted.

Her scar itched; she contorted her arm down the inside of both life jacket and raincoat to scratch, not caring how unprofessional she looked, and turned forward, searching the horizon for Pirongia Island. The cool morning wind slapped her face. She hadn't slept much the night before, seeing the face in the window every time she closed her eyes, and when she had finally drifted off, her dreams were harrowing vignettes that left her sweating and gasping.

Rangiora was maneuvering toward open water. She had been surprised he would captain the boat.

"No worries," he had explained at the dock. "Passed the Boat Master's course. Comes in handy." He had thrown life jackets at each of them; Walker hugged his, but Cooper threw hers back. Glad for the extra warmth atop the loaner rain jacket, Alexa had zipped and buckled silently. She kept waiting for the day New Zealand would warm up, be in the eighties, but it hadn't happened yet.

"Two boaties went missing last year. Lake can cut up on a whim. And one paddleboarder never returned, just an empty board. Keep an eye out." He had laughed callously.

Alexa held her hair back, wishing for a scrunchie. Standing behind the double seat bench in the open craft, she listened to Walker, seated next to Rangiora. Cooper, encased in a whipping police poncho like the DI's, was sitting on the bow, getting sprayed again.

"Two blokes, on a dare, my brother's mates..." Walker was shouting to Rangiora. "Late at night. They took a canoe. Never seen either of them again."

"Yer spinnin' yarns," Rangiora shouted back. "Shut up, bro." But Rangiora didn't smile.

Feet apart, knees slightly bent, Alexa was finding the rhythm of the waves until a big one caught her off guard. Ducking, her eyes landed on the waterproof backpack crime kit tucked under the bench. Conducting a mental inventory was calming: camera, fingerprint kit, tools, gloves, ruler, casting materials, notebooks, flashlight, batteries, forceps and tweezers, BLUESTAR, evidence bags, barrier tape, and rope. What was she forgetting? What exactly were they looking for? According to Rangiora's conversation with Horne, Ngawata had reluctantly conceded to the search. He had claimed shock upon hearing about the "drowning" and explained that Herera lived in a small cabin on the island. They would start the search there.

Alexa looked up from the kit. The island loomed dead ahead. Landing was different this time. Rangiora steered into a smaller cove, turned the skiff around, and backed in deftly. After dropping anchor, he lowered a metal plank that bridged boat and shore. Alexa removed her life jacket as Cooper hopped off first. Lugging the eight-pound crime kit, she lumbered off next. "Positively civilized, Officer Rangiora," she said on firm ground. Neither Ked got wet.

This beach was slightly smaller than the one from three days ago. Alexa did a systematic sweep of rocks, sand, and driftwood. Walker helped Rangiora pull the boat farther in and reset the anchor, and then the group gathered in a circle. Alexa took charge. "Okay. First destination is the cabin, but keep an eye out for anything suspicious."

"Like what?" Walker asked, looking around nervously.

"Signs of struggle. Footprints. Trash. Anything that looks out of place." She unzipped the crime scene kit and removed the camera. "Who wants to be photographer?"

"I will," Walker answered, taking the camera.

Alexa looked at the looming tree line. Why wasn't there a treasure map of the thirty-acre island, with an X-marks-the-spot? All she could do was ask Rangiora if Ngawata had given directions to the cabin.

"This is the beach Herera used," Rangiora answered. "The cabin is through the woods toward the cave. Ngawata said there's a path."

"Did Herera use a boat to get here?" Alexa asked.

"A *waka*."

"A what?"

"A *waka*, you know, canoe," Rangiora said. "In the past, Maori used canoes like cars. The lakes, rivers, and coast were the roads. If he was abducted from the island, it's probably still here."

"Or it could have been cast adrift," said Walker. "Or sunk."

"But this isn't the past," Alexa pointed out, yet she didn't believe herself.

They searched the beach and tree line for a canoe. The waves lulled and weak heat from a shy sun calmed Alexa until two birds, the funny ones that had dive-bombed Cooper, began to screech and come at them.

"Watch out," Walker yelled, waving his hands.

"The birds are nesting," Rangiora said. "We're too close to their eggs." He ducked as one whizzed by.

"Let's get moving," Alexa said. "There's no sign of a canoe."

Cooper, unperturbed, headed toward the woods, and they followed single file.

One by one, they slipped into thick forest. Rangiora and Walker removed sunglasses, and all four stood still in the sudden quiet to let their eyes adjust. The heady fragrance of woody litter infused the air.

"Look at this place," Walker said, placing his hand on the trunk of a towering hardwood. "It's Jurassic Park."

"Let's hope without a T Rex," Rangiora responded. "It's a podocarp forest."

"A pod-o what?" Alexa asked.

"Podocarp. Remnants from Gondwana."

She refused to ask for further clarification. Gondwana was probably some vengeful Maori god.

Cooper pointed to a narrow trail and began walking.

"So your uncle was buds with the guy who carked it?" Walker asked, close on Cooper's heels.

Cooper rubbed her chin as she spoke. "*Whatungarongaro te tangata toitū te whenua*."

"What the hell, Coop?" said Walker. "Speak English."

"A man disappears from sight, the land remains," Cooper translated.

"Still not making sense."

"Herera is gone but not this island. Shut up."

Walker turned and rolled his eyes at Rangiora but backed off. Alexa felt the slight uphill grade in her calves as the foursome wove through the undergrowth of ferns and shrubs. She had read Pirongia was a lava dome island. The forested middle was the caldera. The cliff edges surrounding the caldera had mostly eroded into the lake except for the northeast side. The cliffs were what gave Pirongia a military advantage hundreds of years ago. Warring tribes used the high point as a crow's nest. Sneak attacks weren't possible if guards were vigilant. Below the cliff was the cave where three hundred years ago, Chief Rangituata had been entombed.

This burial site was considered sacred by the Maori. It was also where the archaeological team was digging for artifacts in 2016, Alexa remembered reading. Someone had vandalized the site, and the whole shebang was canceled. Now *Pākehā* were forbidden to approach.

Paul Koppel and his friend had broken the rules.

We are too.

"Were any of you sent here to investigate the vandalism a couple years ago?" Alexa asked. She needed to look closer into that dig. Something about artifacts oozing out of the ground. Was Herera a part of it? Was anyone ever caught?

"Yeah nah," Walker said. "Before my time."

Cooper and Rangiora kept their mouths shut, kept hiking.

"Officers, I asked you a question."

"Coop hadn't joined the force yet. Still in nappies," Rangiora said. He stopped walking and turned to face Alexa. "I saw photos. Dig site was near the cave. The tarp spread over the dig was slashed. Surveying tools smashed. Not much else. Some racist graffiti."

"Were the vandals caught?"

"Nah. Someone just wanted the archaeologists out of there. They got what they wanted."

"But why?" asked Alexa. No one answered.

Unfurling ferns, tiny mosses, leaves, liverwort, and orchids blanketed the forest floor, muting their steps, obscuring footprints. Above the forest floor, a canopy of silver fern, cabbage trees, and tall hardwoods dimmed the light. The scene was similar to the forest she had walked through with Cooper and Ngawata, and yet it wasn't. Disorientation made Alexa wish Walker would say something, anything, to make her laugh.

Why was there no birdsong? Had something scared the birds

off? A predator? Scanning the canopy, Alexa meandered off-path, dodging emerald ferns, and walked to the base of a cabbage tree. She leaned upward following the trunk with her eyes, and was unable to spot any birds. *What gives?* Traipsing back to the path, she tripped on a root.

"Damn," she uttered, embarrassed to be on all fours.

The team stopped and stared but did not offer help. She inelegantly stood, brushed her knees, and tugged the strap of the crime kit, which had become entangled on the root. She pulled, met resistance, and then pulled harder. The kit sprung free, dislodging what looked like...she bent closer...a bone.

A large, human bone.

Alexa put a hand over her mouth to stifle the scream that had shattered the forest quiet.

A femur.

"What the frickin'?" Walker yelled. He stepped back while Cooper and Rangiora rushed forward.

The two officers and Alexa stood looking down at a long, tan-colored bone. Cooper reached down to touch it, but Alexa shouted, "Don't!"

Cooper jerked her hand back. For once, her face showed emotion: fear.

Alexa's mind raced. *Treat this as a crime scene.* She wished she hadn't screamed. Show weakness and the pack attacks. "Let's all take a couple steps back, and then you can photograph it, Officer Walker," she commanded. "I've already disturbed the scene by pulling the object free. Let's not move it further or touch it."

"Take a squizz," said Rangiora. "There are more bones here." He ignored Alexa and was toeing an area of soft earth.

A rib cage poked through dark humus.

"Officer Rangiora, you are disturbing the scene."

Again.

Alexa looked down, tried to calculate the age of the bones. She crouched near the rib cage. No cloth, no shroud clung protectively.

Fibers like linen and wool break down in months and could disappear completely within a year. So the skeleton had been here at least a year. But longer, she'd guess.

Ashes to ashes, cellulose to cellulose.

A few areas near the grave had subsided. She cast her eyes around—no overt signs of digging.

"A bloody skeleton," said Walker, who had moved forward an inch. "We've found our something suspicious." The freckles across his nose stood out against his drained complexion.

Alexa stood and spoke, her voice level. "I repeat. Let's not contaminate the scene. We'll wait over here while you take photos, Officer Walker."

"It's a burial site," Cooper said. "It's not a crime scene. These bones are ancient."

Alexa looked back at the bone she had dislodged. She imagined picking it up, feeling the smooth, hard, calcified surface, probably hollow, the marrow having dried up long ago. But why were the bones unearthed if this was a grave? There were no wild dogs or foxes to dig them up. There were no indigenous land mammals in the land of many flightless birds. She scanned for artifacts near the skeleton. Arrowheads or *patu* or fish hooks. Nothing…

"Look. I'm in charge. We need to photograph these remains and then tape them off. They might not have anything to do with Ray Herera's death, but I'm not sure. It looks as if the grave has been disturbed recently. We'll need a forensics anthropologist out here." Alexa looked at her three colleagues, sensing they were weighing whether to challenge her authority. "Walker? The photos?"

A nod to his fellow officers came from Rangiora, who finally began stepping backward.

"Did that dig take place around here?" Alexa asked Rangiora.

"Nah. It was close to the cave, like I said."

Walker began taking close-up and midrange photos of the rib cage, femur, and general area. No skull or other bones were visible. She fished crime scene tape out of the kit and tossed it to Cooper. Meanwhile, she dug out her cell phone to call in the discovery.

No service. Severed from civilization.

She stuffed the cell back in her pocket and began a crude sketch of the scene in her notebook as Cooper and Rangiora used sticks and saplings to four-square the area and enclose it with tape. The yellow ribbon was stark against the natural environment.

"Use a side measurement for scale." She had stopped sketching and was monitoring Walker. "Here." She dug out the ruler and marker cards. "After the initial midrange photo, start using these placards and numbers."

Shut up. Let the man work.

But she couldn't. "And put the ruler at the same height as the femur so they'll both be in focus."

Walker complied.

"The body might be that of a slave. Slaves were buried in shallow graves," Cooper said.

"The Maori owned slaves?" Walker asked. He was finished.

Cooper looked him in the eye. "Sometimes Maori slaves were *Pākehā*."

"No way," said Walker.

"Way."

"You're joking, eh, Coop?" Walker asked. Cooper turned her back to him.

"What makes you think it's a slave?" Alexa asked. Cooper's knowledge of Maori culture was an asset.

"A commoner would be buried deep or released in the lake. Royals were interred in the cave."

Alexa, surprised Cooper answered right away, decided the DI must have talked with her, told her to act more like a cop. "Do you think this is a burial area?"

Cooper shrugged.

Alexa said they'd better get back to finding the cottage. The forest—darker, warmer, weighted with secrets—continued converting carbon dioxide into oxygen, but Alexa was having a hard time filling her lungs.

Chapter Twenty-Five

"I see it," Rangiora said.

Ahead in a small opening, a weathered shack hardly bigger than a chicken coop blended with rocks and earth. The sole off-center window caught a ray of sunlight and glared. Wedged into the forest edge on the far side was an outhouse.

Rangiora approached the window and leaned in. "Can't see shite." A small tree limb tumbled down from the ragged tar paper roof and made him jump.

"Skeered, Rang?" asked Walker, who was hanging back. The discovery of bones had unnerved them all.

"Shut your hole," Rangiora answered. A wooden latch held the ground level door closed. Rangiora reached to turn it.

"Hey, Officer Rangiora, put gloves on first." Alexa had knelt down and opened the kit. She tossed a pair of gloves to Rangiora, who pulled them on and then turned the latch. The door creaked a quarter way open and then caught in the dirt. Rangiora shouldered his way between the gap into shadows.

Alexa tossed gloves to Cooper and Walker and pulled on her own. She grabbed an LED flashlight from the kit and handed it to Cooper. "Let's go."

Walker forced the door farther back and gained a few inches.

He, Alexa, and Cooper pressed into the dimness.

Rangiora was standing in the middle of the small hut, staring at a three-foot-high totem, a stout figure, tongue distended and bulging eyes made of abalone shell. Its protruding penis was out of proportion.

"Looky here," Rangiora said. "This dude is excited about something. Maybe you, Walker."

"You're an egg," Walker replied.

"The *tiki* should not be here," Cooper said. "It should be guarding the cave."

"What do you mean, Officer Cooper?" Alexa studied the carving. Its lopsided eyes stared back at her.

"It's an ancestor, carved to guard the sacred cave. Someone moved it."

"So you've seen it before?" Alexa pried her eyes from the statue; it chilled her.

Wynne Cooper's blue lips pressed together.

Alexa looked around the cramped shack. Maybe there were other treasures or signs of struggle. A narrow camp cot covered with a wool blanket neatly rolled up at the foot took up the far wall. One chair, high back with a ripped cane seat, stood against the window. A wooden crate served as a table, and cooking equipment, a single metal plate, two cans of Wattie's baked beans, and a half-empty fifth of Blenders Pride whiskey were stored underneath. A shovel, fishing pole, and wooden rake leaned in one corner, the rake tines sharp as spears. Alexa was about to comment when Rangiora pulled a trunk from under the cot.

"Score," he said, ready to open it.

"Let's take that outside. There will be more light," Alexa said. Rangiora grunted and lifted the trunk.

"What the...?" Walker said from a corner. He stared at the rafters. They followed his gaze toward three dangling serpents.

"Snakes." Alexa bit back a scream.

"Tuna," Cooper said, laughing. "He was drying tuna."

"Get out," Walker said. "They aren't tuna." He walked closer, reached up, tapped one. It swung once, twice, stopped.

"Maori name for eel is tuna," Cooper said. "He was drying them. Eel are sacred food. Maori have over a hundred words for eel."

"What? Like whacked, munted, butt ugly..."

"Shut up, moron," Rangiora said. "Start taking photos while we go open this."

Outside, Rangiora discovered the metal trunk was locked. "Maybe the key's under the mat," Alexa blurted. She had the jitters. Snakes, bones reaching out to grab her. What next?

A search for the key was fruitless. They could snap the lock or wait and open it back at headquarters. Alexa took a deep, calming breath and said, "Do we think the contents of the trunk might reveal something about Herera's death?"

"There's a chance," Rangiora answered.

"I agree. Break the lock. But let me dust it for prints first."

All a man's treasures in a thirty-two by eighteen-inch footlocker. Who needed more space anyway? Alexa had been growing repelled by American consumerism: McMansions, megamalls, lines of millennials waiting to purchase the latest iPhone. Hadn't she pared her own life to a single suitcase? A stab of sympathy for the dead caretaker, the bird man, jarred her.

Rangiora sorted through clothing as Alexa watched. The loincloth Herera had been wearing the day Alexa met him at the pools nestled atop a neat pile of worn chinos, faded red swim trunks, two threadbare T-shirts, a short-sleeved button-down, and a fleece pullover.

Underneath the clothes lay documents. Rangiora handed them to Alexa, starting with three birth certificates. "This is for Raymond Fitzgerald Herera," Alexa read. "And this one is for Ramona Marie Caravaner, born the same year: 1971. Maybe his wife? We don't know anything about a wife, do we?" The third birth certificate was for Eleanor Christina Herera, born 1996. "He has a daughter too," Alexa said.

Next came an expired driver's license, a marriage certificate for Raymond Fitzgerald Herera and Ramona Marie Caravaner, and then two death certificates.

"Oh man," Alexa said while Rangiora waited. The first was for Ramona C. Herera and the second for the daughter. "Herera lost his wife and daughter on the same day, blunt force trauma. Ten years ago."

"That would turn me into a hermit," said Rangiora. "Think he killed them?"

"We'll have to check it out," she said, "but I doubt he'd be walking around free if he had. Blunt force trauma is a common cause of death. Might have been a car wreck. Car crashes, pedestrians or bikers being hit by cars, plane crashes, boat accidents, all can cause blunt force trauma." And being attacked with a greenstone paddle.

"Who's been in a boat accident?" Walker asked, appearing suddenly.

Rangiora explained and then continued the trunk inventory. He pulled out a blank envelope, opened it, and counted three hundred eighty-five dollars in cash.

"That's a lot of money," Walker said.

Photos were in another envelope. Rangiora flipped through them and handed them to Alexa. She had to study one hard before recognizing the caretaker she had last seen dressed as a warrior. He was younger, and his arm was wrapped around a small, dark woman. No facial tats. The other photos were of the same woman, and two were of a little girl at different ages. School photos.

"Ouch," said Rangiora, whipping his hand out of the trunk.

"What?" asked Alexa, imagining the sharp edge of a greenstone club.

Rangiora sucked his finger and then felt around more cautiously. He pulled out two intricate fishing hooks and examined them in his large hands. "These are made from bone, not wood."

"What kind of bone?"

Rangiora looked puzzled. "I can't tell. Maybe whale, combined with paua shell. Watch." He held one hook from a short string, and Alexa watched it dangle, the rainbow-colored abalone shell catching light and sparkling. "It's a trawling hook. The paua attracts a fish's attention."

"Are you Maori, Officer Rangiora?" Alexa asked.

"Half," he said. "My father. Why?"

"You know a bit about the culture. Do you speak Maori?"

Rangiora shook his head. "Most Maoris don't. Coop's an exception."

A small carving knife tucked in a leather sheaf. The Holy Bible. Empty binocular case. Alexa continued to watch Rangiora inventory the trunk and thought of Herera with his broken heart guarding the island, scanning the lake with the missing binocs. Perhaps he had spotted Paul Koppel and his partner plying the waves toward his refuge.

"Nothing suspicious unless you count the cash," said Rangiora. He was kneeling and sat back on his haunches. "He probably had no bank account. This was his bank. The fish hooks could be valuable. They look old. But no greenstone weapon."

Or stolen duct tape. "No signs of struggle in the hut or out here either," said Alexa. "Just the totem." She was disappointed there had been nothing to connect Herera with Paul Koppel. Both she and Rangiora eyed the outhouse twenty feet to the right.

"Officer Walker," Rangiora said, "go suss the loo."

Walker frowned. "Are you kidding me, mate?"

"That's senior officer to you," Rangiora answered. "Go check it out."

Cooper, grunting, was wrestling the totem out the door of the shack. Alexa almost said something about not disturbing the scene but bit her tongue. It didn't appear that this was a crime scene. She heard a sudden moan and jerked around. Walker emerged from the outhouse, shaking his head.

Alexa needed to let the DI know about the discovery. She checked her phone, relieved to see two bars, and speed-dialed his direct line.

"Horne here."

"It's Alexa. I'm calling from Pirongia. We've discovered human remains. Old bones."

"Another murder?" came the stunned reply.

"I don't think so. The bones were defleshed. Officer Cooper thinks maybe they were the remains of a slave."

"A slave?"

"Dug up or something. The grave was exposed. We need to get a forensics anthropologist out here."

"I cannot believe we have another body on our hands."

"Bones. Not a body. We secured the area, and now we're at Herera's shack."

Silence.

"Anyway, no sign of struggle. No sign of more than one person living here. A large totem pole was in the shack. And there's a trunk with personal papers, three hundred eighty-five dollars, and clothes. Two death certificates for Herera's wife and daughter. COD is blunt force trauma. Can you check that out?"

"Yes. Tell me about the totem," Horne said.

"Officer Cooper says its place is outside the sacred cave. That it has been moved."

"So Herera was stealing. Or protecting."

"What would you like us to do? Should we continue searching the island?" Alexa looked toward the fringe of trees bordering the clearing and then at the three officers standing around her, listening intently.

"Keep searching another couple hours and then come on in. I'll have to call Auckland for a forensic anthropologist. You're not certified?"

"No. If there is a skull, I can examine the teeth, but I didn't see one. Gone or still buried, I guess. Any word on how Herera died?"

"Autopsy is ongoing. No word yet."

"What about Ngawata? What did he say?"

"He acted shocked about Herera. Said he hadn't been back to the island since the day you met him."

"Did Cooper's uncle show?"

"No. We have a ten-one out for him."

"Ten-one?" asked Alexa.

"Broadcast to all units. Think he's done a run."

"Did Ngawata consent to be fingerprinted?"

"He acted insulted and refused." The DI's voice was strained.

"I'll check in when we get back."

"Be careful, Glock. Whoever killed Herera could be on the island."

The warning made the hair on her neck stand at attention. The team looked at her expectantly. She studied them as she tucked her phone in her pocket. Walker: grim, Cooper: stoic, Rangiora: impatient.

"Detective Inspector Horne wants us to continue searching."

"The cave. That's where we need to search," Cooper said.

"Yeah nah. Not going there," Walker said.

"Orders," Rangiora said, scowling at Walker. He shouldered the footlocker. "I'll put this back in the hut and latch up. We need to get going," he added. "Lead the way, Coop."

Alexa gathered her dusting supplies and samples. She'd lifted three prints from the trunk and secured them back in the kit, along with the documents. They could return for the trunk later. Apprehension, like a storm cloud, cast a shadow. The sacred cave. *Pākehā* were forbidden to even approach. Should she remind the team? But wasn't that folklore or superstition? What did she believe? Standing, Alexa swung the kit strap over her shoulder.

If someone was on the island, the cave would be the perfect place to hide.

Chapter Twenty-Six

First Cooper, then Walker followed by Alexa and Rangiora, single file. The forest they entered wasn't dark or cloistered this time. Midday sun pushed through branches, and birds chattered and twilled, tweeting warnings or welcomes. Alexa scanned the trees, hoping to spot one like Fanny, with its tail spread like a hand of cards: pick one and I'll tell your fortune. Rangiora interrupted her thoughts.

"Looked like Herera was looting."

"Because of the totem?" Alexa asked, turning toward him.

The trail widened, and Rangiora caught up and walked by her side. "Maybe Koppel caught him looting the cave so Herera killed him."

"Maybe," Alexa said. "But then who killed Herera?"

"We only suspect he was murdered, right? He may have drowned. Maybe he felt guilty and threw himself in the water. Couldn't swim. Drowned."

"That's not how men usually kill themselves," Alexa said, thinking of guns, nooses, and carbon monoxide.

"More common for Maori," Rangiora said.

They walked in silence, Rangiora dropping back, a tall presence bringing up the rear.

Just as she disappeared when entering the forest, Cooper vanished again as she exited. The others followed and found themselves at the edge of another clearing, breathing in lake and wind. Across the clearing was a rounded butte spotted with tufts of grass and ferns.

The sacred cave. Not as formidable as Alexa had envisioned.

On either side of it, Lake Rotorua sparkled and shifted.

The team had gathered in a straight line facing the dome as if readying for battle. "So there's some top dog chief buried in there, eh?" Walker said. "There's no way I'm going in. Just so's you know that. I respect Maori rules."

"I see the entrance," Cooper said, pointing at a slit between shrub and rock, ignoring Walker. The narrow black gash looked impenetrable.

"Let's search this area first," Alexa said. "This is where the archaeological dig was, right, Officer Rangiora?"

The senior officer pointed to a flat area flanking the cave. "That's where the tents were. Three of them. The excavation was between here and the *pā*." He pointed to the small hill.

"Pa?" Alexa asked.

Rangiora scowled. Cooper looked from him to Alexa. "Hill fort," she explained. "Strategic for the *iwi*. This was once a great fortress."

"Thanks, Officer Cooper. Let's see if there's any trace of that dig, and then you can show me where the totem was when you last saw it."

All four moved cautiously over the remaining twenty yards toward the cave. Alexa's eyes scanned systematically right and left, right, left. The ground was swept clean by the wind. Nothing out of place. No trace people had camped here and spent days sifting through dirt and rock for clues into the past.

A path wound to several terraces leading to the top of the mount. "Officers Walker and Rangiora—why don't you follow that path? Cooper and I will finish searching this area and enter the cave."

"The path leads up to the *pā* lookout," Cooper said. "The terraces are eroded about halfway up. There have been slips into the lake."

"Maybe Herera jumped," Rangiora repeated.

"Or was pushed," Walker said.

Alexa had not noted abrasions or bruises on Herera's body to indicate a fall, but she kept quiet as the two men set off.

"The totem stood here." Cooper pointed out a flat area to the left side of the cave entrance.

An impression of darker earth was clear. "I'll take some photos of it." Since Walker still had the camera, Alexa turned on her phone camera. "How much does it weigh?"

"I couldn't lift it, and I can bench ninety kilos," Cooper replied. That explained why her uniform shirt was taut against her biceps. "It had to take two people."

"How much is that in pounds?"

Cooper thought for a moment. "Around two hundred. The totem is of Chief Rangituata. His mission is to watch over and protect his people. His absence shifts the maintenance of order."

"Order?"

"No person should defy the laws. Moving the totem is a serious violation. There will be punishment."

Alexa's mouth dropped.

Cooper continued. "The totem protected us. Now we must protect him." Blue lips pressed together; the spirals on her chin lay stark against dusky skin. Cooper walked over to the cave opening.

Alexa had a sudden urge to confess to this young Maori that she was worried about entering the cave. That she didn't want to trespass into the sacred womb and offend the gods. Or meet someone hiding, waiting. But distrust of Cooper kept her silent. "The cave was off-limits during that dig, wasn't it?" she asked, stalling.

"It is *urupā*, a burial site. No one is allowed in."

But now we must ignore custom, Alexa thought. *This is police business.*

"Let's go."

Cooper said something in Maori, possibly a prayer, and then turned her body sideways to enter the small fissure. Alexa followed, glad to be slimmer, but got stuck anyway. The crime scene kit refused to follow, and she had to back out and reenter, kit first. How could anyone have gotten a body or casket through here? Alexa was a cave virgin. Her heart was pumping at high velocity, and the taut red tissue crisscrossing her back itched. Inching forward, neck bent so she wouldn't concuss herself on a rock overhang, her hands on the cold slick walls on either side of the winding passage, the kit banging her thighs, she struggled to keep up with Cooper. If there was any crawling involved, she would be backing out, pronto. Each step brought fading light and cooler temperatures.

They were heading down. After twenty feet, Alexa could no longer touch both sides of the damp walls. Slowly, she lifted her head and stood fully upright in the chamber, an image of Neanderthal evolving into first man. Well, woman. Cooper's broad back disappeared around a bend. Alexa, trying not to freak at being abandoned in the dark, switched on her cell's flashlight, worried about the battery.

"Don't." Cooper's voice floated untethered. "Let your eyes adjust."

Adjust to what? You can't adjust to total darkness.

Alexa switched the light off and inched toward the hollow voice, her left hand on cold clammy rock, the right stretched ahead. The sudden flash of light and its blunt disappearance intensified the darkness. Afraid she would smack into a wall or fall into a pit, Alexa was about to turn the light back on when she edged around a passage.

What the hell?

The ceiling and walls were a spatter of BLUESTAR forensic spray. Yet not. More distinct. Like pinpoint stars on a moonless night. A shimmering turquoise faerie village.

"What is it?"

"Light of the enduring world," Cooper whispered. "*Titiwai.* Glowworms."

"So beautiful." Alexa remembered the guidebook touting these rare creatures unique to New Zealand and Australia. Mary had promised to show her some. "I know a place where you ride boats through a cave and they hang above like stars."

A damp thread caressed her face and returned her to here and now.

"In the beginning," Cooper whispered, "there was great night, dark night, long night. And then—the glowing of the worm."

The two women stood, quest postponed, kinship established, soaking up the magic. Alexa, distracted from fear, felt awash with gratitude for a land so unique, it shone light in its darkest places.

Taking a baby step backward, Alexa reached out to touch the wisp of emerald light.

"Now the glowworm will eat you," Cooper said, her voice back to normal. "They use their light to attract prey."

Alexa dropped her hand.

"Turn on your flashlight," said Cooper, clicking hers on. The glowworms vanished. Alexa did the same, and suddenly, they were standing in a small sanctum of the cave. More beauty astounded Alexa as she marveled over stalactites hanging from the ceiling, limestone icicles reaching for earth. A small pool of water in the corner, still and clear, reflected the formations. And, she noted, an infinite number of places a person could hide.

"The burial chamber," Cooper said, pointing toward another passageway with her light.

It was short and opened to a large chamber that the two women, standing close together, explored with their lights. A center pillar of stone supported the ceiling. Niches in the far walls looked like submarine bunks. A pile of rocks and debris in front of the stone pillar had a dropped-from-the-sky look, jumbled and disorganized. Cooper rushed toward the jumble and began talking in Maori, her voice loud and panicky.

"*Kāo, kāo, kāo.*"

"Stop," Alexa said. "What are you saying?"

"The chief 's tomb has been raided," Cooper yelled.

They scanned the disarray of bowling ball-sized rocks and wooden sticks. Cooper began to thread herself around and over them, Alexa following. A cleared hollow lay in the middle of the helter-skelter as if someone had stood there, lifting and hefting rocks. Alexa remembered Mr. Wright from the Rotorua Museum describing the burial bier's pyramid shape and knew that they had once been carefully placed upon the body of Chief Rangituata. She edged forward, forcing herself to peer into the hollow, expecting skeletal remains.

Empty. Somehow, Alexa wasn't surprised. Dismayed, but not surprised.

"The grave has been destroyed," Cooper said, her voice back to impassivity. They stood and stared. Neither knew what to do. Dank cold penetrated her rain jacket and blouse, and Alexa shivered.

"Water," Cooper said suddenly. "We have to douse the gravesite with water." She flew back toward the passageway, nimbly picking her way through boulders. Alexa followed and promptly tripped, falling hard atop a pile of sharp-edged rocks. Her cell went flying.

"Stupid klutz," she muttered, untangling herself from the crime scene bag. She stood to assess the damage and fish her beaming cell from between two rocks. Her left knee throbbed, and her right wrist was gashed, blood weeping instantly.

Panic at being left alone grabbed and squeezed. She limp-hopped after Cooper, thankful her knee could bear weight, and found the officer kneeling by the small pool in the glowworm area.

"What are you doing?" Alexa asked.

"I need a container. What's in the crime scene kit?" Cooper said.

Alexa dropped the crime kit. "What for?"

"Fresh water can neutralize *tapu*. If we don't douse the burial site, we will meet evil."

"But we aren't the ones who disturbed it."

"We need to protect ourselves and our families and whoever might come after us."

Alexa opened the kit. They used plastic evidence bags, filling them with cave water and returning to the burial chamber. Cooper's voice trembled as she said Maori words and slowly splashed water over the rocks and empty tomb as Alexa shone light. Glistening, the burial ground turned a deeper hue, red and angry. Cooper did the same with the water Alexa had collected. Then she turned. "We need to leave now."

Rangiora and Walker stood like driveway lions on either side of the cave entrance when Alexa and Cooper emerged disoriented and blinking in bright sunlight.

"We thought the spirits had gotten you," Walker said, his face anxious.

"What did you find?" Rangiora asked.

Neither woman spoke. Alexa wanted to hear what Cooper would say, but Cooper didn't say anything. "The burial site, where the chief was, has been disturbed. There's no trace of bones or artifacts," Alexa finally said. "We'll need to tape off the entrance, get experts here to assess the theft. I'll call it in."

"Bob's your uncle," Rangiora said. "Herera was robbing the grave."

No bars.

The team used the last of the yellow tape while Rangiora reported what he and Walker had discovered at the lookout. "Someone had been camping up there. Could have been where Herera was tossed into the lake. We bagged some stuff, but there's something stuck halfway down the cliff, a blanket or a parka," he said. "It's too steep to retrieve. Walker here has volunteered to stay and guard it until we can get equipment to pull it up. Whoever killed Herera could still be on the island."

Walker paled. Cooper volunteered to stay with him before he could protest.

The lake flattened to stainless steel as the police launch skimmed its surface, fast and urgent, to Rotorua harbor. Rangiora and Alexa did not speak.

Chapter Twenty-Seven

"Situation can't get worse," DI Horne said to the reduced team. They had assembled in the conference room at two p.m. after sending reinforcements to the island. He stood at the head of the table; everyone else was seated.

Alexa silently agreed.

"The results of Herera's autopsy...Trimble, share," Horne said. The bespectacled man opened the folder in front of him and extracted several eight-by-ten photos that he centered on the table. Alexa stared at the nearest: Herera's face, covered in tattoos, eyes pried wide, stared back.

"This is Dr. Hill's report," Trimble said. "Postmortem examination reveals bloodshot eyes, visceral congestion, fluid and cyanosis in the blood and tissue, hemorrhages and skin discoloration. Death attributed to asphyxia."

"Strangled?" Horne asked.

"Dr. Hill said smothered. No marks on his neck, but look at his lips." Trimble pointed to a closeup of lips. "They're blue and there's bruising."

Maori women, not men, had their lips tattooed blue—long ago to make themselves beautiful and desirable, today, like Cooper, to express cultural pride and identity. Herera's lips looked like they had been inked. But his blue lips were from lack of oxygen in the blood.

"You can see the impression of his top teeth on the inner lip from pressure being applied." Trimble pointed to a photo of Herera's inner lip turned back. "He was dead before being dumped in the water."

"Any trace?" Alexa asked.

"Mostly washed away," Trimble said. "He was in the water eight hours or more. I took what's left down to the lab."

"Time of death?" Horne continued.

"Between six and eight a.m. He had postmortem contusions on his shoulders and thighs as if he had rolled over something rough."

"Pushed from the lookout, probably," Rangiora said. "We were just there."

Alexa calculated. Herera must have been killed the morning after leaving the bird in her house. Had someone been watching him watching her? Followed him?

The room was silent. Now they knew, not just suspected, they were facing a second murder. Which meant there was always the possibility of a third.

Someone was getting nervous, covering tracks, acting irrationally, dangerously.

DI Horne broke the silence. "Which of you wants to give the lowdown on the island?"

Senior Officer Rangiora seized the opportunity. "I'll recap. First Glock tripped on human bones in a shallow grave. They looked like they had been dug up."

"What?" said McNamara. "Another body?" He was next to Alexa and turned to frown at her.

"A skeleton, right?" Horne looked at Alexa, and she nodded, wishing Rangiora hadn't said tripped. She tried not to wince from pain. Her good black jeans, torn at the knee, were ruined.

"The bones were old, and all we spotted was a thigh bone

and rib cage," Rangiora said. "We secured the scene and went on. Next, we found Herera's shack. Inside was a three-foot totem that Coop says was moved from the cave entrance. Nothing in the cabin had been disturbed. We made a list of items he had stored in a footlocker, which includes death certificates of his wife and kid. Blunt force trauma."

"Senior had me check that out," Trimble interrupted. "Car crash, State Highway Five. Lorry ran off the road and overcompensated. Hit them head on."

Horne bowed his head. Alexa imagined him thinking of his own daughters, gone in an instant, like Mary.

"What next?" he asked.

Alexa interrupted. "I think we should look into the archaeological dig that was halted a couple years ago on Pirongia. There might be a connection."

"What dig?" Trimble asked.

Horne looked surprised. "It was a joint study with some uni profs and the Maori Cultural Association in 2016. Someone spray-painted racial slurs on the tents. The *iwi* closed the dig."

"Had they found anything?" Trimble asked.

"It depended on your point of view. Pottery, adze. Fish bones. Not human remains. I don't see how the dig connects to this, but look into it. Anything else to report?" The DI looked back at his senior officer.

Rangiora continued. "Cooper and Glock entered the cave and discovered the burial chamber was ransacked and empty. Grave robbers."

"For real?" Trimble asked, shaking his head. "This isn't a made-for-telly movie?"

Rangiora nodded. "While they were in the cave, Walker and I hiked to the *pā* above. There's a bunker made from rocks and logs and evidence someone had camped there. A firepit with ashes and fish bones. Too rocky to see footprints. It's steep, and the edge is crumbling. Walker spotted something over the ledge, about halfway down to the water, thought at first it was another body. I think it's a tarp or parka. Coop and Walker are waiting for equipment to retrieve it."

"Any signs of someone on the island? Someone alive?" Horne asked.

"We didn't see or hear anyone," Alexa said.

"First someone kills Koppel, and then a week later, Herera. They both knew something or had something and were killed for it," McNamara said.

"That's a possibility," Horne said. "The exposed bones may or may not factor in. I located a forensic anthropologist in Auckland. I've left a message for her to contact me as soon as possible. And the Ministry for Culture and Heritage is sending someone to assess the cave damage and figure out what's been taken."

"Rawari Wright from the Rotorua Museum might have ideas about where the stolen objects would be taken," Alexa said. Blood was seeping through the Band-Aid on her wrist.

"Go talk to him," Horne said. "I believe he was a liaison for the archaeological dig as well. Ask if he knew Herera." He issued directions to each team member and dismissed them with a wave of his hand.

—

Alexa limped to the lab to check in with Jenny. The young technician was working on the prints collected last night from the lab and exit doors.

"So many were superimposed that the comparator only accepted three," Jenny said. "They match Officers Abel Rangiora and Wynne Cooper." Jenny looked at Alexa to gauge her reaction.

"Rangiora touched both last night," Alexa said. Possibly on purpose. He could have been covering his tracks. But Cooper? Why would her prints be in both places? "Who was the third?"

"There was a match." She gave Alexa a slip of paper. Alexa

scanned it but didn't recognize the name written down. Had this person been the face in the lab door window?

"Thanks. I'll look into this. Have you gotten anything from the Herera autopsy?"

"That officer on loan from Auckland, the one with glasses, dropped off evidence twenty minutes ago. I took a quick look. There's not much—fiber, hairs, some soil."

"Cause of death was asphyxiation, not drowning."

"But water washed away a lot of trace. I'll start with the fiber. It was extracted from the mouth."

"Good. Yesterday, Horne sent a team to search a boat belonging to Paul Koppel's father-in-law. Have you looked at findings yet?"

"Again, there wasn't much. Some soil and trash. Officer Walker said it looked like the boat had been scrubbed down. Which should I do first? Autopsy or boat?"

"Start with the boat. I collected soil from Pirongia this morning. Compare the soil to it and to the mud pits," Alexa directed. "How are you holding up?"

"I'm okay," Jenny said, touching her head. "I'm not happy they shaved my hair."

Alexa smiled. "Survival trumps vanity, I guess."

Jenny's gaze traveled from Alexa's hair to her ripped jeans to her dirty Keds. "You look a bit roughed up yourself."

"Exciting morning." She had stopped by the ladies' to wash up, press a fresh Band-Aid to her wrist, and inspect her knee. But her hair, curled in an every-which-way frizz, had defeated any attempts at taming, so she'd stuffed it behind her ears. One side had liberated itself. "I have to eat something, and then Bruce, I mean DI Horne, wants me to visit Rotorua Museum. I'll take care of the crime scene prints I lifted this morning later on. You've got enough. Go home if your head bothers you."

The officer she had insisted be placed outside the lab doorway was still there. Alexa nodded at him as she left.

Scarfing a yogurt in the canteen, Alexa read a text from Aria, the dispatcher in the Communications Office: Stop by. I have info you requested.

Had Aria identified the person in the hoodie? Alexa slurped the last spoonful and threw the carton in the bin. Time to find out who was caught on camera last night.

Aria Thompson was gone. "Her shift ended at two," another woman in the office said.

"Do you know if she left a message for a Ms. Glock?" Alexa checked her watch. It was a few minutes after.

"She said to give this to a Miss Clock." The woman handed her a note.

"Glock," Alexa said and unfolded the note. "Like the gun." The hooded man who had entered the police station at 8:01 pm last night had been Carl Rogers, the evening janitor. Aria had provided Rogers's address and phone number.

Wait a minute.

She unfolded the paper Jenny had given her: *Carl Winston Rogers.*

Relief. The face in the window had been a janitor. But had he left the exit door ajar? Or let someone in?

Leaving the Communications Office, Alexa wondered who she could get to check into him. Whom did she trust besides Bruce Horne, who seemed forever unavailable for private chats?

The undercover cop from Auckland. Trimble. She found him and explained her request.

—

Rawiri Wright answered on the first ring as if expecting her call. When he heard about the theft from Chief Rangituata's tomb and the discovery of skeletal remains, he insisted Alexa drive to the museum right away. Twenty minutes later, she was seated across a desk from him in his small office. His eyes, behind glasses, weren't sparkling this time.

"Whoever robbed the burial chamber is cursed. The spirits have latched and won't let go." Wright pushed a stack of papers to another spot on his desk for emphasis.

Alexa froze. The pen in her hand was still, her notebook page bare, her thoughts jumping to Herera, washed up like driftwood on a beach.

Wright continued. "Vandalism and theft of archaeological materials are as old as humanity. Think Egypt. King Tutankhamen and that obsessed British tomb-hunter Howard Carter. A predator, he was, claiming the tomb had already been robbed. *Taurekareka*! He was the one who robbed it."

King Tut? Taurekareka?

"You have much archaeological theft in your country. On Native American land. New Zealand is much smaller and newer than your country."

"Newer?" Alexa asked. The man was confusing her, maybe on purpose.

"North America's first inhabitants arrived sixteen thousand years ago. Polynesians arrived in New Zealand only one thousand years ago."

"That's interesting," Alexa said, her page blank except for the word "newer." Time for redirection. "I hear you repeating 'archaeological theft.' What do you know about the dig on Pirongia in 2016?"

"Nothing. I was a liaison on paper only. I was never out there."

"Perhaps you hoped the museum would benefit."

"*Pākehā* should not have been mucking about on Pirongia. It is sacred land."

Now he sounded like Mary's brother. "What about the selling of antiquities that might have been dug up then or later?"

"People must be registered with the Ministry for Culture and Heritage to possess Maori artifacts and can only sell or trade them with others who are registered. I'm registered on behalf of the museum."

"I doubt the thieves were card carriers."

"Or dealing with people who are registered. I agree," Wright said. "We don't have much documentation to the extent that illegal trading in New Zealand goes on. But it happens on every continent and in every nation. Some say it has reached epidemic proportions and helps fund organized crime, terrorist groups, even ISIS." He leaned closer to her and rested his chin on his intertwined fingers. "Think of it this way. Illegally excavated artifacts are easy to fence because they won't be in a stolen objects database."

"What type of artifacts would have been in Chief Rangituata's tomb?" Alexa asked. "A greenstone club?"

"Yes, most certainly, and maybe more than one. Also tools, ceremonial objects, sacred food, and war bounty."

"What would ceremonial objects and war bounty be?"

"Masks and shields. Moa or kiwi feather cloaks. Spears. Skulls."

"Skulls?"

"The belief was that it is better to keep an eye on your enemy, even in death, than turn a back. I have examples of these objects." Wright bowed his head, murmured something in Maori.

"You have skulls? Here in the museum?" Gruesome images flickered across her mind.

"We have three recently returned *toi moko*." He stared at Alexa.

Moko was tattoo. Toi must mean skull.

"They were returned three months ago as part of the government-funded Karanga Aotearoa Repatriation Program. Two from England and one from Ireland. We are testing them to see which tribe they might have belonged to so that they can be properly reunited and buried."

"Are you talking about tattooed skulls? Would tattoos be visible?" The idea was fascinating.

"The Maori tribes sometimes preserved severed heads—either an honored loved one or to offend the enemy. The head is the most sacred part of the body, and the *toi moko* were preserved by smoking and then drying the heads in the sun."

"The skulls aren't on display, are they?"

"It's an insult to even show a photo of one." Wright narrowed his eyes. "Human remains, or *kōiwi tangata*, are not *objets d'art*. Granted, it is a historical fact that some of our peoples participated in the selling and trading of heads taken as battle trophies, but mostly it was Europeans. Greed confuses one's moral compass."

"Would a skull sell in the black market today?"

"Yes."

"What would a person do with a skull and other artifacts he had stolen?"

"Find a buyer, of course." Mr. Wright's face dissolved to a scowl. "If no one was buying, the artifacts would not be stolen."

"Who buys?" Maybe Wright was a buyer. Did he have a private collection? Or what about the museum collection? The greenstone club that had captivated Alexa? Had it been procured legally?

"Buyers are auction houses, antiques dealers, private collectors, museums."

"Have you been approached to buy any Maori artifacts?"

"*Āe rā*!" he replied.

Alexa raised her eyebrows.

"Par for the course. I have been approached many times over the years I have curated for Rotorua Museum."

"Have you been approached in the last few months?"

"No," Wright answered right away, maybe too quickly. "I haven't been approached in several years now." He looked directly into her eyes, and she wanted to trust him.

Who said love all, trust few? "What did you do when you were approached?"

"There are many curators who operate with 'don't ask, don't tell' philosophy. This only perpetuates the black market."

He hadn't answered her question. Alexa stayed silent.

"The provenance of an object isn't always available. If a seller can not provide documentation, I don't deal. This has not always been the case here. My predecessor believed differently."

"How so?" Alexa asked.

"I don't like to speak on someone's behalf. You can talk to him directly. His name is William Dittmer." Wright fingered through an old-fashioned Rolodex on his desk. "Here." He wrote a name and number on a Post-it and handed it to Alexa. "He has an antiques store, Kauri Treasures, on Tarangi Street. He attended that dig."

"Thank you." Alexa sensed Wright was holding something back. "So your predecessor might have been involved in black market activities?" Alexa asked, staring intently at Wright, who merely shrugged. Now she sensed he was ready to terminate the interview. "Why did this man leave the museum?"

"I was never privy to this information, but it happened abruptly."

Worth checking into, Alexa thought. "How does the big picture work? I mean, who is digging up artifacts? Here or elsewhere. Are they the same people who sell them directly to museums or antiques dealers or to someone overseas?"

"No, no. The looting of antiquities is usually an organized, tiered network. It starts with grave robbers or treasure hunters, whatever you want to call them. These people are often impoverished, destitute. Willing to sell their souls for the dollar."

"Okay," she said.

He appraised her. "The Maori people have a higher rate of poverty than *Pākehā*. And a Maori might believe the antiquities were left behind by ancestors who would want them to benefit."

"So maybe a Maori is involved?" *Like Herera.*

Wright ignored her. "A grave robber is paid a pittance by a middleman or trafficker who *then* sells to the higher-ups like auction houses or overseas markets. Most loot is smuggled out of its country of origin. China is a big buyer of antiquities right now, as are Switzerland and the States. Your rich Manhattan hedge fund manager, for example. That sums up the big picture." Wright stood.

Alexa stayed seated. "Did you know the Pirongia caretaker? Ray Herera?"

"Ray? He married a distant cousin. Tragic when she and their daughter were killed. He is finding strength and solace amid sacredness. Don't go blaming him for this."

Wright had not noticed her tense usage. "Please sit down."

He continued to stand, looking down at her.

"Mr. Herera's body was found washed up at Ponga Point."

Wright sank into his chair and bowed his head. When he finally looked at Alexa, his eyes had a misty sheen. "Ray would give his life to defend his ancestors. He is an honorable man."

"Was, not is. I'm sorry to have brought you bad news." Alexa flipped shut her mostly empty notepad and stood. This time, it was she who looked down at Wright. "Please contact me or Detective Inspector Horne if you hear anything about the artifacts or Mr. Herera's death."

There was no pressing of forehead and nose in parting. Once in her car, she wrote down everything she could remember while the conversation was fresh, and then thought of Jenny, back in the lab, busy with evidence from Herera's autopsy and samples collected from the boat. Alexa was torn between stopping by the antiques store to meet the former curator, William Dittmer, or heading back to help Jenny. Her GPS indicated Tarangi Street was only seven minutes away.

Decision made.

Chapter Twenty-Eight

A jaunty red-and-blue-striped awning shaded the double windows of Kauri Treasures. Alexa peered through the glass but couldn't see past her disheveled reflection. The sign on the door read: Open Monday-Saturday, 10–5. A bell jangled, but no one appeared as she entered. It took a moment for her eyes to adjust, focus. The large room was bulging with china, silver, books, porcelain, framed art, masks, furniture, and jewelry. A jolt of panic stabbed Alexa. What if she knocked something over? She cautiously stepped to some shelves, scanning them for Maori artifacts, and sneezed from old-book mustiness.

"May I help you?" came a not quite Kiwi voice from across the shop. Australian, Alexa guessed, twirling around. Kiwi and Australian accents were barely different in Alexa's ears but night and day to a local—something about vowel shifts.

A diminutive man with a shock of dandelion-fluff hair sidled toward her through a row of Toby mugs. "William Dittmer, proprietor," he said. "How may I assist you?"

Panic: she had no plan. Should she act touristy or identify herself?

He didn't wait. "I've just received an exquisite collection of Royal Albert teacups. Would you like a gander?"

"Yes, please," Alexa answered, glad to buy time. She followed the man, who appeared—despite the shock of white hair—to be in his midforties, to a circular display table.

"Look at this Albany Blue." He lifted a delicate cup with both hands and held it up to a chandelier. "So fine you can see light through it." He set it down and selected another. "Buckingham turquoise. Note the gold scrolls along the edge. Hand-painted. Makes you crave a spot of Darjeeling, doesn't it?"

"I prefer coffee," Alexa replied, noting the man's fingernails were shiny with clear polish. "I'm looking for Maori art."

He studied her. "From the States, are you?"

Alexa nodded. "Are you Australian?" A chill danced up her spine. The caretaker on Pirongia, the dead man, had pointed to his head and said, "*ma, ma,* white" when he described Koppel's companion. Maybe he had been speaking of hair, not skin.

"Yes. Melbourne. Much better weather here."

Alexa felt a tweak of danger. "Do you have authentic Maori artifacts?"

The man abandoned his teacups and shifted past brass and copper teakettles, pressed tin lanterns, hookahs, frames, and candlesticks to a display case. He took a key chain out of his pants pocket and unlocked the case with his right hand. "Come see," he said, reaching in and then dangling an object from his palm.

"What is it?" asked Alexa, joining him. She scanned the velvet-lined case and noted pendants, tiki statues, a small bowl with mortar. And two greenstone war clubs.

"I can tell you crave adventure, am I right?"

Alexa tried not to stare at the clubs. She ignored his question and came closer to examine the pendant as it swung back and forth like a snake charmer's cobra.

"Bone *toki* on native flax cord. Symbol of strength and courage over adversity. You've faced adversity in your life, yes?"

The burn scars on Alexa's back tightened.

"Would you be interested?" The pendant stopped swinging, waiting for her decision.

"Talky? What's a talky?" she asked, mesmerized by the small shape dangling from his fingers and his fortune telling prowess.

"A *toki* is an adze, the most important tool the Maori owned. A cutting tool. The pendant is a small adze carved from bone."

"Bone? What type of bone?" She squared her shoulders to break the spell and felt the scarred tissue from right shoulder blade down to mid-vertebrae protest.

"Bird bone. Possibly moa. Feel how light." He handed her the necklace and smiled. His teeth were yellowed, and the odor of cigarette clung to his clothing. "Bone carving was a sacred craft practiced by some of the more warlike native tribes here in the North Island. Sometimes human bone was carved."

"Human bone?" She thought of the fishing hook Rangiora had lifted from Herera's trunk.

"Waste not, want not, eh? But human bone was mostly used for larger items than this. Maybe for shark fishing."

"Is the necklace old?"

"Depends on your definition of old. Are you searching for something in particular?" He reached for the necklace, replaced it, and locked the case. The jangle of bells caught his attention. "You'll excuse me please."

"No worries," Alexa said. "I'll look around."

Dittmer moved soundlessly toward two chatting women who had entered the shop. Alexa could hear a new spiel, something about great bazaars, giving her a chance to study the case. Her attention went to the greenstone clubs. One, labeled twentieth century, had ripples of white washing through it. The second, from the nineteenth century, was larger and darker. An hourglass hole was carved at the handle, and a woven wristband was looped through it. They could have been the same ones she had seen around the waists of the island warriors. Nearby was a flat tiki man, neckless, made of greenstone flecked with brown. Its deep-set sideways eyes leered at her. The card below read "Provenance: Y37667, Bailey & Barre Wellington." Alexa got out her phone and took pictures. A sound made her pause and look up.

Dittmer had returned.

Before he could speak, Alexa said, "I'm interested in the two clubs here." She tapped on the glass. "Would you show them to me?"

"War clubs?" he asked. "That surprises me."

Alexa didn't answer.

"These two are beauts. It took years to polish them to such perfection."

"Yep." She waited as he unlocked the case again.

His child- sized hand hovered over the clubs. "Which would you like to see?"

"The older." In a blink, the weapon was in Dittmer's hands. Alexa imagined its cool, smooth heft.

"See how flat and sharp the edge is." Dittmer ran a finger along its side. "Deadly in battle." His eyes took a gleam. "Particularly when thrust at the temple or neck or, of course"—he looked Alexa over—"the ribs."

The hair on Alexa's neck rose. "How much does it cost?"

"Ten thousand."

"Not cheap," she said. "Where did it come from?"

"I have my sources." Dittmer smiled, showing canines.

"Where did it come from?" she repeated. "I'm part of a murder investigation, and we are looking into possible stolen artifacts that may be connected. Rawiri Wright of the Rotorua Museum suggested you might help us." She dug out her ID.

Dittmer's eyes shape-shifted to smaller, shrewder orbs. "Murder investigation?"

Alexa stayed silent.

"I purchased the club legally." His eyes flitted to the other club in the case and then to her badge. "Is Mr. Wright still with the museum?"

"Yes. He thought perhaps you might have some information."

A bark of a laugh. "He did? How preposterous." The shop bell jangled as the women left. They were alone.

"You haven't answered my question."

Dittmer had not asked who had been murdered or what artifacts had been stolen. Alexa continued. "Many of the items in the case state the provenance, but that one does not."

"I do not have verifiable provenance for this club," Dittmer said, looking down at the *mere* in his hand. "That is not uncommon." He ran his finger along the tapered edge again.

"Why not? And how can you ask so much money for it?"

"If I had the provenance, the price would double."

"You're dodging my question. Where did you get the club?" She held her hand out for it.

Dittmer hesitated and then placed it in her hands. A shock from opposing electrons almost caused her to drop it.

What the hell?

"An estate sale. It belonged to a widow from Auckland who passed on."

Alexa thrust it back to Dittmer and looked at her fingers to check if they had been singed.

What the double hell?

Dittmer replaced the club on the green velvet, whisked a cloth from his breast pocket, and rubbed its glossy surface. "The family was selling her estate, and I came across it. Lucky. This one too." He pointed to the other club and rubbed it with the cloth as well.

"So you have no idea of the clubs' origins?"

"No." He locked the case.

"Do you have a bill of sale for the clubs?"

"I really don't see how that is any of your business. I have a reputable business here."

"Detective Inspector Bruce Horne is running the case and sent me here. Would you like me to give him a ring?"

Dittmer huffed. "That's not necessary. I can check and see

if I can locate the receipt. But quickly. I have an appointment. Come."

He deftly wove through the shop and disappeared through a door at the rear. In her haste to follow, Alexa bumped a tin lantern, knocking it into a copper kettle that she grabbed before it crashed to the ground. She steadied the swinging lantern, noting the tag: Souk, $180.

She proceeded cautiously to a small room where Dittmer was standing behind a desk.

"Have a seat," he said, pointing to a chair. "A Bergère, covered in Fortuny silk."

It took Alexa a moment to figure out what he was on about.

She perched on the edge of the dainty chair, aware of her throbbing knee.

Dittmer stared at the desk computer. "It's slow."

"I'll ask a few questions as we wait."

Dittmer frowned. "I really don't have anything else to say."

"I could come back with the DI," Alexa said.

"That's not necessary," Dittmer replied. "Perhaps I should close the shop so we won't be interrupted."

"Perhaps," Alexa replied. The hair on her neck stood again as Dittmer brushed by. She quickly looked around. There were two framed *Mau Rākau* certificates—Level 1 and Level 2—hanging on the wall. Maybe some type of judo, she concluded and stood to look closer, but Dittmer returned. Alexa sat back down and plunged on. "Mr. Wright indicated that…excavators…know not to approach him to sell their goods, but that you were not so choosy. Is that true?"

Dittmer stayed standing behind his desk. He leaned on it, looking down at her, his steel gray orbs unblinking. "In the four years Wright has been curator at Rotorua Museum, only two objects have been added to the Maori collection. Two! One fell into his lap—a door lintel."

Alexa thought of the carved work of art above the entrance to the Maori collection room.

"The other, a cloak of *harakeke* and feather, is merely on loan. In my tenure, we increased the collection by twenty percent. Wright has wasted many opportunities to expand. This is an injustice to the peoples of Rotorua," he said.

"An injustice? How?"

"When objects of limited or missing provenance are offered to a museum, a curator must weigh the benefits with the drawbacks, do you see?" He finally sat.

"No."

"Let me ask, would you rather an antiquity of exquisite beauty be on display for many to see and learn from—say the three-thousand-year-old bust of Queen Nefertiti that draws more than one million people to the Neues Museum every year—or buried in a cave? A museum knows how to care for and protect such objects." Dittmer slapped his palm on his desk.

"I would rather the object not be stolen in the first place or that looters not profit."

"I hardly see how buried treasures can provide knowledge of cultures and educate the public. A museum's purpose is noble."

"A thief's is not," Alexa countered. "What can you tell me about the dig on Pirongia two years ago? We know you were involved."

Dittmer went still. "Hardly worth the effort. All that was found was broken pottery and fish bone." It was possible that his pale skin had paled further.

"Why did you leave the museum?"

"I make a better living in antiques. I don't see how I can help you with your investigation."

"I need to know if you have been approached recently by someone selling Maori artifacts."

"Ah, the computer is ready. Just a moment." Dittmer appeared to be searching. "Yes. This is it. A bill from three years ago. Shall I print it?" Without waiting for an answer, he left the small room again. In a moment, he was back, standing above her with a sheet of paper. "Here."

"Thank you." She read the printout, noting the Bailey & Barre name again. "I'll share it with the Detective Inspector in charge of the investigation. But wait." She reread. "This is just for one of the clubs. Do you have a bill for the other?"

"I don't see it in my records. I'll keep looking. But I have to leave now."

She stood, and now Dittmer was eye-to-eye with her five feet seven inches. "Have you been approached recently?"

Steel-gray eyes darkened to slate. "No one has come to my shop with Maori antiquities in recent months." He stepped back against his desk.

"What can you tell me about this Bailey & Barre?" The slightest of muscle fasciculation in his left eyelid. Maybe she had imagined it.

"It's an international auction house in Auckland. They specialize in militaria and Maori and Pacific artifacts." He gathered steam. "They handle appraisals, restorations, and estate sales. I make several trips a year to their auctions." He made a point of checking his watch.

"I'm sure you want to help with our investigation. If someone in the area had Maori items for sale and did not proposition you, whom would they turn to?"

Dittmer straightened his compact body. "I don't know. Are we done? I have an appointment."

"A final question. Did you know Paul Koppel?"

Another twitch, she was sure this time.

"No."

Alexa returned to her car parked across the street. It was half past three on a sunny afternoon in downtown Rotorua, the day after Ray Herera's body washed up on the banks of the lake. A woman and a tot in purple gum boots walked by hand in hand, their singsong laughter seeping through the cracked window a reminder that life goes on even in the midst of murder. Alexa knew it was time to head to the lab, but something William Dittmer said bothered her. A niggling irritant.

What?

She jotted down notes, trying to jar her memory, and shifted her throbbing knee.

Nothing.

Just as she decided to head to the station, Dittmer emerged from his shop.

She watched as the antiques proprietor looked both ways down the street, locked the shop door, and scurried around the corner. What was there to do but follow?

Chapter Twenty-Nine

Dittmer's snow-white head bobbing down the sidewalk made him easy to keep an eye on; driving the car at walking pace with traffic breathing on her bumper was not. Should she park and tail him on foot? But what if he was heading to his car? She was about to pass him when Dittmer stopped by a black Honda Accord, unlocked it, and slipped in.

It was then she figured what was bothering her.

Monday afternoon traffic in Rotorua, the fourth-largest city on the North Island, was congested; Alexa took advantage of that by staying two cars behind the Honda and concentrated more on the driving than the mission.

What was the mission? Should she notify DI Horne? If Dittmer was merely getting a haircut or going to the gym, she'd waste his time.

But Dittmer had mentioned antiquities "buried in a cave." That was what had bothered her. *I never mentioned a cave.*

After ten minutes, the Honda turned right onto Queen's Drive near Lake Rotorua. A colorful billboard touted *Polynesian Spa: Open Daily*. The Honda turned into the spa entrance. Alexa waited for two cars to pass before doing the same.

An appointment at the spa?

Slowly cruising the half-full parking lot, Alexa watched Dittmer open his trunk and extract a gym bag. From her rearview mirror, she watched him scurry to the entrance. Parking one row over, Alexa jotted down Dittmer's license number, which she had memorized, and then opened the door.

But wait.

A disguise. He would recognize her. Lucky the Monet scarf from last night was stuffed in her tote. She wound it turban-like around her hair, shoving stray tendrils underneath, put on sunglasses, and, before she could back out, walked to the entrance, trying not to limp.

Inside smelled of sulfur and salt. Bird tweets, palm trees, and reggae music created a pseudotropic. All kinds of people, some in swimsuits and jandals, some in robes, some in street clothes, queued at two ticket lines. Dittmer stood in the left line. A family of four clustered behind him. Two towheaded boys were tugging at their parents' arms, yammering excitedly.

Brightly colored menu boards lined the wall above the ticket windows. A variety of hot pool packages were available: luxury, private, adults only, family fun. Next to this were spa therapy choices. For $180 a person could choose mud treatment body wraps to tighten and tone skin, improve and increase blood circulation, and eliminate toxins.

Alexa, with a surge of anger, thought of Paul Koppel's mud treatment. Of his wife defending him. Of his little boys thinking death was a game and Daddy would come home.

She pushed her sunglasses farther up her nose and crowded behind the family, who were speaking German. Keeping her head down, she edged behind the large mother and listened to Dittmer speak to the agent.

"Private pool number three, one hour." He sounded like a regular. "I have a reservation."

Alexa glanced up and read the description: *The Deluxe Private Mineral Pools Offer Complete Privacy and Open-Air Lake Views, $30 for 30 minutes.*

Bargain.

The ticket agent, who wore a Hawaiian shirt, scanned her screen. "Yes, welcome back." Dittmer paid cash, received key, slippers, towel, and robe, and sidled off toward the men's dressing area.

"The sliding board, Papa," one of the little boys said and then switched to German. "*Gleitbrett*!" The parents debated between themselves, scrutinized the coupons they had in hand, and argued with the ticket agent. Alexa clenched her fists, mentally screaming "Decide, morons."

Finally, they purchased their family fun pack. "How may I help you?" the ticket agent asked Alexa.

"Private pool number four, please, one hour."

"Do you have a reservation?"

"No."

The woman scanned her screen. "That pool is not available." She smiled pleasantly at Alexa. "Would another of our private mineral pools work?"

"Is number two available?"

"Yes, it is." Her smile broadened. "Anything else? A spa treatment? Bathing costume?"

Alexa shuddered at the thought of a rented bathing suit, hated bathing suits, hated anything that showcased her lovely scars. But then she considered the alternative: sleuthing naked. "One suit, please."

"Size?"

Her mind blanked. What sizes did New Zealand use? "Medium."

The agent handed Alexa a locker key, towel, white robe, slippers, and shrink-wrapped red tog and gave instructions. "I hope someone is joining you," the agent added. "It's very romantic."

"Ah, yes, no, thanks," said Alexa, shoving an escaped hank under her turban. She put the sixty-five dollars on her credit card, took a deep breath, and looked around. Danger in a popular tourist attraction with singing birds and fake waterfalls was ludicrous.

In the dressing room, she struggled into the rented tog, worried about *its* provenance. The spandex fought back, and the result was tight in the butt, loose in the bust, and left her upper back exposed. But who would see? Bruce Horne flashed in her mind. She figured he'd be angry at this wild goose chase.

But not if she discovered something important.

Following instructions, she showered, flinching as the spray hit her wrist and swelling knee. She wrapped up in the robe, stuffed her feet into too-small slippers, stowed her tote in a locker, stashed key and cell in her robe pocket, and—finally—stepped into a waiting lounge of dim light, soft music.

Panic.

She looked around. But the lounge was empty.

What if Dittmer had been here? She'd left scarf and shades in the locker.

After a few minutes, a stout Maori woman in a bright red sarong entered. Her lustrous black hair, in a thick braid, hung heavy over her right shoulder. "*Kia ora*. I am Hanna, your escort. Are you ready?" Like Officer Cooper's, Hanna's lips were blue, and spirals covered her chin.

"Yes."

"I'll show you to your personal spa pool."

Alexa followed. "Are most of the private pools rented out this afternoon?"

"Just a few," the woman replied. "Yesterday was much busier."

They were in a narrow hallway with numbered doors lining the left. The woman stopped at Number Two, unlocked it, and stepped inside, saying something about a complimentary drink. Alexa didn't follow but ventured farther down to Number Three and pressed her ear right to the door. Faint music. No voices. She tried the knob.

"I said in here." Hanna stood back in the hall, frowning.

"Oh dear. I wasn't paying attention." Alexa followed her into Number Two. "Long day."

The room was enclosed on three sides by bamboo walls, tropical plants and vines. Straight ahead, it was wide open to the lake.

"It's gorgeous," Alexa said, watching a sailboat skim by.

The spa pool, encased in fake rocks, took up most of the space, and there was no ceiling, just infinite blue sky.

I could get used to this.

"The bath is filled with alkaline mineral water to leave your skin soft and supple," the escort explained, scanning Alexa's face and legs.

Alexa pulled the robe tighter.

"Is thirty-eight degrees warm enough?" Hanna asked.

"Too warm," she said automatically, although the breeze from the lake had given her dampened skin chill bumps.

"I'll turn the temperature to thirty-six then, and the jets to medium. You can adjust the pressure here." A control panel was hidden behind a fern. "Would you like music?"

"No thanks. I like the sound of the bubbles," Alexa said. A seagull flew overhead, screeching. "And birds."

"If it begins to rain, you can close the retractable ceiling, but most guests leave it open." Hanna smiled, her teeth gleaming white against the Kool-Aid blue of her lips. "Here is a menu. Would you like some nosh and drink?"

Wouldn't it be nice to dangle my feet in the water and scarf nachos supreme and a piña colada?

"A water, please."

"I'll be right back," Hanna said, leaving the door ajar.

Alexa had never sat in a spa pool in her adult life. Didn't even take baths ever since "the accident." Showers only.

Deep breath.

She had to act as a tourist for her escort's behalf. She disrobed down to her rented bathing suit. Most people probably soak nude, she thought, tugging the rear material to cover her cheeks and dipping a toe. There were steps and seating in and around the spa. Inch by inch, Alexa descended, and for a moment, stunned by the sensations, she let the bubbles and jets ease her tension. She sank onto a bench seat, her marred back hidden against the fake rocks, water up to her breasts, and stared at Lake Rotorua until Hanna returned with a bottled water.

"Will anyone be joining you?" the escort asked.

What was it with these nosy people?

"No. I'm on my own."

"Here is a buzzer to ring if you need anything." She pointed to a button next to the door. "I'll knock when you have five minutes left. *Kia harikoa.* Be in high spirits." Hanna bowed her head and slipped out, closing the door firmly.

Ah. Why have I been avoiding this?

Temptation was strong to settle and soak. The jet pummeling her scar tissue felt good, therapeutic, and Alexa allowed herself sixty sensuous seconds, sipping Pure Rotorua Spring Water, toying with an image of Bruce—she let herself use his first name—joining her, no rented togs, and then chastised herself for fantasizing about a man she'd known for a scant week and who wasn't particularly friendly.

But those eyes.

The silencing of the jets jarred her back to reality. Why had they stopped?

She waded to the steps and climbed out. Dripping, she pulled on her robe, patting the pocket to make sure her cell was still there, and discovered the jets were on a timer.

Mystery solved.

She jammed her wet feet into the slippers and pressed her ear to the bamboo wall shared with Spa Three. Faint music—Bob Marley, maybe—still no voices. Looking down, she noted a five-inch gap between wall and floor. Spreading out the towel, Alexa lay flat, wincing when her knee hit the concrete floor.

A slice of Room Three: bench, rocks, greenery, slippers. As her ears adjusted, she could hear bubbling jets in addition to the music. No feet. Dittmer was soaking. Just as she was pushing herself up, Alexa heard a knock.

Was Hanna about to open the door?

But the knock was for Room Three. Alexa lay back down and watched dripping pink feet emerge from the spa and walk to the door. "Yes?" she could hear, but not the response. Another pair of feet, bare, larger, hair on toes, entered the room.

"Why are you late?" Alexa recognized Dittmer's voice.

"Not to worry. We were busy at the house," came a Kiwi response. "Let's talk in the pool. Have you ordered?"

Something something paninis, something something smoothie. Was this Dittmer's boyfriend? A robe dropped to the floor, and four feet disappeared into the spa.

Damn.

Trying hard and failing to hear above Bob Marley crooning "No woman no cry" and pressure jets, Alexa scrambled to Plan B. To spy from the open lakeside, she would have to climb back in her spa pool and clamber out the other side, over fake boulders, onto grass. Then she could peer around the privacy wall that jutted out between Spa Room Two and Spa Room Three. Lake Rotorua, eerily flat, lapped the shore meters away.

Placing cell and slippers on the bench, Alexa waded back into the pool, hot water shocking her cooled skin. She tried keeping the robe dry, but at the far end, where she hoisted herself up over the fake boulders, the robe dropped into the water.

What the hell.

She clambered over and crouched down as soon as both feet were on the grass. Inching forward on all fours, ignoring the knee pain, she reached the jutted wall and crouched against it, hoping nobody would choose this moment to sail by on the lake and spy a crazy woman.

"Strawberry kiwi," she heard.

Damn.

Had she risked her dignity to hear men discussing fruity drinks?

"Refreshing," came the reply.

Alexa inched forward and peered around the wall. Dittmer was alarmingly near, his back to her. He was naked, dangling legs in the water, his slippery skin poached red. A sandwich on a plate next to him was half gone. The visitor, the lower half of his body submerged, sipped from a straw disappearing into frothy pink and appeared to be looking directly at her.

She snapped back.

Had he seen her? Alexa held her breath, squeezed water from the robe hem.

That face. Did she recognize that man's face? Fifty-ish, bald, clean-shaved, brown eyes under dark, thick brows.

No. A stranger. She leaned forward again.

"What have you got for me?" the stranger asked.

"Whale bone spear, intricately carved…"

"Whale bone? Do you know the Maori Trojan horse story?"

"But of course, Philip. So clever. Hawke's Bay, right? The warriors lay under black mats to look like beached pilot whales. When the villagers left the *pā* to harvest the whales…"

"Yes, yes. Attack. Violence and death. A second Troy. What else?"

"Club. Greenstone."

Alexa felt again the shock in her hands at the touch of that club in the shop. That greenstone club.

"And…"

Silence except for bubbles.

"Don't keep me waiting, William. You're teasing."

Alexa risked another look. The stranger had stood, water cascading down his sleek toned chest and thighs. His stark nakedness jarred Alexa back behind the wall again.

Dittmer laughed, spouted something about serendipity. "I have a skull."

Alexa thought of the raided tomb and the headless skeleton. She pressed her ear to the bamboo wall, strained to hear more.

The stranger's voice turned animated. "Split twenty thousand.

Pay your source from that." His voice was louder. He must have waded over to Dittmer.

Alexa held her breath.

"No need," Dittmer's voice, bubble, bubble, bubble, "terrible accident."

"How unfortunate," came the bald man's reply. "But a little bonus for you, *n'est-ce pas*?"

The sound of bubbles got louder. Her phone! Why hadn't she been recording the conversation?

Alexa scurried backward and clambered into her pool. She didn't even try to be quiet. Her heart was pounding as she slopped back through and out, grabbing her cell. How much of her sixty minutes was left? Her thoughts jumbled. A couple of photos. Or video. Then to the parking lot. Get the baldy's license number.

To hasten her return, she whipped off the robe and threw it to the floor. Cell phone clutched high, she sloshed back through the water, clambered over, and crawled to her perch.

Just as she peeked, cell camera ready, Dittmer said, "That's the five-minute warning knock." He slithered out of the spa.

Her photos when she scrutinized them seconds later were of a pair of butts, one red, one tanned.

Chapter Thirty

Alexa sped Michael Phelps-speed through her pool and dashed, robeless, dripping, down the hallway through the waiting area and into the ladies' locker room. Then she remembered the locker key in the robe pocket. "Crap." She ran back to her private spa room, nearly knocking over Hanna.

"You've left?"

"Well, I needed to use the facilities," Alexa said, panting.

Hanna blocked her access.

"I need my robe and towel."

"I'm sorry. Your time is up," the escort said. "You can see—"

"Yes! But I still need my robe. The key to the locker..."

Alexa shouldered past Hanna and tried the door.

Locked.

"Let me in!" She hadn't meant to shout.

Hanna unlocked the door and stepped aside. Alexa rushed in, grabbed the robe, and dashed away, Hanna's "I hope you had a pleasant soak" following her down the hall.

She had been tempted to sprint directly to the parking lot but spent three eternal minutes tugging off the clingy tog and shoving damp body parts into decency.

Dittmer's black Honda was exiting onto Queen's Drive.

"Damn." She frantically searched the parking lot for another departing car, not knowing what to look for. In ten minutes, the only people who left were a young couple, arms tight around each other, laughing and nuzzling.

On the chance that Mystery Philip hadn't left the spa, Alexa hustled inside. No handsome bald man in the gift store or having a second smoothie in the café. She couldn't very well search the men's locker room, though she was tempted.

The ticket line was empty. Alexa marched up to the same ticket agent she had earlier. "I need to know who signed in and paid for private spa Number Three this past hour. There were two people."

"I'm not allowed to share that information," the agent responded, her bright smile fading.

"I need to speak with the manager then," Alexa said, digging out her badge. "This is a police investigation."

The manager refused to divulge the information as well and said to come back with a search warrant.

Alexa left the spa, measuring equal parts defeat and victory. Released endorphins coated her brain as if she had run the length of the Kaituna. Instead of waiting until she returned to the station, she sat in her car and dialed, surprised the DI answered on the first ring.

"Horne here," came the familiar bark.

"It's Alexa."

"Where are you? I thought you'd be back by now."

"Rawiri Wright gave me some information that I followed up on. I'm leaving the Polynesian Spa right now and heading back. Will you be…?"

"The Polynesian Spa?" Horne asked.

"I'll explain when I get back. I wanted to make sure you'd be available."

"I'll be waiting in my office."

It was past five o'clock when she parked and entered the station. Sharon Welles was tidying her desk. Her cat eyes raked

Alexa's disheveled appearance. The hint of makeup Alexa had applied this morning long gone, her hair a windblown spa frizz, and—she looked down—blouse misbuttoned, jeans torn at the knee.

"Long day," she said to Welles. "DI Horne is waiting for me."

The DI was on his phone as Alexa knocked and entered. He motioned for her to sit while he finished.

"That was Trimble following up on the mayor's whereabouts the night Koppel was killed. Security cameras confirm she left Tulip Fest at the civic center at 9:05 p.m. Her husband says she arrived home at 9:20. They watched tellie and went to bed."

Alexa was chomping to tell about her afternoon, but she held back. "Koppel's time of death was between nine p.m. and midnight, right?" she asked. "So we have to rely on a husband's alibi."

"Not ideal," Horne replied. His eyebrows scrunched together as he looked her up and down.

"Is Trimble around?" Alexa asked, glad she had aligned her buttons. "I asked him to check out the evening janitor. Carl Rogers. He might have been the face I saw in the lab window last night. He could also be responsible for leaving the basement door ajar."

"Trimble is in the conference room. He asked an hour ago where you were, and I didn't know what to tell him." Horne frowned. "What information did you get from Rawiri Wright, and where have you been?"

Finally.

She took a deep breath and launched into her afternoon, first with Wright, then at Dittmer's shop, and ending with her spa visit.

The DI stayed quiet, his blue eyes intense and unwavering. "I have a photograph but it's from behind. I'm not sure it will be of any use," she finished, cringing at her unintentional pun. Horne's phone rang. He ignored it and continued staring, making Alexa shift.

"I'm trying to process this information. But I'm stuck on the fact that you stepped beyond the bounds of your contract." He shook his head. "You are not a police officer. You have been hired as a temporary forensics examiner."

Alexa didn't speak.

"You deliberately exposed yourself to danger and perhaps put the investigation in peril."

Or perhaps solved it.

"From here on out, you need to limit your activities to the lab. Let's see the photograph."

"It probably won't help," she stalled.

"Do you have a photo or not?" Horne's face turned stony.

She fiddled with her phone and located the picture of the bare butts. Even the heads of the men were cut off. "Here."

After a few seconds of silence, Horne laughed, a chortle first but then a deep eruption, a release-from-tension laugh that left his eyes wet and sparkling.

"I'm sorry. By the time I got my cell phone..."

He ignored her, staring at the photo again, laughter fading. He touched the screen and stared harder. "Look," he said, handing the phone back to Alexa. "I think that's a tattoo."

Wonder of wonders: mystery man had a tiki tattooed on his left cheek.

"Let's head to the conference room," Horne said, springing up. "And make a plan."

Rangiora and a strange woman were studying photos on the conference table. The woman was using a magnifying glass.

"And you are?" Horne asked.

"Marija Robertova, forensic anthropologist," she answered, standing back up. "I have arrived from Auckland." Her accent was foreign, guttural.

"You made good time. I'm DI Horne, and this is Alexa Glock, temporary forensics examiner. She can fill you in on what was found on the island."

"I'm doing that, sir," said Rangiora. "I'll be taking Dr. Robertova to Pirongia early in the morning."

"What do you think?" Horne asked, pointing to the photos of the femur and grave site.

"I cannot judge based on these," Dr. Robertova said. "It does appear the grave was shallow. The disarticulation indicates..."

Alexa caught Rangiora's puzzled look. "Disarticulation is when all the flesh has disappeared, right?"

"That is correct," she answered. "In shallow graves, this process takes between six and twelve months. In deeper graves, it takes longer. Let's hope there's a wider bone field. A skull will help determine ethnicity and gender."

"How come the bones aren't white? I thought ancient bones turned white," Rangiora said.

"The bleaching of bones only occurs if exposed to sunlight. It looks as if the decay process was subterranean."

"All good," said the DI. "We need to know how old the bones are and cause of death. A gentleman from Ministry of Culture and Heritage will be accompanying you. He'll inspect the tomb to assess any possible damage and theft." He looked around. "Where's the rest of the team?" he asked Rangiora. "Are Officers Cooper and Walker back from the island?"

"Yes. They're on the way to the station. Bringing sammies."

"Glock has some information to share, but I'd rather wait until everyone is here. Let's reconvene in fifteen." He did an about-face and left the room.

The short break gave Alexa a chance to talk with the anthropologist. "Do you work at the forensics lab in Auckland?" she asked when Rangiora stepped away.

"No, no. I am working on a second PhD at Auckland University. I am required to take the occasional contract job." The doctor was wide and blunt; her short, dark hair, interspersed with silver strands, swished back and forth as she talked. "I'm studying data-collection protocol."

Alex thought that sounded as exciting as tooth decay. "Did Officer Rangiora tell you the skeletal remains might be that of a slave?

"No, but the shallowness of the grave in Maori custom signals the deceased was not revered; his gods and peoples had forsaken him."

Alexa nodded, impressed.

"However, this is speculation."

"How will you determine how old the bones are?" Alexa knew weather and soil were main factors.

"Estimating time of death is not an exact science, you know. First, I will search for artifacts. Bits of clothing, jewelry, remains of a casket. If those are not available, I will transport the bones to the lab and begin chemical testing. Do you suspect foul play?"

"Keep an open mind," Alexa said. The aroma of deli meat, oil, and vinegar pushed her ravenous button.

"Come and get it," Walker bellowed, setting a paper sack and napkins on the conference table.

The team dug in, and Rangiora introduced Dr. Robertova to Trimble, McNamara, Cooper, and Walker.

"Have a sandwich," said Trimble, offering her the white paper bag.

The doctor declined. "I shall go check into my motel and be back first thing in the morning."

As they sat around chewing, Walker filled them in on what happened after they left the island.

"Coop used a rod and trawling hook to snag what turned out to be a sleeping bag halfway down the cliff," he said, admiration in his voice. "Looked like she was reeling in a big shark."

Cooper's mouth turned slightly upward.

"Where did the rod come from?" Trimble asked.

"Herera's shack," Walker answered, his voice coated with pride. "I remembered seeing it when we were there." He stuffed the last of his sub into his mouth and wiped his hands.

"So you contaminated more evidence?" McNamara growled.

Walker, stunned, stopped chewing.

"Shove it," Rangiora said to McNamara. "Good call, I'd say."

Alexa, reviewing her notes, liked the way Rangiora defended

his junior officer. She had just taken a large bite of roast beef, lettuce, tomato, cheese, and roll when she read the words *mau rākau* and thought of those certificates hanging in Dittmer's office. She chewed and swallowed. "Anyone know what"—she knew she would mispronounce them—"m-a-u r-a-k-a-u is?"

Cooper looked surprised. "*Mau rākau?*"

Alexa nodded.

"It means to bear weaponry." Cooper stared at her. "It's Maori martial arts with spears and clubs."

As the DI walked in, Alexa remembered the deft way Dittmer handled the greenstone club from the glass case.

"There's a sammie left, Senior," Rangiora said.

"No thanks." Horne, all business, walked up to the corkboard. "Ms. Glock?"

Alexa choked down another bite, imagined pepper in her teeth, and hobbled to the board. She needed a swig of water.

"I had a busy afternoon," she started and then stopped. Everyone in the room had had a busy afternoon. "I met with Rawiri Wright, the curator of Rotorua Museum, about looting and selling antiquities. He assured me he didn't deal with looters but his predecessor, a man named William Dittmer, might have."

"Wait. What are you going on about?" McNamara interrupted, his mouth full. "You're wasting time."

"Let Glock—" Horne began to say.

"I dropped in on Mr. Dittmer at his antiques shop on Tarangi Street." Alexa didn't need the DI to run interference. "There are two greenstone clubs in his shop. He argued for increasing the museum's collection, and I believe he practices Maori martial arts." She looked toward Officer Cooper and nodded.

"I followed him when he left his shop and was able to listen to a meeting he had with a man named Philip. Dittmer told Philip he had a whalebone spear, greenstone clubs, *and* a skull."

"A skull?" Rangiora interrupted. "Like the one missing from the bones you tripped over?"

"Well, we can't be sure it's missing until we go back and properly search. But Dittmer's buddy mentioned an overseas buyer."

"Slimy bastards," McNamara said. "Stealing from the Maoris."

"What connects Dittmer to Koppel?" Horne asked.

"Gotta be the money," Trimble replied. "That secret bank account."

"That cashier's check from the account. Who was it made out to?" Horne asked.

Trimble searched his notes. "Wei Zhong. Found him. He's an engineer in town. Works at Concrete Answers. Koppel paid him a deposit to fix the cracked foundation at his house."

"Are you having me on?" McNamara bellowed. "Who risks his jolly good life for home repairs?"

Alexa remembered something and cleared her throat. Everyone turned to stare.

"Dittmer mentioned his supplier had an accident and would no longer be able to assist them."

The room hushed, the team digesting more than sandwiches.

"This Dittmer chap. He could be our man," Trimble said. "Did you tape the conversation?"

"No. Events happened too quickly," Alexa explained.

"Sounds like a smuggling ring," the DI said. "More than one person is involved. Herera either got in the way or was contributing."

"So you don't know who Dittmer was talking to?" Rangiora asked.

"I got a good look at him." *All of him.* "My hunch is that this Philip is connected to an auction house." She checked her notes. "He mentioned 'being busy at the house' and a catalog." She looked at the printout Dittmer had supplied. "Bailey & Barre Auction House. In Auckland."

"Where did this meeting take place?" Trimble asked. "How were you able to listen in?"

"The Polynesian Spa," Alexa replied, ready for what all. "In a private spa. I booked the spa next door and heard the conversation."

"Why didn't you call us?" Rangiora said, scowling. "You aren't a detective."

"I should have."

"You got balls, I'll give you that," McNamara said.

"Ms. Glock got a photo. Would you share?" Horne wasn't asking; he was commanding.

Alexa pulled the photo up and handed it to Rangiora. As the phone made the rounds, Alexa watched the reactions. Rangiora looked at her with disbelief. McNamara shook his head. "Pervs, eh?" When it got to Walker, he squawked, "Bare arses? I'm supposed to ask a suspect to bare his bum?"

Cooper was the one who noticed and enlarged the man's left cheek. She handed the cell back to Rangiora.

"Mr. Spa has a tat," he said, studying it. "Tiki man."

The team formed a plan, including putting a tail on Dittmer, and dispersed.

Alexa dashed after Trimble as he left the room. "Detective?" she called.

"I tried to find you earlier." He waited for her to catch up.

"What did you find out about the night janitor?"

Trimble opened his folder right in the hallway. "Carl Rogers has a record," he said. "Possession of a controlled substance and drunk driving."

"Are you kidding?" Alexa said. "And he works at a police station?"

"He did three months at Mount Edens Corrections Facility. He's part of a recidivism reduction program for nonviolent offenders. Provide jobs for ex-cons, and they're less likely to..."

"Yeah, yeah. Less likely to return to prison."

Trimble frowned.

"Sorry. Go on."

"I spoke with his boss. The guy said Rogers was showing up, doing a good job. He works five nights a week from six until midnight." He paused. "Think he was your face in the window?"

"Could have been. Was he in the station when Jenny was attacked?" Alexa asked. "And have you spoken with him?"

"Not on the list. He'll be coming on duty in a few minutes. I'll talk with him then. I didn't want to spook him into not showing."

"Good thinking. Have you checked his phone records?"

"On it. Waiting on the phone company release."

Part of the plan the team formed was for Alexa to identify Philip via mug shots on the off chance he had a record. Her eyes blurred and her stomach rumbled as she munched the second half of her sandwich and studied an online parade of defiant or desperate faces.

No luck.

Next, she scrutinized the Bailey & Barre Auction House website, but the only names revealed were those of the owners.

Walker stopped by, looking tired, his ginger hair tousled and an oil stain marring his uniform shirt. "Any luck?"

"No."

"Senior said for us to head to Auckland first thing. To check out the auction house and see if we can find your man. Meet me at the station at six a.m."

"You're sure?" Two hours ago, the DI had told her she was restricted to the lab.

"Yeah nah."

—

The cottage felt like a long-lost friend as she unlocked the door at half past eight. After a shower, three ibuprofen, and donning comfy yoga pants, Alexa poured a glass of wine and felt fortified to call her brother, check in, ask about her nephews, fill him in on her decision to stay longer in this isolated island country.

She had never been close to Charlie, but Alexa had been trying to do better in the past couple of years. To forgive and forget. He was always willing to talk—mostly about the boys—but never initiated contact.

Charlie didn't remember their mother like Alexa did. He had only been three when she died. Whereas Alexa resented her stepmother for taking Dad's attention and Mom's place, Charlie, at nine, had latched onto Rita with an intensity and desperation that had unnerved Alexa, made her realize she had pretty much ignored the guy and he was desperate for attention. But still, his leeching had been painful.

When the accident happened, Charlie had sided with their stepmother. "It wasn't her fault, Lexi."

Little traitor.

Alexa started to dial but then realized it was the middle of the night in North Carolina.

Loneliness hit hard. She thought of Jeb and wondered if he had found someone else. She had strung him along, happy to be part of a couple when it suited. Her blunt honesty had freed him.

What was it, though, that kept her from committing? Exhausted, she tried losing herself in a dated copy of *New Zealand Women's Weekly* and a glass of wine, but her mind rebelled, insisting on juggling the island, the skull, the antiques store, the spa, Bruce Horne.

Throwing the magazine down, Alexa took the wine and went to sit on the porch, elevating her knee on the railing.

Emboldened by surviving the day, she felt no fear in the cool darkness and let the river music and melancholic hoot of a nearby owl soothe her soul. What had Horne said? "If you can hear a ruru, you are safe."

Safe.

She sat and thought. Tomorrow, she would return to Kauri Antiques and buy a teacup. A royal-blue teacup. Lifting fingerprints from fine china was a breeze. With a plan in mind, she went inside, locked the door, and headed to bed.

—

"No, no," Charlie screamed, trying to reach her.

"Back. Get back," Rita yelled, holding the kettle, looking down at Alexa, who had slid across the kitchen floor in woolen socks, knocking into her.

"No. Noooo."

The ambulance was a year away. Rita held her writhing body, refused to let her peel away her shirt, and pressed cold, wet towels against her back.

"Let me go. Help me."

Screaming woke Alexa at 3:38 a.m. She was boiling. Covered in sweat. Jerking off the covers, she staggered to the window, yanked it open, gulped cool fresh air.

Chapter Thirty-One

Three days earlier, she had driven to Auckland to lift prints from Fanny. Now she was riding shotgun, retracing the same route. Officer Walker, who was driving, had had two cups of coffee and the unmarked cruiser's heater going when she had arrived at 5:50 a.m.

"Lots of sugar, no cream. Hope that's good."

Alexa's heart sank, but she smiled. "Thank you."

"Did you grow up here?" she asked as they reached the outskirts of Rotorua. The sweetened black coffee was more palatable than she imagined, and the sun, rising behind a hill, was blushing the sky pink. Her eyes were sandpapery; getting back to sleep after her nightmare had been impossible.

Dad, Charlie, the doctors, her therapist, all had claimed that Alexa had slid across the slick linoleum into her stepmother and it was an accident that a stream of boiling water poured across her back, melting her shirt into her skin, her piercing screams rending the air.

But maybe...

Never again would she sit in a hot spa pool.

Walker's reply whipped her back.

"Yeah, eh." He cast a shy glance at Alexa. "I left for a year to attend police academy in Auckland. Other than that—been here all my life."

Alexa asked more to stay awake. The warmth from the heater, the lull of tires on pavement, the smeary morning sky were tugging at her eyelids. Walker, as she suspected, was not married and had no current girlfriend. He rented a flat with a mate, pulled for the All Blacks, but he didn't ask any questions of his own, and after twenty minutes, Alexa quit fighting and let her lids drop. Walker turned on the radio, volume low, pale fingers tapping the steering wheel, and by Matamata, she was out.

The stop-and-go traffic of Auckland jolted her awake. She was startled to see it was almost nine. Rubbing her eyes, she wondered if this trip would pay off. Would she discover the identity of Tat Man? Would she recognize him with his clothes on?

"We're meeting with Karsh Bailey," Walker told her as they pulled into the Bailey & Barre parking lot. "He's the owner."

"Does he know we're from the police?" Alexa asked, flipping down the visor and studying her reflection in the wee mirror: raccoon eyes stared back. She found the gloss in her tote and applied a layer to her lake-chapped lips. At least her hair was behaving.

"Yes," Walker said, slipping into a space. "DI Horne set up the meeting. We're looking into the buying and selling of Maori artifacts. But Senior didn't mention Chief Rangituata's tomb or the murders."

Alexa popped a couple of painkillers, washed them down with cold sweet coffee, and followed Walker toward the warehouse-style building. Short bushes lined the white painted concrete exterior. Double glass doors with *Bailey & Barre Auction House, circa 1918* in ornate letters welcomed visitors. Walker held the door for Alexa. A visitor's desk to the right was staffed by a young woman in bright-red lipstick.

Alexa surveyed the lobby as Walker headed toward the receptionist. An art show jazzed up the interior. Paintings, hanging from exposed pipes or set on easels, were in rows. Alexa was drawn to a large oil of a Maori family collecting clams on a beach, the splashes of color in the ragged clothes worn by the two children and parents, their flaxen bags heavy with their bounty, the sea green and alive. She'd like to invest in art, something peaceful and colorful like this, someday and examined the card under the painting: "Lot 35, P. McIntyre, starting bid $35,000."

So much for that idea.

"Ms. Glock?" Walker stood at the end of the row. "Miss Delaney is ready to show us to Mr. Bailey's office."

She left the painting and followed Walker and the receptionist down a hallway to an office.

"How can I help you?" A fit man in his seventies stood from behind a walnut desk and extended his hand to Walker. His black silk suit hung tailor-made. Walker shook his hand and introduced himself.

"And this is Ms. Glock from our Forensics Department."

"Forensics?" Bailey asked. His withdrew his hand.

"A pleasure to meet you," Alexa said, wishing for a more elegant appearance. In the predawn darkness, she had pulled on rumpled khakis, a black V-neck sweater, and damp Keds. She pulled out her notebook.

Walker took charge. "Mr. Bailey, can you give us a description of your auction house and how many people you employ?"

"Please sit." Bailey pointed to a pair of leather guest chairs, and they did as suggested. "I was told by your inspector that you had questions about Maori artifacts?" He sat behind his desk.

"Yes. But first we need information about your company," Walker said.

"My great-grandfather started the auction house in Wellington in 1918. We're New Zealand's largest auction house and run by third-generation family members. We opened our Auckland house fifteen years ago. I'm head here, and my sister runs Wellington."

"How many people do you employ?" Walker asked.

Mr. Bailey considered the question. "We have auctioneers,

valuers, buyers, a catalog division, insurance personnel, marketers, a warehouse, and shipping department." He tapped his fingers on the polished desk. "And our receptionist."

He's stalling, Alexa decided. He should know how many people work for him.

"Perhaps twenty full-time and ten more part-time."

"We'll need names and numbers," Walker replied.

"What on earth for?"

"The names and numbers are for verification," Walker said.

Bailey looked perplexed. "To verify what?"

"Are your sales mostly from buyers in New Zealand or international?" Alexa asked.

"Both," Bailey said, turning shrewd eyes toward her. "Our auctions attract many overseas buyers. They can look at a catalog and bid electronically."

"Sight unseen?" Alexa couldn't fathom buying expensive art from a catalog.

"Buyers trust us."

"We'd like a copy of your current catalog," Alexa said.

Bailey perked up. "We have several." He whipped around in his swivel chair and opened a drawer of the credenza. "These are our latest."

The catalogs were large and glossy: Fine Wine and Spirits, Estate Jewelry, Antiques and Decorative Arts, and New Zealand Art.

Alexa scooped up Antiques and Decorative Arts while Walker resumed the questioning. "Is it true that your auction house specializes in Maori artifacts?"

"We have evolved into the premier Maori and Pacific artifact purveyors," Bailey said, puffing up. "There is worldwide appreciation of this unique art."

"Do you have Maori artifacts in the warehouse now?" Walker asked.

"We almost always have a supply. Is there something specific you are interested in?"

"Could we take a look at what's in house now?" Walker asked.

"I can arrange that." Bailey did not hesitate. "Meanwhile, browse the catalog. Pages twenty through twenty-four, I believe." Bailey punched a number on his desk phone. "Sheryl, can you locate Lot Seventeen and have it brought to the display room?"

Alexa turned to the pages Bailey mentioned. Pages twenty and twenty-one were headed Textiles. Headbands, flax-woven pouches, *poi* balls, and a feather cloak were artfully displayed. The next couple of pages included two war clubs—one of black stone and the other of whale bone. There was only one greenstone item: a tiki pendant.

"Is it unusual to have so few items made of greenstone?" she asked.

Bailey looked surprised. "Well, yes, as a matter of fact. Greenstone is becoming harder to procure since the Pounamu Vesting Act of 1997. The South Island tribe now owns all mining rights, and the *iwi* have chosen to rest the land, so to speak."

"Does that affect the price of greenstone?"

Bailey nodded. "The price of greenstone has skyrocketed."

"Where do you obtain your Maori artifacts?" Alexa asked.

"Mostly from private collectors and sometimes from estate sales."

"Are you able to provide proper documentation for the items you sell?"

"Not every item has a discoverable provenance. For the ones that do, I am registered with the Ministry for Culture and Heritage to sell and trade. Certain artifacts, like the digging stick with the carved head on page twenty-three."

Alexa looked.

"That item is registered. That's what the asterisk and numbers indicate. It's fifty years or older and has cultural significance, so it cannot leave the country unless written permission is given from the Culture and Heritage committee. A buyer also has to be registered."

"What about this knife?" Alexa asked, pointing to another item on the same page. The wooden blade had serrated teeth embedded in it. "Are those shark's teeth?"

"That's a *māripi*. And yes, those are shark's teeth."

"Is it a weapon?" Alexa asked, a chill zip-lining down her spine.

"It was used for butchering whales, sharks, dogs"—he paused—"sometimes human bodies."

The chill did another run.

"Is it registered?"

"No," Bailey said, squirming enough to make his leather chair squelch. "Our valuers classified it a reproduction."

"Are registered items harder to sell?"

"Yes and no. Certainly, they are harder to buy for our overseas investors. But often buyers seek the authenticity registration provides."

"Does the committee do spot checks on everything you acquire?" Alexa was trying to grasp the concept of registered and nonregistered artifacts and how that might tie in with loot pillaged from Rangituata's tomb.

"Occasionally. But I follow proper procedure, so spot checks are not a concern. Tell me what this investigation is about."

"Who determines which artifacts must be registered?" Alexa ignored his request.

"Our valuers." Mr. Bailey sprang up, buttoned his suit jacket, and moved to the door. "Let's see if Lot Seventeen is ready."

"One more question," Alexa said. "What can you tell us about international smuggling rings? For Maori artifacts?"

"Every transaction Bailey & Barre makes is aboveboard. I don't deal in black markets." He opened the door and waited.

Walker and Alexa followed him into the corridor. "Where are your restrooms?" Alexa asked.

Bailey pointed the way down the corridor. "We'll be in here," he said, stopping at a door that was cracked.

After popping in and out of the ladies' Alexa continued down the hallway, which turned to the right and dead-ended at a door marked Shipping Department. She tried the handle; it opened to a cavernous room packed with shelved boxes and furniture.

A woman was operating a forklift, deftly sliding a box into its nook. Alexa backed out. Bailey & Barre was big business.

She didn't have much time and was about to try another door when she heard a voice.

"Miss?"

Damn-it-all.

Alexa turned. The receptionist, Sheryl, was approaching. "Thank goodness," Alexa said. "I forgot which way to go." She considered the young woman. "I was looking for Philip's office."

"Philip Milchner?" The receptionist scrunched up her forehead.

Alexa nodded.

"Mr. Milchner is in Napier."

"When will he return?" Alexa asked.

"I'm not sure," she said, puzzled. "Probably tomorrow. We have the lot you requested. Follow me."

"I'll need Philip's phone number," Alexa continued.

"It's on the list I gave your boss."

Boss? She followed Sheryl into the display room. Lot Seventeen was arranged on two tables. She gave the artifacts a cursory look and walked over to Walker, who was poking the shark tooth knife like a kid. Mr. Bailey was talking on his phone.

"I got the name," Alexa whispered.

"How?" Walker mouthed back, but there was no time to explain. Bailey had joined them.

Alexa asked, "What can you tell me about Philip Milchner? Your employee who is in Napier today?"

Bailey looked surprised. "Mr. Milchner?"

Alexa nodded. "What's his job title?"

"Philip Milchner is one of my valuers."

"How long has he been with your house?" Alexa asked. "And what's he doing in Napier?"

"Why? It's none…"

"Answer Ms. Glock's questions," Walker said. The *māripi* was in his hands.

"Please put that down."

Walker complied.

"Mr. Milchner started three months ago. He came to us with impeccable recommendations," Bailey said. "Some art deco items have come up for sale at the Masonic Hotel in Napier. Philip is taking a look-see. He left for Napier from Rotorua, where he had business yesterday. Why are you interested?"

Bingo.

"What business in Rotorua?"Alexa and Walker asked simultaneously.

"An estate sale, I believe." Bailey's eyes darted between Walker's and Alexa's. "Why are you interested in my employee? Is there something I should know?"

"We can't share information at this time, Mr. Bailey," Alexa said. "Do you know where Mr. Milchner was on Saturday?"

"I don't know what my employees do on the weekend, unless it's work related."

"Do you know William Dittmer? He has an antiques store in Rotorua." Alexa asked.

Bailey blinked. "That name sounds familiar."

"He was the former curator of the museum in Rotorua," Alexa added.

"And let go, right? I remember now. Some improprieties, I believe. I haven't had the pleasure."

"Do you have a photo of Mr. Milchner?" Walker interjected.

Mr. Bailey's forehead wrinkled. "If Mr. Milchner is doing something illegal, I have a right to know. My company's reputation is at stake."

"This is routine questioning," Alexa said. "You've been very cooperative."

Bailey relaxed. "I believe there was a photo of him in the

Aucklander last month." He fished out his phone and spoke to Sheryl again.

A few minutes later, the receptionist appeared with a copied newspaper photo. The caption read: "Philip Milchner, valuer for auction dynasty Bailey & Barre, nets $40,000 for rare book collection." A man in ball cap and sunglasses was looking away from the camera.

Alexa brought the paper closer, studied it. Maybe it was Spa Guy. Hard to tell with clothes on. "Is Mr. Milchner bald under that cap?"

"Why, yes," Mr. Bailey said. "Bald as an egg. He earned a sizable bonus for that sale."

After advising Sheryl and Mr. Bailey to not contact Milchner, Walker and Alexa thanked them and left.

Were Dittmer and Milchner partners? Had one or both of them killed Paul Koppel? Ray Herera?

Walker took a photo of the news clipping with his iPhone, sent it to headquarters, and then called DI Horne from the parking lot, filling him in and suggesting someone intercept Milchner. Alexa was listening. "I don't agree," she said loudly. Walker frowned and kept talking. She leaned closer and yelled toward the cell, "I don't agree, sir."

She could hear Horne speaking, and suddenly Walker thrust the phone in her face. "Here!"

"Bruce? I mean DI?"

"So you're calling the shots now?"

"Of course not. It's just a suggestion. We might learn more by tailing Milchner than by questioning him. So he doesn't know we're onto him."

"Put Walker back on."

—

They rode in silence for the first hour, Alexa's mind on the teacup. She wanted to get back to that store and buy the teacup. How would she handle it if Dittmer were in the shop? Make up some story about needing a gift. Bridal shower thingy. Did they have bridal showers in New Zealand?

Goodness knows she had been to enough of them in the States, people eyeing her, asking, "When are you getting married, Alexa?" Men were never asked, but a single woman? Fair play. Open season. Who let the dogs out?

Same with baby showers. "Don't you just want one of your own?" some colleague would gush, practically shoving her drooling infant into Alexa's protesting arms.

In a few years, it would be too late to bear a child, which had never bothered her much when it was a choice.

I don't even like kids, remember?

Walker broke her wild goose thread. "You were right. It's better to follow Milchner rather than haul him in. I wish I'd get this police business straight for a change."

"We'll find out which plan DI Horne went for when we get back." A swell of affection for the ginger-headed rookie took her by surprise. "If Bailey is in on the whole thing, he's probably already called Milchner. You did a good job questioning him."

Walker pushed pedal to metal, and the remaining two hours to Rotorua flew in a blur.

—

Bruce Horne was leaving the station as they entered. He looked at his watch and turned around. "I can spare five minutes. Let's talk here." He pointed to the reception bench where Alexa had first met him. Walker filled him in on the details of the visit.

"Good work, Walker." The DI studied the young officer whose cheeks colored. "Go write your report."

He turned to Alexa as Walker hurried away. "I need you to check in with that anthropologist doctor. She's at the morgue. We need cause of death and age of the skeleton. Hurry her up.

She thinks she's writing a dissertation or something. Couldn't get her to comment."

"So you want me to leave the lab again? I thought I was under house arrest." She should have kept her mouth shut.

The DI flushed but was mature enough not to bite. "I'm on my way to Pirongia to meet with the Ministry of Culture representative. He's discovered something of interest."

"I'll head straight to the morgue. What did you do about Milchner?"

"That's my business." He shook his head and left.

Chapter Thirty-Two

A week had passed since Alexa stood in this morgue observing Dr. Hill deconstruct Paul Koppel. His melted face flashed in her mind. Whatever he had done, he had not deserved to be dumped in molten mud.

Dr. Robertova was arguing with someone on her phone. Alexa, dressed in scrubs, booties, and gloves, crossed the room toward the skeleton laid out on a steel cart. No odor of putrefaction or cooked flesh this go; these bones cast an earthy musk.

"Have it ready Thursday," Dr. Robertova demanded and then slid the phone into her pocket. "Imbeciles," she muttered. A surgical mask and a mini recorder dangled from her neck.

The two women looked down at the reconstructed and brushed clean skeleton. The rib cage, laid flat, had long since been capable of expanding and contracting. Two ribs were cracked and, Alexa counted, one pair was missing.

"I've completed the inventory. All bones accounted for except the skull, floating ribs, and three phalanges," Dr. Robertova said. "A complete skeleton is never around when you need one."

Was she cracking a joke? The expert from Auckland was hard to read. "Any artifacts found with the remains?" Alexa asked.

"Some shells and traces of a flax cloak, which I have carefully preserved. Groundwater dissolved most of it. In Maori culture, cloaks are imbued with *taonga* and worn by people of high status. To separate a cloak from the body is said to induce danger."

"Yikes." But wait. Officer Cooper thought this was the grave of a slave, not someone of high status.

"Clothing disguises our flaws but decays and disintegrates more rapidly than that which it disguises, leaving the natural state behind."

Say what?

"How did the bones become exposed?" Alexa asked.

"They were dug up."

"How do you know?" There had been no obvious shovel or trowel marks.

"Impressions had been smoothed over. A dirt pile was covered with sticks. Holes in the area had been refilled, stomped on. Lots of indicators, if you know what to look for."

Was that a dig?

"Your officer took photos of it all." Dr. Robertova shook her head. "There was an impression where the skull had been. Most likely, treasures were taken as well. We will never know the full significance of the loss."

Alexa was angry she had missed obvious signs. The horror of tripping over human remains had clouded professionalism.

"The Ministry of Culture and Heritage representative found a grave marker. A rock with a strange marking. He is searching the area for other graves." Dr. Robertova pulled on her face mask and picked up a wee phalanger. "I am ready to examine the bones."

Alexa looked at the pinkie toe with dismay. One down, two hundred to go. She was itching to stop by Kauri Treasures. "Detective Inspector Horne has just requested sex, age, cause, and time of death. ASAP."

Dr. Robertova looked perturbed. "It is important to be systematic."

"We have a murderer on the loose," Alexa said.

"If you insist."

"Thank you."

The doctor reached for a tape measure and began with the femur Alexa had tripped over. She murmured something about limb length and height into the recorder dangling from her neck and then moved to the pelvic region.

"I can determine the sex with ninety-five percent accuracy," Dr. Robertova said and then looked up at Alexa. "If I had the skull, it would be with ninety-eight percent accuracy."

"Ninety-five percent will do," Alexa said, shivering. The lab seemed to be getting colder and colder.

"The area around the pelvic inlet matches that of a male." Dr. Robertova studied the pelvis with a magnifying glass. She set down the glass and started measuring again. "It's larger, more robust than a female's, and the pubis bone has a triangular shape."

Alexa nodded.

"Look at the iliac." Dr. Robertova stroked the left hip bone. "It's more vertical. And the coccyx…" She leaned over to examine the tailbone. "The coccyx is not an obtuse angle like a female's is for childbirth."

"So…male," Alexa said. "How old when he died?"

"I cannot be precise without proper equipment." Dr. Robertova moved the magnifying glass back up to the ribs and studied them for a moment. "The rib walls are thinning and irregular." She moved to the patella. "No obvious signs of arthritis. Early to midforties, I would estimate."

"How long have the bones been buried?" Alexa prodded.

"I can't say. Bone color is not an indicator. This brown hue comes more from soil and climate than age. I will use carbon dating and nitrogen levels in the lab back in Auckland."

"But from your best estimate, this is not a recent skeleton?"

"Recent?" Dr. Robertova had picked up the pinkie toe bone again.

"Can you take a stab?"

"It is older than fifty years."

"Thank you. What about cause of death?" Alexa said.

"Please give me an hour."

DI Horne's cell went directly to voicemail when Alexa called. She imagined him in the cave on Pirongia, under the spell of glowworms and missing treasures. She relayed the findings and then spent the next hour examining tarsals and tibias with the doctor, first by hand and then by X-ray. In the end, all they discovered was a healed fracture of the tibia. But that was not what had killed the skeleton. That stayed buried in the past.

Chapter Thirty-Three

It was 4:40, and the on-and-off rain was on again when Alexa hurried to her car. Hadn't the sign at the antiques store said open until five? Ignoring her throbbing knee, Alexa drove to Tarangi Street, relieved the cottage umbrella was in the back seat.

From her streetside parking spot, Alexa could see lights and the Open sign on the shop door.

Dittmer didn't know she had followed him yesterday and overheard his conversation with Milchner, yet Alexa was tense; he knew she worked with the police. Word may have gotten to him that she'd been snooping around the auction house, asking questions about his friend, about him. Plus, he knew how to use a greenstone club.

Two men were dead. Alarm bells blared in Alexa's head.

But there wasn't time to call for backup. Alexa took a deep breath, unfurled the umbrella, and ran to the shop.

Jangling bells again. Aged wood and old book mustiness assaulted her olfactories as she leaned the dripping umbrella next to the door and tried not to sneeze.

"Hello," came a faint female voice. "I'll be right with you."

Relief.

Alexa wound cautiously through the narrow passage of

bric-a-brac to the three-tiered display of teacups and saucers. Which one had Dittmer lifted to the light?

"G'day, dear," said a diminutive woman in a floral dress. "I'm about to close, so you'll have to hurry." Ruby lipstick smeared into the bar code lines of her upper lip. Her fluffy white hair looked just like Dittmer's.

"I'm looking for a gift. A teacup. My friend likes the Royal line."

"Royal Chelsea?" the woman asked, her birdlike hand darting toward a violet covered cup.

"No."

"Royal Crown? Royal Albert?"

"Yes. Royal Albert," Alexa said. "Blue."

"Turquoise?" The woman pointed to a blue-edged teacup.

Alexa recognized it and whisked it up by the little handle before the woman could touch it. "My friend will love this," she blurted, her heart pounding.

"Would you like me to wrap it?" The woman held her hand out for the cup.

"No, thank you. I'll take it as is," Alexa said.

"Here's the saucer. Will there be anything else? We have lovely new acquisitions from Haddadine Souk."

"No, thank you. Are you the owner?"

"Oh my," the woman said. "Look at the rain." Water cascaded from the store awning. Turning back to face Alexa, she said, "I help my son two afternoons a week. Or when he goes on buying trips. It's his shop." She wrapped the saucer in tissue and eyed the teacup dangling from Alexa's pinkie.

"Buying trips?" Alexa almost dropped the teacup. "What's hadda…souk?"

"Haddadine Souk? Elegant metal works from the famous bazaars of Marrakesh. Lanterns, teakettles, candlestick holders. My son traveled there recently. Come—I'll show you."

Alexa's pinkie tightened. "Marrakesh? When was he there?"

"Oh—let me think. July, it was. Are you sure I can't wrap that?"

"I have a special gift bag for it," Alexa replied. "How much?"

"Twenty-two dollars." Dittmer's mother started writing a sales slip.

Alexa slipped the cup in a paper bag she had tucked in her tote, fumbled for her wallet, and withdrew cash.

"I hope your friend likes it," Dittmer's mother said and handed her the wrapped saucer.

"I hope so too."

Her heart galloped and her hair dripped. Dittmer had traveled to Marrakesh. Alexa bet the dates coincided with Koppel's trip. Maybe Dittmer was the "investor" Koppel met on the plane, the one Mindy Koppel had mentioned. Had DI Horne filed the warrant for the passenger manifest?

She was about to start the engine when she realized she had left the umbrella in the shop. Should she run back, retrieve it? Dittmer wasn't there. She'd be safe, and the umbrella wasn't hers to lose.

Hard to hear the jangle over the deluge as she pushed the door back open. As she reached for the umbrella, she heard voices, a male's and a female's, and froze. Angry tones rising in crescendo.

From the back.

Should she investigate? An icy raindrop crept down her back. As she took a step deeper into the store, the voices became louder. Nearer.

Someone was coming.

She snatched the umbrella, swirled, and dashed back to the car, locking the doors. From the safety of the car, she dared look toward the shop, and through sheets of rain, a dark figure turned the Open sign to Closed.

She double-checked the locks and started the car, taking off in a jerk. Driving to headquarters, Alexa took deep, slow breaths but couldn't control her shaking. The male voice had been Dittmer's. He may have killed two men and tried to kill Jenny. Had he been watching from the back room? Shivers coursed through her body. The heat, set to high, wasn't helping.

Why had Dittmer's mother said he wasn't there? What had he heard? No matter. What mattered was that she had the teacup to dust for prints. She looked to the passenger seat where the cup was tucked in her tote. Safe. Maybe they matched the duct tape prints she had lifted the day after Jenny was attacked. The secret stash. She wasn't one hundred percent sure the teacup evidence was legally procured, and she didn't want to get anyone's hopes up if the prints didn't match. If they did, she'd run straight to the DI.

Three times, she checked her rearview mirror.

The umbrella now refused to cooperate, so Alexa cursed, chucked it in the back seat and ran into the station lobby, shielding her tote under her sweater. Sharon Welles, slipping on a trench coat, froze at the sight of her.

"Detective Inspector Horne is looking for you," she said, scrutinizing Alexa's drippy hair and lumpy sweater.

"Thanks. I'll run up to his office." Alexa offered her brightest smile and headed for the stairwell.

"He's in a meeting," Welles said to her back. "In the conference room."

Loud voices. Alexa opened the door, slipped inside. Lee Ngawata, the man she had met on Pirongia, was yelling at the DI, while Cooper and Rangiora stood like guard dogs on either side of their boss.

"It is a criminal offense to remove *kōiwi tangata* from a place of burial. You have unleashed danger."

Alexa held her breath.

Ngawata continued to rage. "The Office of Tribal Affairs should have been notified. You had no authority to remove remains from the island. They are *tapu*. You have angered the spirits."

"This is a murder investigation. That is all the authority I need," the DI said, his voice, as usual, calm and steady.

Ngawata, dressed in a black suit, folded his arms across his chest. The swirling tattoos on his face darkened in color like some type of magic.

Horne continued. "The skeleton is being treated with respect and will be returned as soon as our investigation is over. But there were no bones in the cave. The Ministry of Culture rep determined no bones have been in the chief's burial chamber for over two hundred years, although there is evidence of recent disturbance. Someone was looking for them. Were you aware of this?"

A glimmer of a smile appeared on the elder's face.

"Please explain," Horne said.

"It was grand vengeance for an enemy to steal from the tomb of a great chief."

"So enemy tribes looted the cave?" Horne asked. "Centuries ago? And all this time..."

Ngawata ignored him. "A grander revenge was to steal the actual body. Display the skull. Make fish hooks out of the bones."

Alexa and Rangiora's eyes met. The fish hooks in Herera's trunk? Made of human bone?

"To prevent this, remains would be moved, months after an elaborate burial ceremony. The higher the rank, the more the moves."

"Where are the bones now?" the DI asked.

Storm clouds gathered in the chief's eyes. He spoke with gravity. "You tell me."

The men stared at each other. Several moments passed. The silence was explosive. Finally, Horne broke it. "Are you telling me the skeleton we removed was Chief Rangituata's?"

Ngawata barely nodded.

Horne whirled to face Alexa. "Do the doctor's findings confirm this?"

Alexa thought it over: male, forty to fifty years old, buried more than fifty years ago, traces of a cloak. She nodded. "It's possible."

"We had no idea," Horne said. "But a second murder has been committed. There was no time to lift *tapu*. Another life could be at stake."

"A second murder?" Ngawata asked.

"Your island caretaker—his death was not an accident," he replied. "I need your cooperation to find out what happened to him." Horne strode toward the door. "Come with me to the interview room. Officer Cooper will join us."

"Herera was a noble man." Ngawata stood a moment longer. "The spirits had spoken to him. He was preparing to move the chief again." He turned his unblinking snake eyes to Alexa. "You bore witness to *taonga* in spiritual transition."

Alexa flinched.

Ngawata left with Officer Cooper at his side.

Rangiora closed the door and then looked at Alexa again. "What did you bear witness to?"

Unease flitted like an insect around her brain, but Alexa decided it was time to slap it away and trust the senior officer. "When Cooper and I went to the island the first time, Herera and Cooper's uncle had spears and clubs. Maybe that's the *taonga* he's referring to. Maybe they borrowed them from the chief. Played dress-up." She shook her head, trying to absorb it all. "So the tomb has been empty for years?"

Rangiora nodded. "The Culture and Heritage rep wasn't altogether surprised. Relocating skeletons was common. The chief in the cave is urban legend. Must have made the looters mad when they found the cave empty. But how did they find the chief's grave?"

"Someone had to be spying on Herera as he prepared to move the body." She hugged the tote closer to her chest. "Did we ever locate Officer Cooper's uncle?"

Rangiora nodded. "His daughter, Coop's cuz, had a car accident. Taylor Cooper was at the hospital all day and night Saturday. Trimble checked it out. So he couldn't have killed Herera."

"I'm glad," Alexa said. Her clothes were wet, and she was shivering. "Is the cousin okay?"

"Yeah nah. She will be after rehab."

"Gotta check in at the lab," she said.

"You should towel off first," Rangiora said with a nod.

As Alexa walked in, Jenny said in a rush of breath, "I was just about to leave. I don't like being down here alone, even with the guard at the door. I've been busy. One set of prints on the shovel match Herera's."

Alexa stashed the teacup bag on a shelf and followed Jenny to her work station. Evidence was neatly arranged and numbered. She realized Jenny was referring to the shovel taken from Herera's shack.

"The shovel blade matches the marks left where the bones were dug up," Jenny said. She pointed at the photo Rangiora had taken of blade marks in the churned earth.

"That's consistent with information I've learned. He was preparing to move the remains."

Jenny pointed to bags of soil. "The soil collected from Paul Koppel's father-in-law's boat matches soil from Pirongia Island."

"That's strong evidence Koppel had been to Pirongia."

"It gets better," Jenny said, pointing to a large bundle wrapped in plastic. "That's the sleeping bag that was halfway down the cliff on Pirongia. Officer Cooper retrieved it with a fishing hook."

Alexa pulled on disposable gloves and walked over to the bundle. She remembered Walker explaining how Cooper had cleverly fished it up the cliff side.

"Since Herera was smothered and there weren't finger marks around his lips and nose, I figured something soft was used." Jenny, who seemed to forget about heading home, pulled on a pair of gloves too and unwrapped a section of the plastic, exposing blue nylon. "It's a mummy bag. A portion in the top right quadrant has traces of saliva, blood, and tissue. The blood type matched Herera's."

Someone had smothered Herera in his own sleeping bag. The narrow shoulders and hip width of a mummy bag, like a straightjacket, would have made it impossible to fight back. And then he was rolled off the cliff. The bag must have snagged as he slipped out and hurtled toward the water.

Ruthless, this killer. "Excellent work," Alexa said.

Jenny accepted this compliment with a nod. "What I want to know is if I can lift prints from the bag? So we can identify the killer."

"It's hard to secure prints from fabric." Alexa thought for a moment. "It would probably be better if we go for touch DNA. If the killer pressed hard on the fabric, which he did to suffocate Herera, then skin cells would be left behind. Photograph the area first, and then scrape the fabric with a blade. You'll get some fiber and debris, but you'll also get skin cells that you can transfer into a DNA processing tube."

"Do you think the same person who suffocated Herera attacked me?" Jenny asked, studying Alexa.

"If it is, count yourself lucky." A surge of excitement replaced her shivers, warmed her core. The puzzle pieces were starting to fit. "Let's look at the bag together."

The two women worked to photograph and scrape the bag. In thirty minutes, they had collected enough sample to send off for analysis.

"Too bad DNA testing takes so long," Alexa said. In the States, a thirty-day turnaround was considered quick. "Have we gotten Koppel's results yet?"

"Yes. They came in this afternoon. I emailed them to you," Jenny said. "We'll put a rush on this sample. But even with a rush, it takes a week."

Alexa's stomach rumbled. "I'll take a look at Koppel's DNA results. Go home. You've put in a long day."

Jenny didn't resist. "I'll see you in the morning. The guard will walk me to my car."

And then Alexa was alone.

Locking the door made her feel marginally better. At least the strobing fluorescent light in the hallway had been replaced. Alexa decided to look at Koppel's DNA results before dusting the cup. She logged in, noting her hands were shaking, and scanned her email for the report.

Like fingerprints, no two people share identical DNA. The introduction of deoxyribonucleic acid analysis while Alexa was in graduate school had revolutionized forensics. Her professors had been stoked. While fingerprints could be wiped away, criminals often left their twisted ladder genetic makeup behind without knowing. Blood, hair, skin cells, sweat, semen, spit. And now DNA technology was so common that people were using their own spit to trace their roots. Swab your cheek and mail it off to find relatives you never knew existed.

Those ancestry kits were also helping to solve cold cases.

Alexa held her breath and scanned the results, searching for answers to Paul Koppel's murder. What had the real estate agent, councilman, husband, and father gotten himself into? Why risk the Hallmark life, even if money was tight? Those little guys needed their dad.

The analysis was a letdown. The DNA from fingernail scrapings and hair follicles found on the lower part of Koppel's blackened body had been degraded by the heat. Samples from Koppel's teeth and bones only indicated Koppel's DNA, of course. However, there was the cigarette butt found at the mud pots. Saliva transferred from the mouth of the smoker to the butt yielded enough epithelial cells to prove Koppel hadn't smoked it. Who had? Dittmer?

She switched her mind to the art of fingerprinting. Teatime, finally.

Alexa scanned the lab, aware of silence, her own breath gone jagged, and then retrieved the teacup, gingerly removing it from the bag. A pounding at the door made her drop it.

"Shit." Royal Blue was upside down, the handle severed. The door handle jiggled. Flashback. She reached for her cell, in her pocket this time, and then heard a muffled "Ms. Glock."

Trimble. She carefully scooped the cup into the paper bag and stepped to the door.

"Don't blame you for locking it," he said when she opened. "I just finished interviewing the janitor."

Alexa pulled her gloves off and tried to look unruffled.

"Would you believe he got the job as security guard through his parole officer?" Trimble asked.

Alexa shook her head and casually set the paper bag on the desk.

"Sometimes authorities carry these recidivism programs too far." Trimble rushed on. "Rogers said he looked through the lab window Sunday night, said he was checking that the door was secured. That's your face, eh? I asked him about the propped exit door. He denied it. He said the door was locked. But when I mentioned cell phone records, he flat out caved." Trimble thumbed through his ubiquitous stack of papers. "He received a phone call prior to coming to work Sunday evening. Take a stab?"

Cat still had Alexa's tongue.

Trimble looked gleeful. "Kauri Antiques. Your fellow Dittmer's place."

"No way," Alexa said.

"Rogers 'bout cried to Mummy when I showed him the records. He said some dude paid him to leave the door open. Said he never met the guy, just talked to him on the phone. An Aussie."

"Was Rogers working the morning Jenny Liang was attacked?"

"He had worked the night before. His shift ended at midnight," Trimble said. "I have him in a holding cell."

"Have you told DI Horne?"

"Thought you'd want to be the first to know. I'm on my way to tell Horne now," Trimble said, waving goodbye.

"Thanks, Detective."

A celebratory lager would hit the spot. And a medium-rare rib eye and fries. But Alexa knew she was getting ahead of herself. Time to dust the teacup. Hammer a final nail in Dittmer's coffin. The little Alexa knew about fine china was that it was sturdier than it looked, and this piece confirmed it. Only the handle had broken off. The smooth, nonporous surface of the fine china should have preserved the natural oils and sweat Dittmer's fingers left behind.

Black granular powder was best. Alexa was careful not to overapply as she swirled the brush on the side of the cup opposite the handle. In her mind, she saw Dittmer lifting the little beauty to the light, admiring its translucency. Then she thought of how his small hands were skilled in the art of *mau rākau*. Spears. Clubs. Carefully setting it down with trembling fingers, she readied the tape, pressed it to the blackened surface, and lifted.

In "olden days," an examiner would use side-by-side microscopes to compare prints. Alexa had a flicker of nostalgia for the searching of deltas, creases, and scars as she readied the optical comparator for another round. She turned it on and let the National Fingerprint Identification System scan through its millions of prints. An eternity passed in sixty seconds.

Green light.

—

DI Horne was alone. Staring at the corkboard in the conference room.

Where is everyone?

He turned and watched her cross the room. One eyebrow lifted. "Why are you limping?"

"I fell in the cave," she answered brusquely. Any hint of tenderness on Horne's part might unravel her. "Did Trimble tell you about the janitor?"

"He and Rangiora have gone to bring Dittmer in."

"Has anyone located Milchner?"

"He is no longer…a person of interest."

"What?"

"I can't say why. Not at this juncture."

Juncture? Alexa took a deep breath. "I went back to Dittmer's store today to buy a teacup he handled in my presence. The prints I just now lifted from the cup match the duct tape prints from Paul Koppel's body."

Horne stared at her, his mouth dropping. "What?"

"They…"

His eyes went dark, hard. "You went back to the store? By yourself? Without telling anyone?"

He reached into his pocket, and for a crazy moment, she thought he was pulling out a gun. He stabbed numbers on his phone, shouted something about waiting for backup, and then looked at her. "You put yourself and my team in danger. I can't have that." His voice had reverted to steely calm. "Leave. Go home."

Chapter Thirty-Four

Why did I ever come here? Get involved? Alexa fumed as she tore out of the station parking lot. *All the work I've done.*

The rain had tapered to a fine mist, and darkness had descended, cloaking the eerie city, its stinky smells and internal rumblings, in glistening black. Alexa forced herself to slow down and buckle her seat belt.

She'd never been told to "go home" in her entire life. People valued her contributions.

Anger surged through her, came out in a scream, and left when Alexa cracked the window, felt cool air stroke her hot temper.

A sliver of her mind knew the DI was right. She had overstepped boundaries. Again. Why? Was she trying to impress Bruce Horne? If so, her plan had backfired.

Big time.

At the northern tip of the lake, as she turned onto Okere Falls Road, Alexa was startled by car lights in the rearview mirror. The road was usually deserted. Keeping the same distance behind, the car turned too. *Probably Sarah or Stevie Ingall.* The hair on the back of her neck stood despite her reasoning. For a long mile, the car kept its distance. To see what would happen, instead of making the final turn onto Trout River Road, Alexa continued straight. To who knows where. In the mirror, she watched the car turn.

Relief.

It *had* been one of the Ingalls.

After half a mile, Okere Falls Road turned gravel. It took ages to find a driveway in which to turn around, and once she did, Alexa resumed fuming. She had several days left on the Trout Cottage rental agreement, but maybe she'd leave early. Head to Auckland. Contact Mr. Red Sneakers at the forensics lab.

No other cars on winding Trout River Road. Or pulled off on the narrow shoulder. Alexa relaxed and pulled into her driveway. The car lights lit the empty area in front of the cottage. Something long and fast skittered away at the beam's periphery—a stoat, probably. Alexa had read about these out of control weasel-like predators—killing far more than needed, especially baby birds, to satisfy hunger.

And purposefully introduced. People are idiots.

Cutting the engine, she stepped out of the car. "Get the hell out," she growled into the darkness. Slamming the door, she wondered what was happening back at the station. Had they found Dittmer? It was torture not knowing.

She listened for a moment. Silence except for river burble and an engine ping. No hooting ruru or chirping bird. She walked across the drive to the porch.

Hadn't she left the porch light on? Why was she so reckless? And hadn't Bruce said the absence of the ruru's hooting was a warning?

Unlocking the front door and pushing it open, Alexa tossed keys and tote on the bookcase.

Reaching for the light switch, a sudden crash from the bedroom paralyzed her hand. A black shape came barreling at her. She whipped around and ran back out, slamming the door. Dashing to the car, she realized she had no keys. She dodged the Toyota and sprinted toward the river path, ignoring knee pain, hopping over a shrub, and slipping on the wet bank, landing on her butt.

Flipping and rising on primal adrenaline, Alexa caught a flash of illumination as the cottage porch light flicked on and then off, followed by crunching gravel.

Someone was after her.

She hurtled blindly toward the river, glad for the inky blackness of the sweater she had thrown on this morning. The crunch of footsteps dissolved to silence. The intruder was now on grass.

Maybe she could hide and call for help. She felt the outline of her phone pressing against her groin.

River rumble deepened as she neared the track, reached it, veered left, toward the Ingalls' home a quarter mile away. Accelerating, Alexa splashed through puddles, her mind a tornado, her body responding to coursing endocrine. She ran and ran, cutting corners at each bend, scraping wet foliage, eyes darting, ears straining. The river roar was intensifying, the seven-meter falls screaming beside the path, drowning the sound of her heavy breathing, her pursuer.

The path. The side path to the Ingalls' house. Safety. If she could reach it.

Was she still being chased?

Unarmed, alone, she had become prey. She thought suddenly of the stoat, its lethal cunning and stealth, and abruptly halted and darted off path, river side, slipping behind the tall harakeke that reminded her of the bamboo in her Raleigh yard, careful not to step too close to the edge, the river rushing by twenty feet below.

Huffing. Statue still. No moonlight. A crunch. Footsteps running by. A flash of white.

Dittmer.

She held her breath. Dogs barked.

Iris and Echo.

No.

Her damn phone.

She pressed her pocket to stifle the sound. Surely, the roar of the falls had drowned out the ringtone. Pawing. Pressing. Praying.

"I heard that," came a shout. Then closer. "Come out." Dittmer's voice penetrated the thunderous falls.

A rush of air.

Flax to Alexa's right was beheaded.

Whirr.

Foliage to her left decapitated. Suddenly, Dittmer was in front of her, holding a machete—no, a Maori club—inches from her rib cage, his eyes bulging, his tongue flickering. To her horror, the club vanished in the air and then suddenly was at her throat.

"One thrust and your jugular is severed."

The coldness of the greenstone against her naked neck jolted instinct to survive, and she lurched backward.

"I should have killed your lab friend when I had the chance." Alexa involuntarily lurched farther back at Dittmer's words.

Too close. A foot hung over the abyss.

She lunged sideways, into more flax. "But you got Koppel," Alexa shouted, now on her knees.

"Koppel was my golden ticket to the island. He jumped at the chance for a little excitement and, well, payment, of course."

Alexa could not see his face, those crazed eyes, just disembodied white hair.

"You lured him to the mud pots," she yelled.

Flax and ferns above her fell to the ground, sliced from the stalks. "A man who regrets his own actions is too dangerous. A liability. Such a shame."

Alexa crawled back until one foot slipped over the edge and then the other. She was hanging above the falls, digging ten fingers into earthy ledge. Her right foot kicked into roots and rock, and she hauled herself up over the ledge and sprang up perpendicular, through the thicket, swordlike leaves slashing exposed skin, and ran until her sidling intersected another path, a different path. Confused for a moment, Alexa realized this path must lead to the cave. The cave Bruce had promised to show her. The cave closed because a tourist had slipped to her death.

Dittmer's voice filtered through the river racket. "I watched you at the store today." The voice floated, followed her. "Where's the pretty teacup?" A maniacal laugh.

Alexa bounded down the narrower path, ducking and dodging limbs and leaves, tripping on a root, falling hard. Her already injured knee hit a rock; she bit her tongue not to scream and scrambled onward on all fours, walls of rock closing in on either side, her hands groping wet moss and ferns, her eyes latching onto green lights, little green lights down low, leading the way.

Titiwai. Glowworms. Light of the enduring world, Cooper had said.

She stood up, crouched, and followed the emerald dots through a slippery gap. The green points disappeared around a turn, dot to dot leading her to safety. The cave. A Do Not Enter sign was hammered into the ground, and a rope hung across a slim entrance. She ducked below it and stumbled inward, turning sideways to slip inside, joining the spirits of Maori women and children hiding within the womb of Mother Earth from marauding warriors, hiding from pain and torture, from boiling water and stepmothers with hardened eyes. A thrashing. Dittmer was passing, hadn't noticed the green lights, missed the turnoff, and was speeding down the path to the falls, the one she had explored on her first run along the Kaituna.

He would turn around as soon as he saw it dead-ended. That the platform was empty. A plank into an abyss.

She pulled her phone out, saw one bar, and stabbed 111. "Help," she screamed into it. "Okere Falls."

"What is your emergency? This connection—"

The phone screen went blank. Alexa thrust it back in her pocket and made a decision: No hiding. No being a victim… again. She backed out of the crevice, pried the wooden Do Not Enter sign out of the ground, and crept toward the falls.

The roar. The roar of foamy whitewater dropping seven meters deafened her approach, her heart, the pounding in her ears. Dittmer was climbing the three steps to the platform when he spotted her, his mouth opening in surprise.

"Why did you kill Herera?" she shouted, halting.

Dittmer stepped onto the platform and turned, looming above her, the club held at an upward slant. Rain started, sudden, heavy. "A fool," he screamed. "Hoarding treasures to keep them safe. I saw him watching me from the *pā*. Had to return and roll him off the cliff like the munted drunk he was. And now you." With a guttural war cry, he leaped the three steps from the platform, thrashing the greenstone club like a blade, his eyes popping madly out of their sockets, his magnified body flying at her.

The wooden sign sliced the air, hitting the tip of the club with a clack before Alexa knew she had swung. The war weapon arced backward out of Dittmer's wet hand, suspended between days to come and days swallowed up, landed, clattered across the slick platform, hovered over the edge, balanced between earth and water.

Alexa swung again, hitting air, and watched, dismayed, as the warning sign flew from her cold grip and whirled through space. Her weapon. Gone.

Dittmer scrambled back, pulled himself up the platform, his hot desire for greenstone blinding him to anything but greed when Alexa rammed into him. They slid across the wet platform, Alexa clawing for traction on slimy wood, Dittmer breaking through the flimsy railing, his white hair disappearing into detonating darkness.

And then she was alone in the rain.

Chapter Thirty-Five

Deep in an armchair, Iris and Echo on either side, a mug of hot tea warming her hands, Alexa explained again the series of events between leaving the station (or being *ordered* to leave) and banging on Sarah Ingall's front door. DI Horne's eyebrows were bunched, his blue eyes gone navy as he stood looking down at her, waiting for her to finish. Rangiora rocked on the balls of his feet beside him.

"Good on ya," Rangiora interrupted. "We heard him come after you. You left your mobile on."

"I what?" She sat straight. The sound of crashing water still filled her head.

"That was smart, eh. We heard Dittmer say he rolled Herera off the cliff. 'Course he didn't mention suffocating him first. Minor detail."

Her cell was still on when she stuffed it back in her pocket. She sank deeper into the chair, let it support her full weight. Her shoulders, up near her ears in a stiff hunch, eased downward. She wouldn't have to defend her actions.

Rangiora held up a plastic evidence bag. Inside, catching the light from the gas fire Sarah had lit, glinted the greenstone war club. "It was just hanging there, over the edge practically, like water over the brim of a cup. Miracle it didn't drop. Bet it will match Jenny's wound."

Alexa's mouth parched as she stared. Dittmer had attempted to demolish her skull with it. She averted her eyes, sloppily sipped tea.

"Your bedroom window was wide open," Rangiora burst on. "That's how Dittmer got in."

With a jolt, she remembered her nightmare, thrusting the window open in the middle of the night, gasping for cool air.

"The room was tossed. His car was past your driveway, tucked into the woods."

"He was searching for the teacup." Alexa's grip tightened on the mug, the steam and scent doing little to assuage her tremors. Iris knew and pressed her muzzle firmly, warmly on Alexa's thigh.

Horne took over. "Emirates Airline confirmed Dittmer sat next to Koppel on the Dubai-Wellington leg from Marrakesh. That's how they met and hatched their scheme."

Alexa shook her head at Paul Koppel's bad luck and weak character. "Any sign of Dittmer?"

"It's impossible to reach the river from the platform. Just sheer cliff down to a narrow sluice," the DI replied. "The search and rescue team are stringing a wire net across the river downstream of the rapids."

"Is there a chance Dittmer survived?" Alexa asked, her voice cottonmouth hoarse.

"Slim," Horne said. "If no body is snagged in the net, we'll start a search at dawn." He looked over at Sarah, who was hovering at the doorway. "Can Ms. Glock spend the night here?"

"Of course," Sarah said. Iris barked, making Alexa jerk. Hot tea burned through her wet khakis.

Even drained of energy, Alexa bristled at Bruce making plans for her. But she didn't want to go back to Trout Cottage.

Ever.

"Come to the station in the morning," he said. "We'll finalize your statement." His eyes caught and locked with hers, sending a spark daring her to flicker.

Alexa turned away.

—

Dittmer's body was snagged in the net before daybreak; cause of death had been blunt force trauma, his head smashed against rocks in the gorge. He was posthumously charged with Paul Koppel's and Ray Herera's deaths and Jenny's attack.

After giving her statement the next morning, Alexa had driven through pouring rain to Trout Cottage only to pack and thank Sarah Ingall, who, along with Iris, graciously went with her. "These are for you," Sarah said, handing her a pair of greenstone trout-shaped earrings. "Do you always get tangled in messes?"

Alexa thought of the tedious lab work she'd done the past couple of years in Raleigh, all teeth, no bite, her safe fellowship in Auckland teaching future odontologists, and laughed, surprising herself.

"Hardly." She hugged Sarah and then bent down and scratched behind Iris's ear, even though she didn't like dogs.

Chapter Thirty-Six

A week later, in an Auckland coffee shop, Alexa was poring over the *New Zealand Herald*. Mud pot murder news had faded. "Maori Celebrate as Chief's Skull Returned" was today's front page news. According to the article, an international smuggling sting, headed by Customs Agent P. E. Wilkie, confiscated a skull in Singapore and returned it to Rotorua during freak gale force winds. There was a photograph of Agent Wilkie. Alexa looked.

And then looked again.

Still in ball cap and shades, Agent Wilkie looked suspiciously like Philip from the spa.

Bare butt guy was an undercover customs agent.

Alexa laughed and went back to reading the article. The distinctive facial patterns, smoked to permanency two and a half centuries ago, made identification easy. Respected Maori leader Lee Ngawata was quoted: "A traditional ceremony will reacquaint our ancestral chief with his *pito* and *whenua* (umbilical cord and placenta) so that his spirit can sleep the sweet slumber of eternity and then the gales will cease."

Reunification with the rest of the skeleton and ultimate burial would take place in a secret location.

Alexa sipped her flat white coffee and considered Ngawata's

words: only then will the gales cease. She whipped out her phone to check Rotorua weather: severe nor'easters battering Bay of Plenty area; many without power.

A gust of wind blew the café door open. Three hours north of Rotorua. They had better hurry up with the reburial.

Maybe it's time to bury some of my own baggage too?

Alexa picked up the paper to finish. Other items, including human bone fish hooks and greenstone clubs intended for the overseas black market, had been recovered and also would be returned to local *iwi*.

She kept reading. Detective Inspector Bruce Horne was quoted, "Individuals in Rotorua, Auckland, Wellington, and Singapore were participating in criminal activities including conspiracy, trafficking in and possession of stolen antiquities. We are proud to have worked together with national and international agents to end this assault on New Zealand's rich cultural history and to have solved the connected murders of Paul Koppel and Ray Herera."

Buried treasure had lured William Dittmer to kill two men and attempt to kill Jenny. But what about Paul Koppel? Why had he risked his cosmos for a few thousand dollars? Didn't he realize the riches of his ordinary life?

Alexa finished the article and set the paper down. She took a last sip of her flat white and thought about the message she had received two days ago.

"Horne here. Er, I mean Bruce."

Alexa had laughed. *Finally, we're on a first-name basis.* The message had ended with a brief "About that rain check. Give me a ring."

She thought of the glacial eyes and hard body. The man had his own buried treasures and woes. She wasn't sure she wanted to dig them up and so far hadn't returned his call. Her fingers brushed over the numbers, but then she dropped her cell into her tote and looked down at dirty Keds.

Tomorrow.

Time to go. She had an interview with Dan Goddard, Mr. Red Sneakers, at the Auckland forensics lab. Fingers crossed, she headed for the door that New Zealand had flung wide open.

Acknowledgments

Many thanks to the following people who helped shape *Molten Mud Murder*:

First to my agent, Natalie Lakosil of Bradford Literary Agency, who "was intrigued from the start" and "couldn't put it down," and to my editor, Barbara Peters of Poisoned Pen Press, who showed me the beauty of the Oxford comma.

It is a pleasure to work with these smart, responsive women. I wrote *Molten Mud Murder* while in the outstanding Nancy Peacock's writing group. Thank you, Nancy, and to Denise Cline, Lynn Davis, Lynn Harris, and Linda Janssen, all of whom provided guidance and inspiration.

Experts rock! Thank you to Angela Oliver of the Christchurch Writers' Guild, my Kiwi expert. Thank you, Arapine Walker, Poutiaki Rauemi, of the National Library of New Zealand, my Maori expert. Thank you, Janie Slaughter, Department Head/ Criminal Justice at Wake Technical Community College, my forensics expert.

Beverly Koester, my friend, always had keen and gentle suggestions.

Triangle Sisters (and brothers) in Crime provided fellowship and inspiration.

Cheers to all who came to visit while we lived in New Zealand: my children, Scott, Phillip, and Sally Weiner; my niece, Juta Fowlkes; my stepson, Rob Johnson; my sister, Jennifer Fowlkes; and my mother, Sally Freeman.

Some of the places in *Molten Mud Murder* are real and some are made up. All the mistakes are real and mine alone.

Molten Mud Murder exists because one day my husband said, "How would you like to live in New Zealand for a year?" Thank you, Forrest, for that and for being my best friend and best adviser.

About the Author

Photo by Morgan Henderson Photography

Sara E. Johnson lives in Durham, North Carolina. She worked as a middle school reading specialist and local newspaper contributor before her husband lured her to New Zealand for a year. Her first novel, *Molten Mud Murder*, is the result.